S0-ASH-972

MAGICAL LOVE

With a sprinkling of fairy dust and the wave of a wand, magical things can happen—but nothing is more magical than the power of love . . .

Praise for Kate Freiman

"An enchanting ride to make-believe! In *Lady Moonlight*, Kate Freiman conjures a vision of the Fey as whimsical as her heroine's cobweb slippers." —Claire Delacroix

"Kate Freiman has looked inside the human spirit and shares her findings with her readers. Join this wonderful author as she takes her audience to a world beyond their imaginations, a locale where love is the eternal force that binds all human souls together, a place where good things are possible." —*Painted Rock Reviews*

"A wonderful breath of fresh air, the gifted Ms. Freiman wows us." —*Romantic Times*

"Ms. Freiman makes the ordinary extraordinary. . . . A transcendent ride into the wondrous world of love. [She] makes masterful use of the senses, providing her readers with all the tools and props needed to see where and how the characters move through the story." —*Romance Communications*

"From beginning to end this book will keep you captivated." —*Bell, Book, and Candle*

"This riveting paranormal mystery literally leaves you on the edge of your seat to the very end. It makes you relive the feelings of that first love so well, it almost leaves you aching. The author does a fantastic job of melding emotions of days gone by with today's society of young people. Great going, Ms. Freiman!" —*Old Book Barn Gazette*

Titles by Kate Freiman

LADY MOONLIGHT
EARTH ANGEL

Lady Moonlight

KATE FREIMAN

JOVE BOOKS, NEW YORK

MAGICAL LOVE is a trademark of Berkley Publishing Corporation.

LADY MOONLIGHT

A Jove Book / published by arrangement with
the author

PRINTING HISTORY
Jove edition / March 1999

The Penguin Putnam Inc. World Wide Web site address is
http://www.penguinputnam.com

ISBN: 0-515-12465-6

A JOVE BOOK®
Jove Books are published by The Berkley Publishing Group,
a member of Penguin Putnam Inc.,
375 Hudson Street, New York, New York 10014.
JOVE and the "J" design
are trademarks belonging to Jove Publications, Inc.

PRINTED IN THE UNITED STATES OF AMERICA

10 9 8 7 6 5 4 3 2 1

Dedicated to the Memory of
CAROL STEEVES
(1958–1998)

You knew the magic of horses,
the power of dreams.
I miss you, my friend,
my heart's sister.

Prologue

*"... someday you will be old enough to start reading
fairy tales again."*

—C. S. Lewis

ST. HELENA, NAPA VALLEY, CALIFORNIA, MONDAY, MAY 24, 1999

The package from Ireland came by courier just after eight
in the morning. His first impulse was to drop the package
into the trash and pretend he never saw it, but he knew that
wouldn't work. Instead, after setting it on the counter, he
ignored it and ground beans for a pot of coffee. While the
coffeemaker sputtered, he drank a glass of orange juice,
then showered. When he came back to the kitchen, he studied the package from a short distance, simultaneously curious and wary. It looked harmless, but his gut warned him
that anything with his grandfather's return address could be
as volatile as a letter bomb. A glance at the microwave oven
clock told him he only had time for breakfast before he had
to meet his partner in San Francisco.

Without conscious intent, Con fingered the talisman suspended on the thin gold chain around his neck. Most people
assumed it was a good luck charm. The pure gold horseshoe
nail, bent into an imperfect circle, was a unique souvenir

of Ireland, a reminder of memories he preferred not to re-live, a reminder of memories he dared not forget. If it was good luck not to repeat mistakes, then the nail was a genuine good luck charm.

It was impossible not to remember why he'd rather be smart than lucky. *Aisling* . . . The name meant a vision, a dream. The woman, like her name, was an illusion, an insubstantial, quixotic, unobtainable dream. Fourteen years ago, he'd exchanged foolish dreams for substantial, practical, obtainable objectives. Fourteen years ago, he'd sworn *not* to dream, awake or asleep. He'd done fine since then. Damn fine. Almost perfect, in fact. Until this parcel, arriving out of the blue like this, proved that even the thinnest *almost* was as wide as the universe.

Damn! Might as well see what it was, instead of stewing all day about it. With an impatient growl, Con tossed the package on the kitchen table, then poured himself a mug of hot coffee. Sitting at the table, he tore open the wrapping and unfolded a sheet of heavy white stationery at the top. The old-fashioned paper was covered with bold, black lettering, written with a fountain pen, and dated two days earlier.

> *Conlan:*
> *Your mother tells me you've made more millions now that you've sold your business. Money isn't everything. It's time you took a holiday. Your old room only needs airing to be ready for you. Mrs. Penny is eager to bake for someone who appreciates her cakes and tarts more than myself.*

Con rolled his eyes. Leave it to his grandfather to dismiss his only grandson's success, because it was with computers, not horses. An O'Hara who didn't work with horses wasn't a *true O'Hara*. But the part about taking a holiday, and his old room . . . Not a straightforward invitation to visit, but a pretty bald hint. What the hell was the old man up to?

We've unfinished business between us, Conlan, urgent in nature. The memory of that day fourteen years ago has been like an unhealed wound. Each time I've written inviting you to O'Hara House, you've declined. This time, I believe the enclosed articles will compel you to change your mind.

With memories of his last trip to Ireland rushing back like a shower of broken glass, Con set the letter down to think. He and his grandfather had been estranged since his nineteenth summer, but he hadn't forgotten that last encounter either. Ambros Conlan O'Hara IV was a man who left a strong impression. Back then, almost as tall and broad-shouldered as his only grandson, hardly a silver strand in his thick, black hair, his mother's father could have passed for a much younger man. He'd sure been fit enough to give his grandson a black eye after disowning him. Con had limped away from the rock-strewn lane where one of the award-winning O'Hara Irish hunters had dumped him. First Aisling, then the damn horse, then Grandfather—they'd left his adolescent male pride in tatters.

Unfinished business? What an understatement! He'd sworn never to go back.

Still, this letter sounded a shade more humble than previous ones. His mother hadn't said anything, but he wondered if the old man was ill; felt a twinge of worry that he might be. Just guilt at his own stubbornness. Or regret that his family was so small, so broken. Or maybe, in spite of himself, he just cared about the old man. Con idly rubbed the golden nail, the way he usually did while he was thinking, and felt it warm to his touch.

Aisling. She'd warmed to his touch, too. Or so he'd thought.

Damn! He released the ring, letting it fall against his T-shirt. For crying out loud! He'd been a geek of nineteen, a nerd with the social skills of a hedgehog, a slave to his hormones. It had been a real learning experience mistaking lust for love, but it was all in the past. He was over her, had been for more than a decade. Besides, Gramps didn't know Aisling existed, so whatever he wanted couldn't have anything to do with her.

> *I'm seventy years old, and things look different to me now. I don't know how long I have left, Conlan. I don't want to die a lonely, unhappy old hermit.*
> *When you examine the enclosed items, you will understand why I am asking you to come to Ireland.*
> *Once you've made your travel plans, phone me. I also suggest that you refrain from discussing this matter with your mother until you and I have spoken. At the best of times, Corliss tends to be less than dispassionate. I don't wish to alarm her needlessly.*

A postscript followed his grandfather's flourishing signature:

> *P.S. You still owe me a bottle of whiskey, Midleton Very Rare. Bring two, if you expect any in your own glass.*

He would have laughed at the reference to his role in the demise of a bottle of that fine Irish whiskey, but it dredged up another episode Con would have preferred to forget. Equal parts irritated and intrigued, he reached into the well-padded package. Inside several layers of bubble wrap, he found a thin, old-looking leather-bound book with impressive gilt lettering.

He did laugh when he read the title: *True Tales of Irish Family Curses and Enchantments, Book III.*

It had to be a joke, but he might as well glance at the book over breakfast. After detouring to pour a mug of coffee, Con returned to the kitchen table and opened the book to the inside title page. The subtitle made him laugh out loud again: "A History of the Lost de Burgh Family, and the O'Hara Curse."

Gramps had gone to a lot of trouble to break the ice. Might as well find out what this was about. Taking a sip of coffee, Con began to read. After the first page, he forgot about his coffee. He forgot about the meetings set up to finalize the sale of the software development company that had made him and his best friend millionaires before their thirtieth birthdays. He forgot about everything except the story he was reading, and the memory of one magical summer night in Ireland fourteen years ago.

When he reached the end of the book, he felt numb. After staring at the last page long enough to start seeing double, he blinked to clear his vision. Then he noticed a sheet of plain paper folded and tucked inside the back cover. It was a photocopy of an old, faded note. Some of the old-fashioned writing was hard to decipher, but he got the anguished gist of it.

The phone rang, sounding as startling as a fire alarm in the silence of the kitchen. Con jumped, then nearly fell over his chair trying to stand. He grabbed the handset on the third ring.

"Rough night, Sloan?" It was his partner.

"Hey, McKeogh. Not nearly as rough as the morning. Why?" Then he remembered. "Oh, hell! I'm sorry. The meeting with the attorneys. Damn! Something came up here and I lost track of time." He gave the hair falling over his forehead a hard tug.

McKeogh's low chuckle came over the wires. "I've heard that one before. Not to worry. Everything's copacetic. You'll have to get your signature notarized on all the copies, but that's really all you missed."

His partner was one in a million. "Oh, man, I'm sorry. I'll get onto that right away." He paused. "Uh, McKeogh? I'm going to have to go out of town for a while. To, uh, Ireland."

"You finally broke down and decided to see your grandfather? Good. How long are you staying?"

"I don't know. A week. Maybe more." A lot depended on how soon he could find a shrink to treat the old man. "I'll stay in touch by phone and e-mail."

"Hey, take a real vacation. We might be out of work, but we can afford it." Another chuckle in his ear prompted his quick grin of agreement. With the recent sale of their most ambitious programming product to date, they'd gone from broke workaholics at twenty-four and millionaires at thirty, to temporarily unemployed multimillionaires at thirty-three. "When are you leaving?"

"As soon as I can. I haven't started making reservations."

"That quick? He isn't sick, is he?" Con muttered a vaguely negative answer. "Hey, why don't I bring the papers for you to sign today? That'll save you some time."

Time. He glanced at the clock. Just past noon? How the hell did he lose four hours? Still mentally numb from everything he'd read, he muttered his thanks. After promising to bring fresh bagels, McKeogh hung up, and Con went into his office to start making travel plans and piling clothes on the bed for packing.

Nearly two hours later, the turn of a key in the front door announced his partner's arrival. He hollered that he'd be out in a minute, and a fresh pot of coffee would be a good idea. Then, refusing to take the bait of McKeogh's candid opinion of his manners, he finished arranging for a rental car at the Shannon airport. When he returned to the kitchen, the smell of coffee and toasted bagels greeted him. So did the sight of his partner—the only other human being in the world who knew about him and Aisling—engrossed in the leather-bound book. Their eyes met and he waited through a long silence. Finally, McKeogh raised a brow.

"*This* is why you're going to Ireland?"

He scowled. "No, damn it. I'm going to Ireland because I think my grandfather is a few kilobytes short of a meg."

"Un-huh. What about Aisling?"

Sometimes, like now, he regretted ever sharing that part of his history with McKeogh. "*Nothing* about Aisling. Hell, I'm still getting over Melanie."

"Get real, bud. *You* broke up with *her*."

A cave seemed like a really good idea right about then. He hated being on the defensive like this. "So? I care enough about Mel to feel rotten about hurting her. It's like . . ." He searched for an image, then shrugged. "I'm a biohazard, toxic to relationships. I'm tired of feeling like pond scum, but I seem to end up hurting every woman I try to get serious with.''

''So maybe you need to try *not* to get serious.''

Con shook his head. ''I won't do that. Not even to . . .'' He drew a deep breath and let it out slowly. ''Look, forget about all this, okay? I'm just going to check out some kind of—''

''A horse?'' McKeogh gave a sudden snort of laughter that turned into a cough. ''Oh, Sloan! I thought you *hated* horses!''

He glared. ''Could we talk about—''

''No!'' Waving the leather-bound book at him, his partner flashed a wicked grin. ''This says Aisling is under . . . some sort of spell . . . that . . . ,'' another snorting laugh, ''. . . that makes her . . . ,'' a howl of laughter, ''. . . makes her . . . turn in . . . into a *horse*?''

Con winced. The belly-clutching, hooting laughter finally sputtered to smothered chortling punctuated by gasps and whoops. Clenching his teeth, Con waited for the inevitable punch line, but McKeogh couldn't stop laughing enough to deliver it. Finally, between gasping breaths, the words came at him:

''Oh, Sloan! This is too rich!'' Another howl assaulted Con's ears. ''You . . . You l . . . lost . . . y . . . your v . . . vir . . . virginity . . . to a . . . a g . . . g . . . girl who . . . turns into a *horse*!''

Con grabbed the leather-bound book out of McKeogh's clutches. ''I *hate* when that happens!'' Con muttered.

Book One

Once upon a time, long, long ago,
and far away, there lived a
beautiful maiden who believed in
True Love . . .

One

"Hurry, Luna! They're coming after us!"

Aisling bent lower to mold her body to the straining muscles of her mare. The wind caught her words and flung them away, but Luna's burst of speed told Aisling she'd been heard and understood. With no saddle or bridle, her legs and feet bare, not even wearing her riding clothes, but her best day dress, she clung only by her balance, and her hands wrapped the thick strands of Luna's frost-white mane.

The first stone wall rose abruptly out of the mist and gray light of dusk, looming higher than Aisling remembered, and thicker, too. Holding Luna straight between her hands and her legs, she drove her toward the wall, her heart in her throat with fear, yet pulsing with faith. Luna would take her safely over that wall, or die trying, her own horse's heart was that great. Aisling trusted the mare utterly. And from the night of her birth, Luna had let no one but Aisling touch her.

Now Aisling braced herself to absorb the shock of landing, and lifted her head to look forward. In her layers of skirt and petticoats, she slipped a little to one side. The mare shifted under her, keeping her safely balanced. 'Twas always like that between them, the *knowing*, without signals, without words.

How could Da be so cruel as to be selling her own sweet mare, and arranging her betrothal to a horrible old man, all at once and without bothering to ask what *she* wanted?

Well, she was giving him her answer now, wasn't she?

The sunset they raced toward had faded into pinks, violets and smudges of brown. In the distance, she could see the faint glow of lamps in windows welcoming people home. Misty dusk was falling over them like a gray blanket. Luna's legs pulled the ground under them, her body bunching and reaching with each bounding stride. Stinging tears welled in Aisling's eyes, from the wind in her face and the whipping of her own hair tangled with Luna's mane, and from anger. And grief. And fear.

Luna cleared the next wall that loomed out of the mist, but stumbled when her forelegs touched the ground. Aisling's skirts slipped and slid against the mare's silky coat. Her heart leaped in fear even as she clutched the mare's neck harder and righted herself. She mustn't fall! Luna mustn't get hurt! Cautiously, she signaled Luna to slow. At a walk, the mare's lowered head and heaving sides told Aisling they would have to rest. Biting her bottom lip to steady it and hold back her tears, she stroked Luna's heated neck. "Soft, now," she crooned. "Walk a little or you'll cool off too quickly and get yourself colicked."

The mare's hooves quietly brushed the tall grasses as she made her way across the farthest walled paddock of the de Burgh lands. Abruptly, Luna stopped, then tossed up her head and sidestepped. Aisling clutched at the mare's suddenly tense neck. With her heart pounding in her throat, she steadied the quivering horse. What had made her shy?

"Here now!" a reedy voice piped up out of the mist and falling dark. "Where're yer manners?" Luna shied again, forcing Aisling to clutch her neck to stay mounted. "Ye're tramping all over the door to me house 'n' home!"

Aisling gasped. "Wh . . . Who's there?"

"Who's there, she's askin', but 'tis I should be asking who you are, I should."

"This is de Burgh land, sir." She tried to sound un-
daunted, but her voice was trembling with exhaustion,
shock, and fear. "We've not had tenants for many years.
Who are you?"

The wheezy laughter that greeted her question seemed to
come out of the air. Twisting, Aisling peered around the
field, but could see no one. The laughter swirled around
her like the cawing of crows in a high tree. The mocking
sound threatened Aisling's fading courage. Fear made her
angry.

"What manner of coward are you, accosting people in
the dark?"

A sharp snap—a twig breaking—startled a gasp from
her. Luna flung up her head with a snort, but this time stood
her ground. Heart racing, Aisling sought the hidden tres-
passer, but saw no one.

"Acorn Bittersweet is no coward, he's not," that reedy
voice declared, closer now. "The bachelor Acorn Bittersweet, I am, protector of Eire's fine horses, a Leprechaun
shoemaker of renown."

A *Leprechaun*? Aisling was about to admonish the tres-
passer to tell her the truth, but Luna, calmly, curiously,
extended her neck toward something in front of her nose.
Aisling leaned forward to peer between the mare's ears.
Glaring amber eyes met hers. She promptly sat back, her
breath catching as she noted the odd aspects of the creature
scowling up at her.

"Nor is Acorn Bittersweet tenant to any Mortal land-
lord!" A short, wiry figure stood arrogantly in the tall
grasses. He wore neatly tailored green britches and a grass-
green waistcoat buttoned tightly over a white shirt with
cascades of sparkling white ruffles. He looked no bigger
than a boy of nine or ten, but his voice and wizened features
told Aisling this was not a boy. With green ankle-high
pointy-toed boots and cuffs like folded leaves, he did indeed resemble drawings of Leprechauns in her childhood
storybooks. A *Leprechaun*? And was he truly called Acorn
Bittersweet? Or was exhaustion and panic making her see
things? A nervous laugh began bubbling up inside her.

But then, the . . . *Leprechaun?* . . . was clearing his throat loudly, his indignant expression trapping her giggles before they erupted. He tipped his head to one side and regarded her with those unblinking yellow eyes. She tried to stare unflinchingly back, but his gaze was so unsettling that she had to look away after only a few seconds.

"Have ye no manners but bad ones?"

In Aisling's estimation, the bad manners were all on *his* side, but his sudden appearance during her bid for escape compelled her to be cautious. "My apologies for nearly trampling you, sir. I was thinking of other things when you startled my mare." She offered a hesitant smile. "I hope we did you no harm."

Wide lips parted in a smile that revealed very tiny white teeth. "Nicely spoken, you are. I forgive you for trespassin'." He raised his right arm and, with fingers as bent and gnarled as twigs, grasped the brim of his green three-cornered cap. "Acorn Bittersweet, I am, dear gentle lady, and at your service."

With a courtly bow, he swept the cap off, revealing hair like tufts of straw, some red, some yellow, some green. And his ears—! Aisling's smile froze. His ears stood out from his head, wide at the base, pointed at the tips. Following the sweep of his hand, Aisling saw he was standing beside a mound covered by long, darkly green grasses growing in a circle.

'Twas a *rath,* a mound like many others on the de Burgh estate, like many hundreds more all over County Sligo. Scholars claimed the mounds were only ancient remains of the Celts, but the Irish folk—even those who might claim to know better—believed otherwise. 'Twas said the mounds were *Faery raths,* entrances to a magical realm some called Under-Hill.

The blood rushing to and from her head was making her feel now flushed and then light-headed. She'd never thought about Faeries as anything more than stories of magic and mystery, but if this . . . *person* truly was one of the Little People, it wouldn't do to be offering him offense.

Fearing her smile looked sickly, Aisling nodded as cordially as she could manage. "How do you do, Mr. Bitter-sweet? I am—"

His caw of laughter stopped her speech. "Indeed, I know the fair Aisling Ahearn, daughter of the beauteous Fiona de Burgh and the deceiving Eamon Ahearn." Her shock must have shown on her face, for the little man grinned slyly. "Oh, I do know you. 'Tis newly and unwillingly betrothed to Ambros O'Hara, the younger, ye be, of those O'Haras claiming the lands adjoining your own."

Her mouth fell open. At another of those crowlike laughs, she snapped her mouth shut. "And this lovely white mare be Luna, daughter of Midnight and Apollo, that yer own sire means to sell for a broodmare." He winked one amber eye at her. " 'Tis said the mare has Fey blood, as does her mistress."

" 'Tis . . .'Tis true, what you say of my parents, and of my mare's sire and dam, but . . ." *Fey blood?* Words failed her.

Never mind the Faery stories. How could this little man know what she herself learned only hours ago? After drinking tea that was more whiskey than tea, Da had announced that they were deeply in debt. The costs of running the estate had increased more than the value of the funds set aside to maintain it, he'd explained, not looking her in the eye all the while. He'd had to spend every penny of the de Burgh legacy, *her* inheritance, to keep the actual properties from going to creditors, but there was still too much owing. Selling all the remaining de Burgh horses would not raise enough to repay these bills.

The O'Haras, father and son, had generously lent them the funds to pay those creditors, so now they were in debt to their nearest neighbors. Da had arranged to work in the position of stud manager at O'Hara House, at less than the going wage, to repay their benefactors, but his contribution would be but a tiny drop in a large bucket. If Aisling wished to keep the de Burgh lands together for her descendants, and cancel all their debts, she must, Da announced, accept the marriage offer of Ambros O'Hara, the son.

Her own Da was going to sell her into marriage with a

stranger! Ambros O'Hara, the son, was more than twice her
own age, and his gruff demeanor frightened her. So had
the tales of his first wife and child dying mysteriously.
'Twas said he hated women, and had the temper of a
dragon.

In shock had she listened. Da talked only of what he and
what Ambros O'Hara were wanting from her. What of her
own dreams? What of her right to choose her own husband?
Cried and pleaded she had done, and smashed the whiskey
jug against the stones of the cottage, but to no good result.
Shame and anger had hardened his heart to her protests.
He'd locked her in her bedroom until Ambros O'Hara had
arrived to seal their bargain.

But surely, no one had been listening . . . She would
question this little man without answering him. "How do
you come by your information?"

The Leprechaun chortled and shuffled his feet in an awkward sort of dance. "There's magic to knowing things,
there is!"

Unable to think of a suitable reply, Aisling gaped at the
strange being in front of her. The mournful cry of an owl
came out of the dark and the mist, making her suddenly
aware that night had fallen. A shiver rippled through her.
The summer night air had grown cool and damp, and she'd
rushed away too hastily to put a wrap over her dress. Suddenly frightened by all that was happening to her, Aisling
tightened her heels on Luna's sides. The mare gathered herself, ready to spring away.

The little man tipped his head like a bird listening for a
worm and held up his hand. His utter stillness strangely
compelled Aisling to wait silently until he gave her a wide
grin. " 'Tis Eamon Ahearn and young Ambros O'Hara
gaining ground on ye I hear. I can help ye hide, if ye'd
like. For the sake of my sweet Fiona de Burgh's lovely
girl-child, 'twould be."

Fresh hope scattered her fears and suspicions like leaves
on the wind. "Oh! Mr. Bittersweet, I'd be so grateful, truly!
But however will you hide us here? The field is so open."
In daylight or moonlight, from any vantage point along the

thick stone walls, every nook and cranny of this field was plainly visible. The only possible place for her to hide, a stand of trees straddling the joined corners of this field and the next, was too small to hide Luna.

"Oh, a spell it would take/certain magic strong would do/to render you unseen/to them not worthy of you." After chanting his rhyme, he gave a little chortle. "Magic I would do,/I would, for you!"

A spell? She didn't believe in the magic of Faery lore, but she wanted nothing to do with spells all the same! Speaking of the devil always made him appear! But as she parted her lips to decline the Leprechaun's offer, she heard hoof beats thudding ever closer. Her father and Ambros O'Hara were indeed gaining ground on her.

Acorn Bittersweet cupped one hand in front of his pointy ear and pursed his lips. "Almost here, they are. The time for deciding is almost past."

Could she outrun her pursuers? They were in the next field, and as brave as Luna was, their horses were stronger and fresher. There was no time to flee. Truly, she was trapped. Scarcely breathing, she gazed at the strange little man, unwilling to trust him, afraid not to.

Acorn Bittersweet smiled, a surprisingly kind smile. " 'Tis a Leprechaun's pleasure to be helping Mortals," he told her. Then his smile faded. " 'Tis the worst pain of my life to confess I failed to save my beautiful Fiona from the terrible fire. Casting a helping spell for her daughter would be making amends for that, it would."

The tenderness, the sadness in the little gnome's voice sent tears welling up in Aisling's eyes. Her father had saved Fiona de Burgh from that fire, and had married the orphaned young heiress soon after, but Acorn Bittersweet must also have had special feelings for her mother. If he could truly help, Aisling had nothing to lose.

"Hurry, then, Mr. Bittersweet. Please, cast your spell quickly!"

Two

~

The little man raised a gnarled hand. "Spells are not free for the taking, they are not."

Aisling felt her heart sink, and with it her last hope of protecting Luna and saving herself. "I have no money with me," she confessed, bowing her head.

"Give me one strand of the fine gold of your hair, and one strand from the white tail of your lovely mare. A cloak to hide ye both shall I weave."

Her head came up as his words reached her. "Two strands of hair?" It seemed this strange creature would prove to be her protector, frightening though his talk of spells might be. "Truly, 'tis all you ask?"

Did she dare believe his magic would work? 'Twould require considerable magic to weave a cloak large enough to cover them both, using just two strands of hair! The night air was seeping into her bones through the light layers of her summer dress. Even if there were no magic in it, a warm covering of any kind would certainly be welcome. If such a cloak could hide Luna and herself long enough to escape Da and Ambros O'Hara, even just for this one night, she would be eternally grateful.

Acorn Bittersweet smiled. "The strands of hair are what I'm needin' for weaving a magical cloak. The gold necklace ye wear is my price."

Aisling's hand automatically went to her throat to cover

the fine chain encircling it. "But . . .'Tis all I have from my mother," she protested, blinking back the sting of tears.

"And 'twas all she had from me, it was," he countered.

Aisling pinched the delicate chain between her thumb and forefinger, uncertain whether to believe him. Her mother had died shortly after giving birth to her. The necklace had been bequeathed to Aisling, along with the lands and funds her father was given control of. Until that very day, she'd been expecting to receive her inheritance on her twentieth birthday, four long years away. Now it seemed everything she'd believed she owned, everything she'd dreamed of—university, a husband who loved her, and their children to raise—would not be coming to her, whether she gave in and married Ambros O'Hara or no.

If her own father had been cheating her, why would this stranger not be telling her lies, as well? " 'Twas a gift from you?" The little man nodded, but Aisling hesitated. "You'll be proving it, then, before I let you take my mother's only legacy from me."

Acorn Bittersweet made a cackling sound Aisling took to be laughter. "Proving it, will I? 'Tis Fey gold, wantin' to come home! Feel it growing warm? 'Twill burn ye if ye don't release it."

She opened her mouth to deny his claim, but suddenly the slender chain around her neck was indeed becoming hot. Unwillingly, she lifted it away from her skin. The Leprechaun gave her a sly, knowing grin.

"Hand it over quick now, and let me pluck the hairs I need to weave the cloak for you and yer mare. Yer father and yer intended are but a few steps the other side of the wall."

Even before the little man finished speaking, Aisling had unfastened the necklace with trembling fingers. The instant she unhooked the clasp, the chain began tugging against her grasp. Acorn Bittersweet hopped around to stand beside Luna, his twisted twiglike fingers reaching upward for the necklace. Unutterably saddened by losing her last memento of her mother, Aisling released the chain. To her astonishment, it floated weightlessly into the gnarled palm waiting for it, and wound itself around Acorn Bittersweet's fingers like an ingratiating cat greeting its master. Her mouth and eyes grew wide at this proof of the little man's magic.

The sound of Da and Ambros bellowing her name into the mist and darkness startled her. She cast an anxious glance toward the wall separating them from her, then turned her gaze to the Leprechaun, who was watching her with a strange light in his amber eyes.

"Before I'm grantin' ye this spell, I'll be knowing, I will, why yer fleeing Eamon Ahearn and Ambros O'Hara."

Were they all conspiring together? Some Faeries were said to like helping people, but which ones? Was Acorn Bittersweet only distracting her until Da caught up with her, expecting a reward for turning her over to him? Or would he be weighing the merit of her reasons before deciding to help her or not?

She wished she could read his expression, but he was such an ugly, strange creature, it was difficult to gaze fully at him for any time. He was still standing at Luna's shoulder, grinning smugly as he reached up to stroke the mare's neck. Aisling braced herself for her mare's customary explosion. But at the Leprechaun's first touch, Luna, who'd never tolerated anyone but Aisling herself to groom or ride her, sighed and lowered her head. With a muffled chuckle, the little man rubbed Luna's face and scratched between her ears. The mare made a sound like a low moan of pleasure and Aisling felt the muscles beneath her softening. 'Twas the oddest thing she'd ever seen—not including the Leprechaun himself!

He gave Aisling a long, stern look. "She's a beauty, she is. Sensitive and high-spirited, much like the Mortal lass she carries. 'Twould be a shame for either to fall into uncaring hands."

His words spoke straight to her troubled heart. "You're an understanding man, Mr. Bittersweet. Luna has been like a sister to me. I can't bear thinking of her going to strangers who don't know her worth. She's the last of the best de Burgh horses, and should be bred to the best stallion in Ireland."

"Can ye not convince yer intended to buy her from yer father?"

By the saints! The Leprechaun *must* be in league with the two men pursuing her! Hadn't Da suggested she do just that? As if *she,* who'd never been taught the arts of womanly ways, as she would have been if her mother had lived, would know how to twist Ambros O'Hara to do her bidding, even if she wanted to.

"Ambros O'Hara *isn't* my intended! He's a greedy old man who's trying to steal my life as well as my inheritance!"

Alarmed by her shrill tone, Aisling let her voice drop to nearly a whisper and poured her heart into her words. "I've always dreamed of going to university, Mr. Bittersweet, and of marrying for love. Ambros O'Hara wishes to acquire me as his broodmare. He has no love in him, except for things he can own."

The sudden hot sting of tears made her close her eyes before speaking again. "I've love in me, Mr. Bittersweet, like a young bird longing to fly. I don't want to let it die unfledged in the sharp talons of a falcon."

When she stopped speaking, the night was silent around her, except for the swishing of Luna's tail, the lowing of cattle in the distance, and the sound of herself sniffling softly. With her eyes closed, she'd lost sight of the Leprechaun. The sharp sting of a single hair being pulled out of her scalp rudely alerted her to his location. Stifling a yelp, she clapped her hand to the injured spot on her head, then glared down at the top of Acorn Bittersweet's cap. If his magic failed, she'd be pulling more than one hair out of his pointy little head!

He was grinning and humming to himself as he wound the long strand of her hair around his hand and stepped toward Luna's rump. The stamp of a hind foot told Aisling the Leprechaun had pulled a hair from the mare's ground-sweeping tail. If he truly could be weaving a magical cloak to hide them, he would need to be quick, for she heard her father and Ambros along the walls, calling to each other through the heavy mists. With every shout, her pulse raced faster.

"Close yer eyes tight," Acorn Bittersweet instructed, "while I am weaving this spell."

Aisling shut her eyes and pondered her actions this night. She had been very hasty in her flight. If the magic cloak worked, she and Luna would escape from her father and O'Hara. That had been her only intention. But, for the first time, she wondered about later. And tomorrow, and after. Truly, she wouldn't want to hide forever! Just until she convinced Da she was in the right. Just until she shocked the whiskey and the anger out of him. Just until he stopped saying she was a selfish ingrate, when she'd been more mother to him than he'd been father to her, as long as she could remember.

Was it so selfish to be dreaming of restoring the burned shell of the de Burgh great house to its former glory, and of breeding beautiful, strong Irish horses like the ones her ancestors had produced for generations? Was it so selfish to be dreaming of learning, dreaming of seeing more of the world than this little corner, dear as it was? Was it so selfish to be dreaming of loving and being loved? Was it so—

"No dreaming!" She flinched at the Leprechaun's squawked command, but didn't yet dare to open her eyes until he gave her leave. " 'Tis sensitive to dreaming and wishing, magic is, and easy to flummox. Ye must be thinkin' of aught but hiding from yer pursuers and leave the specifics to me, else there's no tellin' what might happen when the spell is cast."

The explanation seemed sensible, if indeed there were such a thing at all as magic. Afraid the magic wouldn't work, and equally afraid it would, Aisling squeezed her eyes shut and tried to temper her impatience at each passing second. When at last he barked, "Open yer eyes, Fiona's lovely daughter, and see what I've made for you!" her eyes flew open.

Even in the misty darkness that had fallen since sunset, she had no trouble seeing what he held across his twisted arms. Aisling gasped in awe. Never had she seen anything

like that beautiful, shimmering cloth. 'Twas indeed a generously made cloak of finest gold threads. Truly, the feat
was astonishing!

"Take this, now, and wrap yerself and the mare, while
I'm casting the spell. No longer can I slow the passing of
time while yer father and yer suitor seek ye. They'll be
climbing the wall any second. Hurry!"

Breathlessly, Aisling reached down to take the gossamer
fabric from him. His warning set her heart beating faster.
The men's voices came ever closer in the darkness, calling
her name through the swirling mists. The pale beacon of
the rising full moon suddenly sent a beam of light through
the fog and darkness, and a jolt of fear pierced her. If the
fog lifted even a little, she—in her white dress on her milk-
white mare—would be as visible as the moon itself.

The cloak felt cool as dew and light as mist. She wanted
to examine its exquisite textures, but Acorn Bittersweet
made hurrying motions with his twisted hands. Still, inde-
cision and fear made Aisling hesitate. In all her sixteen
years, she'd never been away from de Burgh Manor alone,
not even to visit neighbors. Indeed, she'd only gone once
with Da to Dublin, and only a few times to Sligo itself.
She knew how to run a horse farm and a household, but
nothing of life outside her own world. What if she were
fleeing Da and Ambros O'Hara only to run into the arms
of worse trouble? There was an old Irish saying: *Is fearr
pilleadh as lár an atha ná bathadh 'sa tuile*—"It is better
to turn back from the middle of the ford than to be drowned
in the flood." Perhaps—

"There! I see her!" Da's voice boomed across the fields,
jolting her out of her thoughts. "She's all right, I think.
Still on that witch of a mare! Aisling! Aisling, you turn
yourself around and come home!"

"The cloak! The cloak!" the Leprechaun ordered in a
hoarse whisper. "Put it around ye now and count to ninety-
nine and one, or all will be for naught! They're almost upon
us, and they'll take ye home by force, they will. 'Twill be
the end of all yer pretty dreams then!"

He was right. There was no other way out of this. Taking

a deep, shivering breath, Aisling unfurled the cloak. Weightless and cool, shimmering as dew in sunlight, it drifted around her, settling over Luna's sides. Holding the edges together under her chin, Aisling counted to one hundred.

Then she sat waiting for the magic to begin.

Some minutes passed, but there was no flashing of lights, no twinkling of magic dust. She felt no different, only ashamed for believing in magic. She and Luna were as visible as before, standing like a statue in the middle of the open field. Ah, well, 'twas no more than she deserved for trusting a stranger.

What a fool she was! Once Da caught up with her, she'd be facing the consequences of her actions. Somehow, she must find other means to be convincing Da not to be marrying her off to Ambros O'Hara. Almost as old as Da, he was, and so arrogant and condescending. Imagine, grabbing her to kiss without the courtesy of asking, as if he owned her. Her first kiss it was, and more disappointing than even the Leprechaun's magic spell. Ambros's face stubble had scraped her skin, and his groping hands had bruised her flesh. At least, if the cloak wasn't working any magic, 'twas warming her more than Ambros's embrace had done. Truly, if that was the way men in arranged marriage treated their wives, she'd be marrying for love or not at all.

"Where do you say she is, Eamon?" 'Twas Ambros O'Hara's deep voice, closer even than Da's a moment ago.

"In the middle of the damn field! The fog is lifting. How can you not see her?"

Aisling heard the thudding of boots as the two men dropped over the wall into the field. She sat on Luna, in full view of anyone looking. As the mare's ears flicked curiously forward and back, Aisling guided her around so they faced their pursuers squarely. Her heart began beating faster at the sight of the two men, both of them scowling fiercely, but her hands stayed steady.

"The fog is lifting, but she's not there, Eamon. Nor is the mare. Are you sure 'twasn't a trick of the moonlight?"

"Trick of the moonlight? Are you saying I'm old or

crazy? I saw her, I tell you.'' Da turned slowly in a full circle, his gaze sweeping past her as if she weren't there. Then he faced O'Hara. ''I know I saw her,'' he repeated with less confidence.

''I know you *want* to see her. She's all the assets you've left in the world beside your own hard work.'' The man's cold reminder of Da's bargain with the O'Haras made Aisling cringe.

''We'll find her, don't you doubt it.'' Da's voice belied his words. ''With nowhere to go, no money and only the clothes on her back, she won't travel far. She'll be coming home this night, after she tries sleeping hungry on the cold, wet ground.''

How strange! She and Luna were standing right before Da and Ambros O'Hara, yet the men spoke as if they were not there. She waved one arm over her head, but neither man appeared to see. With her eyes growing wide and her heart fluttering wildly, she turned to look at the Leprechaun. Her heart gave a lurch at his nod. Truly, the spell had worked! The magic was real!

He grinned, his wide, thin lips twisting in a most unappealing way. '' 'Tis as you requested, lovely Aisling.'' Acorn Bittersweet gave her a sweeping bow. His mocking manners sent a sudden chill of alarm through her, making her feel ill. ''They'll not be finding ye, they won't, even with ye standing close enough to touch. Just as you wished, it is, pretty Aisling, daughter of my beloved Fiona. Ye'll never have to sell yer beautiful white mare, nor wed Ambros O'Hara.''

At the gloating tone of his reedy voice and the triumphant glow in his amber eyes, Aisling bit her lip and looked away. Oh! What had she done? Why hadn't she listened to her doubts? The misgivings in her heart were fast turning into regrets. Fear, sinking like a frozen rock in her stomach, warned her that he had tricked her with her own desperation.

''My girl is as innocent as the daisies, I told you. Didn't I advise you to court her the way you'd tame a skittish filly? I saw you manhandling her.'' Da planted his feet and crossed his arms across his chest. "You frightened her into running away."

Facing him, barely a stride away, Ambros O'Hara crossed his own arms and squared his shoulders. "You swore the girl would be as easy to lead as a lamb. You promised she'd be biddable and affectionate. Hah! She's as docile as a cornered wildcat."

As O'Hara spoke, he moved steadily toward Da. And, to Aisling's surprise, Da began backing away, his arms no longer crossed, but his hands raised as if to protect himself, to beg the bigger man for mercy.

"Our agreement includes a wife *and* a horse against your debts. With your girl to handle the breeding of that *bahn shee* mare after the wedding, we would credit you a generous sum. Without the girl to control her, we'll have to sell the mare, and no one will pay a fair price for that lunatic. She'd be worth more in France for the table."

Aisling felt sick. The cold, hard way Ambros O'Hara spoke proved there was no mercy in the man Da called his friend and neighbor. Surely, Da would now defend her. Surely, he would tell O'Hara that there was no putting a price on his only child. But, to her shame, Da hung his head, a thing she'd never seen him do in all her life. Even though the de Burghs were not as ancient or wealthy a family, in years gone by they had often bested the O'Haras in competitions from pie baking to horse breeding. Tears welled up in her eyes to think of Da humbling himself to an O'Hara.

"I understand and I'm hoping you'll not be holding my girl's foolishness against me. Daughters are a trial, they are. Can you still find it in your heart to be hiring me to work with the de Burgh horses you've acquired, Ambros O'Hara?" Surely, she was hearing wrong. Da's ingratiating tone shocked her. How could he beg like that?

"Perhaps. You've a rare ability with horses, Eamon Ahearn, and a good eye for breeding great ones. 'Tis a pity you failed to tame that girl of yours."

" 'Twas indeed harsh of heaven to leave me with a useless daughter, then take my Fiona before she could give me a son.''

Her father's cruel words dried her tears before they spilled down her cheeks. Aisling jolted as if she'd been slapped, her breath catching and nearly strangling her.

O'Hara gave a snort. ''If your wife had lived, we'd not be having this problem. 'Tis your own doing that you've lost everything. You've a contract with my father and me, Eamon Ahearn, to settle your debts to us. You've given your word to deliver a willing bride and what remains of her dowry. If the girl cannot be found safe—and marriageable, you understand; I'll not raise another man's bastard as my own—we'll not be bound to those terms. The remaining de Burgh lands and horses will be forfeit, and you'll not be getting any funds to see you comfortably into your old age.''

Aisling's heart gave a painful leap, then sank. How could this be true? How could Da have struck a contract giving her inheritance and herself to the O'Haras? Truly, the law said he couldn't have, but the law wasn't any help out here in the middle of a field. De Burgh Manor, with its burned shell of a great house, the modest cottage where she and Da lived, these walled lands and their strong, spirited horses, had been left to her by her poor mother, with Da as trustee until she came of age. There were some business investments that supported the estate, but she didn't understand about such things—no one ever explained them to her. She'd heard the solicitor telling Da he'd be getting a life interest in the property, and a generous allowance until his dying day. But she'd also heard the solicitor explaining to Da that he hadn't the right to sell any of her inheritance. 'Twas hers alone to sell or keep.

She knew her rights! By the law, Irish women no longer must be handing control over everything from fathers to husbands when they married, as they had in the past. Irish women were entitled to inherit and own property, and someday, Aisling believed, they'd be voting the same as men—only more wisely! Aisling could afford to marry for love, and that she intended to do, or else she'd never marry.

Still, being sixteen and the size of a twelve-year-old boy complicated the getting of her way. If only Da had listened to her! Now look what had happened! And how was she going to get herself out of this enchantment? Truly, there'd be no meeting the love of her life until she was herself again!

As she watched, Ambros O'Hara turned and began striding toward the field where they'd left their horses. Without more than a heartbeat's hesitation, Da also turned and followed, his head still lowered, his shoulders rounded. Before she could gather her senses, they'd trudged a fair distance away from her.

Da had betrayed her trust and her love, but there was no one else to turn to. Somehow, she would make him protect her.

"Da, where are you going? Da! Look at me, Da! I'm standing here as plain as the nose on your face!"

Her voice rose shrilly out of the night. Luna bobbed her head several times. The Leprechaun tugged at his tight waistcoat, seeming about to speak, but only shook his head.

She drew in a deep breath for one last shout. "Da! Mother left de Burgh Manor to me! I'm your daughter! How can you be letting those thieves have their way?"

But Da and Ambros O'Hara walked on, neither giving any sign they'd heard her. Oh, God! Was she only visible to her own eye? Was she truly as substantial as the wind? Luna gave a sudden loud neigh, calling to the horses Da and Ambros O'Hara were mounting just then. The mare nearly unseated Aisling with a great trumpeting call from her deep lungs, but neither the men nor the horses in the next paddock looked in their direction.

Shocked and frightened, Aisling sought answers from the little man standing beside her in the Faery *rath*.

"They can't hear you," Acorn Bittersweet reminded her, rubbing his gnarled hands together and smirking up at her. "And they never shall!"

No! She hadn't meant to disappear completely! She'd only meant to hide, to give herself time enough to convince Da that she'd a right to her studies and a right to choose her own husband. She never should have trusted the Leprechaun! They were said to be helpful spirits, but everyone with even the smallest drop of Irish blood knew that all Faeries were capricious. What a fool she'd been! And now she'd have to be explaining to Da and the O'Haras about how she'd let a Leprechaun enchant her.

Desperately, Aisling clutched at the edge of the magic golden cloak, but no matter how she tugged at it, she couldn't get it to come off. When she tried to slip off Luna's back, to face the grotesque little man at his own level, she found she couldn't. It was as if some giant magnet held her in its invisible grip, keeping her tethered to the mare.

The enormity of her mistake brought tears to her eyes.

"My poor Luna! Oh, please, Mr. Bittersweet, take the spell off us!"

The Leprechaun gave her a long, studying look before speaking. "Ye wish to spare Luna?"

Her heart leaped at the chance of release. "Oh, please, yes! 'Tisn't fair to trap her with me."

Scratching his pointy chin with twiglike fingers, Acorn Bittersweet closed his eyes and rocked back on his heels. Scarcely daring to breathe, Aisling waited. When he opened his eyes again, his wide smile sent her heart leaping with hope and fear.

"Because ye're my sweet Fiona's daughter," he said with a bow, "and ye ask so nicely, I'll change the spell on ye and the mare."

Three

Aisling opened her mouth to thank the Leprechaun, but he lifted a gnarled hand, signaling her to remain silent. Tamping down her impatience, she pressed her lips together and waited as he searched his pockets front and back, muttering under his breath. Finally, he peered into his half-cupped palm, then grinned up at her. She gave him a hopeful smile just to be polite.

'' 'Tis clever I am, I am!'' he crowed, giving an awkward little hop-step. ''This she'll be and you shall be she/ when this I tie on white mare's mane./'Twill be thus till the spell is broke./Then ye'll both be back the same.''

Mystified and increasingly uneasy, Aisling watched him approach Luna's off side. Would she be betrayed yet again this night? The Leprechaun reached for a strand of thick, silky mane. She thought she saw a glint of gold, some magical talisman, perhaps, in his hand. When he stepped back with a pleased grin on his grotesque face, she saw a tiny horse made of gold dangling from Luna's mane. A heartbeat later, Aisling fell to the cold, damp sod as Luna simply disappeared from under her. The shock of landing snapped her teeth together and sent stars dancing in her eyes.

Drawing a deep breath, gathering her pride, she looked at the little man. Acorn Bittersweet gave her a smile and held out his gnarled hand. She thought at first that he was offering to help her up, then realized he was only showing her the tiny gold horse lying in his palm.

It was moving! It was alive!

Her stomach lurched. "By all the saints, what have you done?" she cried as he closed his hand around the golden horse and shoved it into his waistcoat pocket. "What have you done to Luna?"

If she could get her legs under her, if she could stand, she would throttle the horrible little man until he made everything right again.

"'Tis my way to keep yer mare safe and yourself un-wed, just as ye wished it. The mare's spirit will be safe asleep within the trinket, and when the spell is broken, you'll both be as you were."

Aisling gasped sharply. Oh, poor Luna! The Leprechaun had twisted her meaning again! "But that isn't what I wished at all! You've misunderstood me! Please, Mr. Bittersweet, release Luna and me from the spell. I truly do wish someday to marry a man who loves me, not my inheritance. And Luna has done you no wrong. Please release us!"

He doffed his cap again, his serious demeanor mocking her. "In due time, I shall. These next hundred years I shall be seeking gold and treasures. When I return, three hundred and twenty Mortal years my age shall be. Ready to forsake my carefree bachelor days, I'll be. No lady Leprechauns there have ever been, so to marry, I must find a bride of another kind, I must. Eamon Ahearn stole Fiona from me, he did, so his daughter will be my bride in her stead. And the lovely white mare sacred to goddess Epona will be mine as well, she will!"

Aisling listened, sickened by shock. Saints preserve her! She'd jumped from the frying pan into a roaring blaze of a fire! Tears spilled down her cheeks and she felt herself growing faint. "But, Mr. Bittersweet, did you not hear me say I wish only to marry for True Love? 'Twas the very reason I was fleeing Ambros O'Hara tonight."

"Ah! True love! A Mortal thing." Her tormentor's lips stretched into a leering smile. "As ye are mostly Mortal,

then, I shall give ye ninety-nine years and one to find yerself a True Love. Just as ye wished.''

"One hundred years?" Her voice broke. *"Mostly* Mortal? I am *entirely* Mortal. I cannot live that long!''

"No mere Mortal can!'' He chuckled, rubbed his hands
together, and did a shuffling little dance. "But Fiona's child
is no mere Mortal!''

Acorn Bittersweet danced a little jig. Aisling watched in
stunned silence, not bothering to wipe the tears that coursed
down her cheeks. "When viewed by Mortal eyes in the
Mortal world, ye shall appear as the white mare. Only
Under-Hill and in Fey company shall ye appear as yerself.
But I shall spread stories about yer enchantment wherever
I travel. Until the breaking of the spell, ye'll be a whisper
in the shadows, hoof beats in the mists. Ye'll be a rumor
of a lady turned into a white mare, a tale of a white mare
turned into a lady.''

He gave her a mocking courtly bow. "Seek ye thus yer
True Love. But resign yerself to being my bride, and dwelling Under-Hill with me when I return.''

With sickening clarity, Aisling realized that Acorn Bittersweet had never intended to grant her any favors. She
and Luna had been pawns in his game all along. Just as
they'd been in the games Da had been playing. But 'twas
one thing to have the law of the land on her side. 'Twas
something altogether different to be combating mystical
forces.

"Why are you doing this to me, if you loved my
mother?''

The little man gave a cackling laugh. "All wrongs must
be righted. Fair's fair!'' He kicked up his heels and danced
a jerky little jig in front of her.

Fair? Nothing about this spell seemed fair to her, but
perhaps she could appeal to this side of him. "How is this
fair? I've not done you any wrong, have I? If Da did cheat
you, why should I be paying his debt?'' Indeed, she thought
dizzily, that was the question of the evening.

The horrid little creature stood over her, his thin lips
stretched into a grotesque smile. '' 'Tis more than fair of

me, it is, to give ye the chance to win the true Mortal love
ye seek. Ye have one hundred years from this very night
to find the True Love ye crave. If ye do not find a Mortal
in all that time who will both declare and prove his love
thrice, then ye'll be mine.''

He squawked a laugh that made her wince, then began
twirling and leaping in a crooked path away from her. Benumbed, Aisling sat watching the image of the dancing
Leprechaun growing blurred and indistinct through her
tears. For some minutes, Acorn Bittersweet sang of his tri-
umph and danced like a stick bobbing in a whirlpool. Even
when he'd disappeared into the mists, she could still hear
his reedy voice on the wind.

The horror of her situation tore a wail of rage and fear
from her throat. Acorn Bittersweet's muffled chortle, drifting out of the darkness and fog, was the only response.
And then the night fell silent. In despair, she wiped at her
tears. More tears fell to replace those she brushed away,
until she stopped trying and gave in to her sorrow and fear.
Finally, she grew tired of sobbing. All 'twas good for was
giving her a headache, not for solving her problems.

''A curse on that Leprechaun! And a curse on Ambros
O'Hara, too!'' she shouted to the heavens above her. Then,
''Oh, Luna, I'm so sorry,'' she whispered into the darkness.
''I don't know yet what I shall do, but if there is any way
to find love, I *will* break this spell.''

Laughter like the pealing of tiny bells came out of the
mists, startling Aisling. With her pulse leaping painfully,
she twisted to peer through the darkness for the source of
the sound. When she turned forward again, shaking with
fear, the sight of a woman standing in front of her wrung
a startled cry from her.

A shimmer of light surrounded the woman's figure, revealing an exquisitely beautiful face, with delicate features
and dark-fringed violet eyes that smiled as warmly as her
full red lips. Aisling simply stared, scarcely able to breathe,
completely unable to comprehend—or believe—what she
was seeing.

The woman's slender figure was draped in some sort of

white and gold gauzy dress, loosely belted by a chain of white flowers. The same flowers had been woven into golden hair that reached to the woman's ankles. Garlands of white flowers encircled bare ankles above narrow feet. The new stranger extended her arms gracefully, as if offering to embrace her. Diamond rings adorned every slender finger, but it was the sweetness of the woman's smile, the offer of comfort, that brought new tears to cloud her vision. 'Twould be wonderful now, just this once, to receive a soothing, loving touch, of the sort she imagined mothers gave fretful babies.

"Greetings, Niece," the woman said in a musical voice.

Aisling blinked, but the woman still stood before her. "Who are you?" she demanded in a voice that was meant to sound firm, but came out as a wail.

The woman smiled tenderly. "I am Rainbow-and-Silver-Lining, half-sister to your maternal great-grandmother. I was great-great-aunt of your mother, Fiona, and you are also my niece. Your magical name is Remember-Fear-Not, but I shall call you by your Mortal name, Aisling, if that pleases you better. You may call me Aunt Rainbow."

Aisling choked back the sob rising in her throat. "This can't be happening! I've imagined this night, with my father's betrayal, Ambros O'Hara's lechery, and that dreadful Leprechaun and his spells. Now I'm dreaming a Faery queen is calling me *niece*."

The woman calling herself Aunt Rainbow gave another silvery laugh. "Oh, no, child, I'm not a queen, although all The People are of royal blood." Her lovely face grew solemn. "The same ancient royal blood flows in your veins, although somewhat diluted, or else the Leprechaun would not be able to enchant you in this way."

"Forgive me for not being grateful!"

A sweet smile answered her sharp words, bringing a rush of heat to Aisling's face. "If you were only Mortal, child, marriage to the Leprechaun would mean your death. Your Fey breeding protects you." Smiling more brilliantly, even as Aisling gasped at her dreadful words, the woman tipped her head to one side and regarded Aisling for a long moment. "As a more youthful Leprechaun, Acorn Bittersweet adored Fiona. You are the very image of your mother at the same age. 'Tis not surprising he wishes to marry you."

"Da says I'm not even the shadow of her," Aisling argued, ignoring the notion that the ugly little man could love anyone.

Aunt Rainbow's delicate sniff expressed scorn. "Eamon Ahearn is a fool who never appreciates what he has until 'tis gone. He scoffed at the de Burgh family's respect for The People, and ruined several of our favorite *raths*. Worst of all, he caused the destruction of a Sacred Hawthorn tree." She frowned quite fiercely. " 'Tis only right that he should repay his debts, and so like him, even without effort, to find someone else to do so for him."

Aisling wanted to defend Da, but she knew the beautiful Faery was speaking the truth about Da's easy shirking of any responsibility, except for his horses. And his scorn for the Faeries was legendary. With her own eyes, she'd seen him plow over a Faery fort that lay where he'd intended to build a chicken coop. Build the coop, he did, but not a single egg did the chickens within it lay.

The Faery woman—'twas nearly impossible to think of her as a relation!—offered her a sad smile. "Over the years, Eamon Ahearn has gambled away all the de Burgh properties your mother left you, and many of the fine horses in your stables, as well."

The words sent daggers of pain into Aisling's heart, but after hearing Ambros O'Hara speaking, she had no reason not to believe they were true. "None was his to wager," she protested.

"Nor his to lose," the Faery agreed gently, "but his gambling acquaintances don't scruple over such details. The O'Haras, father and son, have purchased all of Eamon's debts from various men, and now they are sole creditors of all he owes."

"So that is why Da arranged to marry me to Ambros O'Hara, to give the appearance that he hadn't stolen my inheritance." The woman claiming to be her aunt gave a sad nod of confirmation. "That can't be true! The law says

I'm free to be managing my own property and marrying whom I choose! De Burgh Manor belongs to me still. Ambros O'Hara shall never own it, nor shall he wed me.''

Aunt Rainbow sank beside Aisling on the grass and pressed a gentle hand on her knee. "Oh, no, Niece, 'tis all too true. Your father has left you penniless, and at the mercy of a man who has no love in his heart. 'Twould be charitable to believe Eamon was seeking a way to secure your future, but he knew you would be the price of it. The O'Haras would have allowed him to remain in the cottage, hovel that it is compared to the poor burnt great house where your mother was raised. Eamon would have been comfortable until his dying day, without a remorseful thought for all he'd done.''

Aisling bit her lower lip to steady it, while considering everything that had transpired that night. 'Twas true, she'd been terribly betrayed, terribly disillusioned by her father. But she'd loved him so long that 'twas difficult to stop, even after hearing the facts. She felt honor bound to defend him.

"But, Aunt, Da could have sent me to an orphanage when my mother died. Instead, he kept me and raised me, doing the best he could. Surely, that must count for something on the positive side of his accounting?'' A sick, sinking feeling washed over Aisling. "I could have repaid Da for keeping me, by agreeing to marry Ambros O'Hara. Instead, I've spoiled everything by running away, and getting myself enchanted.''

"You, spoiled anything?'' Aunt Rainbow's golden eyebrows rose and her violet eyes widened. "Tell me, child, why did you flee?''

"To keep Da from selling Luna.''

"And?'' A teasing smile accompanied a gentle squeeze of Aisling's knee.

"And to be convincing him I mean to marry only for love, as he did?'' Aisling answered uncertainly.

Aunt Rainbow took Aisling's hand in both of her own. "And so you shall, Niece. So you shall,'' she declared.

Hope fluttered like a fledgling bird within Aisling's heart.

"Oh, Aunt! Then you can take away this horrid spell!"

Aunt Rainbow sighed and shook her head, making her silken hair ripple like a shawl stirred by a breeze. "There are many rules governing the use of magic, child. Acorn Bittersweet has indeed chosen to employ strong measures, but he is a powerful and respected Leprechaun, and he did truly love your mother. 'Twould not be politic for me to break the spell he has cast on you and your mare."

Aisling's heart sank. "But even one hundred years can't be time enough to find True Love as a *horse*! Oh, Aunt! 'Tis hopeless! I shall die first!"

"Nothing is hopeless if you know how to hope," Aunt Rainbow corrected. " 'Tis truly in your power to break Acorn Bittersweet's spell if you honestly believe in the power of True Love."

"Of course I believe in the power of True Love!"

Aisling's declaration seemed to echo in the mists, and for a moment she was sure she was only dreaming. A frightening dream, to be sure, but none of it was real. When she awoke, all would be well. She would find herself in her bed, quilts pulled to her chin against the night chill, and Luna would be in her warm stall, knee-deep in fresh straw. No matter what she might dream, 'twas just illusion that would evaporate in the dawn. De Burgh Manor would still be hers, and there would be no arranged wedding with stone-hearted Ambros O'Hara!

Ah, but if 'twasn't a dream . . . ?

Dream or no, Faery relatives or no, she'd no desire to be sitting alone in the middle of a horse field in the middle of the night. Aisling squared her shoulders.

"Indeed, I do believe in True Love, Aunt Rainbow," she declared firmly, hoping she believed *enough*. Although who in the world could love her as Luna, she couldn't begin to imagine. " 'Twill have to be a man strong enough to love either an old mare, or an old hag." She smiled as bravely as she could. "Can your magic find such a man?"

The Faery squeezed her hand gently. "I cannot remove the enchantments on you and your mare, Niece. But as I was standing by when Acorn Bittersweet was working his magic, I took some liberties with his spells.''

Aisling's startled gasp prompted a mischievous Fey grin. Eyes widening, heart fluttering, she listened to her Faery aunt's pronouncement. ''You shall age but one month for every Mortal year. At the end of one hundred years, your age will be just four and twenty Mortal years. On each full-moon night, from dusk until dawn, you shall be visible as yourself to any Mortals you happen to meet.''

The Faery gave Aisling's hand another gentle squeeze, then released it to gesture toward the mists swirling around the woods at the edge of the pasture. ''Dawn approaches soon. Come, my dear Remember-Fear-Not, and I will bring you Under-Hill. You shall live with me, and with the others of the Moonstone Circle. 'Tis always the present in the Faery World, so Mortal time is as slippery as water. You must be careful not to overstay the allotted time, but I shall help you all I am able. In the search for your One True Love, however, you must help yourself.''

Feeling slightly dazed, Aisling rose and followed. At the edge of the woods, where the mists grew thick and seemed to pulse with their own energy, she hesitated. Aunt Rainbow continued without her. Finally gathering her fast-ebbing courage, she stepped into the thick forest just before the vision of white and gold vanished into the thickets. Panic seized her heart. She didn't dare risk being left behind.

''Wait, Aunt!'' She lacked the fleet grace of her Faery aunt, but she tried her best to keep the exquisite, darting figure within sight. A glimpse of Aunt Rainbow's filmy gown led her toward an opening in the hedge. The silvery peals of Faery laughter echoing delicately in the fog drew Aisling farther into the unknown.

**THE PADDOCKS, O'HARA HOUSE, CO. SLIGO,
MONDAY, AUGUST 21, 1899**

''It's been a month, Eamon. Give it up, man.'' Ambros O'Hara clapped a hand to one of Ahearn's bent shoulders. The older man didn't seem to register the contact, or his words. "Do you hear me, Eamon? She's gone."

It was pathetic the way Eamon stood in the middle of that pasture night after night, waiting for his daughter to return. A full thirty days, the man came nightly to that field that used to belong to his wife's family, to stand in the mist and wait. Just stood there, looking, listening. He didn't even call her name. Was he *willing* her to come home? With each passing day, Ahearn became more stooped. Ambros suspected the only thing keeping him alive was the hope that his errant daughter would come back.

A vain hope, that, in Ambros's opinion. Suspecting at first that father and daughter had been trying to swindle his own father and himself out of the de Burgh holdings, he'd sent men to look for the girl and her horse. Not even the Travelers had seen them, unless the mare had been disguised, and the girl likewise. Still, they were too striking to ignore.

Ireland was small, and the horse world even smaller; rumors were impossible to control. Someone must have seen that milk-white mare and the beautiful, golden-haired girl before any rescuer or abductor would have had the chance to conceal them. His men had offered money for information, but no one had any to sell, except for one old woman—rumored to be a witch, of all the foolishness!—who claimed the Faeries had carried away the girl and her horse.

Faeries! Hah! True, Sligo had more than its share of legends and tales of mythical and magical beings. With all the ancient Celtic sites, superstition thrived. Carried away by Faeries! Stupid little twit had probably gotten her neck broken and the mare stolen by whoever found her. If not, she'd ended up having to sell the mare for a fraction of her true worth, or starve.

Unless, he thought darkly, she'd sold herself to feed the mare. The girl was devoted enough to her horses—that mare in particular—to do just that. Aisling Ahearn had a way with horses that was as close to magic as he was willing to believe. It was one of the reasons Eamon's proposition had appealed to him and his own father. The O'Hara stable would benefit from the acquiring of one of the best stud managers in Ireland, and the prime pasturing lands they'd been coveting long before the de Burgh manor house had burned to the ground.

His own reasons for approving the terms seemed like so much ashes now. His first marriage had been for love, but he'd lost his wife and their son in childbirth. He'd sworn never to risk that pain again, but he'd been alone nearly as long as Aisling had been alive. For some time, he'd considered her an ideal choice for the mother of his future children, the heirs to the O'Hara holdings. From a discreet distance, he'd watched her grow from a lively child into an exquisite young woman. He knew the horses she trained were considered among the best. He'd believed her to be as dutiful and biddable as her father claimed.

Something wild and dying shrieked in the darkness. Ambros suppressed a shudder and jammed his hands into the pockets of his canvas jacket. Aisling had certainly proven herself to be as wild and *un*biddable as the white mare no one but herself could touch. Perhaps it was best that she'd disappeared. Marriage to her would no doubt be a constant struggle for dominance. The girl was beautiful enough to shame the sun, but the pleasures of possessing such beauty, of getting his own sons with a wife so finely made, mightn't compensate for the work he would have to do to tame her.

Ambros grunted. Aisling's beauty wouldn't last long in the world, nor would her innocence. It was a shame to lose the bloodlines, but he had no interest in used goods. No matter, now. Thanks to Eamon's gambling fever, he and his father owned the lands the girl would have brought to their alliance anyway. He hadn't had to search for another suitable young woman, as soon as word got out he was thinking of marriage. The fathers of girls with bloodlines and beauty not as fine as Aisling Ahearn, but of far more docile temperament, had sought him out, offering the hands of their daughters. He'd had his choice, and was satisfied now.

Once again, Ambros prodded Eamon's shoulder. "Come, man. She's gone. Time to get on with your life. We've

horses to train and sell. Sybil Mullany has agreed to marry
me, so I'll not be following you out here again.''

Eamon stared at him. ''She was right about you all along.
You've no love in you.'' Ambros snorted in protest, but
Eamon's bleak gaze silenced him against his will. ''You
dream of what you can buy. I dream of what I can win.
She only dreamt of what happiness she could give.''

Ambros turned to leave, but Eamon's iron-hard grip
caught his shoulder, fingers tightening until they dug like
talons into the muscles of Ambros's shoulder. Pain shot
down his arm. Stifling a gasp, he tried to shake Eamon off,
but the other man's strength surprised him.

''The price of all and the value of none,'' Eamon muttered. ''You'll live to regret this as I have, Ambros O'Hara.
You and all your get. I should have believed Fiona about
the Faeries. Now we'll all pay, each in our own way. And
my innocent daughter will bear the highest cost of all of
us.''

Eamon released his grip on Ambros's shoulder abruptly
and spun away. *Faeries!* Cursing the man for a lunatic,
Ambros watched him disappear into the darkness, then began making his own way back to the house. *Faeries!* He
was a rational man, and there was nothing rational about
talk of Faeries and curses. He'd not be drawn into this
superstitious foolishness.

Nevertheless, Ambros decided to give wide berth to one
of the so-called Faery forts directly in his path. Irritably,
he dismissed the faint bell-like sounds as the complaints of
some creature disturbed in its sleep. There was no one else
but himself out here, and it certainly wasn't him laughing
like tiny chimes.

AT THE EDGE OF THE FAERY REALM, EVER-THE-PRESENT

For a moment, Aisling couldn't see a thing through the fog
and, in her panic, forgot what her aunt was saying as they
traveled. She turned around several times, making herself
dizzy. Suddenly the fog cleared and a path through an un-

familiar grove opened before her. Impatient to rejoin her
Troop at a distant gathering, Aunt Rainbow beckoned her
onward without pausing to wait. Confused and frightened,
Aisling followed at a near run until she drew close enough
to the small, gracefully gliding Faery woman to feel safe
at a rapid walking pace.

Surely, these events must be happening in a dream, a
horrible, fantastical nightmare! Hadn't she cried herself to
sleep after Da locked her in her room before Ambros
O'Hara's arrival? Perhaps even those events had been a
dream, and when she awoke, Midsummer Day would just
be dawning, a blank page for her to fill in the usual ways.

Oh, but what if everything—the Leprechaun's enchantments, her invisibility, a Fey great-great-aunt—were real?
Remembering the comment her aunt had made about the
next hundred years, Aisling suppressed a shudder. If this
were all a dream, there was no harm in asking. And truly,
if this were no dream, there was desperate necessity in asking!

"Aunt!" Her voice seemed to echo around her. "Can
you really cast a spell on a Leprechaun?"

"Oh, yes!" Aunt Rainbow's laugh chimed. "Solitaries
are serious folk, and seldom enjoy a joke at their own expense. They believe utterly in their own infallibility, and
never admit to mistakes. But I shan't be casting a spell on
Acorn Bittersweet."

Disappointment pierced her hope that Aunt Rainbow
would be using her own magic to free Luna and herself.
Something snapped a twig deep in the forest, and Aisling's
sinking heart gave a startled leap. She stopped to stare into
the dense, dark trees. Again, her aunt left her behind on the
path. With the fog seeming to follow as they went along,
Aisling opened her mouth to beg the hurrying Faery to slow
her pace.

"Remember-Fear-Not, your Fey name gives you great
courage," her aunt called before she could say a word.
"Worry not for the safety of Luna. A white mare is revered
above all sacred horses in the Faery realm. And no Leprechaun has ever harmed a horse."

The ring of truth in the Faery's voice brought a bit of comfort into Aisling's heart. But what of her own fate? Would she ever be reunited with Luna? Would she ever find her True Love? Or would this nightmare end in disaster? What would become of Luna then?

The exquisite Faery creature paused while Aisling hurried to her side. Her questions were on the tip of her tongue, but once again, her aunt seemed to know what was on her mind and in her heart. The gentle touch of those slender, white fingers on her cheek brought tears to her eyes, and a trembling smile to her lips. It was a simple enough gesture of affection and concern, one she'd always yearned for but never experienced from the women Da had hired to raise her, nor, indeed, from Da himself.

Aunt Rainbow smiled. "As you are one of us, though mostly Mortal, The People will protect you, as well. Never forget your name, Niece. If your heart is strong, you will find True Love." With another smile, her aunt pressed a tender kiss to her forehead and patted her shoulder, then turned and darted away down the winding path.

With a little more confidence, Aisling followed. For the first time in memory, she felt cared for in a special way—she felt *mothered*. A warmth, some sweet, unnamable emotion, seemed to envelope her heart. And with it, the blossoming hope that if this was not a dream, she would find the True Love that would free her.

Soon, she noticed a tang of pine, a hint of rosemary, a waft of lavender in the air, but none of the scents she knew equally well, particularly that of horses and cows. Dark and foggy as it was, with not even a sliver of sky, no twinkle of stars or glow of moon appearing through the dense canopy of the trees overhead, Aisling discovered she could see as clearly as if it were early dusk.

"Where is the light coming from, Aunt? Are there torches hidden behind the trees?"

Her beautiful Faery aunt looked back over her shoulder, delicate brows arched. "You've Faery eyes, Niece, although not so sharp as mine, nor even your poor mother's.

You are only a fraction Fey, but there is magic in your blood.''

Aisling stopped and stared at her aunt. A moment later, the Faery seemed to notice she was alone again. This time, instead of entreating Aisling to hurry, however, she suggested they rest. When Aunt Rainbow took a seat on a fallen log, she gestured for Aisling to sit beside her, then put her arms around her in a comforting embrace. Unable to recall another such heart- and soul-warming moment, Aisling nestled closer. Immediately, her eyelids began to droop. Exhausted, she welcomed the chance to sleep. A soft laugh, accompanied by the sound of tiny bells, startled her eyes open again.

''Did you never wonder at your way with horses?'' Aunt Rainbow stroked Aisling's hair, another simple gesture that brought tears to her eyes. ''Eamon has a Mortal's skills for the training of them, although he's better than most. But you—like your mother before you—need only a word and a touch to tame the wildest of them. 'Tis the reason Luna will only allow you near her, the way her sire and dam would only allow Fiona's touch. 'Twas the reason Fiona came to the attention of both Eamon Ahearn and Acorn Bittersweet. She was just your age now when both of them vowed to have her. Their rivalry caused terrible events to occur.''

Sleepily, Aisling promised herself to ask her aunt later—providing this wasn't all a dream—about those terrible events.

Aunt Rainbow pressed another gentle kiss to Aisling's forehead. ''Rest now, Niece, and rest easy. Everything shall soon be set to rights.''

Closer to the image of her mother than she'd ever felt, snug in her aunt's comforting embrace, Aisling fell into an exhausted sleep. Vaguely, she sensed she was being carried, then carefully lowered, but still, she slept. Images of being a small child again, of being with the mother she'd never known—transformed now into a vibrant woman—swirled through her mind. She saw herself as a girl budding into a young woman, laughing with her mother over the antics of a white filly foal. Arms linked, they were as alike as sisters, even to wearing similar violet-sprigged white dresses.

Then, at a misty distance, she saw a figure approaching, and her mother disappeared from her side. Striding across the grassy paddocks of de Burgh Manor came a young man so handsome Aisling's breath caught at the sight of him. Tall and broad of shoulder he was, with long, powerful legs and beautifully shaped hands. Black Irish he was, with ebony hair spilling over a noble forehead, and bold, laughing blue-gray eyes. Ever closer he strode, a smile curving his generous mouth in undeniable joy at the sight of her. Oddly clothed he was, neither a gentleman nor a farmer, but she dismissed this as the strangeness of a dream. As he drew near, Aisling's heart began to race with recognition: 'Twas he! 'Twas her own True Love!

He spread his arms wide, and Aisling darted toward him, eager for his embrace. His solidly muscled chest absorbed the impact of her greeting, and then, as she looked up into his dear face, he bent his head, with tantalizing slowness, to kiss her. His name . . . ? What was it? Surely, she knew his name? Of course, she knew the name of her own True Love! It was . . . It was . . .

Something jolted Aisling awake. Oh, what a dream!

Four

Ambros O'Hara thanked the boy who'd brought him the message, then dropped a coin into the child's outstretched, dirt-grayed palm. Shutting the door against the driving rain and wind of an autumn storm, he stood in the dimly lit foyer and broke open the seal on the smudged notepaper addressed to him. The signature was Eamon Ahearn's. The sight of it on All Hallow's Eve, the day after he and his father had attended the man's funeral, raised the hairs at the back of his neck. Ambros had to read the shaky, uneven lines several times before their meaning sank in. When he finally understood what Eamon was confessing to, he folded the note and leaned against the heavy oak door, his eyes unseeingly focused heavenward.

After a long, blank moment, he roused himself and turned toward fire blazing in the library hearth. Then he hesitated. Part of him wanted to destroy the note, but . . . The truth couldn't be destroyed. It would always try to surface, like a damp spot under whitewashing. If Aisling Ahearn ever returned, it was her right to know the truth. Until then, no one else needed to know.

Fortunately, his father hadn't seen the note delivered. After tucking the paper into the pocket of his trousers, he walked toward the door leading to the cellars. Somewhere in those labyrinthine rooms and hallways, there must be a safe place to hide a piece of paper.

A GATHERING PLACE, THE FAERY REALM, EVER-THE-PRESENT

"At last, Niece, we've caught up with the Moonstone Circle," Aunt Rainbow announced, gesturing toward a clearing filled with shimmering light and bustling with activity. Silvery music and laughter echoed lightly around her. Aisling couldn't ever recall dreaming in such vivid detail.

It was a dream, wasn't it?

"Come in, Remember-Fear-Not. This is one of the favorite gathering places for all the Irish Circles of Trooping Faeries. 'Tis particularly well suited for festivals and competitions. There will be tournaments later, when the other Circles arrive."

Aunt Rainbow held her hand out to Aisling. Clutching her aunt's delicate hand for security, she stepped forward to enter the clearing, then breathed a long sigh of amazement. The trees surrounding the clearing arched overhead to form a vaulted, leafy canopy festooned with garlands of flowers in every color of the rainbow. Diamonds and colored jewels glittered like dewdrops on the leaves. Wherever Aisling looked—gawked, although she tried not to be rude—there were beings like her aunt, graceful, exquisitely beautiful whether male or female, garbed in gossamer and flowers. Their voices sounded like the chirping of night creatures, and their laughter rang like silver bells on the wind. When they noticed the arrival of Aisling and her aunt, however, sudden silence fell over the clearing.

"Ah! 'Tis our Rainbow!" a musical male voice called out. A moment later, the silence dissolved into a symphony—soon, becoming a din—of joyful greetings. Suddenly, all those beautiful Faery beings were swirling around her, touching her hair and her clothes, smiling, speaking in their tiny, silvery voices. At her side, Aunt Rainbow murmured introductions into her ear, as quickly as each new

Faery appeared. Aisling kept her composure through the
first few rapid presentations, although the names were so
odd, she suspected she would never remember half of them.
But when a beautiful copper-haired Faery woman said she
remembered Fiona, Aisling succumbed to the sobs that had
been building inside her.

"Oh, dear! You mustn't cry! We only enjoy laughter,"
the Faery chided sweetly. " 'Twould be unforgivable of
you to spoil our merrymaking."

Aisling recoiled at the Faery's hurtful comment, but no
one else seemed to think it was insensitive. To her relief,
Aunt Rainbow stepped in and shooed everyone away, then
led her to the far side of the clearing. Immediately, conversation, laughter, and music swelled to fill the glade with
a distinctively happy symphony.

"We are only gathering here for a time," Aunt Rainbow
explained, "on our way to another festival. That is mostly
what we Trooping Faeries do, you know." She touched
Aisling's hand with cool fingertips. "We aren't as indus-
trious as you Mortals, perhaps because we are so accus-
tomed to using magic or guile," she continued, smiling
ruefully. "Or perhaps because it's our nature to simply enjoy life and avoid unpleasantness whenever possible."

"Oh," Aisling said, thinking that sounded rather childlike. "But what about me?" Her voice wavered. She swallowed. "How am I going to find my True Love if I am
here with you and the other Faeries?"

"Do not fret, Remember-Fear-Not. I will assist you
whenever you wish to go to the Mortal realm. I am certain
you shall find your True Love on a full-moon night, but I
cannot tell you how many of your hundred years will
pass."

Aunt Rainbow tipped her head and gave Aisling a long,
considering look. "To break a Leprechaun's enchantment,
one's True Love must prove his love thrice by deeds and
thrice by words. It is not such a simple task to find a Mortal
man willing to prove his love even once by word and deed.
Many of them would prefer to be tortured instead. 'Tis

possible Acorn Bittersweet will prove to be the better choice after all.''

"Aunt!" Aisling wailed, stricken by the horrifying thought. "How can you say that? I thought you were helping me escape him!''

Rainbow smiled sweetly. "Ah, Niece! We Faeries do prefer taking the easiest ways whenever we can.'' Then she frowned slightly. "The complementary magic I wish to employ to alter Acorn Bittersweet's enchantment must be cast just so. I have minor concerns about some of the fine details of my spell—nothing you need worry about.'' A dazzling smile lit the Faery's face, and when Aisling managed a weak answering smile, Rainbow patted her shoulder gently.

Abruptly, Aunt Rainbow darted to another part of the bowerlike room and began sprinkling fine powder in the air. "Faery dust," she told Aisling with a mischievous grin. "There is a Wise Mortal—some of her people call her a witch—who knows much of these matters. I shall enlist her aid in our endeavors. I shan't be gone long in Fey time.'' Aisling opened her mouth to protest, but the Faery glided to her and patted her cheek, silencing her. "As you will be among most entertaining company, you will hardly miss me," Rainbow added brightly.

Biting her lower lip, Aisling barely managed to contain a new threat of tears. She didn't understand any of Rainbow's talk of magic and witches. All she understood was that she looked like a horse to all Mortals except herself, and Aunt Rainbow was leaving her alone in this beautiful but strange place, with beautiful but terribly rude and noisy strangers. Exhaustion, fear, and confusion broke down the last of the fragile composure she'd tried so hard to preserve. She gulped and desperately clung to the delicate hand that lightly held hers.

"Aunt, please don't leave me!" she wailed.

Aunt Rainbow cupped Aisling's chin in her cool, slender hand. Her dark violet gaze met Aisling's. "Never forget the power of your magical name, Remember-Fear-Not, Niece. All shall be well. What comes around, goes around. Those who have offended The People, those who have injured you, my dear niece, shall suffer pangs of remorse until amends are made.'' Reminding Aisling of a bird, the Faery tipped her head. ''Remorse is not a Fey emotion, of course, but, like True Love, we recognize it when we see it.''

With one of her sparkling smiles that always seemed to have the power to draw an answering smile from Aisling, the Faery stepped back. There were no mirrors anywhere that Aisling could see, but Rainbow didn't seem to notice the lack. She gave a quick tug to straighten the drape of her gossamer dress. Then, while Aisling wrung her hands and blinked her tears away, she glided toward the bejeweled and garland-decked arching doorway.

''The O'Haras won your inheritance with little effort,'' Rainbow said over her shoulder, ''but winning you shan't be quite so simple as buying your foolish father's debts. Ah, no, they shall have to work for their reward.''

The Faery's declaration sent a chill of unease through Aisling. ''Wait, Aunt! What do you mean?''

Aunt Rainbow stopped in mid-stride and turned to smile at Aisling. It was a sweet smile, but there was something in her aunt's expression that made Aisling suspect she wasn't going to like the explanation. *Please be a dream*, she prayed.

''I have cast a spell on the entire O'Hara line. To ensure that the de Burgh inheritance isn't lost to you, they shall prosper in all business endeavors. But none of them shall love happily until you are released from your enchantment.''

''But, Aunt, the O'Haras are already prosperous. I hardly think they would believe themselves to be particularly cursed by conditions that vary not the least from their current status.''

Again, Rainbow flashed one of her dazzling smiles. ''You misunderstand me, Niece. The keystone of my complementary spell is this: One of Ambros O'Hara's descendants shall fall in love with you, and you with him, within the next hundred years, or their line will die out when Acorn Bittersweet claims you.''

Aisling's jaw dropped, but when she tried to speak, only a choking noise came from her throat.

" 'Tis brilliant, I know." With a trill of silvery laughter lingering after her, Aunt Rainbow darted into the passage-way.

Aisling shook her head. She couldn't have heard that right! Aunt Rainbow surely didn't . . . She wouldn't . . . No matter how she repeated the words in her mind, the meaning came out the same. With enormous effort, she leaped toward the leafy doorway, but halted at the sight of the dense fog filling the tunnel-like corridor.

"Aunt! No!" she wailed after the rapidly disappearing Faery. "I hate all O'Haras!"

She stamped a foot for emphasis. All the nearby Faeries paused in their activities to stare at her. Aisling glared back. Shrugging, they all turned away and continued their games. She followed her aunt along the foggy path as far as she dared, then stopped.

"I *don't want* to fall in love with an O'Hara! I *won't* fall in love with an O'Hara! I won't let an O'Hara fall in love with me!"

With each declaration, her voice grew more shrill, but there was no sign her aunt heard. The fog was closing in on her now, and her knees were shaking with fear, but she wasn't ready to admit defeat. She took a deep breath, determined that the entire world would hear her this time.

"A hundred years isn't long enough to make me fall in love with an O'Hara!"

LONDON, ENGLAND, DECEMBER 20, 1965

"Look, Jonathan! There's a chapter about my family in this book!" Corliss O'Hara Sloan held the leather-bound volume up for her husband to see. Immediately, he left off sorting through a bin of architectural prints across the little shop and came to her side.

"True Tales of Irish Family Curses and Enchantments, Book III," she read from the gilt-embossed spine of the book. Opening the cover, she read the elaborately decorated

first pages. "It's one of a series," she told him with a laugh in her voice. "Oh, my! It concerns Ambros Conlan O'Hara the second, Da's father . . . No, his grandfather. An unpleasant man, if my own grandfather's tales are even half-true. I wonder what that scoundrel got himself into."

"Let's see what it says." He took the open book from her hand and cleared his throat. She leaned against him, content to listen to his resonant voice. "Hmm. *The Legend of Lady Moonlight*, subtitled, 'A History of the Lost de Burgh Family, and the O'Hara Curse,' " he read in solemn tones that made Corliss giggle.

She poked his ribs. With a snort of laughter, he hugged her tightly. Corliss snuggled close, burrowing inside Jonathan's down jacket, savoring the sinewy strength and spicy scent of her handsome husband.

"Funny me even picking this up." She held the book up. "I was looking for vintage cookery books." Corliss gave her husband a self-mocking smile. "But isn't that how we came by that lovely silver tea service, looking for a sofa? And our favorite sofa, looking for a clock?"

"And a pair of Siamese cats while looking for an office chair." Chuckling, Jonathan kissed her temple. "Find the shopkeeper, then. I'm starved."

"You're a bottomless pit, you are!" With a laugh, she stepped out of his embrace and plucked the book from his hands. "Get us a place at the pub while I pay for this. We'll look this over at lunch."

As Jonathan made his way across the street, Corliss turned to look for the owner of the quaint old bookshop they'd been exploring. The sudden appearance of a young woman—an exquisite blond woman wearing a white gauzy, loose-fitting dress, pink-tinted glasses, and sandals with gold cord straps—startled her. With nearly every other female in London—possibly the world—either in bell-bottoms or miniskirts, the woman would have been noticeable even if she hadn't been so beautiful. Fleetingly, Corliss wondered at how anyone could dress so skimpily at Christmas in London, but the woman didn't seem to notice the chill that made Corliss shiver even in a heavy sheepskin jacket.

Corliss caught herself staring with rude openness, imagining for a moment that she was looking at a fairy tale princess come to life. She couldn't recall ever seeing any woman more incredibly, stunningly, gorgeous. The young woman gazed serenely at her through those pink-tinted, wire-rimmed glasses, then smiled brilliantly, infectiously.

"You'll be taking that, will you?" The woman spoke in a liltingly Irish voice, making Corliss glad she was on her way to her homeland. " 'Tis a lovely series of wonderful, true tales. We Irish do love our magical stories, do we not?" Incongruously, Corliss noticed the faint tinkling of bells, perhaps a recording of Christmas music playing softly at the back of the shop. The woman flashed another brilliant, slightly conspiratorial, smile.

Corliss held the book toward her. "Yes, please, I'll take it. How much?" Her abrupt, un-Irish, direct question sent a flush of heat to her face.

Without taking the book from her, the woman gave Corliss a long, considering look. Corliss fought the urge to fidget like a naughty child in Sunday school.

Finally, the woman smiled—a little slyly, Corliss thought. "Ah, 'tis priceless, truly it is. A unique item."

Corliss had been around horse trading all her life. She shrugged and kept her tone casual. "If 'twere priceless, it would not be moldering in this drafty old bookshop."

The woman's silvery laugh harmonized with the ringing of those bells. "There's truth in that." She tipped her head to one side, regarding Corliss through large, dark eyes behind those rosy glasses. " 'Tis true, you're an O'Hara." Cautiously, Corliss nodded to confirm the woman's statement. "And descended from Ambros O'Hara, of County Sligo, himself, you are."

A little distressed now, that this stranger knew so much about her, Corliss nodded curtly.

"Then truly, although 'tis priceless, you've already paid. No money is needed. The book is yours." The shopkeeper gave a dismissing wave with one pale, slender hand. "Compliments of the season! Happy Christmas!"

Puzzled and a little suspicious, Corliss reached into her purse. "Oh, no! I can't just take it! You make your living selling things. Name a fair price and I'll pay you."

The woman put a delicate hand on Corliss's, the light contact drawing her attention away from searching for her wallet. " 'Tis yours, my dear, truly. 'Twas meant for an O'Hara to find it, although in truth, 'twas meant for an unmarried O'Hara son." She frowned. " 'Tis most puzzling." Then, after patting Corliss's hand, an incandescent smile lit her exquisite face. "Ah! Perhaps everything will happen as 'twas meant, after all."

The woman's odd words increased Corliss's nervousness. "Th-thank you. And happy Christmas to you, too."

Strangely, she couldn't move her feet, although she desperately wished to be anywhere but this musty, odd shop. The woman removed her pink-tinted glasses and gazed into Corliss's eyes so directly, with eyes an astonishing shade of purple, that Corliss began to feel almost faint. Finally, the woman nodded and replaced her glasses.

"You'll be going home, then?" The question came gently, with typical Irish interest in another's travels. But the woman's next words, accompanied by more of those silvery bells, stunned Corliss. "You'll be telling Ambros Conlan O'Hara the fourth, that a grandson is on its way? 'Twill be welcome news to him."

Corliss's jaw dropped. She snapped it shut and glanced around for Jonathan. When she turned back to the woman, to demand how she knew anything so personal, there was no sign of her. Nor was there any sign in the shop of the old books and prints she and Jonathan had been browsing through. She was instead standing in a tiny grocery store, and instead of the exquisite, mysterious woman who had given her the book, a well-upholstered middle-aged woman sat in an old rocking chair beside the battered black antique cash register, her crochet hook moving with machine-like precision as she worked a lace doily.

Dazed and a little frightened, Corliss wrenched open the

shop door, then let it fall closed by itself behind her. She raced across the street and flung herself into Jonathan's arms, still clutching the leather-bound book. Unable to describe the unsettling incident coherently, she allowed her husband to diagnose her condition as hunger, and to prescribe a cheddar cheese sandwich and half-pint of bitter.

Later, after reading the story of Aisling Ahearn and the so-called O'Hara Curse, Corliss decided to keep it all to herself. When they arrived at O'Hara House, she hid the book in the farthest, darkest corner of the manor house wine cellar. 'Twas a warning, she was sure, but she daren't share her fear. It would make her sound utterly mad, to speak of magic and curses. Da and Jonathan would laugh at her for being so superstitious, or they would dismiss the tale as the ravings of a pregnant woman.

Besides, the legend had nothing to do with Jonathan and her. Nothing could threaten their love.

Book Two

A long, long time later, a young and handsome prince of the Bufonidae Family came to this enchanted place . . .

Five

Clutching the neck of a nearly full bottle of Gramps's best Irish whiskey, Midleton Very Rare, Conlan Ambros O'Hara Sloan set out across the moonlit fields to celebrate the worst day of the worst summer of his sixteen years in an appropriate way. He was going to get stinking, roaring, falling-down, forget-his-own-name drunk.

When he reached the center of the farthest field, the one on the far side of the tumbled-down stone wall, he tipped his head back and took his first gulp. He wasn't ready for the fire that filled his mouth and scorched its way down his throat to his belly. The heat consumed his breath, leaving him bent double and gasping. Man, that stuff was strong!

Cautiously, he straightened and took two deep breaths of the cool night air. His throat felt raw, his lips tingled, and his chest felt like he'd been hit by a truck, but already a pleasant warmth was pooling in his gut. Con grinned. Sheesh! No wonder Gramps kept this stuff locked in the gun cabinet! It was Irish dynamite! Turning a slow circle in the center of the overgrown pasture, he peered through the dark even though he knew he had to be alone out there in the middle of nowhere, in the middle of the night. Satisfied, he tipped his head back and turned in another circle, raising the bottle to salute the nearly full moon peeking through a veil of clouds.

"*Sláinte!*" he bellowed, toasting the sky in the only Irish word he'd learned in his first week. A hiccup spoiled his effort to get his North American mouth around the correct pronunciation, *slauntcha*. With a snort of disgust, he downed another swallow. This time, the trail of fire following the whiskey down his insides only made him wince. A third swallow went down almost painlessly, although it gave a little kick when it hit his gut. Hey, once you got used to this stuff, it wasn't so strong!

He tipped the bottle again, but the whiskey took a wrong turn on the way down his throat. It seared places it hadn't found before, places he hadn't known he had. Tears flooded his eyes. His ears burned. Coughing caught him and twisted him down to his knees in the wet grass, ripping the air out of him, not letting any back in. When he finally managed to draw a breath in through his clenched teeth, the cool air burned almost as badly as the heat of the whiskey. Guess he wasn't quite used to it enough.

Several painful breaths later, he struggled to stand. His legs ignored his brain and buckled under him. Cursing, he landed hard on one knee. Fortunately, his right hand stayed locked around the neck of the whiskey bottle. Wouldn't want to waste a drop! Not when he had serious drinking to do. Nothing else was going right, but he should be able to get stinking drunk without screwing up. Man, being sixteen sucked mud!

Kneeling, Con lifted his face to the heavens. "I hate being sixteen!" he muttered. Was it his imagination, or had the moon winked at him? After another quick swallow, and another breath drawn in between his teeth, he let out a wolflike howl. Somewhere in the distance, dogs barked an answer. He drank a toast to them, then sank down to sit on his heels. With the bottom of the bottle propped against his thigh, he peered through the darkness again. This was not how he'd pictured the summer after his high school graduation.

"*I hate being sixteen!*" His bellow rang in the air, but

then his voice broke. Taking a healthy swallow of whiskey, he wrestled it down, and drew in a harsh breath.

"I hate girls and I hate horses!" His voice came out strong that time. "I especially hate Irish girls and Irish horses!" At the crack in his yell, a sudden film of tears clouded his vision. Damn! He wouldn't cry! Even drunk, they couldn't make him cry. It was his battle cry, or maybe his mantra. He'd repeat it till he got it right, or passed out trying. "I hate Irish girls and Irish horses, and I hate my parents!"

Another sip went down easier than before. Maybe he was getting used to it. Or else he was numb inside. That would be a good thing, being numb inside. Then things wouldn't hurt him so much. No, not *things*. Things couldn't hurt him the way people could, especially people he cared about. Well, he wasn't stupid. The solution to getting hurt by people was to stop feeling, stop caring. Then they couldn't shred his heart and stomp on it and cut it into little pieces with a dull blade and . . .

"Damn you, Maddy Molloy!" he muttered. "You and your stupid horses! Nearly broke my neck for you!"

But it wasn't his neck that ached inside. It was the part of him that had pounded with anticipation and pleasure when pretty Maddy Molloy had made it plain last evening that she wanted him to take her for a walk and kiss her in the shelter of the old garden. It was the part of him that had clouded his brain today, making him forget his antipathy for horses, making him want to show off for her. Then Maddy had told him he kissed worse than he sat a horse, and had torn that part of him with the jagged edge of her laughter.

Con raised the bottle to his lips again, but when he tipped his head back, he lost his balance and landed hard on his butt. The jolt, dead center on the worst of his horse-inflicted aches, rattled his teeth and sent a few drops of whiskey skyward. The scenery rocked like a raft on white water. With a grunt, he propped the bottle against his thigh to wait for the earth to stop rolling.

His second evening here, Gramps had pushed him into

the pub to "meet the young people" at a traditional Irish music night the locals called a *céilí*. Maddy had introduced herself and tugged him across the pub to a booth where several other kids already sat. Crowding onto the bench, she'd pulled him with her, then leaned her full breasts against his arm and looked into his eyes like he was the only guy in the world. She'd let him pay for her tiny bottles of Coca-Cola, and for her plate of chips, which turned out to be greasy French fries. When he'd figured out the cost in U.S. dollars, he'd nearly had a heart attack. But Maddy made it feel like a privilege to spend his money on her. She made him feel special.

For days after, with her leading him a little farther each evening at the pub, he'd been in an agony of anticipation. Sure, he was totally, perpetually horny and hopeful. That was an occupational hazard of being sixteen. But Maddy made him think she was just as interested. How was he supposed to know she was putting him on? Being two years younger than his classmates for the past four years, he didn't have much—okay, he didn't have *any*—dating experience. He needed something to take the sting out of his parents' divorce, so he played right into her hands.

When the *slagging* at him started, with each one in the group of local kids taking a turn, competing for the best insults, the sharpest verbal barbs, he thought it was the usual *craic,* the good fun they always seemed to have. At first he didn't notice the difference from the friendly teasing they aimed at each other every night. They went from his accent to his ignorance of rural life, to his presumed lack of sexual experience, shredding his ego. The next thing he knew, he was taking a dare to ride Maddy's father's stallion the following day. How was he to know a groom from the O'Hara stud had told someone from the Molloy farm that he was afraid of horses?

After another swig of whiskey, Con squinted at the moon, now shining almost as bright as the sun. Nothing to see out there, though. No lights from houses or streets. Nothing but fields and farms and stone walls and more fields. And wet grass, which was soaking the seat of his jeans.

He *wasn't afraid of horses,* damn it! He just plain didn't like them, and after today, he hated them even more.

The nightmare sequence of events played like a bad movie in his memory. Maddy had kicked her horse into a gallop before he'd gotten both feet into the stirrups. The damn stallion had bolted after the other horse, then picked up speed before stopping short in front of the wall Maddy and her horse had cleared. He'd shot out of the saddle like a cannonball, his face just missing the pile of rocks that passed for a fence. His shoulder was already turning sickening shades of purple and green. Did Maddy care? Ha! She'd laughed.

"Shouldda quit then," he muttered. "Got back on, like an idiot." He took a swig of whiskey, swallowing with hardly a grimace. "Here's to being an idiot. No, an *eejit!* That's how they say it. And here's"—he waved the bottle toward the sky—"to the mud flats." The mud flats near Sligo Harbour deserved two hard swallows of whiskey.

Con closed his eyes against the memory of seeing an enormous lake of glistening, sucking mud, with ships out beyond it. *Ships!* That should have been his cue to turn the stupid horse around, and to hell with Maddy, but the way the damn thing was dancing around and pulling at the bit, he probably would have lost the battle anyway. Damn Maddy, out in front, didn't get a drop of mud on her, but her horse spattered him with globs of stinky black ooze from the first stride. Then his horse had made a sharp left. He'd continued straight, headfirst into the mud and water. The stupid stallion had kicked up its heels and galloped home, with Maddy shrieking curses at him for letting the horse run loose. She'd gone off after the horse and not come back, leaving him to limp back to his grandfather's house.

With a grunt, Con let himself lie back on the cool grass. The world inside his head began to swirl and the ground lurched. He popped his eyes open, which stopped the internal rolling but didn't do anything for the way the earth was rocking under him. Was Ireland floating? Or was he? What was that pounding? Ba-da-bump! Ba-da-bump! His pulse in his ears? Or . . .

Hoof beats? Nah. Horses didn't run around in the middle of the night. They slept in stables at night. Didn't they?

Con struggled to sit up but gravity was too strong—or he was too drunk. He was stuck lying on the grass, and damn it, there was a horse galloping out there! No mistaking the sound now. Ba-da-bump! Ba-da-bump! Ba-da-bump! Every hoof beat echoed in his head, louder, louder, closer, closer. Oh, hell! He was gonna get trampled by a horse with insomnia!

Why did he have to die before he could get laid, even once?

He squeezed his eyes shut and held his breath, braced for the inevitable. The colored lights inside his skull swirled and streaked and hummed, and the earth rocked and rolled and spun under him. His lungs burned with trapped air. Con made himself breathe. Against his will, he drifted into a stupor.

Something brushed his chin. Con jerked awake and stared at the white horse towering over him. Its feet dug into the damp earth beside his head and chest, its muzzle lowered to sniff at him. Warm, moist breath tickled his neck. Drunk as he was, he knew enough not to move suddenly with those hooves so close to his head. Warily, he stared up at the beast until he realized he was staring at three white horses. He blinked and two of them melded into the third. Watching the images made him dizzy. He closed his eyes again, but stayed acutely aware of the horse.

Or so he thought, until he jerked awake.

"You'll be giving the angels more than their share of fine Irish whiskey tonight," a voice said, a sweet, lilting voice. A *woman*, not a horse. Definitely a woman's voice. "That bottle needs closing, and you need putting to bed."

Con knew his eyes were open, but he couldn't see a thing. It took him several seconds of panic to realize he hadn't gone blind. The mist from earlier in the evening had thickened into fog and settled over the ground like the thick down duvets on his grandfather's beds. *Soft weather,* Mrs. Penny, the housekeeper, called it, too wet for fog, not wet enough for rain. Whoever was there was completely hidden by the fog, and there wasn't a thing he could do to find her. Lying still made him aware of the dampness that had seeped into his jeans, sweater, and shirt. Turning his head only set the tilt-a-whirl ride in his brain in motion. Sitting up was out of the question.

"Caoch ólta," that sweet woman's Irish voice said. " 'Tis blind drunk you are." Way too sweet to be Maddy. So who . . . ?

Gritting his teeth, Con gathered himself for one supreme effort and pushed himself up onto his elbows. Slowly, he sat up, every inch of movement setting off explosions behind his eyes and making him seasick. He strained to see through the mist, but he could hardly make out his own shoes on his feet.

Moonlight sliced through the fog, and Con felt his heart stop. The most beautiful girl—woman—female—he'd ever seen stood smiling down at him. He blinked, expecting her to be a figment of his imagination, a trick of moonlight and mist, but the vision remained. He swallowed hard.

"I'm seeing things," he croaked.

Her laughter sounded like sweet music. "You're seeing me, to be sure."

He shook his head. Fireworks exploded with blinding pain, but when he opened his eyes, the vision was still there.

"I'm hearing things, too. I must be dreaming."

Again, she laughed, a soft, sweet sound. "Ah, well, you were asleep beside a Faery *rath*. Perhaps you've been enchanted."

If he wasn't before, he sure was now! He couldn't stop staring at her. Was she real? Hell, she looked like a picture of a fairy princess in a kid's storybook. Her hair was pale gold, so long that it flowed all the way down to her hips like a shawl, and her skin was pale like moonlight. It was too dark to see color, but he'd guess her eyes were dark blue. And her mouth . . . Soft-looking lips, just full enough to make them kissable.

Not that he personally expected, in this lifetime, to find out.

Anyway, weren't Faeries supposed to be tiny, firefly-like things, like Tinker Bell? Lying there looking up at her, he guessed she'd come up to his chin, but she was definitely a full-grown girl . . . woman. She wore some old-fashioned kind of long white dress, tight around the top and full at the bottom, and there was enough moonlight see how tiny her waist was, how nice her . . . figure was. Enough moonlight to send the blood rushing to his loins and his face.

"May I sit with you?" she asked.

Con's face heated. Great first impression! Drunk and rude! Damn! He rolled onto his side, waved crookedly at the patch of grass beside him, then gawked as she sat gracefully down.

"My name is Aisling." She had the most wonderful voice. " 'Tis an old Irish name meaning a poem, a vision, a dream."

"You probably are a dream," he muttered, then wanted to kick himself for saying something so stupid. She laughed softly, but it didn't sound like she was laughing *at* him. Not like Maddy.

"Well, I could be a dream, but I'm real enough, too. And do you have a name, or are you part of *my* dream?"

"I'm Sloan," he answered from habit. It was the only name he'd had to answer to in all his years at private schools and camps.

"How do you do, Sloan?"

There was probably some answer to that question, but his brain hurt too much to consider one. Right now, he was on serious sensory overload. He'd never been so close to anyone so gut-churning, heart-pounding beautiful. He wanted to touch her to see if she was real. Wanted to draw her down beside him so he could feel her stretched out along his body. Wanted to kiss her mouth, and feel her hair against his skin. And that was just for starters. But a girl this gorgeous would never let a toad like him touch her.

His fate was sealed. He was gonna die a virgin.

Letting himself roll over onto his back again, Con stifled a groan. "Was that your horse?" he asked, alarmed by how slurred his voice was. "Where'd it go? Don't wanna get stepped on."

"Ah, you needn't worry yourself about being trampled by Luna. She'd not hurt you." There was a short pause, and then she said, "Tell me, Sloan, what makes you so sad on such a beautiful summer night?"

Drunk as he was, he knew he shouldn't tell her he was horny and didn't see any serious chance of getting laid this century. There wasn't much he could tell her, without coming across like a loser. He wouldn't spill his guts to a total stranger who would probably laugh at him, anyway. He could tough it out by himself. He didn't need pity. He was fi—

"Sloan?"

"I hate it here. My parents are splitting up, so they sent me here for the summer, to get me out of their way. And my grandfather hates my guts." He gave a short, bitter laugh. "I'm covered with bruises from a lunatic stallion, I spent too much money on a girl who thinks I'm a loser, and I'm so drunk I can't see straight. I hate horses, I can't use the car, there are no computers anywhere, and . . . Did I tell you I hate horses? Other than all that, hey, everything's copacetic."

Flat on his back, he didn't see Aisling move, just suddenly felt her fingertips, cool on his cheek. He drew in a quick breath and froze, focused on a butterfly touch that was gone too soon. But then he felt her touch his hair where it curled at his shoulders. His scalp tingled.

"Lovely hair, like the old-fashioned heroes in my storybooks." Her whisper made him ache inside.

Not daring to let himself believe she wasn't fooling, he snorted. "My grandfather says it makes me look like a girl."

She gave a little musical laugh. "Then your grandfather needs new spectacles! To my eyes, you look nothing like a girl. You've the look of a young warrior about you, Sloan.

Have you as much fight in you as you have whiskey?''

Aisling's flattering words were more intoxicating than all the whiskey he'd consumed. He turned his head to look into her eyes. The movement brought his cheek against her hand. Con expected her to jerk her hand away, but she didn't. He prayed he wouldn't barf on her. She met his gaze, her eyes dark and luminous in the moonlight. He let his gaze drift to her lips, soft and full, then met her eyes again.

"Do you believe in magic, Sloan?" Aisling's voice came to him as softly as the whisper of a breeze.

He could, he thought. He must, because this had to be some kind of illusion. Smoke and mirrors, or something like that. It couldn't be real, and there was no such thing as real magic. "No. There's always a trick to it," he muttered.

Again, she gave a soft laugh. "Of course! 'Tis the magic!"

"No such thing as magic."

"How can you be saying that, and you being Irish!"

Oh, great! The girl of his dreams was a patriotic fruitcake. That figured. "Just because I'm Irish doesn't mean I have to go around seeing Faeries under every bush, does it?"

Aisling actually turned her head and looked around the dark field. Then she looked into his eyes again, smiling playfully. "And a good thing that is, because you'll not find them under every bush. The Good People are more particular than that."

"You don't really believe that fairy tale stuff, do you? You're pulling my leg, right?"

She took her hand away from his cheek, held both palms up as if for inspection, and frowned. "I didn't do any such thing to your leg! Perhaps one of The Good People is trying to get your attention."

Oh, man, she thought he meant she was literally . . . Guess either that wasn't an Irish expression, or she was a little slow. Finesse would be a good thing to have right about now. No hope for that. He tried to sit up, but only got as far as propping himself up on his elbows. A sharp pain circled his skull, then dulled to an ache somewhere in the back of his head.

"I mean, you're teasing me about believing in Faeries." Aisling gave a quick little shake of her head. He stifled a groan. "You're not teasing me. You believe in magic and Faeries?"

She gave him a brilliant smile. "Why wouldn't I believe in something that's true?"

Now he did groan. "Aisling, I'm a computer scientist. Or I will be when I finish my degree. I believe in things I can prove. Magic is just a bunch of superstitions from before people figured out scientific explanations. Anyone with a brain knows that."

The instant the words were out, he knew he shouldn't have said them. The air between them seemed to get colder. Aisling abruptly stood up. Framed by moonlight, she was a graceful shape above him, but he could feel her frowning.

" 'Tis the heart you should be looking to for your proofs."

"Don't go!" he croaked as he pushed himself into a sprawled version of sitting. He couldn't make his legs obey the simple commands for standing. The sensation of being stabbed by broken glass assaulted his brain. He caught his breath, then forced himself to his hands and knees. Ignoring the pain in his head and the rolling of his stomach, Con fought gravity and whiskey to stand up. When he finally succeeded, his vision suddenly turned to blackness, with shimmery streamers of lights teasing the edges. He prayed Aisling would still be there when his vision cleared.

She was. And he'd guessed right; the top of her head came to his chin. With her head tilted up and her eyes looking straight into his, she radiated intensity. He fought to stand without swaying, but every steadying breath brought him another dose of her sweet scent. The rush of blood to his loins threatened to bring him to his knees again.

"I'm s-sorry," he stammered. "I'm an inte . . .

intellectual s-sn-snob. No so . . . social skills. It's the curse
of being pre . . . preco . . . precocious.''

Aisling nodded solemnly. ''Ah, yes. 'Tis all too familiar
I am with curses. Is there no way to free yourself?''

Oh, hell! She thought he meant a real curse! Like someone waved a magic wand and changed him from a prince
to a nerd! What a loony toon! Con opened his mouth to
correct her, but remembered just in time that arguing about
the existence of magic was what got her upset in the first
place. No one could say he didn't learn from his mistakes.
But what was he supposed to say to this gorgeous creature
who took magic and curses seriously?

Inspiration struck. ''Maybe you can help me.''

To his astonishment, she smiled as if he hadn't just
handed her the most obvious line. ''I'd be pleased to try,
Sloan.'' He thought she blushed, but he couldn't be sure
because the moonlight washed the color from everything.
''And perhaps you'd be kind enough to help me break the
spell entrapping me and my mare, Luna.''

Suddenly, he didn't care that she was a little crazy, with
her insistence on magic and spells. All he cared about was
that she was asking him for help. *His* help. She wasn't
setting him up and brushing him off the way Maddy had.
She was asking him to be a hero, to go to battle for her.
Something inside him, that part of him he'd thought Maddy
Molloy had thoroughly shredded, stirred with new hope.

''Anything. Just ask. I'll do anything. I'd crawl over broken glass for you.'' He didn't feel even a little foolish.

The touch of Aisling's fingers on his sleeve felt like the
brush of a butterfly. ''I don't believe that will be necessary,
although surely there will be tests and trials. The breaking
of spells is not to be undertaken lightly.''

''What—'' A sound like tiny bells made him pause.

''Sloan, I must go.''

Aisling slid her hand down his sleeve, drawing away
slowly, as if she didn't want to. It was all the encouragement he needed. Impulsively, he caught her hand in his and
held her back when she started to turn from him. He must
have tugged on her a little harder than he realized, because

she ended up right under his chin, her slender body a scant inch from touching him. Her hair brushed over his hands, soft as silk threads, and her scent filled his head. His whole body ached to feel her against him, but he didn't dare try. A girl . . . woman like Aisling wouldn't want a sixteen-year-old sex maniac like him groping her!

"Sloan, I must go," she whispered, but she didn't move.

He released her hand, but she didn't step away. "Aisling," he said softly, just to taste her name on his lips. Then he told himself to get real. She must be about twenty. Why did he have to meet her when he was only sixteen, and not worth her taking him seriously? Life wasn't fair.

She tipped her head up and looked into his eyes. Their faces were so close, all he had to do was bend a little and he could be kissing her. She had to realize that, but she wasn't moving away. Suddenly, he felt stone-cold sober. The clarity of his senses stunned him.

"I could believe in magic if I could kiss you."

Con didn't realize he'd turned his thought to words until he heard them hanging in the silence. Man, how stupid could he get? How could he insult her like that? He saw her raise one hand and braced himself for the sting of a slap across his face. But then she raised her other hand.

Her light touch felt both warm and cool on his cheeks. Transfixed by the depths of her eyes, he let her draw his head down until he had to close his eyes. The touch of her lips on his was cool, hot, over before it had begun. Con kept his eyes shut, certain that if he opened them, he'd find himself standing alone in the middle of a moonlit field. Then he heard her sigh.

Praying he wouldn't fumble, Con reached for her. She was so little, his hands closed around her waist. He could overpower her so easily, could take what his raging hormones demanded. Resisting the urge to drag her hard against himself made him tremble. He didn't want to resist. He wanted to give in to the storm rising inside him.

Bending toward her again, he found her lips with his on the second try. He was shaking so hard all over that he might as well be standing at ground zero in an earthquake.

Breathing in her sweet scent, he kissed Aisling softly, lingering a little to memorize the feel of her lips against his, to absorb her sweetness. She swayed, closing the slight distance between their bodies, and the gentle press of her small, firm breasts wrenched a groan from the depths of his soul. He gathered handfuls of her long, silky hair and increased the pressure of his mouth on hers. She nestled closer. The brush of her middle against him sent a jolt of pure animal lust to his already straining lower body.

Con couldn't believe this was happening. That Aisling was *letting* this happen. She tasted so sweet and felt so good! Would she let him . . . ? She was older; she had to know what was happening between them. If Aisling didn't stop him . . . He shouldn't go on, but he couldn't make himself stop. A groan of misery and hunger rose in the back of his throat. Her body stiffened in his arms, but his body was on autopilot. He felt her trying to draw away, but he didn't want to let her go. Not yet! He wanted . . . He needed . . .

Pain exploded in his head.

She was pulling his hair. Hard. He got the message. With a grunt, he tore his lips away from Aisling's. Breaking the kiss so abruptly felt like being punched in the gut. A rush of air ripped into his lungs.

"Sorry." Speaking hoarsely, he released his hold on her waist. "Sorry, sorry, sorry."

Through half-closed eyes, his entire body aching, he watched her step back from him. His scalp hurt like hell, but in a funny way, the pain made him feel everything more acutely. There was some satisfaction in hearing her breathe as rapidly and shakily as he did. But only a little. Mostly, there was embarrassment that he'd gotten out of control. And frustration that she'd broken the kiss.

She was so beautiful! Her hair swung like a curtain when she ducked her head, then rippled with streams of moonlight when she looked up at him again. Her eyes were like the sky—dark, fathomless, luminous. Even after kissing her, he had trouble believing she was real. He stared down at her, his breath heaving like ocean waves in the silence

of the night, and prayed she'd be smart enough to run before his hormones turned him into a beast.

"Sloan, I must be leaving now." She sounded reluctant,
but a second later, she bolted away.

"Can you come back tomorrow night? Aisling?" Without answering, she continued sprinting toward the shadows
of the stone wall. "I'll wait for you anyway."

He watched until she disappeared into a swirl of fog, then
bent to retrieve the bottle before starting back to the house.
The effects of the whiskey flooded back so swiftly that Con
sank to his knees with a groan. Falling face-first onto the
cool, damp turf, he moaned with self-loathing. All that
whiskey couldn't wash away reality. He was still the black
sheep of the O'Hara family, still unwanted, a world-class
misfit.

Sinking into seasick oblivion, he accepted the coup de
grâce of the evening: the encounter with Aisling had to be
a drunken hallucination. A girl that beautiful wouldn't stop
to speak to him, let alone let him kiss her.

But if she was real? If she really had let him kiss her?
If she'd really kissed him back? Maybe that was proof that
magic really did exist!

Nah. With his luck, he'd spend the rest of his life as a
toad.

Six

"Aunt Rainbow, please hurry." Miles away from her ancestors' lands, Aisling waited impatiently for her dainty aunt to complete a wreath she was fashioning from flowers and bits of ribbon. Without Faery guidance, Aisling couldn't make her way safely or accurately between the world of reality and the world of magic. The Moonstone Circle traveled—Faery *rades,* they called their grand parades and pageants—frequently and far, often joining other Circles for festivals and tournaments all over Ireland. Or rather, all *under* Ireland. Several terrifying trips into unknown territories had proven that Aisling's much-diluted Fey talents and Faery eyes were insufficient to protect her.

Rainbow tied a gold ribbon around the stem of a wayward forget-me-not, then looked up with the sweetly bland expression that always meant her aunt would follow her own inclinations, no matter how Aisling pestered. In spite of their childlike behavior and unrepentant pursuits of selfish pleasures, adult Faeries, she had discovered, were very much like Mortal adults. They always thought they knew best for youngsters—usually, of course, younger Faeries—and always insisted on offering advice. Their advice could be utter nonsense, but they knew their magic world better than she ever could.

Fortunately, Aunt Rainbow was one of the most sensible of the Moonstone Circle. Her timely warnings had saved Aisling from several potential disasters. Nevertheless, Aisling chafed at having to defer to yet another adult in this matter of falling in love. She'd known the instant she'd seen Sloan lying drunk in the paddock that he was the man she'd seen in her long-ago journey dream. Or rather, he would be, once he actually became a man. That transformation would be wrought by time—Mortal time—and True Love, but if her estimations were correct, she had little time remaining, although she felt certain True Love was infinite.

For now, however, her recognition of Sloan as her future One True Love must be her secret, for she feared Aunt Rainbow would interfere. Her aunt would insist that only the True Love of an O'Hara, descended from Ambros O'Hara himself, could undo the entwined spells. She dared not confess to kissing Sloan, either. Sloan had tasted of whiskey, certainly, but under the whiskey, she'd tasted something elusive that had compelled her to allow him to hold her for more kisses. To be sure, his unbridled hunger and bold strength then had frightened her away. He himself had seemed overpowered by his own reactions, and her responses to him, but surely she wasn't ready for . . . that.

She was sorry if pulling his hair so hard had hurt him, but she hadn't known what else to do to get his attention. Later, thinking about the encounter while she tried to sleep in a quiet corner of the Faery palace, she'd realized his hunger and his strength had also fascinated her. There was so much about men and women that she didn't know. 'Twould be helpful if she could confide in someone more knowledgeable than herself. Someone who had no particular stake in discouraging her interest in Sloan.

"Aunt Rainbow?" Aisling prompted, after noting the dreamy expression in the Faery's purple eyes. Faeries, she had also learned, tended to become distracted altogether too easily. She needed her aunt to heed her and help her. "Please show me the way out. I know the moon is waning tonight, but Sloan will be waiting for me." Rainbow opened her mouth to speak, so Aisling rushed her next words out. "Oh, I know I shall appear to him as Luna, but if I can pass some time in his company, I shan't mind too much."

"*Sloan?*" Aunt Rainbow pursed her lips and repeated the name as if Aisling had uttered something terribly rude.

"I like him, Aunt, and I believe he likes me. I know he's rather young, but surely he'll age faster in the real world than I will here."

Aunt Rainbow shook her head very emphatically. Then she crossed her arms in front of herself and gave Aisling the sternest look she'd ever worn. "No, no, Niece! You must not dally with this Sloan! You have not met the *O'Hara* man whose love will set you free."

"Then the spell will never be broken!" Aisling stamped her foot, expelled an exasperated breath, threw her hands into the air, then slapped them down at her sides. "I don't want an O'Hara to break the spell! I want someone I can love back, and I could never love an O'Hara! I hate all the heartless, greedy sons of all Ambros O'Haras! They are the source of all my trouble! Why can't I be choosing Sloan now, and saving everyone the bother?"

Rainbow smiled. "The rules of magic must be obeyed to the letter, Niece. *O'Hara* says the spell, so another will not do."

" 'Tis your spell. Will you not alter it? To spare me the agony of having to be near any descendant of Ambros O'Hara?"

Her aunt shook her head, scattering rose petals that had fallen onto her long golden hair. Several of the petals turned into butterflies and fluttered upward toward the flowered ceiling of her aunt's Faery parlor. "Trust me, Niece, that I act in your best interests. 'Tis key that only an O'Hara of Ambros's line may break the complementary spell."

"Oh!" Aisling stamped her foot again, marched some distance away, then marched back again. "I'd rather marry that horrible Leprechaun than marry an O'Hara!"

Aunt Rainbow set down her wreath and gave Aisling a long, appraising look that Aisling met with her chin in the air. She was so tired of this waiting and wondering and trying to abide by rules she didn't understand. Why must she seek help—in the form of True Love, no less!—from the very people responsible for her plight? Why should she help the O'Haras break Aunt Rainbow's spell so the O'Hara line could love happily in the future?

"Be careful what you wish for, Niece. Time is passing. Do you remember that sweet boy-child you saw one evening with his grandfather, Ambros O'Hara? He is now a grandfather himself. You haven't much time to fulfill the requirements for breaking the spell on you." Aunt Rainbow gave a delicate shudder. "Acorn Bittersweet doesn't mean to be cruel to you, dear Niece. Like most males—and all Leprechauns are male—he isn't thinking about this matter with either his head or his heart."

Puzzled by this assertion, Aisling frowned. What else could males think with? Oh! The heat of a blush tingled in her cheeks as she recalled how Sloan's lust had nearly overcome his manners and her good sense. Fanning her face with her hand, she waited for Aunt Rainbow to continue speaking.

"Most Leprechauns are content to remain bachelors. The ones who wish to marry usually choose a wife from the Fey races, but some have married Mortals. Alas, it never ends well for either. Mortal women who marry Leprechauns become pitiful creatures who never see the sun, never hear music, never smile. Some do bear a half-Leprechaun child, but they all eventually wither away and die. Usually, the widower Leprechauns die of grief soon after."

"Then why do some Leprechauns insist on Mortal wives, if they can find Fey wives and live happily for hundreds of years?"

Aunt Rainbow laughed. "Try to convince a Solitary Faery that he isn't the sole authority on something! Once a Leprechaun has made up his mind, very little in the natural or Mortal world can change it. They would sooner die than admit to a mistake."

"Then I shall run away!" Aisling declared, forgetting for the moment that running away from an arranged marriage was what had gotten her into this situation.

The Faery folded her hands in her lap and gave Aisling another of those long looks. "Do not be hasty, Niece. Even for a Mortal with some Fey blood, the penalty for escaping the Faery World without properly breaking the spell is withering death."

A terrible, numbing cold spread inside her as her aunt's words sank into her mind. By all the saints, she was doomed! Doomed to die whether she escaped or married the Leprechaun, unless an O'Hara became her True Love!

For a moment, despair held her captive, until a wickedly rebellious thought popped into her head. 'Twas a fact, her fate couldn't get any worse than dying under the Leprechaun's enchantment. So if she slipped out of the Faery Realm and met Sloan in the paddock, it shouldn't affect the ultimate outcome in the slightest. She wished she could appear to him as herself, instead of as Luna, but this could be her only opportunity to see him again. The old Irish nanny who had cared for her many years ago always said, *Is fearr fuigheall ná bheith air easbuidh:* "Better to have the leavings than have nothing at all."

As soon as she could figure the way out . . .

O'HARA HOUSE, CO. SLIGO, FRIDAY, AUGUST 6, 1982

"And where is it you're sneaking to at this hour?"

His grandfather's bellow startled Con as he was about to slip outside through the servants' entrance at the side of the manor house. He stopped, but didn't turn around.

"Out."

Gramps gave a loud bark of laughter. "You're neither too old nor too big for me to take over my knee. Now, go on back up to bed. You'll not be traipsing around outside in the middle of the night."

Furious, Con spun and faced his grandfather, his fists clenched at his sides. "Why not? Think the Faeries will carry me away?" That had always been the teasing threat uttered during his childhood visits to Ireland.

Gramps lifted an eyebrow. "That would suit me, although your mother, for some foolish reason, might be distressed. But Faeries won't trouble themselves with a lazy, sullen oaf who steals good whiskey and doesn't have a horse-loving bone in his body.''

The words came at him like punches. ''Hey, don't sugarcoat your feelings, Gramps. I can handle the truth.'' His own sarcasm came out forced, but he couldn't let his grandfather see how much he'd just been hurt. ''And don't think I care what you think.''

Wrenching open the door, Con leaped down the cement stairs to the gravel lane and immediately picked up a steady jogging pace. Every stride jolted his bruises and pulled at his sore muscles. He cursed Maddy and tried to ignore the pain. It was easier to ignore Gramps shouting for him to go back. Putting his head down, he continued toward the fields where the horses grazed by day, where he'd met Aisling two nights before. He hadn't been able to think about anything else, except seeing her—and kissing her—again.

The need to see her was like a giant bruise inside him. The fear that he wouldn't was like a rope around that bruise.

Would she come back tonight, after he'd stood her up last night? Assuming she'd showed up. He didn't know. Gramps had made him work off his hangover by mucking out horse stalls and sweeping cobwebs in the barns and sheds, in retribution for stealing the whiskey. He'd fallen into a dreamless sleep at dusk. He would have slept till noon, if the old man hadn't poured a glass of water on his face at half past eight this morning. After another day in the barns, this one spent cleaning harnesses, saddles, and bridles, his cramped and waterlogged fingers ached along with every other part of him. Showering twice hadn't erased the smell of horse and leather and beeswax from his nostrils.

God, he hated horses!

By the light of the nearly full moon, Con jogged into the farthest of the original O'Hara fields, then paused to open the rusty iron gate in the thick stone wall. Dodging shadows and unexpected dips and bumps, he ran. More quickly than he expected, he was across the first field his ancestors had added at the end of the last century. One more old gate, this one left open, and he was in the last of the former de Burgh fields, the one where he'd met Aisling while drowning his sorrows. Staggering to a stop, he bent, with his hands propped on his knees, and panted.

As his breathing steadied, Con lifted his head to look around himself and listen to the night. There was a slight breeze, enough to chill his sweaty skin now that he'd stopped moving. Leaves of the trees in the corners of the pastures rustled. Or maybe the rustling came from an owl or night-hunting bird. He didn't know. Wildlife wasn't his thing; logic was.

There he was in the middle of a dark field, a day late for a date with a girl—a woman—he didn't know anything about. A woman who could be a whiskey-induced hallucination, who had talked about magic and Faeries as if they really existed. A woman whose kisses he couldn't stop thinking about, and whenever he thought about her, the blood rushed from his brain to his . . .

Logic didn't seem to apply now.

Con trudged in a circle in the grass, exploring his environment as well as he could in the near pitch-blackness. Several times, he tripped over uneven ground and almost fell on his face. He should have brought a flashlight—a torch, they called them here—to supplement the moonlight. And a blanket to sit on. He hadn't thought of that till now. All he'd thought of was seeing—and kissing—Aisling again. God, he was such a jerk!

Why did he have to be sixteen?

Something made a shuffling, rustling noise in the distance and Con shivered. At least he'd worn his jacket. He pulled the zipper tab up farther and tugged his sleeve cuffs over his fisted hands. The days were warm, but sometimes the nights got cool and damp. A branch snapped, sounding close enough to be in the next field. He heard footsteps on the sod. Step, step, step, step. Two people or one . . . What? Wolf? Ogre?

Horse! Con couldn't believe his eyes, but the white horse

he thought he'd hallucinated the other night was coming toward him across the field. So either he was hallucinating again now, or he hadn't been then. He supposed, that if the horse wasn't a figment of his imagination, that was a relief. As it came closer, he studied it as carefully as he could in the poor light. With the little bit of moonlight shining down, the body of the horse cast a darker shadow on the dark ground. So it was probably a real horse, not a sign that he'd lost his mind. It was the first time he could recall being glad to see a horse.

The horse walked right up to him as if it knew him. It extended its neck and sniffed at his jacket, ears flicking forward and back. Con stood still, waiting to see what would happen next. He wasn't afraid of horses. He just plain hated them. If his parents had spent all their time and attention on parrots or dogs, he'd probably hate them, not horses.

This one, for example, was kinda cute. He ducked down and peeked underneath. A mare. That wasn't surprising. She was very fine-boned, and her head was small and pretty, with huge, wide-spaced dark eyes. The mare nudged his chest with her nose, a gesture he figured he understood.

"Pushy little thing, aren't you?" he murmured, not really annoyed. The bobbing of her head, as if she were nodding agreement, made him laugh. She gave a soft snort, laughing with him. Raising one hand to rub her velvety nose, he asked, "What are you doing out here so late at night? Aren't you afraid of wolves? Or horse-nappers?" With a sigh, she burrowed closer.

For a while, Con continued petting the white mare and murmuring nonsense to her. Well, not exactly nonsense, but his future plans. Things about his ambitions and dreams that he'd never shared with any humans. It felt good to get the words out, even if his only listener was a horse. At least she was a nonjudgmental listener. Being in the middle of nowhere in the middle of the night felt so otherworldly that he found the passage of time taking on a strange, unreal feeling. When he paused to shake the circulation back into his arm, a wide yawn got his attention. He glanced at the phosphorescent numbers on his watch, surprised to see that he'd been out there over two hours, with only the white mare for company. He felt as if he'd been somewhere else.

"I don't suppose you know Aisling," he muttered to the mare. "Wouldn't make any difference if you did. You can't exactly give her a message for me. Damn! I wish I knew something about her." The horse snorted and bumped his chest with her nose. Con smiled and rubbed the velvety coat. The horse thanked him with a warm, wet tongue across his palm. Yuck! He didn't want to get that intimate with her!

He yawned widely again. If he didn't get back soon, Gramps would probably dump a bucket of water on him tomorrow morning.

"Hey, I gotta go." He started to move away.

The horse grabbed his jacket with her teeth. He batted her nose away. "Quit it!" The mare tossed her head and snorted, but she didn't try to use her teeth again. "You should be home, too," he told her. "Someone must be looking for you."

The mare pressed closer and rubbed her muzzle over his hair. He started to laugh at how she was petting him, but she closed her teeth on his hair. Before he could free himself, she tugged. "Ow! Hey!" At his shout, she opened her teeth and released him. Rubbing his scalp, Con pushed at the mare's chest. "Man, for a while, I forgot how much I hate horses. Thanks for reminding me."

When he pushed her away, the mare answered with a low nicker. "Go home." He made his voice stern. "I'm outta here."

Without looking back, Con started the long trudge back to the manor house. Facing into the breeze made him acutely aware of the chill in the night air. He folded his arms across his chest to warm himself, thinking again of how nice it had felt to hold Aisling in his arms. Would he ever see her again?

The little white mare quietly appeared at his side, keeping pace with him as he walked. For a few minutes, Con ignored her. After a while, the steady beat of her footsteps in the grass became impossible to ignore. He stopped. She stopped beside him, nickered, and wiped her nose on his sleeve.

"You can't follow me home like a stray dog. Whoever owns you is gonna have me arrested for horse stealing. That's all I need. The old man would probably let me rot in jail." He waved his hands at her. She moved her head out of his way, but stood her ground. "Go on! Go home!"

The damn mare didn't budge. Cursing, Con started walking, determined to ignore her if she kept following him. He thought he'd been successful in discouraging her, until he felt her breathing warmly on the back of his neck. He stopped and turned around. The mare stopped and nuzzled his cheek. Feeling just a touch guilty, he pushed her face away from his. She let him, then swung her head right back and tried to lick his cheek. This time, he pushed her away and kept his hand on her neck until he felt her stop trying to return for more. Maybe the creature was lost and lonely, and he was the only person she knew was around. He could relate to that. But that didn't mean he was willing to get slimed.

"Look, mare! This isn't gonna work! Go away, now!" He waved his hands under her nose and whistled sharply. She danced around, but didn't seem willing to leave. Just his luck to get followed home by a beautiful female, and it turns out to be a horse.

A light came on upstairs in the manor house. To anyone else, at any other time, the yellow glow behind the windows might have been a welcoming sign, but to him, it felt more like a reproach. Great. His shouting woke Gramps up. Con could imagine the old man's reaction to seeing him coming home with a stray horse. Damn! If he didn't have bad luck, he wouldn't have any luck!

Grumbling under his breath, Con turned and marched toward the house, not looking to see if the horse was following. He'd gone some distance before he realized he was walking alone. Relieved that he wasn't going to be facing charges for horse theft, he sighed and relaxed his pace. He was only one walled field away from the yard surrounding the house when he heard hoof beats pounding up behind him. The mare cleared the wall he'd had to clamber over. He wondered how the hell she could see where she was going with almost no light, but she landed and galloped toward him, stopping only inches from him.

A flash of memory so brief he couldn't grasp it with his conscious mind teased him with the image of an iron-gray pony, following him. Not surprising, considering how horses ruled his parents' lives, that he'd been around them as a little kid. The rest of the memory didn't come to him, so he shrugged it off.

Then, lunging toward the mare, he shouted and slapped her rump hard. She gave a shriek of alarm, then bolted away and, to his relief, leaped back over the wall to the other field. Rubbing his stinging palm on his jacket, Con turned on his heel. This time he closed the distance to the back door of the house without being accosted by his equine stalker. Discovering the door wasn't locked against him was a pleasant surprise. He let himself inside quietly and crept up the stairs to the guest room. As he tiptoed down the second-floor hallway, the line of light under his grandfather's door blinked and went dark. Guess there wasn't any point in lying about what time he'd come back.

Without bothering to turn on his own light, Con peeled off his jacket and jeans, then stood by the window to unbutton his shirt. The moon was nearly down now. It looked small and cold against the black sky. He could hardly make out the shapes of the fields and the walls beyond the first pasture. In a distant field, he saw a pale shape, saw movement. The little white mare was finally retreating slowly into the darkness.

AT THE EDGE OF THE FAERY REALM

Fighting to hold back her tears, Aisling watched Sloan disappear into the big stone manor house, very much like the ones the de Burghs and O'Haras had lived in a century before. Then she walked slowly back to the tunnel passage in the Faery *rath* where she'd emerged earlier, and made her way back to her aunt's chambers. As she passed through the entrance to the magical world of the Faeries, her form shifted from that of a white mare to her own familiar young woman's shape. She rushed to her aunt's rooms.

Had Rainbow noticed her absence? Her aunt's sweet smile of welcome revealed nothing. Aisling had counted on the games the Faeries had been playing to distract them from seeing her sneak away. Knowing them as she did, she still couldn't predict whether any of the Troop would alert her aunt, or simply ignore her. So much depended on their moods and whims, and on what appeared to be the most entertaining at any moment. Nor could she anticipate her aunt's reactions if she were caught sneaking out of the Faery *rath*. If she were ever going to find her True Love before the end of her one hundred years, Aisling knew she couldn't afford to anger her aunt and lose her as an ally. Tonight's encounter with Sloan had certainly proven to her that, as a white mare, she would have no success finding a man to love her.

Sinking onto a flower-strewn chaise, Aisling adjusted her position with care. Her left haunch smarted from the slap Sloan had administered to the white mare. Even sitting on the softest of Faery furniture was going to cause her discomfort.

"Perhaps a soak in a nice sage and mugwort bath will ease your aches," Aunt Rainbow commented. Aisling cast her a startled glance, and blushed to see her aunt's eyes sparkling with humor. "Oh, Niece! Did you think to outwit me?" The Faery's silvery laughter made Aisling cringe with guilt and embarrassment. "Foolish child, I would not let you wander unprotected between worlds! Fey I am, but I am still your aunt and guardian."

Tears of shame clouded Aisling's vision. "Then you know about Sloan."

Again, Aunt Rainbow's laughter pealed like tiny bells. "Oh, Niece! I know *all* about young Sloan!"

Aisling hoped her aunt's knowledge didn't include how Sloan kissed! Surely, that was far too intimate, even for a

Faery guardian, to know about. The quick frown on her aunt's face worried her. Then Rainbow smiled brilliantly, like sunshine and rainbows after a storm, and Aisling relaxed a little. But she still needed reassurance that her aunt was not angry with her.

"Then you understand my wanting to be with him?" she asked hesitantly.

"Understand, I do. But I fear Sloan will disappoint you, Niece. Remember-Fear-Not, 'tis my duty as your guardian to warn you that Sloan is not the man you would like him to be."

Her aunt's words piqued Aisling's curiosity. What could the Faery know about Sloan that would disappoint her? 'Twas true, he was young. With her Mortal time ebbing quickly away, might he not have enough time to become a grown man? Could Rainbow discern whether or not Sloan had courage and True Love in his heart? But that was not fair. He had not even been tested! When he'd stroked her mare's coat and spoken of his dreams, she'd recognized his passion to do something grand even as she'd felt his loneliness. She believed he had courage and love aplenty, waiting like an oak tree in winter, for the right time to show his leaves.

Aisling adjusted her position again so she could work on her needlepoint. "Surely, Aunt Rainbow, Sloan has to be a better choice for a husband than the Leprechaun. *Anyone* is a better choice than the Leprechaun . . . except, of course, an O'Hara."

Her aunt smiled and Aisling's heart eased a little.

Seven

His grandfather, for whatever reason, didn't mention their argument over his night crawling again. Taking his silence for deliberate ignorance, Con snuck out to the far paddock every night. Leaving the house just before midnight, he'd pray for Aisling to come back. With a blanket stuffed into his knapsack, a big, old-fashioned flashlight in one hand, and a kerosene lamp in the other, he'd trudge along the path he'd worn in the grass. Twice, he'd been soaked by rain. Mrs. Penny had taken his soggy jeans away for washing without a word. She never mentioned the food he swiped from the pantry for his midnight prowls, either. He had a feeling she deliberately left pastries for him to take.

Aisling hadn't come back again. The *wanting* was so intense that he felt numb. He'd sit in the field, in the dark, and try to picture her in his mind. Or he'd light the lantern and hope she'd find him by its yellow glow. When he finally made his way back to his bed, memories of Aisling's face and voice and kiss haunted his dreams. It hurt to want someone so much! The hell of it was, he didn't even know exactly what he wanted from her. He just wanted her to come back, wanted her to be there with him.

He spent the days trying to fill the hours until the nights,

so he could sneak out and hope to meet her again. It didn't
matter what he did to pass the time, as long as it didn't
involve riding the damn horses. Since his grandfather's entire existence revolved around breeding and selling them,
he had to be creative to avoid the old man's attempts to
get him mounted. He had no desire to repeat the experiences he'd had on that hellish ride with Maddy. His grandfather's scorn, and the *slagging* he got from the stable
workers, backed him even more into a corner about it.

Whenever he had a choice, he worked on the farm's
books, in the wood-paneled library on the main floor of the
manor house. When he couldn't get out of barn work, he
cleaned the stalls, cleaned the tack, even cleaned the horses
if he had to. The other grooms eventually realized he wasn't
afraid of the beasts, could, in fact, handle them just fine.
He *just didn't like them*. He didn't want to know their
names, or their parents' names, or their favorite places to
be scratched, or anything else that made them individuals.
And he really didn't want to ride. Horses were sensitive
enough to pick up his dislike the instant he mounted. He
couldn't blame them for being hostile in return, but he
wasn't about to change his feelings. He hated horses. Period.

The only horse he could tolerate was that little white
mare. But, like Aisling, she hadn't come back. After almost
three weeks with nothing much happening, he'd have welcomed a visit from the mare, just to prove he hadn't hallucinated her, too.

For tonight's trek, he decided to vary his routine. He
headed to the ruins of the old house that used to belong to
a neighboring family. He'd been there a couple of times
during daylight, poking around out of idle curiosity. The
stones of the remaining foundation and partial walls looked
like they'd been blackened in a fire. It had probably been
a big, fancy house like his grandfather's, but now the place
just looked sad, the moss-covered shell of a huge house,
with tangled plants and birds' nests everywhere. Hoping he
wasn't disturbing anything more dangerous than a field

mouse, Con cleared some vines away and spread his blanket on the tiles of the foyer.

Stretching out on his back, he crossed his arms behind his head and stared up through the trees and decrepit stone arches. Must have been a hell of a fire to take down a place this big. Getting enough water would have been almost impossible back then. All the wood paneling and draperies in one of these mansions, hundreds of books—a lot of them rare and old—in some of those estate libraries . . . And stables full of hay, straw, wood. And horses. God, the fire must have seemed like hell had opened up.

The first time he'd discovered the ruins, hidden by overgrown bushes and trees, he'd asked Gramps about the place. The old man grumbled that no one knew. Con figured that was code for *Don't bother me,* so he didn't ask again. But it didn't stop him from being curious. Who had lived there? Was anyone hurt or killed in the fire? Where did the survivors go afterward? Did they live in that wreck of a stone house? Being there at night felt different from the daytime. Whispering sounds. Moving shadows. It was almost like the place was trying to tell him its story.

Man, he'd been around too many Irishmen spouting their blarney! He was starting to think like them! Now, *that* was a scary idea for a guy who thought in binary code!

He'd spent the day grooming horse after horse. They were big horses. He ached all over. Hard and uneven as the tile floor under his back was, it didn't take long for him to fall asleep. Damn if he didn't dream about horses! Dozens of horses milling around him as he slept. Their hoof beats shook the ground in his dream. He could even *smell* them.

A tickle on his cheek wrenched him awake. Before he could take stock of his situation, he became aware of a snuffling sound, and the feel of warm breath on his face. The little white mare was back, nuzzling him like she was a big dog. Then she gave him a sloppy lick across his face. Wasn't he the lucky one?

He brushed her nose away from him and sat up. Fishing a wooden match out of his shirt pocket, he lit the kerosene lantern. The mare swung her head away when the match flared, but as soon as he'd closed the glass door of the lantern, she stuck her nose back in his face and took another swipe at him with her tongue.

"Hey, mare, cut it out!" With both hands, he wiped horse spit off his chin. "What are you doing here? This isn't a safe place for you. Don't you have someplace to live? You look too valuable for someone not to miss you."

The mare snorted and shook her head. Con laughed as he got to his feet. "Okay, which one of us is crazier? Me, for talking to you, or you for trying to answer?" When she rubbed her chin on his shoulder, he grunted and patted her neck. "You're right. I'm the crazy one, hanging around out here every night, waiting for Aisling. Stupid, huh? A girl like her wouldn't be interested in a geek like me. Not in a million years."

The mare bumped his chest with her nose, then pawed the foyer floor with her right forefoot, her metal shoe making a loud clank against the tiles. The sound drew his attention downward, and a flash of metal in the glow of the lantern caught his eye. It looked like a loose shoe nail. Moving beside her shoulder, facing her rump, Con bent and ran his hand down her slender leg to her foot. No way she could be one of the O'Haras' solidly bred hunters. There was no trace of Irish draught horse in her. She was too small for a Thoroughbred, too fine for a Connemara pony. Her coat was as soft as mink, and her bones delicate. An Arabian, maybe.

While he pondered the mystery of her breeding, she lifted her foot, letting him cup the hoof in one hand while he felt around with the other. Her feet were tiny compared to the feet of the O'Hara horses, and she wore thin shoes, like the lightweight ones on racehorses. One nail had pulled loose from its clinch, but instead of falling out, it had gotten bent under the pressure of her foot. The shiny nail was reflecting the lantern light.

"You have to belong to someone, mare," he muttered. "Wild horses don't wear shoes." Propping the mare's foot on his thigh, Con searched his pockets for his nine-in-one-gadget. He opened the pliers and closed them on the nail.

When he started to pull on it, the mare shifted her weight, leaning more against him.

"Hold still, girl. You don't want to get this caught on something and break your leg."

While he worked at the nail, straightening it enough to pull it out of the shoe, the mare nibbled at his jacket and rubbed her chin on his back. No question that she was as comfortable around humans as a house cat was. Did she belong to Aisling? If she did, why was she wandering around here? Why wasn't she sleeping in a stable somewhere? Where did she go when she wasn't hanging out with him? And why the hell did he care? She was a horse!

But in her quiet way, the mare was a real character. She was making him break his rule about treating any horse like it was a person. Suddenly, he felt awkward calling her "mare" and "girl," but she didn't wear a halter with a handy nameplate attached. If she had a name, maybe he wouldn't feel so stupid talking to himself. Ironic that the only horse whose name he *couldn't* know was the only one whose name he *wanted* to know. Well, Aisling had called her horse "Luna," so that's what he could call this one.

"You have to have a name, but I don't know it. I'll call you Luna, okay?" Under her fine coat, the mare started to quiver. "Easy, Luna." He ran a hand over her warm, silky neck and side to calm her. "Easy, baby. I'm not gonna hurt you. Let's just get that nail out, okay?"

But she was either tired or frightened, or both, because she continued to tremble. With one last hard pull, Con freed the nail, staggering slightly from the sudden lack of resistance. The mare made a soft noise, as if she was glad to have the bent nail out from under her shoe. He let her foot down and closed the knife, then looked at the horseshoe nail. In the glow from the lantern, the nail lying on his palm didn't look like a normal horseshoe nail. Peering closer, he frowned at it. Nah, couldn't be. What he thought he saw didn't make any sense. His eyes were playing tricks on him in the shadows. But moving closer to the lantern only confirmed his first impression.

"Shit! This thing is gold! Who the hell uses gold nails on horseshoes?"

The only answer he could think of was so totally bizarre to anyone any working brain cells that he couldn't say the word, even to scoff at it.

Aisling couldn't control her trembling. To be sure, she was grateful to have that bent nail pulled out of her shoe. It was the touching all over that Sloan was doing that had her insides turning to jelly. Young he might be, but he had a man's hands! And the feel of them! Gentle and firm his hands were, stroking her skin, holding her foot steady while he pulled the nail!

And his voice, low, soothing. Strangely flat it was, and lacking the music of Irish voices, but she liked hearing it anyway. She had snuck out of the Faery Realm to find Sloan. She knew she was risking possible capture by some other Mortal, or a firm scolding by Aunt Rainbow. But this having to find an O'Hara for her True Love, when there was a perfectly fine young candidate right under her nose, was too silly. What she needed to do, then, was learn something good about Sloan that would win Aunt Rainbow's approval.

Instead, she'd found herself being seduced by the way he touched her.

Only, it wasn't herself he was touching, but herself as Luna that he could see and feel. Only in the Faery Realm was she always herself, Aisling the young woman. In the Mortal world, except on full-moon nights, outwardly, she *became* Luna. So there she was, a woman inside and horse outside, feeling his hands on her neck and face and breasts and leg. Oh, it felt terrible. And wonderful! It was shameless of her, but she wanted more of his stroking touches. And all she could do to tell him was bump him with her nose and lean against him, and hope he wasn't too dense to understand.

She had to turn her head to look at him. Getting the feel for the way a horse sees had taken her some time and numerous collisions in the early days of her accursed enchantment. As a horse, it was possible to see almost completely around behind herself, but she couldn't see something right under her very nose. Seeing in the distance was a matter of lifting her head to the right height, but by the time she got to where she could see, what she wanted to look at was under her nose and she couldn't see it anymore. Nor could she see color through Luna's eyes.

Her sense of touch, however, was heightened, so that she could feel the individual legs of a fly as it strolled across her skin. Or the stroke of a young man's hands. As well, her hearing and her sense of smell were so acute that it took great effort not to be startled by every little sound, and overwhelmed by every unpleasant odor. Ah, but Sloan smelled very nice. She would know his scent if she had to choose blindfolded from a hundred men. And the taste of his skin, too. 'Twas a very heady power.

Now Sloan was studying that horseshoe nail in the light of the lantern. Until he had spoken, cursing something awful over it, she hadn't thought about it. All she'd known was that the loose nail, bent under like that, was bruising her foot. Wasn't that just like a Leprechaun, to use golden nails in a horseshoe? As Sloan said, it could have made her trip. And if she'd broken her leg? What would happen to her? To Luna? Aunt Rainbow had warned her that the penalty for escaping, without breaking the curse properly, was death. Could she die while still enchanted? Would her death mean Luna, too, would die? The questions set her to trembling again.

Sloan's touch could comfort her, she knew. Aisling nudged him. He ignored her. Well, she had no words, no hands, to get his attention. She tried again, plucking at his jacket sleeve with her teeth. He shook her off with a swat on the nose! Aisling stamped her foot. How dare he? And the bruise on her haunch just healed from the time he'd slapped her rump! But how was he to know that whatever he did—for good or ill—to the white mare, he also did to the woman inside? Oh, if only she could tell him!

She bumped his shoulder again. "Hey, Luna, cool it!" His tone was gently rebuking, but also soothing. "Don't push your luck. I really, *really* don't like horses.''

At his words, Aisling felt her heart sink like a stone, and her luck—and what pathetic little luck she had!—sinking with it. *He truly meant he didn't like horses.* How could a man who didn't like horses save her from this terrible curse? *How could a man who didn't like horses fall in love with a woman who was one?*

Unable to voice her misery, she stamped her foot again. Oh, truly she was cursed!

And Sloan was daft! How could he not like horses? Nearly everyone liked horses. Some were afraid of them, but Sloan surely wasn't. She'd felt the confidence in his touch, heard it in his voice. And respect, too, for her comfort and her safety. He *knew* horses. She heard knowledge in his words, felt sensitivity and understanding in his touch. How could he not like horses?

She would have to teach Sloan to like—and to love—one particular horse. It would be like courting! But it wouldn't do for Sloan to fall in love with her as a *horse*! Oh, no! She shook her head. That wouldn't do at all. Oh, dear! How could she—?

The warmth and weight of Sloan's hand on her neck stopped her thoughts dead. He was working his fingers up under what he thought was Luna's mane, but to her it was as if his hand were really under her own hair. The sensations he was creating with his touching and rubbing made her shiver in delight. Oh, this was so confusing! But, oh! It felt so lovely to be touched like this. So lovely, and wanton, and delightful! She couldn't help twisting her neck to encourage him to continue. He laughed, but he didn't stop the wonderful way he was moving his fingers over her neck.

''Luna, you're a hussy!'' He gave her a firm pat on the shoulder that sent shock waves all through her bones. ''Too bad it's not Aisling. She was one foxy lady. Maybe a little too old for me, though. It's hard to tell with chicks. Can't make them show their teeth.''

He chuckled. Aisling didn't think his comment was the

least bit amusing, and stamped her foot to tell him so. Too old, indeed! Perhaps she was, a bit, for a boy of sixteen, but she wasn't yet twenty and three . . . if one didn't count in true Mortal years. Certainly, she was a woman, and sometimes a horse, but not a vixen or a hen, and anyway, everyone knew hens didn't have teeth.

Sloan chuckled again. Aisling liked the sound of his laugh. Then he touched her face, and gently rubbed her forehead and between her eyes until she was nearly fainting with pleasure.

"Ah, hell! Maybe I should practice on you. I can rehearse my lines, in case I ever meet Aisling again."

'Twas a perfectly splendid idea! Aisling sighed and brought her nose to Sloan's cheek to express her approval. His skin was warm, and she did so much like his scent. He rubbed under her jawbone, which felt much better than when she rubbed her jaw along her knee or on a fence board to scratch. What a pity horses couldn't purr like cats.

A sharp whistle split the night. Sloan swore and took his hand from her face. Startled as much by his voice and movement as she was by the sound, Aisling jerked her head up and searched the darkness. She could see nothing but shadows and the stone walls of her ancestor's home. Everything was just darker blackness against the night. But with Luna's ears, she could hear the distant footsteps on gravel, and knew someone was searching for Sloan. Whoever it was mustn't find her.

Sloan swore again and turned his head toward the direction of the footfalls. Hesitating only a fraction of a second—for the sake of one last look at him, for fear that she might not find him again before it was too late—Aisling leaped off the foundation of the ruined de Burgh mansion. Then she bolted toward the Faery *rath* in the remains of the formal garden. She heard Sloan shouting at her as she searched for the entrance.

His voice followed her down the passageway, growing fainter as the distance between them stretched. It was a distance that miles and clocks couldn't measure, the distance between their worlds. It was the distance between a dream and reality. It was a distance that grew farther as, every day, the time she had left grew shorter.

Eight

When the mare shied away from him, Con turned toward the source of the sound. Great. Gramps was whistling him back, like he was a runaway dog. Over the tops of the pasture walls, Con could see a faint golden light coming from where the house stood like a dark gray mountain against the black of the night. Another shrill whistle, and again the mare's hooves clattered and scraped on the broken floor tiles. If she didn't settle down, she could slip and fall. Figuring he might as well calm her, then lead her to their stable for the night, he turned toward her.

The mare was gone.

Just vanished, like a puff of smoke. Like Aisling.

He caught up the bail of the lantern and raised it above his head, but all he saw was the ruin of the old manor house, and the empty fields beyond. No hoof beats, or the rustling of brush, or the crackling of twigs. The night was totally silent. It was like the ground had opened up and swallowed her without a sound. Like he'd imagined her, except he had proof she was real: streaks on the tiles where her feet had slid, and that damn golden horseshoe nail in his fist.

Hell, it was more proof than he had about Aisling.

Maybe he was cracking up from studying too much. Or from listening to the stable workers telling lies about everything from horses to women to fishing trips. Or maybe being perpetually horny was dangerous to his mental health.

Tucking the nail into the front pocket of his jeans, Con gathered the blanket, lantern, and flashlight, and picked his way over the stone walls and across the fields. Predictably, when he reached the back door of the manor house, Gramps was waiting, in his pajamas and a plaid robe that reached to his ankles, and scowling. Instinctively, Con braced himself for a verbal attack.

"Do you mind telling me what you're doing out there night after night, acting like some sort of werewolf skulking about?"

Con walked past his grandfather. He paused and turned around in the middle of the mud room, then shrugged. Gramps latched the back door, then stood facing Con. "That doesn't answer my question. What are you doing out there? You're not performing some kind of pagan rituals with live animals, are you? I've heard stories, and no self-respecting O'Hara would do those sorts of things."

The temptation was too much to resist, even though mouthing off would get him in more trouble. "Yeah, I was doing something with a live animal." Red patches flared in the old man's cheeks. Con didn't want to cause him a heart attack. "Relax, Gramps." He offered a grin. "I found a stray horse, a little white mare. It was too dark to see if she was tattooed or branded. I figured I'd bring her to the barn for the night, so we could find her owner in the morning. She bolted when you whistled."

The old man's face went chalk white, and then the red patches came back and flared even redder. For a second, Con was afraid Gramps was going to have a heart attack. Then he drew himself up and glared at Con. "Nonsense! There is no stray white mare in those fields. You were dreaming, and you should be in bed for that."

The words came out in a growl that made Con hesitate about showing the nail in his pocket. He found himself staring into gray eyes so like his own, but so cold with anger that a shiver slid through him.

Scowling, Gramps brushed past him, flicking off the light switch as he went into the kitchen, and leaving Con in the darkened mud room. After giving the old man a head start, Con followed him. From the kitchen, he made his way in the dark up the servants' staircase to the second-floor bedroom he used. Taking the main staircase from the foyer, Gramps arrived at the same time. They paused outside their rooms, a hallway apart, and exchanged a long, silent look. No matter how he tried, in the sleepless hours until the housekeeper called him for breakfast, he couldn't understand his grandfather's reaction: anger and denial. All he knew was, he damn well *did* find a stray white horse, and he had a golden horseshoe nail on the dresser to prove it.

Someday, somehow, he'd find out where the mare came from, where she ran away to. And he'd find out why Gramps had gone nuts when he'd mentioned her.

A PALACE, THE FAERY REALM, EVER-THE-PRESENT

Aunt Rainbow tsked over the loose right heel of the cobweb-and-gold dancing slippers she'd given Aisling. "We shall have to take them to a Solitary Faery for repair."

Aisling bit her lower lip, praying her aunt wouldn't ask her how she'd damaged her slipper. She didn't want to lie, nor did she wish to confess that she'd snuck out of the Faery Realm alone to meet Sloan. She'd realized too late that when, in the form of a horse, she'd caught the edge of her shoe on an old piece of metal in the field, loosening and bending the nail that Sloan later removed, her Faery slippers had been similarly affected.

If she had to explain about her escapade and mishap, then she would also have to explain that Sloan had kept the golden nail. She was not at all eager to learn the consequences of that. Her conscience, which had enough of a struggle simply to exist in the Faery Realm—The "Good People," as some of the Irish folk called them, in fact had *no* consciences at all!—reminded her that if ill were to befall Sloan, and she could prevent it, she must do so, no matter the cost to herself. But the voice of her conscience spoke in a very modest whisper these days. For the moment at least, Aisling preferred not to voice her question.

"Of course, you know Acorn Bittersweet is one of the best Solitary shoemakers," her aunt commented, startling Aisling badly. There was an odd light in the Faery's purple eyes when she added, " 'Tis fortunate he is traveling far and wide these hundred years, as he would likely inquire how his intended came to damage her lovely slipper."

It seemed her aunt had her own suspicions about the cause of the damage. Aisling tried her most pleading expression, the one that had, with one unfortunate exception, always persuaded Da to give in to her. "Please, Aunt, do not remind me of the existence of Acorn Bittersweet." A shudder ran through her at the thought of encountering the horrible Leprechaun again.

Aunt Rainbow's silvery laughter rang through the leafy sitting room, drawing echoes from other Faeries, who joined in simply because they enjoyed laughing. Mirth for them was like sunshine for flowers. They turned their heads to soak it in, no matter from whence it came.

It had taken Aisling a long while to learn that they were seldom laughing *at* her—although they did that on occasion, such as when she'd asked about their "work," or about Fey notions of "right" and "wrong," and "good" and "evil." Even though they preferred to live in present moments, some of Aunt Rainbow's Troop were descended from the ancient Faery storytelling families. These individuals had excellent memories, and often recited, with embellishments, the tales of Aisling's silly Mortal notions. Toddler Faeries reluctant to take their naps could be sent running for their beds by the terrible specter of acquiring a Mortal conscience!

Her Mortal conscience needled her again now, as her aunt smiled a sweet Faery smile. "I quite understand your revulsion, Niece. 'Tis true, Acorn Bittersweet is neither as grotesque nor as rude as some of the Solitaries, but he lacks a certain charm. And as he considers himself your future husband, 'twould be awkward for you to explain that you damaged your slipper while trysting with the young man you hope will break the enchantment."

Aisling's jaw dropped. Again, her aunt's laughter trilled

and pealed around the sitting room, and again it was echoed by others, surrounding Aisling with silvery music. It would have been pleasant to hear such sounds, like tiny bells in the windblown grass, except that she felt terribly foolish for thinking she could deceive her clever aunt.

"Oh, Niece! Of course I followed you last night! 'Tis my sworn duty." Rainbow gave her a rather naughty grin. "I wished to see this Sloan myself. For a young lad, and one not called O'Hara, he acquitted himself surprisingly well. 'Tis a pity his home is so very far away. 'Tis possible, however, *if* he proved himself worthy of being your One True Love, the golden horseshoe nail might draw him back in due time. Faery gold—"

"—always returns to its rightful owner," Aisling interrupted impatiently. "But, Aunt, I don't have any. Acorn Bittersweet took away my mother's necklace, the only Faery gold I've ever had." Recalling that cruelty still brought tears to her eyes.

With soft clucking sounds, Aunt Rainbow gathered Aisling into her sparkling embrace. "Oh, child, you've inherited a lovely pot of gold from your maternal great-great-grandsire, my own grandsire, to use in your lifetime. No one can truly own the wealth of the earth, you know, although Mortals like to buy and sell and write deeds to this and that. But favored Mortals may use our gifts, so long as they don't break our rules."

Aisling considered this information, trying to understand this contradiction of what she'd learned very early in her stay in the Faery world. "But that would imply a great deal more forethought than I've witnessed in my time with The People."

With a tinkling laugh, Aunt Rainbow sat on a soft cushion and drew Aisling down to sit at her feet on the velvety carpet. "True enough, Niece. We Fey ones aren't generally concerned with the past and the future." Her exquisite features became unusually somber. "But some of us are of a more ancient lineage than the others. Although we seldom speak of this, as it distresses the others." Her aunt's voice suddenly became a mere whisper. "I am one thus blessed, or cursed, with what Mortals call a sense of duty. 'Tis only those Mortal descendants of my sire, Quicksilver Mistletoe, your Fey great-great-grandsire, who prove worthy of the gold, and the good luck it brings, who may receive it. 'Tis my responsibility to protect the gold from those who are not.''

Intrigued, indeed eager, to learn about her ancestors, Aisling settled herself to listen. Whenever she had asked Da about her mother's family, he had stiffly said he'd been an outsider. His marriage to Fiona, within months of the fire that had orphaned her and destroyed their great house, had lasted under a year. When Fiona died in childbirth, at the age of seventeen, whatever she could have told her daughter had died with her. Da had seldom taken her to visit their neighbors, and never let her go without him, so Aisling had had no opportunities to ask those who might have shared her family's history with her.

Rainbow ran gentle fingers over Aisling's brow and smiled. ''Do not forget, Niece, that Faeries make rather poor historians.''

Aisling smiled in answer. ''None of the papers and journals belonging to the family survived the fire, and I know little about any of my other relatives. Whatever you can tell me will be welcome, Aunt.'' 'Twould give her something to share with Sloan, when they met on the next full-moon night.

''Well, then. The first de Burghs were Anglo-Normans who came to Ireland in time the Mortals call the twelfth century. William Fitzadelm de Burgo of Suffolk, England, was a Norman knight. His descendants may call themselves de Burgh, Bourke, or Burke. Ismenia, your mother's mother, was from another old Norman family, *Ó Duilleáin,* now called Dillon, tracing to Sir Henry de Leon.''

''And my half-Fey great-grandmother?''

Rainbow's purple eyes became even more soft and dreamy than usual. ''Ah, my dear half-sister. She was also called Aisling, after her mother. A flame-haired beauty she was, a wonderfully sweet and playful girl. She married into a great horse-breeding family called *Mac Eochaidh* in Irish.

Not quite as illustrious as your Fey ancestors, of course, but grand enough for Mortals.''

After a pause and a teasing smile, Rainbow continued. ''During the terrible potato famine, your great-grandmother, Aisling, used her Faery gold, her gift from our Fey sire, to feed many of the starving poor around her husband's estate. Her daughter, your grandmother Ismenia, had a gift for creating beauty. Even as a young girl, she left treats we Faeries adore—sweet cream and bonbons and biscuits—where we were certain to find them. She taught her daughter to do so as well.

'' 'Twas Ismenia who married into the de Burgh family. Kind she was, to The People, and less fortunate Mortals. Always food, or clothing, some small job to earn a coin, should anyone needy come to the gates. And what lovely horses her husband, your de Burgh grandsire, bred! Many of them share the bloodlines of our own Fey horses. Luna descends from such breeding.''

''So Acorn Bittersweet implied. 'Tis one of the reasons he covets her.'' Regretting her mention of the Leprechaun, Aisling sighed and leaned her cheek on her aunt's knee. ''I wish I might have known them all.''

Rainbow stroked Aisling's hair gently. '' 'Twas indeed a rare day of mourning in the Faery Realm when your grandparents and great-grandmother perished in the de Burgh fire.''

Aisling shuddered. ''Now tell me of my mother, Aunt.''

With a deep sigh, Rainbow took Aisling's hand in her own. ''Eamon Ahearn was a handsome, bold young man of twenty and four when he came to work in your grandsire's stables. He had his eye on Fiona even though she was but fourteen years old when he first saw her. The fire that destroyed the great house left poor Fiona a homeless orphan, although heir to the family's lands.''

Aisling pushed away a feeling of terrible foreboding.

''No one knows how the blaze started, but it spread like a storm at sea. Acorn Bittersweet, not knowing that the house as well as the stables was in flames, thought to prove his devotion to Fiona by rescuing the de Burgh horses.

'Twas Eamon who raced into the burning house to save
Fiona, and they married as soon as she was out of mourning
for her parents. You were born within the year, just past
the seventeenth Mortal anniversary of her birth.''

And, as Da liked to remind her when he had had
enough—or rather, too much—whiskey, her birth had
caused Fiona's death. ''Did my mother receive the gold
after her parents died?''

Aunt Rainbow stroked Aisling's hair. ''The gold did go
to her, but Eamon Ahearn was a reckless gambler. Upon
his marriage to Fiona, he would have claimed her inheritance. Mortal laws allowed that then, as if females were too
feebleminded to manage themselves. 'Twas a fortunate bit
of Fey influence that your grandmother persuaded her husband to have their solicitor safeguard his will, proving
Fiona had only a life interest in the de Burgh estate. And
at her marriage to Eamon, the gold left Fiona.''

The gold left . . . ? Despite the sad tale, Aisling couldn't
stop the giggle that bubbled out of her at the absurd image
of a fat, black pot filled with gold running away on its three
stubby legs. Aunt Rainbow clasped her shoulder and looked
into her eyes. ''Faery gold only rewards those who respect
its true value, and Eamon did not.'' She spoke as sternly
as a Faery can. But then she gave Aisling a gentle shake,
and a sparkling smile.

'' 'Tis true, Da lost everything,'' Aisling acknowledged,
''so the gold showed its wisdom.'' Would the gold approve
of her, she wondered, or would it find her unworthy, for
getting herself enchanted? Somewhat afraid of the answer,
she refrained from asking Aunt Rainbow's opinion.

''You, sweet Niece, are next in line, and the only heir
to the gold. Now, I've heard it said that Ismenia had a twin
brother who went to America when he was barely more
than a boy. 'Tis nearly a century and a half later with no
trace of him or any descendants, if, indeed, he sired any
children. Therefore, you and your descendants are the only
ones in line for the gold.''

Her descendants. Her children, and her children's children. Who would be their father? Surely not Acorn Bitter-

sweet! She couldn't . . . Ugh! She shuddered. 'Twould be unthinkable to . . . to do anything that would result in her becoming the mother of half-Leprechaun children! When she thought of her own children, she pictured chubby, cheerful boys and girls, some with golden hair and blue eyes, some with black hair and gray eyes. And all of them riding horses and going to universities, of course!

Her aunt touched her finger to the tip of Aisling's nose, and smiled. "Remember-Fear-Not, you shall receive the gold next." Rainbow stood and smoothed imaginary wrinkles from her gossamer dress. Then she held her hand out to Aisling and drew her to her feet. "You must love wisely, and use the gold wisely. Else 'twill turn to dust in your hands, and return Under-Hill until another Mortal descendant of Quicksilver Mistletoe proves worthy."

After blowing a smiling kiss toward her, Aunt Rainbow darted away toward the sounds of merriment coming from the great hall. With some trepidation, Aisling pondered her aunt's words. *Wisely?* When had she done *anything* wisely? She hadn't been wise to run away without any sort of plan. She certainly hadn't been wise to get herself enchanted by Acorn Bittersweet. Aunt Rainbow seemed to believe she was unwise to want Sloan to be her own True Love. And her earlier attempt to slip away to the Mortal world, unnoticed by her Faery guardian, had been exactly the opposite of wise.

Truly, wisdom seemed to be a quality she had too little of.

THE VILLAGE, CO. SLIGO, FRIDAY AFTERNOON, SEPTEMBER 3, 1982

He was leaving tomorrow, and he'd only seen Aisling once all summer. From the instant Gramps woke him this morning, that fact lay like a stone in his gut. As he stumbled to the barn before dawn, still half-asleep, he turned it over in his mind, like someone playing with a piece of broken glass, daring it to slash him, knowing it would eventually.

Only one night left for him to slink out to the far field, hoping Aisling would come back.

It was dumb to keep going out there every night, but the far paddock drew him like a magnet. Some nights, he wasn't sure he hadn't imagined Aisling and the white mare. The gold nail he'd pulled from the mare's shoe had disappeared from the dresser in the guest room. He felt stupid about asking Mrs. Penny if she'd seen it, so now his only proof the mare existed was gone. The whole summer was beginning to feel like one long, foggy dream.

Con spent the morning holding horses while the farrier worked on their feet. He might as well have been a lamppost. The farrier hardly spoke, except to tell him which horses to bring out and when to take them away again. By lunchtime, he was about to explode from boredom. Otherwise, he wouldn't have agreed to go into the nearby village with Gramps. Waiting for the old man to do his business in the drugstore and meet him in one of the two smokey, beer-y pubs, Con scuffed along the main street. The village was totally dull. No video arcade or movies.

Except for two things, he wouldn't be sorry to go home: First, what if he never saw Aisling again? And second, with his parents separating, what was home anymore, anyway? Stanford?

He stopped at the door of one of the most ancient shops in the village, a junk shop, really. Without thinking about it, he put his hand on the old-fashioned door latch. The age-blackened wood door suddenly swung inward, pulling him with it. He stumbled, caught his balance, and looked to see who had nearly decked him. A smallish woman, older than his mother but younger than Gramps, blinked up at him through round, wire-rimmed glasses. Her hair was a mix of gray and brown, with almost white patches around her ears. It was tied back in a knot that was coming loose, and the white at the sides, combined with the glasses and her blinking, made her look like an owl.

"Oh, dear! So sorry I am. I didn't see you there," the woman said in a rush. "You're the O'Hara grandson, are you not? Come in, come in!" She had his elbow in one hand, and was waving him inside with the other.

"I've been wanting to get a good look at you, but Ambros hasn't given me a chance. Come have a cup of tea and tell me how your mum is. I used to watch Corliss when she was a wee one, so her mother could have a bit of time to herself." It was more conversation than he'd had all week, maybe longer, even if he wasn't getting a word in edgewise. After six weeks of brusque treatment from Gramps, being welcomed, even by an odd-looking stranger, was a nice change.

Con looked around as the woman led him to two unmatched, well-stuffed old chairs near a battered wooden table that held a vintage cash register. The shelves and tables around the rest of the shop overflowed with . . . junk: really ugly porcelain cupids and bulldogs, a dented tuba, plates painted—very badly—with famous landmarks like the Eiffel Tower and Big Ben. The teapot the owlish woman produced from a little closetlike room behind her cash desk was painted to look like a cabbage. The cups she brought out next were the fussy kind with saucers, none of them matching any of the others. The sugar bowl was a giant pottery bee, and the milk pitcher was shaped like a black-and-white cow. The chocolate chip cookies and wedges of shortbread, on the heavy pottery plate painted and shaped like a giant lettuce leaf, looked homemade. His stomach growled at the sight of them.

The woman waved him into one of the overstuffed chairs, and she sat in the other one, then blinked and smiled at him. Con realized he was smiling back and enjoying himself, even though he didn't have a clue who this woman was.

"Oh! I forgot to introduce myself! I'm Enid McDermott, Enid to you. No standing on ceremony for us. Help yourself to the biscuits, please. Do you take milk and sugar?" Before he could answer, she laughed. "Sugar, of course. Two. No milk. Yes?" She spooned sugar into a cup, poured tea on top of it, and passed the cup and saucer to him.

He grinned. "Thanks. You read my mind."

"Yes, I know."

He'd meant she'd made a lucky guess. She'd responded as if he'd meant it literally. He frowned and bit into a chocolate chip cookie. Its flavors exploded in his mouth. She laughed.

"Now"—she lifted her own cup—"tell me, are you enjoying your stay? How is your sweet mother, and your handsome father?"

He could feel his face get warm as he shook his head, mutely trying to convey that he couldn't speak at the moment. Enid laughed and waved at him to finish. He swallowed. "Everyone's okay. Everything's been fine. Thanks."

Except for not seeing Aisling again, and his parents' divorce, and his grandfather being such a pain in the butt about everything. And except for the horses, and Maddy, he thought.

Enid's brows rose, reminding him of his mother's ability to question him without saying a word. Maybe his short answer was a little rude, but he didn't feel like going into details. Enid frowned, and Con shrugged away the uncomfortable impression that she expected more from him. He took another big bite of cookie. It was almost as sweet as kissing Aisling.

"It's not about horses at all," Enid announced, out of the blue. Confused, Con blinked at her. She smiled. "Everyone thinks it's just about horses, even yourself, but it's something else entirely. One day, you'll understand. If you are courageous enough, then everything will start to come right again."

The hairs on the back of his neck bristled. He put the last bit of his cookie on the saucer. "Uh, Enid, I don't know what you're talking about, but you're kinda spooking me out."

To his surprise, she laughed. "Here I am, forgetting you don't know about me! I've a gift. The sight, we call it. 'Tisn't reading minds word for word like a book, but seeing impressions, like pictures of feelings. People hereabouts know my family has always had one child every generation born with the gift. It doesn't always pass from mother to child. I got my sight from my mother's sister. My own son,

Phelan, did get his talent from me, but it's always different in the males. They're more for doing than for seeing.''

The woman was a fruitcake. Harmless, and she made great cookies, but totally, absolutely nuts! Con grunted as if to say he understood, then stuffed the rest of the cookie into his mouth to keep from having to speak.

Enid gave him a big smile. ''And is Ambros telling you grand stories about the O'Hara family?'' Con shook his head. Enid sat forward in her chair, her expression shocked. ''Surely, he's been telling you about your ancestors, and all the legends?''

Con shrugged. ''Not really. He mostly tells me what to do.''

With a smile, Enid sat back and sipped her tea. ''Ah, well, you're young yet. The next time you visit, come for tea again, and I'll tell you stories. Maybe you'll meet my son then, and he can show you around.''

Just what he needed, Con thought. One fruitcake to tell him stories, and another one to play tour guide. ''Sure,'' he said anyway, trying to be polite. It must have fooled Enid, because she gave him another smile over the rim of her teacup.

A clock somewhere in the piles of junk in the shop chimed. He looked at his watch and rolled his eyes. He'd be late meeting his grandfather at the pub, of course, and catch hell for it. Setting his cup and saucer down on the rickety table, he looked at Enid. ''I better go. I was supposed to meet Grandfather in the pub by now.''

Enid chuckled. ''Ah, well, you're on Irish time now, aren't you? If he's at the pub, he'll be with his friends, and hardly noticing the time passing.''

''I better go anyway.'' He stood up and flashed a grin. ''Thanks for tea. The cookies were great.''

''Come back, Conlan Ambros O'Hara Sloan, and I'll tell you the legend of Lady Moonlight. 'Tis a mysterious and romantic tale,'' Enid told him with a funny smile. She stood and followed him to the door of the shop. He stepped outside, and Enid started to close the door behind him, then opened it again. Wanting to be polite, Con paused and looked at her. She really did remind him of an owl, with those round glasses and the white hair at her temples.

"And I'll tell you all about the O'Hara curse." She gave him a very toothy smile. "Perhaps you shall be the one to discover the ending to the story of Lady Moonlight."

The door swung shut with a click, leaving him standing on the sidewalk with his mouth open.

Nine

Con checked his watch again, but time was crawling and he was bored out of his skull. Judging by the shouting and the laughing and the singing, everyone else in the place was having a great time. This *céilí* at his grandfather's usual pub, with traditional music and singing, was something the locals did one or two nights every week. If he hadn't been obsessed with Aisling, and if he hadn't been positive Maddy and her friends were still howling at him over the stallion incident, he might have mellowed enough to enjoy his last night in Ireland. Even his grandfather loosening up enough to buy him a pint of Guinness didn't feel like the big deal it probably was.

The far paddock of the O'Hara estate was a fast half-hour walk away. He figured it was better to know that she hadn't showed up, than go home thinking maybe she had. After working his way through the crowd to the men's room, he just went out through the delivery entrance at the end of the corridor. If anyone noticed, they sure weren't running after him.

The night was still warm, the moon full and shining like a lamp overhead. A few dogs were out, barking at stray noises, but they were probably tied or penned. He broke into an easy jog and let the steady pumping of his legs carry him along the paved road, down the dirt lane, and into the fields from the back way. He made a standing jump to catch the top edge of the outer paddock wall, then scrambled up the mossy, slippery rocks until he could get one foot over and haul himself the rest of the way. Panting, he sat on the top of the wall and looked around. The moonlight lit an empty field. Well, hell, he didn't expect her to show up just because he wanted her to. So he shouldn't feel disappointed, should he?

Calling himself an *eejit* for hoping, he turned, bracing his hands on the wall, and pushed himself away and down to the ground. She wasn't coming. He stood facing the wall, his forehead resting against the cool, moist stone. He'd never see her again. Might as well go to bed, and give his grandfather some lame excuse for leaving the *céilí* early.

He heard a soft rustling behind him and every nerve in his body jerked awake. Not daring to believe, he told himself it was a hedgehog scurrying for cover, and didn't turn to look. The night pulsated around him, like it had its own beating heart.

"I was hoping you'd think to come when the moon is full."

The soft, musical voice from behind him could only be Aisling's, but where had she come from? Only a few seconds ago, the field had been empty. He hadn't heard a sound until she spoke. It didn't make sense. But so what? She was there!

He turned around, half-expecting her to be a figment of his imagination. She stood in the middle of the field, with the moonlight shining on her like a spotlight. She was wearing the old-fashioned white dress she'd worn the first time, and her hair was like a gold aura. All he could do was stand and gawk, struck dumb by how beautiful she was.

"Sloan, you're looking at me oddly. Is something amiss?"

He had to swallow before he could speak. "No . . . Nothing's wrong. I just . . ." He shrugged and gave her a crooked grin. "I'm glad you're here. I didn't think you would be."

Aisling came toward him. The light breeze played with her dress and her hair the way he wanted to. When she was close enough to touch, if he dared to reach out with his hands, she stopped. Frowning, she looked up at him, then her frown turned into a smile and he felt his heart take a swooping leap. He held out his hands and she took them with hers, her skin so soft and cool that he was afraid the roughness of his would hurt her.

"I waited out here for you every night," he blurted. "The only one who showed up was your horse."

Her smile faded, and her fingers tightened slightly on his. "Oh, Sloan, I'm so sorry!"

He shrugged. "Hey, it's no big deal. When you took off, I thought maybe I missed hearing you say you'd come back. I didn't want you to think I was standing you up."

"I wasn't able to meet you like this until tonight's full moon. After tonight, I'll be gone until the next full moon." She gave him a sadly sweet smile. " 'Tis an inconvenience, I know, but there is nothing I can do to change the circumstances."

"Doesn't matter now, anyway. I'm leaving tomorrow afternoon." He couldn't force himself to say he was going home. It wouldn't be home without his parents being together. And anyway, he would be living in a dorm. "I don't know when I'll be coming back again." *Or if,* he added silently.

She wasn't smiling anymore. "Leaving?"

"Yeah. Flying back to California, where I live. I'm starting college in a couple of weeks, and I've got stuff to do to get ready."

Aisling's mouth—that very kissable mouth he'd been dreaming about all summer—dropped open. "You can *fly?*"

He couldn't help laughing a little, even though he knew by now that she wasn't joking. Aisling seemed to know even less about the world than the other kids he'd met here. No wonder, if she could only come out once a month. It wouldn't be fair—or smart, if he hoped to kiss her again— to laugh at her or tease her.

"Not by myself. In a plane." He jerked his head toward the sky.

She nodded. "Oh, I understand now! I thought perhaps you had the talent to fly magically."

He squeezed her hands gently. "Can we drop the magic talk? Last time, we ended up arguing about it, and that's dumb. My parents argue all the time over the stupidest little things, and now they're breaking up."

She smiled up at him. "You're a wise man, Sloan."

Heat rushed to his face. He wasn't used to being called a man, let alone a wise one. Unable to think of anything to say, he released one of her hands and drew her to walk beside him. She smelled like flowers and sunshine, and he ached with missing her already. He wanted to sit and hold her all night, not saying another word.

At the spot where he usually spread his blanket, Con stopped. Because he'd come straight from the *céilí*, he couldn't pack a blanket. The grass was damp. His jeans didn't matter, but Aisling was wearing that fancy white dress. If they sat on the sod, she'd get her dress wet or grass-stained. Impulsively, he unbuttoned his denim work shirt and spread it on the grass, then bowed to Aisling, inviting her to sit. She did, then looked up at him. At his bare, sixteen-year-old, hairless, practically concave chest. Wishing he had chest hair and muscles, he dropped down beside her and crossed his arms over his knees. They weren't touching now, but he could feel the heat of her body in the air between them.

"I envy you, Sloan. I once wished to attend university, too, in Dublin," she said softly. " 'Tis a dream I've long since abandoned."

The sadness in her voice bothered him. "You shouldn't give up. You can apply for scholarships and loans."

She tipped her head and laid it on his shoulder. The warmth and light pressure, the brush of her hair on his skin, set off explosions along his nerves. When she sighed, he tightened his grip on his elbows to keep from grabbing her.

" 'Tis not the paying for school that stops me."

"So why not go for it?"

She hesitated, and he got the feeling he was going to get an edited version of the truth. "I live with my aunt," she finally said, "and she and her friends seldom stay long in any one place."

"Hell, you're an adult. Why do you have to move around with your aunt instead of doing what you want to do? If I was staying here longer, you could live with me." Another wave of heat stung his cheeks. "I mean, you could stay at my grandfather's house. He's got lots of extra rooms."

Was he insane, or just stupid? She had to be around twenty, and he was just a goofy kid of sixteen. Sure, she'd jump at the chance to move in with him and the old man! Like there was a real future in that for her.

" 'Tis truly sweet of you to make such a generous offer, Sloan, but I'm sorry to say 'twould be impossible."

He let out the breath he'd been holding."Yeah, I guess I'm kinda young for you," he muttered. He hadn't expected her to say anything else, so why did he feel so bad anyway?

Con would have been fine if Aisling hadn't put her hand on his bare arm. The instant her fingers touched his skin, something inside him flared up like a lit match, and he stopped thinking about age or distance. A groan caught in his throat. He let go the stranglehold on his elbows and scooped Aisling into his arms, tipping them over onto the grass. She had only enough time to squeak in surprise before he covered her mouth with his.

For a second after her little yelp, he panicked. Was she going to think he was attacking her and start screaming? But the squeak turned to a sigh, and he felt her lips, her whole body, soften under him. Wonder of wonders, he must be doing something right!

Kissing her, tasting her and breathing in her scent, feeling her body pressing against his, her skin on his skin, trying to get even closer, trying not to crush her, afraid to frighten her, every nerve in his body on fire . . . Con started to shake. He didn't feel like a goofy kid anymore. She sure wasn't responding like he'd thought she would. Aisling's hands kneaded his back and shoulders, her fingers cool on his bare skin, and her mouth opened to his. She shifted and

her breasts pressed against his chest. The lace on her dress
tickled him. He clutched her through layers of dress, guiding her lower body closer to his. He had to feel her against
him, but he wasn't ready for the jolt of lightning in his
loins.

He was so hard. She had to be able to feel him, even
through all her clothes. Too much, too soon? Would she
get scared? He tried to tame his approach, expecting her to
push him away, to pull his hair again. But Aisling didn't
try to end their kissing. He wanted to keep going—all the
way. He knew he shouldn't, but he couldn't make himself
stop kissing her and holding her as close as he could get
her. Oh, God! She tasted so sweet! She felt so good! Those
soft little noises she was making . . .

He shouldn't do this . . . He didn't know if he could
stop . . .

How the hell did a guy control losing control?

For a few more minutes, he didn't think he'd have to
worry about control. Aisling seemed as eager as he was—
he was going to have some interesting marks on his back!
Taking a chance on the next step, Con fumbled for the edge
of her skirt. It was pinned under her, but she moved against
him, freeing the material. Just as he caught the hem in his
hand, she froze, then broke the kiss. He was about to ask
her why when he heard a rustling noise.

"Aisling!" A woman's voice came out of the dark. Con
froze at the sound. "Aisling, where are you? 'Tis time!"

With a groan, he pressed his forehead to hers, their breath
mingling in gasps. "Who's that?" His voice came out as
a croak.

" 'Tis my aunt, searching for me. I . . . I didn't exactly
tell her where I was going."

Aisling touched her fingertips to his cheek, then wiggled
out from under him and got to her feet. Con watched her
from the ground, too turned on to stand up yet. He didn't
want her to get in trouble, but the fact that she'd snuck out
to meet him made him feel pretty good.

Aisling slapped at her skirts and shook some leaves out
of her hair. Moonlight rippled on her hair the way it did

on water. She looked at him, her expression between a smile and a frown. "What a mess I am!"

The moonlight was turning her to silver. Her mouth was moist and swollen from kissing him. Her eyes were dark and huge. "You look beautiful to me," he muttered.

Aisling gave him a quick, sweet smile, then sighed. "I must leave you now, Sloan. Perhaps it's for the best that you are departing tomorrow. I truly enjoy kissing you, but I'm not . . ."

Her voice trailed off, which was a good thing, because every one of her words was hitting him like a bullet. He could finish the thought for her: *I'm not really interested in you as a boyfriend.* She was being kinder than Maddy, but it hurt worse.

"Aisling! Where are you? You must hurry!" The woman's voice, and some kind of little bells ringing, seemed to float on the wind, coming from everywhere, but not from anywhere in particular.

"Oh! My aunt has come to fetch me!" Aisling said. "Sloan—"

Con sat up and looked in all directions, but couldn't see anyone in the field.

When he turned back to Aisling, to promise to come back for her, to ask her to write to him, she was gone. He scrambled to his feet and searched every inch of the enclosed pasture, but Aisling had disappeared. Without another sound, without a trace, as if she'd never been there. Just *gone.*

A GREAT HALL, THE FAERY REALM, EVER-THE-PRESENT

Aisling glared up from the floor of the Faery festival hall. "Oh, Aunt! How could you do this to me?"

She'd been whisked back into the Faery World so quickly that she'd landed hard on her bottom. All the Faeries who were present in the hall seemed to think her abrupt arrival was the funniest thing they'd seen all day. Their laughter rang like chimes inside a small room, echoing un-

pleasantly in her ears. Even Aunt Rainbow, who was unusually *nice* for a Faery, was laughing.

"I'm sorry, Niece, but you did make rather a comical
entrance." Rainbow took Aisling's hand and helped her
stand.

Aisling dusted her skirts and shook leaves out of her hair
for the second time in very few minutes. "You didn't allow
me time enough to say a proper farewell to Sloan."

Aunt Rainbow fussed with the collar of Aisling's dress.
"No need," she said lightly.

"No need?" Aisling gaped at her aunt. "How can you
say that? He's leaving tomorrow for the far side of America."

Her aunt's laugh rang gaily. "And a good thing that is,
as you were both enjoying his kisses more than you should
do. He's just a boy."

Furious with her aunt's insensitivity, Aisling glared mu-
tinously, then marched away to the farthest corner of the
Faery *rath*. Crossing her arms, she sank down onto a fat
mushroom cap to sulk. Sloan wasn't *just a boy*! Boys didn't
kiss like that! Did they? No, it wasn't possible that a mere
boy could stir her feelings the way Sloan had. She could
still feel the way his hard body had pressed against her,
both frightening her and thrilling her with his hunger. He
had held her so gently, for all the heat she could feel raging
inside him. His heart had pounded wildly, and so had hers,
like two *bhrodran* drums being played in the same rhythm.

Besides, hadn't she dreamed of him? So long ago that
she could hardly recall when and where, she had dreamed
of her One True Love. She'd seen a man with black hair
and gray eyes, tall and broad-shouldered, with a gentle
heart and a sweet smile. She had dreamed of Sloan.

Aisling wrapped her arms around herself. But blast it!
Aunt Rainbow was right. A sixteen-year-old boy, no matter
how sweet and exciting his kisses, couldn't be the man to
free her from this horrid curse. She'd tried, hadn't she, to
explain about the enchantment trapping her? But he
wouldn't open his ears—or his heart—to magic. Aunt
Rainbow was right, and her dream had been wrong. Sloan

couldn't be her One True Love. Had she been very cruel, then, letting Sloan kiss her? And kissing him? She hadn't meant to be cruel. She hoped he would forgive her.

Smiling, her aunt beckoned her to rise. They linked arms and began walking farther into the Faery Realm. The Moonstone Circle Faeries were preparing to travel to a distant *rath* for yet another *fleadh,* a festival of dancing, singing, banqueting, and silly games. Truly, their never-ending amusements were tiresome, but she dared not stay alone and risk getting lost.

Aunt Rainbow stopped them in their tracks and turned Aisling so their eyes met. "There is still some little time remaining of your hundred years."

"But so far, I've only met one Mortal man, and you have convinced me that he can't be the right man. The odds are worse than any Da must have faced when he was losing everything."

"Remember-Fear-Not, you must keep believing in True Love," Aunt Rainbow chided gently. " 'Tis a most powerful kind of magic when wielded wisely."

"Methinks love and wisdom inhabit different worlds," Aisling announced as she climbed over a fallen log. Rainbow's silvery laughter gave her back her smile briefly, but her despondent mood was not ready to forsake her. "Oh, Aunt!" She sighed. "I fear I shall never find the man to end this wretched enchantment, if he must love me as I am, and must be someone I can love . . ."

"And don't forget, he must be of Ambros O'Hara's line."

An inarticulate sound of rage burst from Aisling's throat. "O'Hara! O'Hara! I will never fall in love with an O'Hara! I'd rather marry the Leprechaun!"

ST. HELENA, NAPA VALLEY, CALIFORNIA, TUESDAY, JUNE 25, 1985

"Con! I'm home! Come downstairs. There's someone I'm wanting you to meet."

His mother's voice crackled over the intercom speaker,

invading the peace of the spare bedroom he'd turned into a home office. He was in the middle of writing custom software for a client of his fledgling consulting business. Irritated at being interrupted, he waited a full minute before pushing back his chair from his desk. As he stomped out of the room, he heard the hiss of the intercom nagging him. Standing at the top of the stairs, he took note of the suitcases in the foyer. The two tapestry ones were familiar. The tan leather one wasn't.

"Hey, Mom." He called his greeting from the upper landing.

His mother appeared at the foot of the stairs, her expression a mix of warmth and her own irritation. He knew why, and for once he wasn't going to let her work her usual guilt trip on him.

"Con, please come downstairs. I haven't seen you for weeks."

"That was your choice." He kept his feet anchored to the landing. She asked him to repeat himself. "Welcome home, Mom."

The hurt that crossed her face poked his conscience hard. So much for his get-tough-with-Mom policy. He exhaled and started down the stairs to make amends, and a smile lit her face. He marveled at her ability to shift emotional gears so quickly. He was like his father, shifting moods slowly, in a narrower range of emotions, than his volatile mother. In fact, he mused as he reached the foyer and caught her in a bear hug, he liked a zero range of emotions. Less complicated, less room for screwing up.

His mother smelled of Chanel No. 5 and horse; she'd probably stopped at the stable to check on her horses before coming home. She was as fit as a woman half her age, and her return hug was firm and strong. After kissing his cheek, she stepped back, laughed, and lifted a hand to rub away the lipstick. Their greeting ritual never varied, no matter which one of them was coming home. More often than not though, as far back as he could recall, Corliss was the one coming back, the way she was now, from horse shows, or from teaching, or riding with hunt clubs in North America and Great Britain. He was surprised she still knew her way around the house.

This time, she lingered a few seconds extra, then brushed at the hair falling across his forehead. She smiled into his eyes. "How was the graduation ceremony?"

Con shrugged and looked away. "It was okay," he lied.

Corliss didn't seem to notice his tone. She tucked her arm through his and started towing him toward the kitchen. Briefly, her arm tightened. "*Summa cum laude!* I'm so proud of you. Did your father take lots of photographs?"

Con restrained the rude snort that threatened to come out in answer. "He took a couple before he got paged to deliver a foal."

She halted and looked up at him, her eyes troubled. "My poor boy." She pressed her lips together in a thin line, and her eyes narrowed. "Jonathan knew I wouldn't be home in time. He *swore* to me that he would be there for you."

"Yeah, well, he *was* there." Only long enough to soft-boil an egg, but at least his Dad had showed up. Con shrugged. "Tad Butler asked him last-minute to cover his practice so he could get to his daughter's graduation at Yale. The vet who usually covers for Tad was away, and Dad didn't get anyone to cover him. It was the mare's first foal, and the owner was nervous."

Corliss's eyes got bright, like she might cry. "Oh, darling, I feel so sorry for you being left alone like that."

"It's okay, Mom. I'm a big boy now. Tie my own shoes and everything." She frowned, apparently not pleased with his tone. He shrugged again. "We're not talking life-and-death here. So I had to graduate without either of you there. Big deal. It's not the first time you guys haven't been around." Man, he sounded like a whiney little kid. What happened to his don't-care stance?

The hurt look came back to her eyes. "Now, Con, that isn't fair. You yourself told me not to pass up the chance to take Bodhrán to as many qualifying shows as possible this year. You yourself encouraged me to detour to San Diego, so the youngsters could work with a wonderfully talented trainer from Ireland. It really was a marvelous opportunity, but if you'd asked, even the day before, I could have found a way to come home."

He caught himself about to apologize. How did she do that? How was *he* suddenly at fault, when she was the one who missed his graduation? Bodhrán, a big, bold Irish hunter stallion bred by his grandfather and trained by his mother, was an equine star with a trunk full of blue ribbons. But Corliss was also training and showing two green horses, and a clinic with some hotshot trainer had been scheduled for the same date as his graduation from Stanford. Asking her to come home for him would have forced the issue, making her choose between her horses and him. To avoid hearing an answer he might not like, he'd done what he'd always done in similar situations: He let her off the hook.

The way he was going to do again, now. He gave her a phony smile. "You're right, Mom, I did say that." Another tactful fib, but why argue with the way she remembered it? "I'm really okay about it. Honest. Some of my friends' parents took pictures and promised to make extras. Okay?"

Corliss's answering smile was like the sun breaking through the clouds. No wonder people bent over backward for her. When she smiled like that, she could break your heart and you'd thank her for it. And somehow end up believing it was your idea, too. Was that a particular trait of Irish women, Con wondered, or one spread randomly through the female population? If any woman could do those things to a guy, then all women had to be approached with extreme caution. The problem was, even knowing he could get tied in knots at any minute, even watching it happen, didn't give a guy any defenses. One of life's little jokes, that the most dangerous of anything was almost always the most attractive, the most seductive. The most unforgettable.

Still beaming up at him, Corliss patted his arm. "Now, then, I've two lovely surprises for you. There's someone I'm wanting you to meet, and there's something special for your graduation present. Come with me into the kitchen."

Recalling that unfamiliar suitcase, Con had a sudden gut feeling he wasn't going to like either of her surprises.

A GREAT HALL, THE FAERY REALM, EVER-THE-PRESENT

Aunt Rainbow fluttered into the flower-strewn ballroom where Aisling was passing the time watching some of the Moonstone Faeries dancing. Irritating as they could be, with their spontaneity and irresponsibility, they also could be quite amusing. She wasn't certain exactly how many of her hundred years she'd spent living with her aunt's Troop, but she was seldom bored. Now, as usual, she welcomed Rainbow's company.

"I've some unfortunate news for you, Niece."

Aisling's smile turned to a gasp. Her aunt had never before spoken so gravely. She jumped to her feet, her heart racing.

"What is it, Aunt? Has Acorn Bittersweet done something to change the spell? Is he going to make it more impossible to break than it already is?"

"Oh, no, nothing like that!" Aunt Rainbow gave her one of those odd Faery glances that Aisling still didn't know how to interpret. "But there is unpleasant news I must impart."

Aunt Rainbow paused. Aisling waited breathlessly. She loved her Fey aunt dearly, but all The People enjoyed creating and witnessing drama. Although she was somewhat normally less irritating than most of the others, her aunt was no exception. Rainbow was a true Faery, with all their beauty, magic, and grace, and all their thoroughly irksome qualities.

With a nod, Rainbow finally began to speak. " 'Tis so difficult to mark Mortal time here in the Faery world, and it has been running faster than we suspected. 'Tis *three Mortal years* since young Sloan went away, and no one else has come to break the curse. I've sent messengers to seek out all of your Ambros's descendants, and their news is not encouraging. There is only one O'Hara descendant—

but we've no magical way to bring him here."

Aunt Rainbow actually looked rather glum for a Faery, but to Aisling, this was good news. She still favored Sloan above any unknown possibilities.

"He was never *my* Ambros, nor was I ever his." Aisling blew a stray strand of hair off her forehead. "Anyway, Aunt, I've told you and told you, from the very beginning, *I will not fall in love with an O'Hara!* Not even to save myself from that awful Leprechaun."

Rainbow continued to regard her with unusual gravity. "These last three Mortal years here passed in the blink of a Faery's eye. Indeed, nearly ninety Mortal years have slipped by since you were enchanted. By my count, Niece, you've no more than fourteen Mortal years remaining before Acorn Bittersweet claims you."

Aisling's heart sank. "*Nearly ninety years* already?" It felt more like ninety *days*! "Truly, time does pass too swiftly here." Her knees began to wobble. But then the precious talisman of her Fey name steadied her, and she lifted her chin.

"I am Remember-Fear-Not, Aunt Rainbow. I'll find some other way, something that does not require loving an O'Hara, to escape the Leprechaun's wretched curse."

But what? Aunt Rainbow watched her silently, her lovely purple eyes still troubled, as Aisling pondered possibilities. There were all too few solutions, indeed, that did not require an O'Hara or end in her death. In her opinion, both fates were equally unpleasant. She would be as miserable married to an O'Hara as she would be shackled to the Leprechaun. Marriage to either would be a torture to her soul!

Aisling brightened at a sudden inspiration. "I have it, Aunt! I've heard men say that an unruly wife is a terrible trial to a husband, and the ruin of a marriage. Serves them right for trying to rule their wives, I say! Marriage should be a partnership, not a kingdom!"

Aunt Rainbow tipped her head and frowned. "You're changing thoughts faster than a Faery, Niece. What are you talking about?"

A tiny, gleeful laugh escaped Aisling's lips. " 'Tis quite

sensible, Aunt. Does not Acorn Bittersweet wish to have a docile, pleasant helpmate, a loving mother to his grotesque offspring? Well, then, I shall be completely unruly, utterly disagreeable! I shall make such a terrible wife that he'll gladly send me back to my own world to get relief!"

Even as Aisling was speaking, Aunt Rainbow was shaking her head. "Oh, Niece, the penalty for that sort of behavior would be a rather unpleasant death. Have you forgotten Solitary Faeries are fiercely proud, Niece? They insist upon being right. Acorn Bittersweet would likely choose death for himself, as well, rather than admit he'd chosen a bride mistakenly."

As her newborn hope plummeted, tears welled up and spilled down Aisling's cheeks. Rainbow sighed and dabbed at them with a delicate handkerchief made of finest silk and cobweb lace. "Take heart, Niece. I cannot remove my complementary spell entirely, but I can alter it just enough to spare you falling in love with any man called O'Hara."

Grasping her aunt's hands in hers, Aisling gave a sobbing little laugh through her tears. Perhaps Sloan would return to Ireland in time! But no, Aunt Rainbow was always insisting Sloan wasn't the man she wanted him to be. That must mean she must find another, even more pleasing than Sloan, to love truly enough to break the Leprechaun's curse. 'Twould take someone special to make her forget Sloan. Aside from his youth, which time would solve, he had only one flaw. . . .

"My One True Love must be a man who already loves horses, so that he will accept me as I am now." Rainbow nodded, and Aisling saw that her aunt understood she was forsaking her idle hopes for that man to be Sloan. "Then, once I find such a man, you will cast a spell to make him fall in love with me. 'Tis a perfect plan."

Aunt Rainbow's sudden frown erased the fragile hope Aisling had been trying to nurture. "Ah, Niece, you've been reading too many fairy tales! 'Tis a violation of Mortal free will to cast a spell that changes their emotions. Love is particularly volatile." The Faery shook her head. "Something terrible would surely happen to all of us if I did so. 'Twould likely make marriage to the Leprechaun look like a bed of roses.''

That wasn't what Aisling was hoping to hear.

Book Three

"It is good to have an end to journey towards;
but it is the journey that matters in the end."
—Ursula K. LeGuin

Ten

Reluctantly, Con followed his mother into the kitchen. The man sitting on a bar stool in the kitchen looked remarkably like his father. Corliss didn't have to say anything; this was surprise number one. It was obvious the guy was her new *significant other*. If she couldn't see that all the men she dated resembled his father, he wasn't going to risk full-scale war pointing it out.

"Con, this is Leon St. Pierre. Leon, my brilliant and handsome son, Conlan O'Hara Sloan."

He met the other man's eyes and offered his hand. Leon gave him a firm hand clasp and an assessing look, then reached out to Corliss. His mother stepped past him, to stand at Leon's side, smiling, making it clear where her alliances lay. He hadn't expected anything else, so he didn't know why it bothered him. Hell, she was entitled to be happy. Or to try to be.

Corliss turned her smile toward him. "Leon owns a lovely construction firm, building marvelous luxury houses, and he keeps an aged hunter at my stable." Her smile widened. "We've a wonderful surprise for you. Leon wants to buy a young hunter from the O'Hara stud, so we shall all be going to Ireland for July. As a special favor to me for you, Leon has arranged V.I.P. tickets to the Live Aid Concert on the thirteenth, plus a week in London.''

He processed the information. "Ireland for a month? Sorry, Mom, but I'll skip.'' Before she could start in on his heritage and his roots and his grandfather, or he could start thinking about Maddy and Aisling, he added, "You probably haven't noticed, but I've got a life here. My consulting business is just getting off the ground. I can't just disappear on my clients. If I get behind in the jobs already contracted, I'll be scrambling to catch up just when grad school starts.''

His mother gave him a stricken look. It was one of her better tactics. "Oh, darling! You work altogether too hard. That's all the more reason for you to take some time off over the summer. You're going to ruin your eyes and your posture, hunched over those horrid computers all the day and night. Look how pale you are! I've read articles about all the poisonous gasses and rays they emit, and I'm sure your health is suffering.''

He opened his mouth to protest that he wasn't exactly a troll, but there was no point trying to talk. Corliss was on a roll and wouldn't notice. He could guess what was coming next.

"And no social life at all! Too busy working and studying to take a girl on a date! It breaks my heart to think of you lonely and alone, with nothing but those stupid machines for company. You're turning into a hermit.''

His mother seldom allowed logic to interfere with her assertions, but this one was less sensible than usual. It was probably too late to tell her about Maddy and Aisling, or inform her he had done some dating this year. Probably futile to expect her to be rational now. Her mind was set. "So dragging me to the boondocks of Ireland for a month is supposed to lighten my workload? And turn me into some kind of cool social dude, too?''

Her hands went to her hips and a spark flashed in her eyes. "You're so far behind the rest of the world socially, even in the back-of-beyond you'd have to run to catch up!''

Con controlled his wince. A direct hit. Score one for

Mom, and in front of the bozo, too. He should have known better—he *did* know better—than to argue with her over emotional kinds of things. If he didn't get out of the kitchen fast, he was going to break something. Time for a strategic retreat.

"Nice try, Mom, but I'll pass." He looked at Leon, now standing with one arm draped over Corliss's shoulders. "Thanks for offering the concert ticket, Leon, but I'll catch it on TV."

He turned away, and was almost to the kitchen door when his mother called his name. He barely hesitated, but it was enough to leave him open for a flank attack. Leon cleared his throat. Con halted in mid-stride.

"Conlan, your mother is offering to spend time with you. But she wants to see her father, too, and would like you to get to know him better, as well. Can't you see your way to a compromise between your wants and hers?"

He turned back around. "And what's your role in this?" he challenged, giving Leon his darkest glare. He was acting like an immature jerk, but he couldn't seem to control it. Just because his father had decided to let Corliss go didn't mean Con had to accept some other guy in his place. He was an equal opportunity immature jerk, 'cause his father's bimbo couldn't hold a candle to the woman Jonathan had left behind.

Leon stayed cool; Con gave him grudging credit for it. "I've asked your mother to marry me." He paused, his gaze steady. Assessing his audience, Con guessed. "Corliss has asked me to meet her father before she gives me her answer. She would like you to be included in her decision."

He shifted his gaze to his mother, who was looking like a little girl outside a pet store. "Please, Con? It would mean so much to me. And to Da. You're his only grandchild."

Con tuned her out so he could think. His options? Hang tough and stay home. Or give in and trot along to Ireland like a good boy. If he stayed home, he could work on his first few consulting contracts, play poker with his buddies, catch a baseball game. Hell, maybe even risk asking a girl for a date. And, family bottom line: make his mother unhappy.

If he went to Ireland, his mother would be happy, and then she and Gramps would gang up on him about the damn O'Hara horses. No computers. No poker buddies. No baseball. No girls he already knew were safe to talk to; with his luck, he'd run into Maddy Molloy . . . or Aisling. Twice as much work to do when he got back, fulfilling his consulting contracts and going to grad school full-time. The Live Aid Concert would probably be cool, but then he'd owe Leon, and he'd be stuck watching him hang all over Corliss the rest of the month.

Besides, going to Ireland would set him back more than time. It had taken him most of the past three years to stop dreaming about Aisling every night. He was totally over her now. He'd finally given up comparing every girl he met to Aisling. The last thing he wanted to do was start moping after her again, but being in Ireland would guarantee it. That was *his* bottom line.

He opened his mouth to refuse, but looking at his mother, talking to him, but snuggling with that near-clone of his father, changed his mind. If he didn't go to Ireland, his mother would probably say yes to Leon right away. If he did go, he'd have a chance at breaking them up. When he looked at the situation that way, it was a simple decision.

"Okay, I'll go." Corliss was still arguing to convince him. "Mom? I'll go." She gave a little shriek and leaped to hug him.

Somehow, he'd deal with Leon and the O'Hara legacy and even with Aisling. Hell, if he felt the urge to go skulking around the paddocks at night, he could always handcuff himself to a bedpost.

A PALACE, THE FAERY REALM, EVER-THE-PRESENT

Bells chimed, alerting Aisling to her aunt's approach. "There's a rumor that would interest you," Rainbow announced as she breezed into the clearing. "The Hawthorn

Troop is passing by, on their way to a festival in the land the Mortals call County Mayo.''

Aisling looked up from her page. She was reading *Anne of Green Gables,* which one of their Troop members had ''borrowed'' for her. Although Faeries didn't believe in the human concept of ownership, they never actually *stole* anything. Faeries simply took what they wanted or needed, moving things around quite creatively and leaving what they were finished with. They usually chose the belongings of children and people who were ordinarily careless or absentminded, so no one suspected the real cause. Eventually, the owner of this book would find it in some spot she'd searched several times without success, and assume she'd simply overlooked it. Until then, Aisling could enjoy the story.

She smiled at her aunt's merry face. ''Ah. I was wondering what that rustling and whistling was about.'' An unpleasant thought erased her smile. ''We aren't going with them, are we?'' Oh, how she hoped not. The trumpets and the rushing around gave her such a headache. And much as she resented being trapped in the Faery Realm by this enchantment, she disliked even more not having a place to call home. Whenever she could, she persuaded Aunt Rainbow to stay in the *raths* nearest her former Mortal home, the de Burgh estate. 'Twas some small comfort, cold as it was, to be Under-Hill of her own land.

Now her aunt laughed and twirled gracefully, scattering bright streamers and Faery dust over the boughs nearest the main door. When she seemed pleased with the results, she turned to Aisling, her expression—for a Faery—unusually watchful.

''Several of the Hawthorn folk told of encountering a tall young Mortal with black hair and gray eyes. He nearly smothered some of their number by spreading a blanket on the grass where they were resting. To the poor fellow, they appeared as angry bees, and he believes he narrowly avoided being stung.''

Aisling's heart leaped. She dropped the book and jumped

to her feet. Trying to contain her eagerness, she clasped her hands together in front of her.

"Sloan?" His name on her lips tasted like honey.

"Perhaps." Aunt Rainbow studied her for a long moment. "I have altered my spell, as I promised. Now you must decide what to do, Niece. But I must caution you again, my dearest Remember-Fear-Not: Sloan is *not* the man you're wanting him to be."

O'HARA HOUSE, CO. SLIGO, IRELAND, TUESDAY, JULY 2, 1985

"You should have come riding with us, Con," his mother said when he met her in the kitchen of his grandfather's house. She was preparing a tray with appetizers and wine for her and Leon. He shook his head when she pointed to the tray, inviting him to join them. "It was glorious. Da has a quiet gelding you'd have—"

"No, thanks." He found a plate of butter tarts in the pantry and grabbed a couple of the miniature pies, then poured a tall glass of milk. Leaning against the counter, he stuffed a tart into his mouth, then washed it down with swallows of milk. His mother fussed with the food on her tray, and he knew she was waiting to say something. He wondered if she'd ever let go of the idea she could somehow nag him into liking horses.

"You'll ruin your appetite for dinner," she scolded without looking. He didn't answer. She knew nothing ruined his appetite—except being nagged about horses. When she didn't add anything right away, he stuffed the other tart into his mouth. Then, with her back still turned, she spoke. "I wish you'd only consider—"

Mouth full of pastry, he interrupted anyway, "Mom, just drop it, okay?" He swallowed. "I'm the black sheep. Every family has one. Call it the price for being an overachiever. Just 'cause I don't feel like riding a thousand-pound herbivore over obstacles for an adrenaline rush doesn't make me a troll or a total failure, does it?"

Corliss glanced over her shoulder. "You're putting words in my mouth." She turned away, fiddling with the tray of food in front of her. " 'Tis not failure, Conlan. 'Tis disappointment." Honesty, he reflected, was one of Corliss's traits. Tact wasn't.

"Look on the bright side, Mom. I'm employable, respectable, relatively self-sufficient, and I've never been arrested. I shower daily, and I don't spit on the sidewalk. I'm polite to little old ladies and I've never crashed the car."

His mother stood like a post through his little speech, her back still toward him.

"I know all that." She bit off the words. Her knuckles were white around the neck of the wine bottle. She was probably ready to explode, but he couldn't resist one more prod. At this point, he didn't have anything much to lose.

"Mom, can't you appreciate me for who I am? So what if I don't do horses? Unlike some of your friends' offspring, I don't do drugs and hookers, either."

"Stop it, Con! Stop it now!" She turned briefly, her eyes blazing. "You deliberately refuse to understand!" Then she jerked the tray off the counter, bouncing one of the wineglasses onto the floor. It smashed in an impressive spray of shards.

"Blast and damn! This family *is* cursed!"

She didn't stop to clean up. Just stepped over the mess and walked out of the kitchen, kicking the swinging door shut behind her. Con found a broom and swept up the broken crystal. Then he finished his glass of milk and went back into the library of the old manor house. Hours later, with another strained "family" dinner behind him, he was checking his watch every couple of minutes, waiting for night. He'd forgotten the sun set later this far north. Finally, it was dark, and everyone else had gone out for the evening. When he looked out an eastern-facing window, an almost orange full moon was just rising over the horizon. Time for yet another night of stargazing, and feeling like a fool for hoping he'd see Aisling again.

Well, so what? Everyone said Ireland was the place for magic and romance. Why should he be the only one left out in the cold?

With an old blanket over his shoulder and a flashlight in

one hand, he stepped outside. It was an incredible night. The moon hung so huge and bright in the black sky that he didn't bother turning the flashlight on. He probably could get out to the field blindfolded, anyway.

The air was warm, and smelled sweet. Someone must have been cutting hay earlier, and the light breeze carried the scent of it. Looking at the moon was blinding—wasn't there something called "moon blindness"?—but away from its brightness there were millions of stars. As he tramped through the fields, farther and farther from the house, he heard signs that he wasn't alone out there. An owl hooted. Something rustled branches. When he opened one gate to step into the next field, a bristly hedgehog curled into a ball of spikes, waiting for him to leave. Con paused and studied the little creature, wondering exactly how they did mate. Very, very carefully, he supposed.

In the distance, barking dogs challenged each other. A car sped along a gravel road beyond the last walled field, windows open, Prince's "Purple Rain" pouring out the windows. A tinkling crash—a bottle thrown out the car window, probably—the roar of a badly tuned engine, tires spitting gravel, and then the night was back to its own sounds.

Con hoisted himself over the cool stones of the last wall and dropped down into the field. He stood still, listening, letting his eyes adjust to the moonlight, breathing in the sweet air. Aisling hadn't come last night. Would tonight be any different? Anticipation pushed at him from inside, until he couldn't stand still any longer. He walked in a large circle through the tall grass, drunk on the fresh air. A laugh rose in his chest, then burst from him. The sound of his laughter came back to him, softened by the breezes.

Maybe this feeling—like anything was possible, like everything was good—was what people meant by magic.

"Ah, Sloan! 'Tis sweet to see you again. Have you forgiven me, then, for rushing away like the wind, without a word of farewell?" A woman's sweetly musical voice came from behind him.

"Aisling!" he whispered. His heart froze, then did a slow roll that trapped the air in his lungs. Feeling almost light-headed, Con forced himself to exhale. Suddenly, his heart was pounding against his ribs like a wild thing caught in a cage. He was shaking all over, inside and out. His feet refused the command to move, to let him turn around. His skin turned into a force field of awareness. If she blinked, he knew he would feel the shock waves from her lashes fanning the air between them.

"Sloan? 'Tis you, is it not? Although you've grown taller and broader in the time away. Ah, your hair is not so long as a storybook hero's. No matter. 'Tis inside where a man is a hero."

Without moving, he drank in the sweet, musical sounds of her words. Her voice slid over him like a silk scarf, arousing nerve endings, awakening senses, teasing. Part of him was afraid that if he turned around he'd discover he was imagining her there. Another part of him was equally afraid to discover she was real.

"Sloan?"

She whispered his name as a question. So she wasn't sure about things, either. He'd sort of hoped she would be, so she could tell him what to do next. But then, he sort of hoped she wouldn't be so sure, so he could feel like he knew what he was doing. But then, he'd sort of feared he didn't, and prayed he could figure things out without looking like a fool.

One of them would have to do something soon, or they'd stand there all night wondering.

He was the guy; he should make the first move . . .

Should he make the first move? What the hell was the first move, anyway? Girls these days said they didn't want to play by the old rules, and no one seemed to know any new rules. He didn't want her to think he was a wimp or a male chauvinist pig. Saying hello was probably a safe start. He tried to speak but couldn't make his voice work.

Oh, shit! How did anyone *do* this?

"Sloan? 'Twould please me to be seeing your face."

He absorbed her words as if every nerve in his body was raw and exposed. When she paused, he felt his skin expanding, thirsting for more. He swallowed past the sensa-

tion that his throat had turned to splintered glass. Before
he faced her, he had to know: "Will you disappear again?"

"I promise I shan't disappear immediately."

He waited for her to add something, anything, but that
seemed to be all the information she was willing to share.
Hoping Aisling wouldn't see that he was shaking like a
leaf, Con closed his eyes and turned. With a breath trapped
in his chest, he opened his eyes. She stood watching him,
looking the same—no, more beautiful than he remembered.
The breath rushed out of him.

She took a breath. "I wondered if we would ever meet
again."

Her confession broke through some of his defenses. "I
didn't plan to come back to Ireland. My mother wanted to
visit her father." His eyes stayed locked on hers as he
spoke. "Three years ago . . . When you took off like
that . . ." He shrugged. "I figured there was no point thinking you'd want to see me again."

She smiled a little sadly. "Then you were thinking
wrong, but you could hardly know that, could you? 'Twas
my aunt who didn't approve of my . . . seeing you."

Did her slight hesitation mean she was thinking about
the way they'd kissed that night? In the moonlight, it was
hard to tell, but he thought she might be blushing. Damn,
his face was hot now, too! He was nineteen, and a college
graduate, for crying out loud! This felt like being sixteen
all over again, and he'd rather be tortured than go through
that even in memory. Somehow he forced himself to meet
her eyes.

"What about now?" His voice was too gruff. "We're
both three years older. Does your aunt still have as much
power over you?"

Aisling's lashes fluttered down and her head tipped
slightly, so their eyes were no longer meeting. "We remain
very close, Aunt Rainbow and I," she told him softly.
"She's all the family I have left, and I'm her only niece.
But she as good as promised to leave us to ourselves tonight."

He swallowed. "Tonight?"

She nodded. The half step he took toward her felt like a giant stride. At least she didn't back away. Her chin lifted and she looked up into his eyes. In the dark, with the moon reflecting in her eyes, they seemed as fathomless as the sky.

"Only tonight?"

Slowly, she nodded again, making moonbeams flicker and flow on the ripples of her gold hair. He wanted to gather handfuls of her long hair and feel the silky strands on his skin. To keep himself from reaching for her right then, he clenched his hands into fists and kept them at his sides.

"Only the night of each full moon, remember," she added softly. " 'Tis the only time we can meet like this."

He wanted to ask why, but his gut warned him he wouldn't want to hear her explanation. So what? Just being near Aisling dismantled his reason, defied his logic.

"There's a second full moon this month. I'm going to London for about ten days, but I'll be back in time." Nothing ventured, and all that. "Will you meet me here then?"

The smile she gave him shone brighter than the moon. "Oh, indeed, Sloan, I will!"

He felt a weight lift from his heart. "How much time do we have . . . tonight?"

Once again, Aisling turned her face away. Her hair flowed forward like a golden shawl, so he couldn't see her expression. "I must be gone before dawn begins breaking," she murmured.

It was more than he'd hoped for; dawn was nearly four hours away. The possibilities . . . ! And the possible disappointments . . .

Needing to touch her, dreading rejection, Con reached out and stroked the side of her face with fingers that shook. Aisling tipped her face up, her eyes meeting his, her cheek nestling into his palm. With a mysterious little half smile on her lips, she closed her eyes, allowing him to stare at her without feeling foolish. After a moment, his hand at her cheek wasn't shaking as much. Her hair drifted over his wrist and forearm, cool, silky, almost alive in its sensuous movements. Her long lashes cast shadows—moon shadows—on the pale skin of her face.

He studied her full, slightly parted lips. The memories of kissing her came rushing at him like previews of a feature movie. Guess he hadn't put her out of his mind the way he thought. No wonder he'd ended up graduating with a lot of female friends. None of the college girls he'd dated over the past three years had offered much temptation to get involved.

Get involved? Now, *that* was a loaded phrase! How could he *get involved* with a woman with the schedule of a werewolf? Even if he lived here in County Sligo, that was only thirteen nights a year together. And he still didn't know *why*. What did she do, where did she go, in the twenty-seven days between full moons? He searched but there were no answers in her face. Her eyelids lifted; when their eyes met, she looked like he felt: a little dazed. Hell, maybe he should just take whatever she offered and stop questioning everything.

That decision made, he gave in to impulse and stroked her face with the side of his thumb. She smiled sweetly, dreamily. "What are you thinking?"

Con grinned and offered her a half-truth. "That it's a good thing the moon's orbit doesn't take any longer than twenty-eight days."

Straightening, breaking the contact between them, Aisling laughed. "Ah, Sloan! 'Tis indeed fortunate! Fortunate, too, that the nights are no shorter. Dusk falls late and dawn rises early here in the summer. Is it like that where you live?"

It took him a few seconds to catch up with her abrupt change of mood. "Yeah, except dusk isn't so late, 'cause I'm at a lower latitude." He swallowed, geared himself up for the next step. "I brought a blanket this time. Come sit with me and I'll tell you more about California."

He pointed to the folded blanket waiting for them on a grassy knoll. The expression on Aisling's face changed from joy to alarm. Without a word, she made a dash for the blanket. Left behind, startled and confused, Con watched her for a moment.

Scooping the blanket up, she walked away from the knoll, glancing around the field as if she was looking for something. With a nod, she strode about twenty feet away and spread the blanket on the grass there. Then she walked back to the knoll and, bending slightly, spoke as if there were someone there. He shrugged. She knew the area better than he did. Maybe he'd dropped the blanket on a bunny nest, or something like that. Puzzled, he walked closer. She was waving her hands and speaking in rapid Irish. He couldn't understand a word she said. Moving closer until he stood at her side, he scanned the knoll. There didn't seem to be anything in the tall, shadowed grass that looked like a nest. God, he hoped she wasn't delusional!

"Aisling, what are you doing?"

"Apologizing for your carelessness is what I'm doing, Sloan! You dropped that heavy, coarse blanket on a Faery *rath,* covering the entrance. I was explaining that you've a good heart but an empty head. And then I was asking the Good People you've nearly smothered to forgive you and not seek revenge."

Con gaped at her. She couldn't be serious! Could she?

Eleven

Con gave in to the laugh that rose in his chest. She couldn't be serious! Nah, she was just having a bit of *craic,* as they said here, having some fun at his expense.

Or was she?

Instead of laughing with him, Aisling put her hands on her hips and scowled up at him. She *was* serious! Uh-oh! He tried to hold in his laughter, but it kept sputtering up to the surface and erupting into snickers and snorts. Aisling continued to frown fiercely. Finally, he clapped his hand over his mouth.

"You'll be undoing all my work with your rude laughter," she scolded. "Don't be surprised if something unpleasant happens to you that you can't be explaining any other way than saying Faeries caused it."

The Good People? He couldn't believe it! This beautiful woman was a total lunatic! *Revenge? Faeries?* Aisling was abso-effing-lutely nuts, more than a few sandwiches short of a picnic, and *she* was mad at *him* for noticing! Okay, he didn't have to laugh in her face. He could try to be subtle. He could—

Another snorting laugh escaped.

Aisling gave him a tight, unamused smile. "I've heard there are wicked bees around here. Would you be knowing anything about that?"

"*Bees?* Give me a break, Aisling. Bees aren't Faeries,

they're insects.'' How did *she* know about the bees he'd fought off the other day? Good news traveled fast out here. ''Faeries don't exist, except in kids' books.''

She lifted her chin and narrowed her eyes, but didn't say a word. He began to sense, from years of dealing with his equally Irish mother, that he'd gone more than a step too far. Making his point wasn't worth hurting her. ''Sorry. Okay. I was just teasing you, honest.'' He reached for her arm. She pulled away before he could touch her, and he winced. ''Aisling, I'm sorry. I'm being a jerk. Let's move away, so I don't make things worse.''

This time when he reached for her, she stood quietly and let him close his hand around her upper arm. At the instant of contact, his hand began shaking. Hoping she wouldn't notice, trying to be gentle, he turned her toward the spot where she'd placed the blanket. She felt so stiff he was afraid he might hurt her without realizing it. Gritting his teeth to regain control of his nerves, his impatience, his anger at his stupidity, he softened his touch. After a couple of reluctant steps, her resistance started to relax. He let himself breathe again.

She still looked a little huffy when they reached the edge of the blanket, but not so much like she thought he was a lower life-form. Now he really didn't dare ask her how she knew he'd run into a rabid swarm of bees! That would probably get her going again on Faeries. If he couldn't keep her distracted from her Faery theories, he'd end up howling again. She might take off for good then. Damn it, he'd waited three years for tonight. He didn't want to have to wait three more years for a next time. He didn't want to ruin his chance that there'd even be another time.

Con waited for her to sink down onto the blanket and get comfortable, then lowered himself beside her, close enough to touch her, not close enough to be touching her yet. After he sat down, she started rearranging her skirt— layers of skirts—without looking at him. His mind started working enough to recognize her dress from three summers ago. Then her movements distracted him to her feet peeking out from the edge of her skirt. She wore skimpy sandals made of gold leather. Expensive-looking sandals—with a vintage secondhand dress?

Why the same dress she'd worn three years ago? So he'd recognize her? Or because she was poor, and it was her only one? What did he know? Hell, what did he care? Women's clothes were probably a mystery to any guy his age—just like women were. He liked the way she looked, anyway. She was different from all the girls he was used to—so feminine, delicate, and very, very sexy—all that cloth concealing and teasing at the same time. It was a real turn-on. A nice change from the tight jeans and short skirts it was supposed to be sexist to notice. Or those business suits with wide shoulder pads that made women look like football players. If his reactions made him a male chauvinist pig, well, *Oink! Oink!*

Aisling looked at him, her eyes luminous, mysterious. "Sloan, will you tell me about your home?"

Her question unknotted a little of the tension in his gut. "Sure." His voice cracked. He cleared his throat. "What do you want to know?"

She tilted her head to one side and looked past him, a dreamy expression in her eyes. With a sigh, she looked at him again and shrugged one shoulder. "I know little about America, except that many of the starving Irish went there during and after the Famine. 'Tis said my grandmother de Burgh, who was born Mac Eochaidh, had a twin brother who went to America about then, but as no one heard from him, 'tis presumed he died. Whatever you'd like to be telling me about your home, I should like to know."

His mind went blank, and when he opened his mouth, no sound came out. Heat flared in his cheeks. As if she understood, Aisling gave him a gentle smile. "Perhaps you could start by telling me about the city where you live."

Hell, why didn't he think of that? "Good idea. St. Helena, where I've lived most of my life, is a really small town. The population is about five thousand, so Sligo Town is way bigger. Probably at least five times older, too." Wondering if he was on the right conversational track, he paused and raised an eyebrow at her.

"Go on, Sloan." She laughed softly, and he found himself grinning back. "Tell me about the town and the land, and your house, and the people who live around you."

Clearing his throat, he started describing St. Helena, branched out to the Napa Valley and the mountains, then a little about the California wine industry. After telling her about the California Gold Rush, he talked about San Francisco, and about the Pacific coast and the otters and orcas. She kept staring wide-eyed into his face, like a little kid listening to a fantastical story. It was flattering, but it made him nervous as hell, too. He didn't want to bore her to tears. She gasped when he told her about the San Andreas fault line and the earthquakes. When he mentioned that he'd been through a couple of impressive tremors, she gripped his arm as if she thought she was rescuing him. Then she gave a funny little laugh and dropped her hand, which made him sorry she'd noticed. The place she touched stayed warm.

It was intoxicating to have a beautiful woman listening so intently to every word he said. Aisling asked few questions, and she never took her eyes off his. He couldn't remember ever talking so much, at one time, to only one person. Self-conscious again that maybe he was talking too much, he stopped and looked up at the stars. Any second now, she'd probably yawn and excuse herself to go home to bed.

"You've been at university these three years?" Her question brought his attention back to earth. He nodded. "Did you study the computers you were telling me about?" At his second nod, she gave him a teasing smile. "And what are these computers of yours good for?"

It didn't take her many questions to guide him from a general description of computers and the computer industry boom, Silicon Valley, to his own personal ambitions. Suddenly, he felt like he'd gone from a high-tech suspension bridge to one made of vines and planks. He'd given enough presentations and lectures to be a pretty smooth speaker even at his age, but academic and business speeches didn't get into his psyche. Aisling's gently probing questions could strip him down to his emotional jockey shorts before he realized what was happening. Finally, in self-defense, he paused again.

She was quiet for a moment, looking past him with a lost expression in her eyes. Wondering what he could have said to make her sad, he touched her fingers with his. Tipping her head toward him, she smiled, but he still saw shadows in her eyes.

"And are girls allowed to attend American universities? To be learning about the computers and other things?"

The question totally caught him off guard. "Sure," he answered. "It's the eighties, not the Dark Ages. A lot of my friends are women I met at Stanford." Because he couldn't help comparing all of them to her, he could have added, but didn't. She didn't have to know that.

Aisling's chin rose, and she caught her lower lip between her teeth, her eyes narrowing as she studied him. Finally, she said, "I see," in a frosty tone. He did a mental double-take. Could he be reading her right? Did she think he meant something more than *friends*? Did that mean she might be interested enough in him to be jealous of the other women he knew?

Controlling the silly grin threatening to take over his face, Con closed his fingers around her hand. Impulsively, he drew it toward his lips. She resisted for a few seconds, then let him lift her hand for a light kiss on the soft skin of the back. Still following impulse, he turned her hand over and placed a kiss in her palm, then closed her fingers over it. When he looked at her face, her lips were parted, and he could see by the rise and fall of her chest that her breathing had quickened. Her eyes had gone wide and dark, and they were fixed on his, drawing him like a magnet. His own pulse and breathing accelerated. A telltale rush of blood to his loins warned him that parts of his body were about to go on autopilot.

All that time he'd been trying to forget about Aisling, something had been taking root in him. Three years ago, he'd been a horny kid. This time everything felt different. *He* was different. Still horny, yeah, but the hunger he felt was for more than sex. He felt . . . Raw? Naked? Unprotected. He wanted something more than sex from her this time. He could get hurt this time. Not just disappointed or confused. Hurt in something besides his ego. Ripped up somewhere deep inside, like he'd had open-heart surgery without benefit of anesthesia.

This time—Oh, God! The thought scared the hell out of him!—he had a lot more on the line than adolescent hormones. He had a sinking feeling he was going to end up offering her his heart, whether he wanted to or not. Whether she wanted it or not. There were too many possible mistakes. He didn't want to make any. Was she signaling encouragement? Or was he misreading her? Damn, this was no time to be socially dyslexic! What did she want him to do?

Unable to decipher the gamut of expressions crossing Sloan's face, Aisling simply stared at him, enjoying the sight of him. Aunt Rainbow must be wrong! How could he not be the man she thought he was, when she was thinking he was wonderful! Wonderful to be living in such a place as St. Helena, California, and to share it with her in his stories. Wonderful to know so many things about the world and about the machines called computers. Wonderful to hold her hand so gently and smile so sweetly.

Her palm tingled where his kiss lay tucked beneath her fingers. Wherever his fingers touched hers, her skin felt heated. The things he spoke of amazed her, stirred her. His love for his home brought his words alive. She wanted to see his mountains, that—so he said!—made Ben Bulben look like a stone wall in comparison. She wanted to see his Pacific Ocean, grander than the Atlantic, and taste the fresh fruits growing all the year around. She wanted to hear the music called rock, and see the computers.

But she didn't like thinking about Sloan's women friends! To be sure, she had no right being jealous. But it wasn't fair that they were allowed to study at universities and choose their friends and their lovers, while she was roaming the countryside as a white mare twenty-seven nights out of twenty-eight! Oh, and with Sloan's hand holding hers, his kiss tingling in her palm, it was too tempting to be thinking about being lovers with him! Her face grew as hot as if she were standing too close to a fire, a luxury she hadn't enjoyed in nearly ninety years!

Ninety years! The weight of all those years suddenly crushed down on her. All this time she'd been under Acorn Bittersweet's enchantment, the world around her had been changing. Nothing in the Faery World changed. Time passed so quickly in the Faery World, and yet, it was always the present there. Only a few of The People, such as Aunt Rainbow, had the special talent for recalling the past and thinking of the future. Even those Faeries only did so when they must.

But Aisling was mostly human, mostly Mortal. She understood what a past and a future meant. Once upon a time, she'd eagerly planned a dream future, an ideal life. Now what sort of future life would there be for her, if indeed she escaped the horrid spell the Leprechaun had cast on her? She knew nothing of the modern world, except the little she'd gleaned from reading, and what Sloan had told her. Her few friends and family outside of the Faery Realm had been dead many years. She had no home, no means to live. Her inheritance belonged to the horrible, greedy descendants of Ambros O'Hara. If she escaped this curse, what would she do? Or might she escape only to be still cursed?

"Aisling? What's wrong?" Sloan's voice gently drew her back to him. "You looked like you were miles away and thinking about something awful. Did I say something wrong?" He still held one of her hands. With his free hand, he stroked her cheek.

She blinked away the tears welling up in her eyes and shook her head. "No, Sloan, it wasn't you. 'Twas thinking about how little I know of the world that was making me sad."

Without warning, Aisling found herself in Sloan's arms. He gathered her closer and held her against his chest. After a startled moment, she relaxed and let her head rest on his shoulder. She breathed in his scent and felt his heart beating against his ribs. He'd grown broader and deeper in the three years since she'd last been in his arms. His strength and warmth surrounded her and seeped into her until she felt as if the two of them had begun to blend together.

Oh, how she hoped Aunt Rainbow was wrong about Sloan!

"Aisling, I won't kiss you until just before you have to leave," he murmured, his lips brushing her hair. "I want to, but if I start now, I don't know how I'm going to stop at just kissing. Okay?"

Despite her tears, her despair, Aisling felt a laugh bubbling up inside her at his rueful words. "Oh, Sloan! I don't want to agree, but I don't dare to say no," she confessed. "Talk to me, Sloan. Tell me more about California. You didn't mention horses. Are there none?"

She felt his short laugh before she heard it. "Horses in California? Thousands of 'em. Maybe millions. All breeds, all sizes and kinds. Riding, showing, rodeo, cattle, driving. More horses now than when they were the main means of transportation and farm work. My mother keeps her hunters at a stable a few miles away from her house, but in some places, there are horses grazing in backyards just like here."

"And do you like horses any better now?" she dared to ask. So much depended on his answer!

"You want the short answer?" He gave her one of his crooked, charming grins, but she sensed she wouldn't like what he had to say. "Still don't want anything to do with them."

Each word felt like a slap. Aisling winced, but tried to ask politely, "Why don't you like horses, Sloan?"

His shoulders moved in a shrug. "I just don't. Dumb, smelly, expensive, useless beasts."

Surely, he couldn't mean that! "There *must* be a reason. An intelligent person doesn't just dislike something without a reason. And horses are the most magnificent of all the world's creatures! They're so beautiful, so generous of heart."

Her voice swelled with indignation and passion, but she

didn't care if he thought her shrill and shrewish. This was too important to play the shrinking violet. She must convince him!

"You're not a stupid man! How can you think otherwise?"

A quiet chuckle rumbled in Sloan's chest. It felt . . . odd, feeling that vibration working its way through him to her.

"Interesting debating style you have," he muttered, his lips moving against the hair at her temple.

"There's no point in debating a point that's so obvious it would bite you if it had teeth!"

"Uh-huh. Something else I forgot I don't like about the beasts. They bite."

A terrible suspicion occurred to Aisling. "You're not saying you're afraid of horses! A big, strong Irishman like yourself!"

Sloan recoiled as if she'd hit him, and his back went stiff. She feared she'd pushed him too far, but the gentle hold of his arms didn't slacken.

"No, damn it, I'm not afraid of horses!" His words came out in a growl. "Why does everyone think that?"

Daringly, she placed her fingertips on his jawbone, where she could feel from its set how angry he was. A moment after she touched his face, she felt him relax slightly in his jaw and his spine. "Because everyone knows that most people saying they *dislike* horses are really saying they're *afraid* of them."

"Well, I'm not most people." The stiffness came back into his body. "And I *just don't like horses*."

A sadness, a despair, washed over her at his declaration. How was she to escape Acorn Bittersweet's wretched curse if the only man in all these years who had seen her as herself, not just as the image of Luna, was a man who hated horses?

Aunt Rainbow had warned her that Sloan wasn't who she wanted him to be. Well, she wanted him to be the man whose True Love would be the key to unlock the curse. Much as she hoped her aunt was wrong about Sloan, Aisling feared she would have to find another man—one who did love horses—to break the spell.

But how could she love another man, how could another man be her *One True Love*? Her heart, her mind—and, most certainly, her body!—were fascinated by Sloan. How could she love another when she was drawn by the hunger she sensed in him? When his hunger stirred a yearning inside her? All of her was filled with craving for his touch, his taste, the sound of his voice and the sight of his face. His kisses vibrated within her memory as if his lips had just released hers.

If finding True Love was the only way to save herself from a slow, dark death as the wife of a Leprechaun, she would have to feel this way, the way she felt about Sloan, about another man. She would have to love that other man truly, and feel the same fascination, the same craving, the same resonance Sloan stirred in her. Could there be another such man as Sloan, in all the world? She couldn't imagine—

"Hey!" He spoke softly, but his voice nevertheless startled her. She tipped her head up. His eyes were troubled, but his smile was sweet. "You went away again. Now you look like someone just died. Is it *that* important for me to like horses?"

"It could be, yes." She would have to tell him about the enchantment on herself and Luna sometime. True Love required honesty. But Sloan clearly wasn't ready to accept tales of magic. She would have to wait, choosing to tell him when he could—would—believe her. True Love also required trust.

"Well, hell." He shifted his hold around her so she was nearly lying back in his arms, her head on his shoulder, her body cradled between his chest and his bent knees. With the moon now behind them, his face was in shadow, but she sensed him smiling. "Are you planning to tell me why?"

"Perhaps." She smiled. "Are you planning to tell *me* why?"

Sloan drew in a deep breath, which pressed them closer

together. Then he exhaled sharply and shook his head. ''Do
you have brothers and sisters?''

His question surprised her. ''My mother died soon after
birthing me, and I was her first. Why are you asking?''

''Your father raised you? Or did he remarry?''

''He liked the ladies, my Da did, but I don't believe he
ever got over losing my mother. He hired a local woman
to take care of me, widow of a working man.''

''But your father? Did he spend time with you? Check
your homework, take you places?''

She didn't understand exactly what he was asking, but
she considered her early years. ''I don't remember much
about being young, except having an old nanny take care
of me. And Da teaching me to ride as soon as I could walk.
Later, Da taught me how to train ladies' horses to saddle
and to cart. If he wasn't too tired''—she didn't want to
mention the drink as the cause of Da's weariness—''we
might play games of cards or darts in the evenings, or read
stories aloud. Sometimes, especially when his musical
friends called, he would play fiddle and we'd sing.'' She
looked into his eyes, trying to read his reaction to her
words. ''Is that what you mean?''

''Yeah.'' He was silent then, for so long that Aisling
wondered if he meant to speak again. She tried to read his
face in the shadows, but she couldn't see well enough. After
what seemed like many minutes, he let out a breath and
said, ''My father is a horse doctor. My mother trains and
shows hunters. They claim I was riding before I could
walk.''

He paused, giving her time to ponder what he'd told her.
But the pause stretched longer than she expected. Aisling's
instincts told her he was having some trouble with the
memories he was probing, so she resisted the temptation to
prompt him to continue. His smile, when it came, rewarded
her patience.

''For the first years of my life, horses were a big part of
my world. When I was really little, I'd go with my father
on barn calls, and watch him take care of horses. He got
busier as his reputation got established, and then he started

teaching at a veterinary school, too. He'd leave the house before I got up for school, and sometimes didn't come home until I was asleep again. There were weeks when I hardly saw him from one day to the next. Once, I said hello to him in a store and he didn't recognize me.''

Aisling drew a sharp breath. Even when Da was nearly dead drunk, he'd always recognized her! ''What of your mother, then?''

''She took me with her, too, when I was little. I'd hang around the stable, hoping she'd ask me to do something to help. If she was competing locally, she'd take me and the nanny, and I'd watch her ride. Sometimes, she'd let me sit on a horse she was cooling out. When I went to school, I started bringing my homework to the stable, just so I knew where one of my parents was. A couple of times, she drove home without me, and didn't notice until she couldn't find me at dinnertime.''

His light laugh amazed her. She couldn't imagine a mother forgetting her own child! And his mother had only the one to care for! She touched his face, then placed her hand on his arm. Again, she waited through a long pause, during which the pulse of the night and the breathing of the man holding her seemed to become one rhythm. She could feel something happening within Sloan, sensed he was feeling his way through unfamiliar thoughts and emotions.

''They gave me a pony for my first birthday. By the time I was three, I was showing him in pony hunter classes. But it wasn't a passion for me, the way it was for them. I didn't want to be a vet like my dad, and I didn't want to just show horses, like my mom. When I got into school, I started doing things I liked instead, things I was good at, and gave up doing things with horses.'' He shrugged. ''And I never missed them.''

Again, he paused for a long moment. When she realized he wasn't going to say any more, she ran her fingertips along the strong line of his jaw.

''Oh, Sloan! You loved your parents, and wanted their attention.'' Aisling spoke softly to the hurt child locked inside the young man. "You've been blaming horses for taking your parents away from you."

Under her side, Sloan's chest rose and fell in a slow, deep breath that was followed by a short laugh. "No way. I just one day realized I don't like horses, and stopped trying to fake it."

Aisling cupped his cheek in her hand. "Do you think you can start liking them again, now?"

He let out a snort of a laugh, then put his hand over hers where it lay against his face. "It's not like a light you can switch on or off, you know."

She saw her opportunity. "Gradually, then. Would you be willing to make friends with my own lovely mare, Luna? Perhaps you already saw her on your last visit. She sometimes wanders at night."

"If she's a pure white mare with sharp teeth, I've met her."

A giggle escaped her when Aisling recalled how, three summers before, appearing as Luna to all but the Faeries, she'd caught at Sloan's jacket to get his attention. "Surely, she didn't bite you!" she teased. Then, with heat rising in her cheeks at her boldness, she added, "Luna has a most affectionate nature, and loves being petted and stroked."

"Yeah. I noticed. She was pretty pushy about it."

She caught her protest before it took voice. It wouldn't do to get indignant about that. Sloan really believed he'd been dealing with a horse. "She knows her mind, Luna does."

"I called her Luna because you said that was your horse's name, and it seemed to fit her. Wild horses don't wear shoes, so I figured she'd gotten out somehow."

"That she had." Hesitantly, Aisling moved her fingertips over Sloan's cheek, fascinated by the heat of his skin, the slight roughness where he'd shaved, the shape of the bone.

"It was the weirdest thing, about her shoes." His fingers combed through her hair, setting her scalp to tingling in a deliciously shivery way. "I pulled a loose nail from her front foot, and I'd swear it was solid gold." He snorted softly. "I can't prove it, though, 'cause I lost it somewhere.'' His shoulder moved under her in a quick shrug.

So that was why he hadn't taken the bit of Faery gold home with him! If Sloan were her One True Love, if he were the man who could save her from becoming Acorn Bittersweet's bride, he would have to return for her in time. She must contrive to ensure that the golden nail accompanied him back to America.

''Imagine! A golden horseshoe nail! If you find it again, 'twould make a lovely good luck charm.''

His fingers brushed her ear, trailing sparks over her skin, sending shivers down her spine. ''Yeah. I could use some luck.''

Impatience finally caught up with Aisling. ''Sloan, might you find a little bit of room in your heart for Luna? To start you liking horses again?'' *Please,* she prayed silently, holding her breath to await his answer. After the way he'd opened his heart to her, 'twould be terribly difficult to think of any other man but Sloan being her One True Love.

He turned his face and brushed a kiss onto her palm. She felt his lips curve into a smile. ''Okay, okay. If it means so much to you, I can try.''

Raising her other hand to hold his face between her hands, she looked up, knowing he could see her in the moonlight, even though his own face was deeply shadowed. ''Oh, Sloan, it means more to me than I know how to tell you,'' she breathed. ''My aunt has warned me that you aren't the man I want you to be. But especially now, I'm finding it very difficult to heed her.''

The long silence that followed her declaration sent flutters of panic through Aisling. Sloan wasn't answering. He didn't even seem to be breathing. What was he thinking? Was Aunt Rainbow right about him, and she mistaken about him, after all?

Twelve

Con felt like he was standing at the edge of a cliff watching the ground under his feet crumble away. Falling was inevitable. It was just a question of when. *The man she wanted him to be?* What the hell could that mean? Was she looking for some sort of hero? Him? What a joke! Someday, somehow, Aisling was going to find out she'd tried to put an imposter on a pedestal.

Meanwhile, Aisling was lying in his arms with her hands on his face, her touch as light as a butterfly. The moonlight shone cool and pale on her, and he could see that her eyes were full of hope. Slowly, he let out the breath he'd been holding. Before his voice would work, he had to clear his throat twice. Each time, Aisling's lashes fluttered as if he'd startled her. For a moment, he let himself get lost in the depths of her eyes.

But then, curiosity got the better of him. "What exactly do you want me to be?"

Anticipating an answer he wasn't going to like hearing, the kind of answer that would probably ruin the rest of the evening, his voice came out sounding a little choked. The innocent-looking smile she gave him didn't do much to relieve his anxiety. What could she want from him? He wasn't even twenty, and he had nothing but more studying lined up for the foreseeable future. What could he offer her besides sex? And disappointment? She could get both of those here in Ireland, without the added hassle of the distance between them.

Damn it, he didn't want to be a hero for her anyway. The most heroic thing he could do for her would be to get the hell out of her life before things got complicated. So what if he still had this little obsession for her? She deserved someone who could love her and take care of her and live with her, make a future with her. Have a family with her. Isn't that what girls—women—wanted? He couldn't give her any of that, not for years. Anyway, he'd pretty well decided that that whole pair-bonding-for-life thing wasn't for him. So far, he hadn't been very good at it, and his parents sure hadn't been great role models. He didn't want to hurt anyone, especially Aisling, but he didn't want to be on the receiving end, either.

She gave him a serious look. "I've been thinking you're a good man, with a true and deep heart."

He loved listening to her soft, almost musical voice, her accent, the way she phrased things. As usual, it took him a few extra seconds to process her words, because he was too distracted by the way she said them. When he finally understood what she'd said, he was stunned by how deeply her praise had touched him.

But even as he felt his face getting hot, sudden doubts deflated his ego. After years of witnessing his parents' battles and manipulations, he couldn't help an attack of cynicism. He was a lonely, horny younger guy, and she was a gorgeous woman. Was there some hidden nefarious reason she was flattering him? Something as harmless as getting some adoring male attention? Or something less benign, like robbing a bank? Did he need to get laid badly enough to find out what her ulterior motives were?

He should try asking first. "And if I'm the kind of man you want me to be, then what? Is there something I'm supposed to do for you?" His sharp, suspicious tone stole the soft sparkle in her eyes. Damn it, he was as sensitive as a Sherman tank! "Sorry. I didn't mean that the way it sounded."

Aisling didn't say anything, but the light came back into

her eyes, and her lips curved into a smile. He was so focused on her face, the touch of her fingertips stroking lightly down his cheek, then down his neck, startled him. The delicate contact sent little sparks of pleasure along his nerve endings. His pulse started to pound in his throat. From deep inside him, a wave of heat rose, making his skin feel taut. A rush of sensations where their bodies pressed together trapped his indrawn breath in his lungs. He got so hard so fast, he ached. Aisling's breath caught, too, and her midnight eyes widened. Guess there was no point in hiding his condition now.

He tried to read her expression. In the moonlight, her eyes reminded him of the sky at night, luminous black and fathomless. Was she offended or frightened? Was she amused by the effect she had on him? Was she going to get up and run? Or was she going to stay? And tease him? Or stay and—*Please?*—not tease him? He still couldn't breathe well enough to talk, to ask her if she was all right.

As he stared at her, she ran the tip of her tongue over her full lower lip. Unbelievably, he felt another rush of arousal, and had to catch his breath so he wouldn't groan.

Her hand came back to lay flat on his cheek. "If you're the man I'm wanting you to be"—her sweet, quiet tone implied she already thought he was—"then all I'm asking you for is your help in breaking a terrible curse placed on me."

She said the punch line so seriously, with such a sincere expression in her eyes, it took him a moment to realize she was teasing him again. Or maybe his mind was slow because most of the blood had left his brain. Granted, that stuff about the Faeries and bees had caught him off guard, and he'd ticked her off by laughing. But, contrary to what his mother thought, he had learned a few things in the last three years, in the crucible of university dating. First, he caught his lip between his teeth until he could trust himself not to crack up and laugh like a hyena. He'd just play along and see where she went with this gag.

Brushing a wisp of her silky hair away from her face,

Con matched her solemn tone. "What would I have to do to break that terrible curse?"

She gave him a sweet smile. "I can't be telling you, for that would be influencing something that must be pure and true, or else it can't break the spell."

Now he let himself smile a little. "That doesn't make sense. How can I do something without knowing what it is?"

"That's the way magic works." A tiny frown line creased the pale skin between her golden eyebrows. "You can't change the rules to suit yourself, you know."

Con nodded. A laugh nearly escaped as he began to speak, but he forced it into a grin. "Right. I was just testing you." Aisling smiled back. She was so good at this little game, he didn't even feel guilty for teasing her. "So, what exactly is this terrible curse on you?"

Her smile faded and she sighed softly. The expansion of her rib cage brought her closer to his chest for a brief moment. Their hearts seemed to be beating to the same rhythm. He totally forgot what they'd been discussing.

"I don't think I should be telling you the nature of the enchantment just yet." That brought him back to earth. " 'Twould be almost the same as telling you what you must be doing to break the curse." She gave him another one of those sweet, apparently guileless, smiles that were beginning to make him nervous. "If you're truly the right man, then your heart will be guiding your head and your hand. If you are the man my aunt cautions me that you are, then your heart will not be speaking to you at all."

He should have seen that one coming. How many times had he heard his mother snap at his father that if he didn't know what he'd done wrong, she wasn't going to tell him, or if he didn't know what she wanted, she wasn't going to say? Guess that was one of those universal mysteries about women. He could accept it, but he didn't have to like it.

"Okay, I get it." Well, he did, and he didn't, get it. And curiosity was becoming an itch that needed scratching. There had to be some way to get her to talk. "One more

question. Can you tell me what will happen to you if I don't
break this . . . curse?''

Aisling closed her eyes for a moment, and Con stared at
the violet shadows the moonlight cast under her long
lashes. She gave another long sigh, then opened her eyes
again.

''If I cannot find the right man to help me break the
curse,'' she answered, looking straight into his eyes, speaking without a hint of irony, ''I shall be forced to marry a
terrible, ugly Solitary Faery from under-the-hill. He has
kept me enchanted nearly one hundred years, since the year
1899, disguising me from Mortal eyes as a white mare. The
punishment for escaping is death, if the curse is not broken
and the Leprechaun claims me, never more will I enjoy the
beauty of the Mortal world.''

Oh, God! Her straight-faced delivery was so perfect, he
almost took her seriously! *A Solitary Faery from under-the-
hill?* His gut clenched in silent laughter. *Disguised as a
white mare!* Another silent convulsion strained his ribs,
bending him in the middle. *Enchanted for a hundred years!*
A snort of laughter burst from his tight chest. *Marry a
Leprechaun?* Oh, man, she was priceless! Another snort of
laughter erupted, then turned into a howl that rang through
the night. He ran out of air, gasped for breath, and howled
again. Tears leaked from behind his tightly squeezed eyes.

Aisling was squirming against him. Oh, hell, he must be
squashing her. Con tried to control himself enough to protect her, but another convulsion of laughter nearly doubled
him over. He caught his breath, and managed to sputter
''That's awful!'' before howling again.

Suddenly, Aisling turned into all flailing elbows and fists.
He was laughing too hard to gather the strength to hold her.
She fought her way out of his arms, hitting him in the face
and chest until he released her. He felt her scrambling to
her feet but couldn't see her with his eyes closed so tightly
he could see flashes of colored lights behind the lids.

Oh, God! He couldn't remember the last time he'd
laughed so hard! His gut clenched and tears slid down his
cheeks. Without Aisling across his lap, he rolled over to

protect his straining belly muscles, and howled until he was gasping to breathe. Taking deep, wheezing breaths, he got his laughter down to sputters, snorts, and gasps. That was when he noticed the silence vibrating around him. Wiping at his wet face, too weak to move more than his head at the moment, he looked up. His heart sank.

Aisling's face registered shock. Shock and hurt and betrayal. She stood over his spent body, looking like an angel with her moonlit golden hair streaming behind her. Her body shook with tiny tremors, but she definitely wasn't laughing. Her lower lip, caught between her teeth, quivered, and tears like liquid diamonds slid down her pale cheeks.

Oh, God! She was *serious*! And he'd made her cry. Oh, hell.

"Don't cry. Please?" Keeping his gaze locked on hers, he pushed himself up until he was sitting. "Aisling, please don't cry. I thought you were joking. I didn't mean—"

A muffled sob silenced him. She glared at him for a long, hollow moment. Another little sob escaped her. Then her chin came up and her eyes flashed. She was so beautiful right then, like some kind of Celtic avenging angel gilded by moonlight, haloed by stars in the black sky. He considered telling her how he saw her, then decided that might be a dangerously stupid thing to say at that very moment. With his brain stunned by the sight of her, he just stared up wordlessly, throat exposed in surrender, expecting the coup de grâce at any second.

She drew a breath. "Aunt Rainbow was right about you!" Her usually sweet, soft voice came out in a thin, high wail. "You're nothing like the man I was wanting you to be! How can you call yourself an Irishman when you've no magic in you? Oh! I wish I'd never met you!"

He felt like he'd just committed a gratuitous act of cruelty or violence. Guilt stabbed him at the sound of genuine pain in her voice. He'd hurt Aisling, made her cry. He was the lowest form of life on the planet. Lower than that. He had to do something to soothe her, to convince her he was even half as sorry as he really was. But how?

First, he'd have to calm her down enough to listen to

him without planning homicide. Con stretched out one hand
to her, inviting her to sit with him again. He tried the kind
of pleading smile that always seemed to work in movies.
With her hands still propped at her tiny waist, she shook
her head in a very definite *no*. Her silky long hair flew
around her in the moonlight, making her look even more
like an angel. The flash of hurt anger in her eyes made him
feel like some kind of devil.

"And there I was thinking about kissing you! Hah!" Her
voice was steady now, and contempt rang in her tone. "I
would rather kiss a goat!" Aisling gave a toss of her head
that set moonbeams dancing off her hair.

"Aisling, please sit and let me—"

"I never want to see you again!" Her words came at
him like darts. She bent forward a little, leveled a fierce
glare at him, then straightened and stood stiffly. Con had
an unsettling feeling that he was watching a play, sitting
too close to the stage. Any second now, he'd find himself
drawn in by the actors, without knowing the script. He'd
have to fake his lines or ruin the play and make a fool of
himself. The trouble was, he didn't have a clue what the
story line was.

Aisling sighed heavily. For an instant, she seemed to
relax, and he smiled, thinking that, whatever mind games
she'd been playing with him, she was finished. " 'Twould
be better to marry Acorn Bittersweet, and live the rest of
my days as the wife of a Leprechaun, without the warmth
and light of the sun," she said in a small, sad voice.
"Good-bye, Sloan," she added in an even smaller voice.
Then, head slightly bowed, she turned away as if she had
no energy left.

The joke had gone too far. Jumping up, he grabbed her
arm and pulled her around to face him.

"Aisling, cut it out, will you?" he bellowed.

With a shriek, she wrenched her arm out of his hold and
took a half step back from him, then hugged her arms
around herself. Appalled that he'd scared her, he stepped
back, too. He'd forgotten how small she was compared to
him. Small, but tough. She stood her ground and glared up

at him. Con crossed his arms over his chest and glared right back.

When he spoke again, he lowered his voice a few decibels, but didn't ease up on the anger. "How gullible do you think I am? There's no curse or enchantment, and no Leprechaun called . . . Acorn Buttercup. So stop trying to get a rise out of me, okay?"

In the cold moonlight, Aisling's face glowed pale as white marble, and her eyes were flashing sparks. She kept glaring at him while he spoke, then slowly began to smile. Even given his relatively limited experience with women, it didn't look like the kind of smile that signaled a truce.

"Getting a *rise* out of you was dead easy." She snapped the words out crisply, then lowered her gaze briefly but pointedly to the front of his jeans.

A heat wave rushed up his neck and stung his cheeks. When she met his eyes again, she was smiling in that superior way women have. The smile that always leaves a guy feeling like he just went through a duel of wits unarmed. At least, with his back to the moon, his face was in shadow, hiding his red cheeks. He drew a breath to suggest they lower the steam on their argument.

Aisling shook her head. "Finding a heart in you now, that would take the skills of a quarry man! And right now, truly, I'm thinking it isn't worth the bother!"

Con felt as if Aisling had slugged him in the gut. She thought his heart was made of stone. Worse, she didn't think he was worth the trouble of finding out if it wasn't. It surprised him how much her words hurt. Okay, it wasn't her words so much as the thoughts behind them that hurt.

She looked more sad than angry. He still didn't understand exactly what had happened between them, but obviously he'd hurt her feelings. Maybe it was rude to make fun of the way she told her story. But she was so dramatic, it was funny. Totally far-fetched, and funny. Maybe he laughed a little more than the joke warranted, but the way she'd overreacted . . . Aisling was too smart to really take all that Irish magic BS seriously. Wasn't she?

He didn't want her to run off again. Not until he had a

chance to apologize. Exhaling slowly, still looking into her dark, sad eyes, he took a carefully small step toward her. She flinched, and quickly took a hasty and equal step back from him.

Did she, or didn't she, believe in curses, Faeries, and Leprechauns? He didn't give a flip. But did she, or didn't she, believe he had a heart of stone? Right now, it felt like crystal shattering under her doubts. Couldn't she hear it break?

"Aisling, take it easy, okay? We don't have much time together, remember? Why don't we sit and talk about this, okay?"

Without intending to, he used the same tone of voice his father used on a difficult patient, and occasionally, with disastrous results, on his ex-wife. Unfortunately, now Con was discovering for himself that what sounded soothing to horses sounded patronizing to women. Aisling stiffened her back, lifted her chin even higher, and frowned at him even more fiercely.

Don't tell her to calm down, he warned himself. *Don't imply she's unreasonable or stupid.* He took another slow breath, then exhaled. "We come from very different places. All this talk about magic and curses . . . It just sounds . . . funny to me. Sure, I'm Irish, but I'm a scientist. I just don't take things on faith. I trust facts I can test, not beliefs with no proof. That's the way I am. But just because I don't believe in Faery tales and superstitions doesn't mean I'm heartless, does it?"

Once again, he tried taking a small, careful step toward her. She didn't flinch this time, but her eyes still expressed hurt and anger, so he waited quietly, praying for a signal that he was doing this right. When a long, charged moment passed and she didn't step away from him, he took another small step in her direction. If he reached for her now, he could easily take her in his arms. Instead, he kept his hands at his sides. After another moment that seemed to vibrate with expectations, he spoke softly.

"I can't help being who I am. Don't hate me for it, okay?"

She lifted her right shoulder in the tiniest shrug. "I don't hate you, Sloan. I pity you. A heart without magic is colder than a stone."

Con winced as if she'd hit him. Her luminous eyes reflected his hurt. "Then help me, Aisling?" The words came out in a rush, in a hoarse whisper, as if they couldn't wait to be said. To his astonishment, he meant them. "Help me find the magic."

She broke eye contact then, lowering her head. When she looked at him again, fresh tears had welled up in her eyes. Afraid he might scare her away, he clenched his hands into fists to keep from touching her. But he swore, if even a single tear slid down her face, he was going to kiss it away.

"You think I'm an ignorant little simpleton, and don't know the difference between what's real and what's make-believe." The hurt in her voice and her eyes fueled his guilt. He'd really been a jerk. " 'Tis true, we live in different worlds, and believe in different things, but that doesn't mean what I believe is wrong."

He wasn't aware of moving toward her, but his knees were now brushing against her skirt. "Sometimes, I'm not very good about saying the right things. Sometimes, I'm better at saying the wrong things." Oh, God, if she didn't forgive him, he'd never forgive himself!

He tried a smile. Her expression softened a little and the tightness in his chest eased a bit. "I don't think you're an ignorant simpleton. I think you're very intelligent." He tried another smile. "But you are little." Her lips twitched, as if she were trying not to smile back. Hope stirred. "And I thought what you said about kissing me was extremely intelligent."

As she tilted her head and studied his face, one golden eyebrow rose. He wanted to stare at her all night, until the image of her face was burned into his brain.

"That I'd rather be kissing a goat, instead of you?"

He bent his head toward her, pausing so she wouldn't feel crowded. Her breath teased softly at his cheek. "No. The part about how you were thinking about kissing me."

His voice came out choked. Without shifting his gaze from her eyes, he lifted his hand to her arm. "I was thinking about kissing you." Her eyes widened. Bracing himself against possible ridicule, he took the risk. "I've been thinking about kissing you for three years."

Her lips parted. "Oh, Sloan! I've thought of kissing you all that time, too."

Her whispered confession unlocked something tight around his heart. Con took a long, slow breath, then reached his other hand up and gently cupped his fingers around her shoulder. The tremor that shivered through her raced through him.

"I think we're both brilliant to be thinking about kissing each other." His voice grew huskier with each word, as his temperature rose and his breath caught in his throat. Lowering his head to hers, he touched his lips to her cheek. "I'm sorry I hurt you," he whispered against her skin.

Her answer was a muffled sigh he took for forgiveness. Moving carefully, Con drew her closer, until he could slide his arms around her back. She held herself stiffly for a moment, then made a tiny mewing sound and leaned into him. He raised a hand to tuck her head under his chin and against his chest. Her hands slid up his arms, past his shoulders, and linked behind his neck, bringing her tighter against him. There was no resistance in her now, only softness.

He was hard already, had become so with almost paralyzing speed, from the second he'd touched her again. Her breasts were small and pressed into him, her middle taut against him, the rest of her hidden by her skirt. Deep inside, he felt as if a volcano was about to erupt. The effort to stay standing, to keep from dragging her down to the blanket and tearing off her dress, made his muscles quiver as if he'd just run a marathon.

He said her name in a shaky whisper. She stirred and pulled away from his chest to tip her head up and look into his eyes. Con stared down at her and felt some part of him take a giant leap into the unknown. He was falling, and he sensed she would fall with him if he only knew how to ask. Were there words to say what he was feeling? He didn't know. All he could think of was showing her how he felt without words, with his kisses, with his body.

When he bent his head, Aisling rose up to meet him. He found her lips with his and a shock of hunger nearly knocked his feet out from under him. Her lips were soft and moist, and they parted for him as soon as he touched his tongue to them. She received the slow thrust of his tongue, making a soft sound in her throat and tightening her arms around his neck, then delicately used her tongue to answer his. The sweetness of her mouth made him hungry for more. The surging of his pulse made him tremble. The tiny tremors running through her fed the tidal wave rocking him.

His knees started to buckle. The blanket was right there for them . . . Somehow, he lowered her without breaking that kiss. With shaking hands, he guided her slender body into the shelter of his, then cautiously let her feel his weight. He swallowed her gasp and waited for her to get used to the pressure of his arousal against her belly. After a few seconds, he felt her sigh. Then her hips flexed, pressing her against him, and his pulse went crazy. He hadn't thought he could get any harder, until another rush of heated blood flooded his loins.

Without warning, icy cold rain poured down on them.

Thirteen

The shock of the cold water startled a cry from Aisling. Con let out a howl of rage. The rain stung like tiny hailstones. He tried to shield her with his body, but within seconds they were drenched to the skin. Hastily, he yanked at the blanket they'd been lying on, until he managed to free half of it. With one arm, Aisling clung to him, shaking, using her other arm to help him hold the heavy wool blanket over their heads. Thunder rumbled in the distance, and then the rain pelted them harder, soaking the blanket. He held her close against him, his jaw clenched to keep his teeth from chattering in the sudden chill.

A deep breath, intended to restore a little calm to his system, filled his head with the odor of wet wool. The rain was seeping through it anyway, so it was like being in a tent with a soaked sheep. At least the blanket muffled the bite of the wind. Disgusted that he hadn't noticed any warning signs of a storm, Con exhaled sharply, then muttered, "Damn!"

Aisling uttered a sound he figured was agreement. He placed a quick kiss on her cool, wet face. She curled tighter against him, and something inside him warmed a little. Under the noise of the rain, she said his name, but he could hardly hear her. He bent a little lower and felt her lips brush against his ear, her breath kiss his skin, when she spoke again.

Lightning flashed, blindingly close, followed almost instantly by an explosion of thunder. With a little shriek, Aisling jumped, her head just missing his cheekbone. He tightened his hold around her, hoping he was helping comfort her, even a little. They couldn't stay in the middle of a wide-open, rain-soaked field with a thunderstorm overhead. If there was a strike anywhere near, they'd end up as crispy critters. They had to get to some kind of shelter, and then he could sneak some towels for Aisling. The keys to his grandfather's car were always hanging on a nail inside the door to the mud room. Chances were good no one would notice him borrowing it to take Aisling home. If his luck held when he came back, he'd be able to sneak up to his own room without getting caught. Even if he got busted, it would be worth the risk to make sure Aisling was safe.

"C'mon!" he yelled over the storm. "We can walk along the walls to the yard, and I'll drive you—"

"I cannot! I must go to my aunt alone!" Her hand, chilled by the rain, touched his face and lightly held him for a kiss. He tried to deepen the kiss, but she pulled away too quickly. In the dark, he could feel her looking at him, but he couldn't see her except as a shadow. She spoke close to his ear but a rumble of thunder interrupted her. When the thunder faded, he thought he heard her say, ". . . who's responsible for this." That made no sense at all, so he must have heard her wrong.

"Didn't hear you," he told her between rolls of thunder.

"If you see my mare Luna wandering at night, remember your promise to make her your friend."

He laughed softly and hugged her tightly. She was as horse crazy as his mother, but for some reason, he didn't mind. In fact, he thought it was kind of . . . cute. As soon as the next clap of thunder rolled away, he hollered back, "Okay, but I'd rather see you wandering at night!"

She dropped her corner of the blanket and threw her arms around his neck. Her mouth was wet from the rain, soft and warm, sweet and eager on his. He released his corner of the blanket to lock his arms around her. The blanket fell over them, muffling the sounds around them, wrapping them in a steamy cocoon where touch and taste were more acute than sight or hearing. He even forgot about the wet-sheep smell of the blanket. With her mouth on his, her cool, wet body plastered against him, and her thick, long hair tangled around him, the sweet woman scent of her filled his senses.

Lightning flashed so brilliantly, so close by, he saw streaks of light from behind his closed eyes. The thunder, exploding barely a heartbeat after, shook the ground under them. Con was positive they were going to die at any second. If it had to happen like this, at least he was with Aisling, but damn it, why did he still have to be a virgin?

Aisling pushed at him, catching him off guard, breaking his hold. "I must go! Next full-moon night, Sloan!"

The blanket engulfed him, and Aisling scrambled to her feet while he was struggling to find the edge and get free of it. Still on his knees, he grabbed for her, but she jumped out of his reach. The soggy blanket fell over his face again, and by the time he'd pulled it off and struggled to his feet, she'd disappeared.

He stood in the rain, staring into the darkness, hoping for some clue to where she went, how she got away so quickly and thoroughly. Suddenly, as if someone had turned off a giant sprinkler, the rain stopped. It didn't slow down, like the clouds were empty. It didn't peter out, like the storm was passing overhead. It just stopped. The full moon appeared like a giant lamp got switched on in the sky.

Con shook his head. If he hadn't been there, he wouldn't have believed how fast the weather could change. It was literally like someone had pulled a rug out from under him. Or like aliens had abducted Aisling. Poof! She was gone. Poof! The rain was gone. If he didn't know what the consequences were likely to be, he'd break into another bottle of Grandad's Midleton Very Rare Old Irish Whiskey and get himself totally plastered. Then, at least, his hallucinations would be legitimate.

Finally resigned that Aisling wasn't going to come back, and he wasn't going to find any answers to some of the questions he wasn't sure he even wanted to ask, he rolled up the blanket and tucked it under his arm. Moonlight shimmered on the wet grass. The stone wall was cool and slick, making getting over it harder than usual. Swearing again under his breath, he dropped into the next field. The grass here was cool and moist, but there wasn't a sign of the rain that had soaked the field behind him.

That was impossible.

Muttering, he hauled himself back over the wall and dropped to his feet in the field where he and Aisling had been drenched. It should have been soggy from the heavy rain that wouldn't have had a chance to soak into the ground yet. It was the same as the other field. The grass was cool and moist, the earth also. But not a drop of rainwater. The moon was nearly set in the far west, and the blackness of the sky sparkled with stars. Lots and lots of stars. And not a single cloud.

Stunned beyond thought, he lifted one hand to push his hair off his forehead. Something else was very wrong: His hair was dry. Feeling a little frantic, he patted his shirt. It was as dry as when he'd put it on earlier in the evening. His jeans were dry. Even the damn sheep-stinking blanket was dry! He started toward the house feeling as if he was sleepwalking, seeing but not comprehending.

On the top stair to the back door, he turned to look out at the fields once more. In the sky, the stars twinkled. Above the fields, fireflies flashed and glowed, performing a natural light show. Not a cloud, not a glimmer of lightning. Somewhere out there wind chimes tinkled, but no thunder rumbled. He felt the blanket, his hair, his clothes, again. All of it, dry as a bone.

Maybe he hadn't mistaken what Aisling had said before she ran off. Something about someone being *responsible* . . . If he didn't know better . . .

He'd thought he did know better. He hated to entertain the possibility that he'd been wrong, but . . .

Nah. Impossible. Irish weather was just . . . volatile. Yeah, that was it. Unpredictable. Nothing *cosmic* . . . Well, *literally* cosmic, as in the *cosmos,* but not *figuratively,* as in . . . *magic.*

A GREAT HALL, THE FAERY REALM, EVER-THE-PRESENT

Aisling rushed through the magical passage into the *rath* so quickly that she tripped over a flower root, got her foot caught in the wet hem of her skirt, and fell face-first into the leaves that covered the floor of the spacious great hall. As she fell, she uttered a yelp of dismay and outrage. All the Faeries amusing themselves there gathered around her even before she'd landed. Landing flat drove the breath out of her, and with it, another cry. While she was struggling to regain her breath, the laughter of the Faeries, like the pealing of hundreds of tiny bells, swelled to such a din that her ears began ringing. Giving in to a soft moan, she folded her arms above her head so that her arms muffled some of the cacophony.

Trying to compose herself, trying to regain her shredded dignity, trying not to cry, Aisling lay on the soft ground with her face cradled in her arms. Faeries were so distractable, she reasoned, that they were sure to lose interest in her humiliation and turn their attentions back to their normal pursuit of selfish pleasures. She need only wait them out, and then she could sneak away to the seclusion of her aunt's private bower.

The laughter continued unabated, however, long past the point of acceptable rudeness even for the most insensitive Faery. Aisling finally lost her struggle with the tears stinging her eyes. Keeping her forehead pressed to her arms, she hid her face and let the tears flow. She hadn't felt so wretched since the evening that Acorn Bittersweet's enchantment had changed the course of her life for the worse. This time, the pain was even more acute. She'd been so close to realizing the one thing she'd been seeking for nearly ninety years: True Love.

Until someone had cast that magical downpour, cruelly stealing the little precious time she could have with Sloan.

A gentle touch on her shoulder broke into her cocoon of misery. Sniffling, she cautiously lifted her head and noticed that the laughter finally had resolved into the familiar musical din of the Faery Troop's normal activities. She blinked away the tears clouding her vision and found Aunt Rainbow at her side, her violet eyes reflecting concern. Silently, her aunt helped her to sit, then, while Aisling sniffed, smoothed her tangled, wet hair off her face. Rainbow's motherly tenderness inspired another flood of tears, so when Aisling finally quieted enough to get to her feet, her head ached with all that crying. Her eyes burned and her nose was stuffy, and she knew her face was blotchy and swollen. Fortunately, Aunt Rainbow's capacity for affection was greater than her Fey need for beauty, Aisling thought, or else she'd have no one at all in the Faery World to turn to for sympathy.

"Poor Remember-Fear-Not," her aunt murmured. "Come with me, Niece. I'll give you a hot nectar tea. Then we must see about your appearance, and quickly, for the troop travels soon to a flower festival." Aunt Rainbow clucked softly while shaking her head. "Such a fierce storm. I wonder what went wrong."

Gathering her sodden and bedraggled skirts in her hands, Aisling trailed after the swiftly moving Faery toward a far area of the *rath*. Wherever they stayed, Rainbow maintained a private suite of rooms for herself, as befitting her ancient and noble lineage among The People. Aisling was never more grateful than now for the privileges of her aunt's status. For nearly ninety years, she'd had to tolerate Faery intolerance of her un-Fey clumsiness, lack of talent at Fey arts, and her foolishly Mortal notions of right and wrong. She'd smiled in the face of their ridicule, bitten her tongue to refrain from offending any of them when their casually spoken insults lacerated her feelings. 'Twasn't simply the graciousness of a well-born young woman, but the wisdom to protect the little that remained of her pride.

She, better than any other Mortal, understood the prudence of avoiding Faery favors. It seemed that for every

Faery kindness, she'd had to endure an equal Faery thoughtlessness.

'Twould have been better to comprehend all these matters before she'd let the Leprechaun cast his spell, but becoming enchanted was likely the only way she would understand them correctly. *Is maith an fáidh deireadh an lae,* her old nanny used to say: "The end of the day is a good prophet." And wisdom, she'd learned for herself, preferred the *following* of consequence, rather than the preceding of it.

Now Aisling lifted her sodden skirts and scurried to catch up with Aunt Rainbow, determined to vent her anger. "I'll be telling you what went wrong. Some accursed prankster—and when I discover the culprit, whoever 'twas shall regret ever being born!—opened the sky above Sloan and myself and nearly drowned us!"

Her aunt led her into their private suite and brought her a cup of sweet, hot nectar. Smiling her thanks, Aisling moved to a velvet-covered log to rest while she drank. "Don't sit, child!" Rainbow scolded, stopping Aisling before she could settle herself on the log. "Fey rain is real enough here, as is Fey mud. Drink up quickly. We must see to your toilette immediately."

It seemed that even Aunt Rainbow had limits to her tolerance, although they were far more generous than those of most Faeries. No one ever saw a dirty or disheveled Trooping Faery, Aisling knew, although some of the Solitaries could be absentmindedly careless about their attire. But, unlike gremlins and imps, even the most oddly dressed of the Solitaries was always clean.

Acknowledging she was a frightful mess, Aisling gave a resigned sigh and remained standing to sip at the reviving tea. By the time she'd finished, Aunt Rainbow had summoned a deep bathing tub filled with warm water and fragrant essences of flowers and herbs. After Aisling stripped off the cold, soggy layers of her clothing, she stepped into the tub and let the soothing heat and scents seep into her chilled flesh. Her aunt sent her dress, petticoats, and undergarments out to the laundress Faeries who tended to the clothing of all the Circle members.

After sending Aisling's dress to be cleaned, Aunt Rainbow helped her wash her hair, tsking all the while. As soothing as her aunt's ministrations were, Aisling's agitation and indignation lingered. There would be no mercy for whoever had spoiled one of her only two precious summer nights with Sloan.

"Calm yourself, Niece," Aunt Rainbow advised in gentle tones. "Sloan must be safely in bed by now, and should be dry as a bone, so there's no harm done. 'Tis only that you are Under-Hill that you are so untidy." Rainbow gave Aisling a pat on her cheek. "But we shall remedy that quickly enough. What's done is done, and can't be undone."

" 'Tis precisely why I'll *not* calm myself, Aunt!" She felt far too agitated to reply in the same quiet manner. "Tonight *was* undone. Now I must wait until the next full-moon night to meet Sloan again, and so briefly. How could anyone be so heartless?"

Even a Faery, she added silently. She didn't wish her sentiments to insult her aunt, whom she truly did love, and who did have fewer Fey shortcomings than most. Throughout the duration of the enchantment, Rainbow had guided her, comforted her, advised her, and mothered her. Aisling trusted her and valued her opinions about everything—everything except the topic of Sloan. But, as kind and loving as Rainbow was, even her sympathies sometimes seemed somewhat shallow.

"Aunt? Do you really believe I shall meet anyone more suitable than Sloan to be my One True Love, and break the spell?" She didn't try to disguise the doubt in her voice.

"You are a most single-minded young Mortal!" Rainbow muttered as she swished fresh water through Aisling's hair.

Aisling smiled at her aunt's tone, but her own reply was made earnestly. "I am not so young, Aunt. By my latest estimate, I'm at least one hundred years old! 'Twould be a shame to live so long without once experiencing True

Love.'' Especially if she were doomed to die, or marry the Leprechaun. A quick shudder raced through her at the thought.

Aunt Rainbow came around from behind her. With an unusually solemn expression in her purple Faery eyes, she cupped Aisling's chin in her hand, forcing her to look up. For a long moment, Rainbow silently studied Aisling's face, one perfectly arched golden eyebrow lifting when her gaze lit on her niece's kiss-swollen lips. A blush stung Aisling's cheeks and she lowered her gaze.

'' 'Tis one thing for Faeries to frolic on a summer's night,'' her aunt said sternly. ''We never find ourselves dealing with unfortunate consequences of a night of physical pleasures.''

Although she'd grown up surrounded by the mating activities of farm animals, Aisling suddenly realized no one had ever spoken to her about relations between men and women. Her father would have sent her in ignorance into marriage with Ambros O'Hara, letting her think of herself as little better than a broodmare to be mounted and bred. She still remembered how Ambros's rough kisses had conveyed his disregard for her innocence, his disdain for her tender emotions.

Ah, but Sloan's kisses . . . To be sure, they expressed his hunger, but also his tenderness, his desire to share the experiencing of passion. Sloan's body had grown hard against her, the way Ambros's had, but she hadn't felt *threatened* in Sloan's embrace, the way she had in Ambros's clutches. Indeed, her own body had responded eagerly. Oh! Another blush stung her cheeks. Perhaps they'd been rather nearer to . . . *physical pleasures* . . . than she'd truly understood at the time!

Rainbow gave Aisling's chin a little shake, forcing her to look up again. ''Faery lore is replete with tales of beautiful Faery women taking Mortal men as their lovers. And there are as many stories of handsome Faery men seducing pixie-led Mortal women seeking adventures. 'Tis why you yourself are part Fey.''

''But, Aunt, Sloan is no Faery!''

Rainbow released her chin and smiled. "No, indeed, he truly is not." A solemn expression replaced her smile. "But that only increases the risk you both take. Offspring, such as your own half-Fey great-grandmother, may result from such affairs. When they are wished for, as she was, both Mortals and Faeries rejoice at their births. Too often, however, children thus conceived are not welcomed. All children, whether Fey or Mortal, or a little of each, deserve to be wanted and loved."

Aisling nodded her agreement. Rainbow shook her head and patted her cheek. "Remember-Fear-Not, forget not that you do not yet know all you need to know about your Sloan. When you do, you may decide he is not the man you wish for your One True Love."

"Oh, Aunt! I can imagine nothing about Sloan that could make him appear worse than an O'Hara! If you knew him, you would understand how I find it so difficult to think of meeting anyone else to love." She frowned, then added her oft-repeated position regarding the complementary spell her aunt had cast. "*Especially* a descendant of Ambros O'Hara!"

Stepping back behind the tub, Aunt Rainbow poured cool water scented with herbs to rinse her hair. "So, you have decided not to heed my warnings about Sloan?"

Aisling ignored the twinge of guilt at her aunt's question. "I *am* heeding your warnings, Aunt, but I'm heeding them with a pinch of salt." She smiled, hoping to prompt an answering smile from Rainbow. When her aunt failed to return her smile, Aisling tried to explain her reasoning. "Sloan is three years older now than when first we met, and less of a boy. Before long, he'll be a man. A strong, brave, and good-hearted man. I've no doubt he could be my One True Love, if only we had more time together."

"Ah" was Rainbow's only response before she moved away from the tub. At her aunt's magical behest, a crisp length of purest white Irish linen appeared, floating by itself in front of Aisling. As she stood in the tub, the cloth wrapped itself around her and the free end dabbed at the moisture on her neck.

Seizing this opportunity to speak candidly with her only confidant, Aisling said softly, "It was quite lovely being with Sloan. He's a gentle man, but there's passion in him. When he was telling me of his home in America, and his university studies, I could have listened to him all the night long. If only someone hadn't spoiled the little time we had tonight. Blast it!"

The petulant stamp of her foot in the tub sent a splash over the side. The magical linen cloth nearly strangled her in its attempt to simultaneously dry her and mop up the spill she'd created. Aisling yanked the free end of the cloth back into place around her, then quickly stepped out of the tub, before the linen made another attempt to dry the floor and pulled her out headfirst. Like wishes and wisdom, Aisling had discovered during her decades in the Faery Realm, magic had its shortcomings.

Still wrapped in the linen drying cloth, Aisling obeyed her aunt's smiling summons to perch on the velvet log while having her hair combed and dried. As Aunt Rainbow stroked a comb gently through Aisling's hair, a fan made of wide leaves responded to her aunt's command and stirred a warm, drying breeze.

"And how did you *listen* your lovely hair into such terrible tangles?"

The deceptive innocence of Rainbow's tone didn't fool Aisling. Obviously, her aunt knew they'd indulged in more than simple conversation! The stinging heat that flared up Aisling's neck to her cheeks was painfully different from the wondrous waves of heat that had flared inside her when Sloan was kissing her. Unable to think of an answer that was truthful, yet not altogether truthful, she decided to remain silent, rather than prompt another lecture.

Still working the knots out of one section of Aisling's hair, Aunt Rainbow sighed. "It's difficult to believe that there are Mortals with less forethought than the most foolish of Faeries have. If you intend to be outsmarting Acorn Bittersweet, you must be both clever and patient. Tonight, you were neither."

Her aunt's disapproval stung. After a few more minutes,

Aisling decided her hair was dry enough. She rose from the velvet-covered log and, feeling restless, began pacing, musing over Rainbow's words. What if Sloan failed to return at the next full-moon night? What if he had to go back to America before then? She might not see him again except when she must appear as Luna. While she believed he would keep his promise to befriend the white mare, should he find her between full moons, 'twas no way to conduct a courtship!

Oh! And he'd lost the golden horseshoe nail, which would ensure his return. She might not ever see him again! Even though he was very likely her One True Love, she might never have the opportunity to escape her enchantment with him. What's more, if Sloan were indeed her One True Love, there could be no *other* One True Love. But if Sloan were not her One True Love . . . If she trusted her aunt's advice to wait for another man, she might not find him before her time ran out. Then she would have to marry the horrible Acorn Bittersweet!

As if by magic, her freshly cleaned and pressed clothing suddenly appeared at the doorway, accompanied by a chime of delicate bells and Juniper Bilberry, a shy Faery laundress. With a smile and a handful of sweets, Aisling thanked the girl, then asked after her mother, Candleberry Burtree, the most skilled seamstress of the Moonstone Circle. The little Faery favored her with a surprisingly bright smile and a quick curtsey, then hurried away.

As Aisling slipped the sheer batiste chemise over her head, the drying linen obligingly unwrapped itself and floated to the edge of the bathing tub. Next, she climbed into her pantalets and tied the drawstring around her waist, then pulled her two petticoats on, the one with the most lace on top. Rainbow held her dress for her and helped her find the sleeves. The scent of sweet wildflowers surrounded her as the layers of cloth drifted over her head and floated down over the petticoats.

Aisling would have liked a mirror for the finishing touches to her hair and her dress, but there were none in the Faery World Under-Hill. This had surprised her at first, because she'd found Faeries to be extremely vain. Her aunt had explained that it was because of their vanity that Faeries usually avoided mirrors. As in the myth of Narcissus, the Good People could become so fascinated by their own images that they were in danger of pining away for unrequited love of the exquisite but aloof beings reflected back to them. Eons ago, therefore, a wise Fey ruler had decreed that no mirrors could be brought to Under-Hill.

Of course, Aisling didn't need a mirror to know she looked much better than she had when she'd fled from Sloan. Would that he remember her as she'd been before the rain, instead of like a drowned rat, until they met again. 'Twould be awful if his last vision of her—as herself, not as Luna—was of her soaked to the skin, with her hair plastered to her! Oh, how could she bear it if she never saw him after tonight? If she never again touched him, or heard his voice or breathed in his scent as he held her in his arms? Kissing Sloan, being kissed by him, feeling their bodies pressing together, had awakened a hunger inside her that still gnawed at her.

Oh! What horrible, painful, *terrible* things she would like to do to the Faery who caused that storm!

At the beginning of her enchantment, she'd thought a hundred years to be an impossibly long time. Now she knew even so many years could slip away in the blink of an eye. Time could not be slowed, and once gone, there was no recapturing of it, except in memories. Perhaps her aunt was right to advise her to use caution with Sloan, but caution couldn't appease her sense of urgency. Time was running out for her, and if she failed to find her True Love before it was too late, she would not have even memories.

Fourteen

~~~~

The door to Aunt Rainbow's suite swung open, and laughter, music, and the neighing of Faery horses drifted to them. These Aisling recognized from more experiences than she cared to recall, were the sounds of a pleasure-seeking Faery Troop preparing to depart. Within a span of a few heartbeats, she knew, there would be no standing idly, musing about her fate, or Aisling could find herself left behind. At her aunt's magical command, all the pretty decorations and comfortable furnishings in the rooms they'd shared folded themselves into invisible bundles. Once the bundles had rolled themselves into secret storage places among the roots under the *rath*, there would be no outward signs of Faery occupation. Upon the Moonstone Circle's return, a few magical spells would reverse the process and within seconds, the various rooms and passages within the *rath* would be filled with the luxury and beauty the Good People required. Being exceedingly lazy, no self-respecting Faery would be carrying bundles and parcels from one place to another, when magic was so easy for them.

Aunt Rainbow had just sent away the last of the richly embroidered tapestries when the trumpet blasts to signal their departure rang through the halls. As she always did when the Faery horns played, Aisling covered her ears to muffle the shrill notes. The rushing and swirling of Faeries of all ages, sexes, sizes, and types soon engulfed her and swept her along like a leaf in a whirlwind. In fact, they moved so quickly that, to an untrained eye, a windstorm was what they would have seemed to be.

During her first Trooping experience, Aisling had learned that the Good People placed far greater importance on everyone else showing good manners, than they did on their own. Several times during that journey, she had lost sight of her aunt when Faeries swirled around her, pushing her first one way, then another. Now Aisling no longer panicked, but simply did her best to keep up, while keeping her ears covered. She knew that no matter how often they might be separated, Aunt Rainbow always managed to find her again.

Sure enough, her aunt rejoined her as she was lagging behind most of the Troop. A male Faery called Raven, handsome and extremely cocky, trooped by Rainbow's side with impressive masculine grace. And didn't he just know it, Aisling thought. Raven had recently joined the Moonstone Circle. She found his swaggering and his presumptuousness very irritating. He seemed to think Rainbow should feel flattered that he wished to seduce her, and should obligingly throw herself at his feet. To Aisling's relief, her aunt had thus far consistently kept Raven at a distance, as if she considered him just an attractive nuisance. However, the Faery male was proving himself distressingly persistent.

Now, as they trooped, the two exquisite Fey creatures appeared to be holding a rather heated conversation. Rainbow was speaking rapidly, waving her graceful arms in the air, and shaking her head often, while Raven was smiling and making conciliatory gestures far more often than he spoke. Aisling wondered if they were having a lovers' quarrel, although her aunt had never given the slightest hint that she had given in to his seductive entreaties. Between the cacophony of the Faery *rade* and her hands clamped tightly over her ears, Aisling was unable to hear anything of their conversation as she followed the two hummingbird-like creatures in front of her.

Finally, the whirlwind of activity ceased, and all the Faeries of the Moonstone Circle began casting a new habita-
tion. When the dust and leaves and other odd bits settled,
however, Aisling recognized this *rath* as the very one
they'd just left. With a resigned sigh, she sat on a log to
watch the Faeries magically assemble their "new" palace.
The first time she'd witnessed this same error, Aisling had
foolishly commented on it, then laughed. Since then, not
wishing to spend any more time itching from head to foot
from millions of invisible stings, she carefully refrained
from eye contact with anyone, and tactfully refrained from
comment and laughter. This time, she was perfectly happy
they hadn't set themselves up halfway across Ireland.
'Twould be virtually impossible for her, as Luna, to meet
with Sloan between full moons if the Troop had traveled
so far.

If Rainbow and Raven had noticed their destination was
a little more familiar than it should have been, they gave
no sign. Instead, to Aisling's surprise and fascination, they
were still talking while her aunt was casting spells to fur-
nish and decorate her suite. Aisling guessed that Rainbow's
obviously increasing irritation with Raven probably ac-
counted for the slight tilt to some of the wall hangings. She
would love to know what they were arguing about, but
she'd been raised to believe eavesdropping was terribly
rude. Besides, they were just a little too far away, speaking
a little too softly, for her to hear them.

Aunt Rainbow abruptly raised her arms in an apparent
gesture of surrender, but when she lowered them, Aisling
could see that her aunt's purple eyes looked quite stormy.
When she spoke now, her voice carried to Aisling's ears.
"Raven, I regret ever entrusting you to carry out such a
simple task, and no amount of excuses and flattery will win
me to your side."

The handsome male Faery shrugged, then, to Aisling's
surprise, jerked his head in her direction. "She's none the
worse for her drenching, is she?" Raven's path across
Rainbow's sitting room lost some of its swagger when he
caught the toe of his boot on a curl in the carpet her aunt

hadn't cast correctly. He recovered his grace in time to strike an attractively arrogant pose in front of his frazzled hostess. "You asked for my help, Rainbow darling. That piddling little drizzle you cast was hardly going to protect your niece's virtue, was it?"

As the meaning of Raven's words sank into her trooping-benumbed brain, Aisling gasped. At the sound, both Faeries stared at her. Raven smirked, his conviction in his own superiority writ plainly in his expression. Aunt Rainbow's exquisite face went so pale that she was nearly transparent. Her luminous purple eyes conveyed unspoken distress, but Aisling was too shocked, too hurt, to care. 'Twas her aunt, not Raven, who had betrayed her, the one who had robbed her of her time with Sloan, and likely, her chance to find True Love.

Aisling felt her spirit deflate. Rainbow had been her only family, her only ally, her only friend, her only teacher for nearly nine decades. From the start of their relationship, Aisling had trusted her aunt implicitly. She had maintained hope, maintained her belief in True Love, because she believed Aunt Rainbow's assurances that all would be well. But all would not be *well*. All would be *horrible*! Her aunt never meant to help her find True Love, because Faeries didn't know what love was. 'Twas only an elaborate joke, for the amusement of her Fey friends.

How could she have been so foolish not to see the truth? But of course, she knew it was because she'd needed to believe in her aunt, or else give up her hope. Without the hope of finding her One True Love, a Mortal love, she would be doomed to marry Acorn Bittersweet. But now she understood that her hope had been an illusion. At the end of the remaining years of her enchantment—years that, in the Faery world, would pass as swiftly as the blinking of an eye, the single beating of a heart—that wretched, ugly Leprechaun would claim her for his bride. No wonder he'd been laughing so heartily as he'd left her to while away their century-long betrothal.

Benumbed by her discoveries, Aisling turned away from the two Faeries, who were still arguing over how much rain had truly been required to separate Sloan from herself. With nowhere else in the whole of the Faery *rath* she could go for privacy, she simply stood there with her face turned away, too devastated even for tears. She hadn't felt so alone, so betrayed, so helpless, since that long-ago day that her father had announced he had promised her in marriage to Ambros O'Hara.

How ironic to discover she might have been better off had she gone docilely to that fate, than she was now, thinking—and fooling herself all the while—that she could change her destiny.

O'HARA HOUSE, CO. SLIGO, FRIDAY, JULY 26, 1985

Finally, it was dark enough to go outside.

On his way past the library, Con heard his mother and Leon talking behind the half-open door. He paused, trying to think of some excuse to interrupt their cozy after-dinner tête-à-tête. If he was being childish, so was Gramps. The old man didn't like Leon, either. Too slick. Treated horses as commodities, not as a sacred trust—Gramps's words, not his. Con agreed with the old man's appraisal, even if he didn't care what Leon's attitude toward horses was.

He still didn't like Gramps as much as he recalled doing as a little kid. The old man was arrogant and cold. Whenever he could, he used his razor wit to express contempt for Con's choice of computer science over horses. But the tacit acknowledgment that they were on the same side about Leon made the old tyrant more tolerable.

Con didn't want to hurt his mother; he wanted to save her from making a serious mistake. He had to be pretty subtle about his subversive intentions, so Corliss would never suspect him. Gramps, though, could use that crusty-old-man routine of his to get away with little things that made the point very clearly, without a word. And Con could tell old Ambros enjoyed every opportunity. Con's personal favorite incident was Gramps's refusal to pour any of his precious Midleton's Very Rare Irish Whiskey for Leon. He'd hidden his supply, under lock and key, in his bedroom. Corliss had argued and cajoled, then given in to buy their own bottle, which Gramps was then happy to share.

God! He couldn't smell Irish whiskey without acutely reliving the night he'd met Aisling. Impatient now to get out to the far paddock, on the chance that she'd show up, he was about to walk away when he heard Leon say his name, followed by something too quiet to hear. He hesitated. Stay, or go? Getting caught eavesdropping wasn't his idea of a good time. But the sound of his mother's gasp decided him.

It was impossible to hear everything they said, although after Con caught the phrases *something furtive, personality disorder,* and *positively antisocial,* Corliss's voice rose like a *bahn shee's.* He couldn't understand much of what she said, but she was vehemently disagreeing with the amateur shrink's opinion of her son. Normally, his mother was so agreeable to Leon, it was sickening. This was the first time he knew of them arguing. He pictured Leon cringing at this new side of Corliss, and smiled.

The voices went on for a while—his, hers, his again. Then Con heard footsteps across the hardwood and old carpet of the library floor. Leon's voice again, answered by Corliss, even more hushed. Con strained to hear, but couldn't make out a word. The sound of a kiss told Con his mother had decided against killing Leon with her bare hands. At least the kiss had been quick.

Corliss was speaking now, her voice too low for him to hear her say more than *a bit of a lone wolf* and *obsessed with academic achievements.* Con winced. *Lone wolf? Obsessed?* Guess she wasn't defending him as vigorously as he'd first thought. The murmuring from behind the library door turned into laughter. More kissing sounds indicated that Leon had managed to handle Corliss. Worse, the creep made him sound like a loose cannon! He didn't need to hear any more to know Leon had outmaneuvered him, crushing his hopes of bringing Corliss and Jonathan back together. His father was living with a bimbo not much older than Con, but she'd come on to him a couple of times, so he figured she'd be dumping Dad soon. He'd always thought his mother was the one who would resist another relationship, in case her ex suddenly smartened up and came back. Guess he was wrong.

With a hollow feeling in his gut, he left by a side door.

AT THE EDGE OF THE FAERY REALM, EVER-THE-PRESENT

''Do you think it wise, Niece, to torment yourself like this?'' Aunt Rainbow's dark purple eyes reflected the strain of their relationship ever since Aisling had discovered her aunt's betrayal.

Pausing in the passageway between the Faery World and the Mortal world, Aisling looked at Rainbow and felt a twinge of guilt. She longed to see the sadness fade from the Faery's eyes. She longed to be comforted, longed to hear the musical laughter that had sustained her spirits for nine decades of uncertainty in the Fey nether-realm. But she refused to accept solace from one of the sources of her misery. With difficulty, she hardened her heart to the Faery's pleading expression.

''*Wise*, Aunt? 'Tis an odd question to ask one who has done little that can be deemed *wise*.''

Rainbow shook her head. ''Ah, Niece, everything you have done is more wise than you know. It pains me to see your resolve beginning to unravel. Where is your belief in True Love?''

Aisling laughed dryly. ''My belief in True Love is as constant as a Faery's loyalty,'' she replied softly.

This time, Rainbow's hurt look caused her no guilty twinges. Like all Faeries, her aunt had no loyalty, except to herself and her own amusement. The expression of regret in Rainbow's eyes was also counterfeit. Faeries had no regrets, either.

''Raven has given you his word, the thunderstorm was his own idea, intended to impress me. He did swear this on a branch of Sacred Hawthorn. Will you not believe him?''

''Raven's word?'' Aisling laughed sadly. ''Why should

I believe his word about anything? He sees me as a rival for your affections. Exaggerating your rain spell gave him the double pleasure of tormenting me while doing this deed for you. If you tell him to swear his veracity on twenty Sacred Hawthorns, he will do so, because he wishes to win your favor.''

'' 'Tis true, Raven is impetuous and arrogant.'' Rainbow sighed. '' 'Tis also true, he has some affection for me, and wishes to court me. Gentlemen swearing falsely for the ladies they fancy is a tradition older even than the mountains.''

This time, when Aunt Rainbow's lips curved into a gentle smile, Aisling could not restrain a small answering smile.

''Remember-Fear-Not, you still do not know all you need to know of your Sloan. Hear me. Raven mistook the intention of my spell. I only wished to slow the fires you and Sloan were stirring, not douse them. 'Twould take more than Faery magic to extinguish the heat between you.''

A blush crept up Aisling's neck and cheeks. She searched her aunt's face for any sign of mockery, of deceit, and saw only affection and concern. ''Swear you will not try to separate us again? The Mortal time remaining for us to meet is so short—less than a blink in the Faery World.''

Rainbow opened her arms and gathered Aisling into a warm hug. Aisling felt a great, gray weight lift from her heart, for she did truly love her aunt.

''I swear I will not, dear Niece.'' Rainbow spoke earnestly. ''Nor will I allow anyone to be my agent in separating you. If Raven will swear he cast the storm spell to dazzle me with his powers, I shall bid him leave the Moonstone Circle as proof his word is true. But if he swore falsely, he may stay.''

Aisling stepped back and stared at her aunt's face, beautifully solemn in a Fey way. ''Aunt, the test isn't fair! You mustn't send him away to prove he swears truly! If he does prove true, you will lose him. If he does not, you will not be able to lose him!''

A chiming laugh burst from Rainbow's lips. ''You see

how wise you are, Niece? I confess, I am curious to see what Raven chooses to do.'' She gave another laugh. ''Never fear. If he swears truly, he will find a way to return.'' With a light pat on Aisling's cheek, her aunt spun away, singing in a clear, bell-like voice. At the other end of the passage, Rainbow halted, twirled toward her, and made shooing motions with her hands.

''Go on, lovely Luna,'' she said with laughter in her voice and eyes. ''Teach Aisling's One True Love to love horses.''

For the first time in nearly nine decades, Aisling did not shed even a single tear as she crossed the threshold from the Under-Hill Faery Realm to the Mortal world in the guise of the sacred white Faery mare Luna.

THE PADDOCKS, O'HARA HOUSE, CO. SLIGO, FRIDAY, JULY 26, 1985

The gate in the first fence closed behind him with a loud clack. Con stopped to glance back, checking for telltale lights, or curtains moving, then, when he didn't see either, he continued sneaking across the field. He felt like an idiot skulking around the fields every night, but he couldn't stay away.

The moon would be full in five more days. So far, he'd seen no sign of Aisling, no sign of Luna. She'd said the next full moon, twenty-seven days from the last one. He could count. Grandfather had an almanac. But what if she came back early from wherever she'd gone with her aunt? He didn't want to take the chance of missing her. With his luck, Aisling would appear the one night he stayed in bed.

Anyway, being in the house with Leon and his mother acting like a pair of hormone-crazed teenagers made him feel like a caged animal. Being out here alone, lying on his back on the ground, watching the moon and stars through his grandfather's binoculars, gave him a sense of peace. He'd spend a couple of hours thinking and playing tapes on his Walkman, Springsteen's *Born in the U.S.A.* tonight, cranked right up to deafening.

Out of the dark, something warm and wet slid across his forehead, startling the hell out of him. Ripping the headphones away from his ears, Con scrambled to his knees and found himself face-to-face with Luna. She gave a soft snort. Probably a polite horse laugh. With his heart pounding harder than any drum solo, he sank back onto his heels and let out a weak laugh.

"Jeez, horse, you scared the stuffing out of me!" he muttered. As he stroked her nose, he added, as if she could understand a word he said, "Never mind. I can use the company."

Getting to his feet, Con patted the mare's silky neck. She nickered and bumped him with the side of her head. When he didn't respond quickly enough to her invitation to rub her ears, she bumped him again. In self-defense, he reached up and gave her a vigorous ear massage. When she closed her eyes with a long sigh and her jaw went slack, he surprised himself by laughing.

"I'd like to have the same magic touch with Aisling," he confided under his breath. "I'd love to have her melting in my hands like this." Luna shook her head gently. Con decided to interpret that as a request to rub her elsewhere, instead of her opinion of his intentions toward Aisling. He chuckled and ran his hand down her neck. "Okay, you're right, I probably won't start with her ears."

Thinking of what he wanted to do the next time he saw Aisling, Con hardly paid attention to what he was doing right then. He stood with one hand absently stroking the underside of Luna's neck, down to her chest. Suddenly, the mare butted him in the belly and sent him backward onto his rear. The shock of landing on the ground banged his teeth together. Adding insult to injury, the damn horse bobbed her head up and down like she was nodding, and snorted a couple of times. Another horse laugh.

"Guess I hit a ticklish spot," he muttered, glaring up at her, "but you don't have to knock me down. You're a regular biohazard, aren't you?"

Once more, he got to his feet, while Luna eyed him suspiciously. Standing quietly with his hands out, palms up, he waited for her to come toward him. When she took a step in his direction, he stepped toward her. This time when he touched her, he slid his hand up to the crest of her neck and rubbed the roots of her thick, silky mane. Her reaction to his massage was to lower her head and let her eyes drift closed. Then she made a sound somewhere between a sigh and a groan.

"I think Aisling liked the way I touched her, too." Luna made that low sound of pleasure deep in her chest. "I wish you could tell me where she is." The mare lowered her head a little farther and nuzzled the knee of his jeans. "Hey, that tickles," he told her, but it was such a familiar sensation that he didn't try to stop her when she nuzzled him again.

Suddenly, a vivid memory assaulted him so hard he couldn't breathe for a moment. A horse . . . no, a pony, solidly built and dappled gray with salt-and-pepper mane and tail, nibbling at his clothes. *His* pony. A rush of remembered affection for that pony—*Sergeant Pepper*! Must have been his mother's silly idea for a name—welled up inside him. He leaned his head against Luna's neck, picturing himself with Pepper. How old had he been? Two, maybe three, when they'd entered their first show.

"God, I loved that pony," he told Luna, as if she'd been following his thoughts and could understand what he was saying. She jerked her head up and flicked her ears at him, almost as if she had. He shrugged. "I used to talk to him, too."

He couldn't remember what had become of Pepper. It was like he'd torn a page out of his memory. Restlessness stirred in him. Moving away from the mare, he began to pace. After a couple of trips back and forth, he noticed that Luna was watching him, following him with her head and ears. She probably thought he was nuts, walking around with no purpose. But walking always helped him think, and anyway, what did he care about what a horse thought about him?

·   ·   ·   ·

Aisling watched Sloan walking slowly back and forth, so deep in his brooding that he was ignoring her, as if she didn't exist. It wasn't so easy for her to ignore him! There he was, free as could be with his hands, thinking he was patting Luna, when it was herself he was making free with. She'd had to do something to stop the man from molesting her like that. What a shock to feel his hand slide from her neck to her breasts. A lovely and interesting shock, 'twas true, but one that would take some getting used to. He looked so funny when she knocked him down. A pity that, being a horse, she couldn't laugh.

Aisling decided Aunt Rainbow had been right to slow the fire between her and Sloan before it consumed them. It would take some time to get used to the feel of his hands on her like that. Of course, she didn't mind the notion of practicing! 'Twas the only way to learn something well! Her little laugh came out of Luna as a nicker. Perhaps horses could laugh after all.

Sloan was pacing still. Back and forth, back and forth, muttering to himself and swearing. If he didn't stop soon, she'd have to be following him, or she'd soon be getting dizzy. Anyway, she couldn't offer him sympathy if he was there and she was here, could she? And he needed comforting something fierce. Something awful must have happened to turn him from a little boy who loved his pony, to the young man who claimed to hate horses. Oh, how she wished she could speak!

Sloan stopped abruptly and turned toward her. "I remember now. I was about nine, maybe ten. Poor old Pepper colicked badly, but my mother was away at a show and Dad was out on barn calls. The housekeeper left messages for him, but he didn't phone back. So I walked Pepper for hours, until I fell asleep on my feet. By the time Dad got home, it was too late to save Pepper."

Aisling touched his face with her lips, offering silent comfort, silent empathy. Sloan jerked away and stared at her, then began laughing. Puzzled that he could laugh at such a sad story, Aisling tipped her head to convey the question she couldn't ask. Strangely, Sloan laughed all the harder then.

"Sorry, mare," he finally said when he'd stopped laughing. "I just realized I'm standing in the middle of a field, in the middle of the night, telling my life story to a horse."

Shaking his head, Sloan moved toward the blanket he'd left on the ground a good distance from the Faery *rath* he'd nearly smothered before. Scooping the blanket up, he tucked it under one arm. He took up the odd little box she'd heard music coming from earlier—and such strange music it was, this rock!—and the silver-colored light wand he used to guide himself to and from the field. Then he stepped toward her.

"Self-pity stinks. I'm outta here." Sloan shifted the things from his right hand into his left. "You better get home before whoever takes care of you notices you're missing. I don't feel like getting lynched for horse stealing. Go on!"

He lifted his free hand. Aisling didn't wait for him to slap her haunch the way he had once before. She stamped a hind foot, whirled around with a swish of her tail, then dashed away toward the secret entrance to the Faery *rath*. From the cover of the grasses and wildflowers disguising the passage opening, she paused and turned to watch him making his way across the fields. He walked steadily, and didn't look back. Not once.

True, tonight he thought he was only walking away from an eccentric and friendly mare. But what of the next time they met, on the full-moon night, when she was herself? She didn't dare reveal her dual identity yet, so she could not offer him true comfort over losing his pony. Over feeling betrayed by his parents, who should have loved him and protected him better. Who must have taught him all he knew—or didn't know—about love. They had taught him a terrible, false lesson: that there were other obligations more important than love—of family, of mate.

It chilled her heart to think he might leave her behind with as little thought as he now left the white mare behind, with walking away without longing, without regret.

Fifteen

Tonight was his last chance to see Aisling again on this trip. All day, every clock or watch he looked at ran in slow-motion. Waiting, waiting, waiting. Waiting for sunset. Waiting for moonrise. The full moon had come up before eight, but that left hours until everyone went to bed and he could sneak out.

Con couldn't sit still. His fingers drummed on tables. He tapped chair legs with his feet. His mother nagged him to stop fidgeting. Leon smirked. His attention wandered. Everyone had to repeat what they said to him. Gramps suggested a hearing test. Leon hinted at drugs. Corliss scolded both of them, then snapped at him for whistling under his breath. He tuned them out and retreated to the solitude of the wood-paneled library as soon as he was excused from the dinner table.

Anticipation twisted his gut. Doubts stung him like mosquitos. What if Aisling didn't show up this time? What if she did? He'd snuck a bottle of Chardonnay from the wine cellar into the back of the refrigerator. Maybe he should have filched a red wine instead. Should he have gotten some flowers to give her? Music? Sharing the Walkman would be cozy, but what if she didn't like his taste in music? Would he need the lantern, or was the moonlight bright enough? He'd optimistically smuggled condoms from home, since buying them in Ireland was impossible. How many should he take with him? Would she be insulted or grateful about the condoms? What if he never got the chance to find out?

"Con, I've been looking for you." His mother didn't sound any happier now that she'd found him.

He looked up from the book on his lap, waiting for her to share whatever was on her mind. She frowned pointedly until he stopped bouncing the foot he'd propped on the opposite knee. He hid his impatience with a phony smile, but the energy had to go somewhere. His fingers started drumming on the padded leather arm of his chair.

With a sigh, she said, "Leon and I are going to the pub one last time. Da is there already, demanding a rematch of yesterday's chess game, no doubt. The man's a terrible loser." She gave him a quick smile. "There's trad music tonight. You seem restless. Care to be joining us?"

Con hesitated before answering, only so she'd think he was considering her invitation. The traditional Irish music was starting to grow on him, but spending any more time than he had to with Leon was not high on his list of priorities. And getting away from the pub would be harder than sneaking out of the house, so he wasn't tempted. He gave her a smile to soften his refusal.

"Thanks, Mom, but I'm okay. I have to finish packing."

She swooped down to kiss his cheek, and Chanel No. 5 engulfed him. Straightening, Corliss tilted her head to read the title of the book lying in his lap. "*Archaeological Inventory of County Cork*? You aren't seriously reading that, are you?"

"Yeah. You said you wanted me to get into Irish history."

"O'Hara history," she corrected. Then, with a quick smile, she ruffled his hair. "Ah, well. 'Twill do to start anywhere that doesn't have computers. Don't be staying up too late. We've a fair drive to the airport. Our flight leaves at five in the evening, and Leon likes to be punctual."

Con didn't really care what Leon liked or didn't like, but he didn't want to upset his mother any more than necessary. He made a grunting sound she was free to interpret as an affirmative answer. She must have, because after another quick kiss on his cheek, she hurried away. He waited a full ten minutes after the taillights of the rental car disappeared around the last bend in the long, winding drive leading from O'Hara House to the road.

As soon as he thought it was safe, he packed the wine, two glasses wrapped in tea towels, his Walkman, and a few tapes into his backpack. After a brief debate with his conscience, he took two condoms from the lining of his suitcase and slipped the packets into his back pocket. Having them didn't mean he had to use them. Didn't mean he expected to use them. Better to have them and not use them, than not have them and need them . . . like an umbrella.

With the blanket over his shoulder and the flashlight in a side pocket of his backpack, he stepped outside at the back of the house. The moon sat halfway up the sky, shining down like a huge spotlight. It was a clear, cloudless night, warmer than usual. With no city lights for miles around, moonlight turned everything to silver and shadows. On his way to the far paddock, he felt drawn to take a quick detour. He took the long way around the walled fields, past the ruins of the old great house that stood like a solid shadow against the black sky and tangled trees. It looked sad and mysterious in the moonlight.

When he'd come back from his ten days in England, his ears still ringing from the Live Aid Concert in London, he'd gone to ask the owlish junk-shop woman, Enid McDermott, about the ruins. He'd remembered her promise to tell him about that so-called O'Hara Curse, and figured she might know the history of the ruins. Her shop had been closed, a hand-lettered sign promising to return the following week. Every time he went back, the shop was closed, so he finally gave up. It wasn't that important.

Aisling might know about the ruined manor house, but he didn't want to waste their last night together talking about history. He'd save it for his next trip to Ireland—

next summer, if he could swing it. Ten months was a long time between dates, but now that he'd found Aisling again, he didn't want to let her go. Or, he didn't want whatever they had between them to end. Or . . . Oh, hell! He wanted to see her again, period!

Turning away from the crumbling stone walls silhouetted against the sky, Con settled into a slow jog across the first field. The moonlight was bright, the air sweet. Anticipation hummed in his veins and clutched at his breath. Thinking about seeing Aisling, holding her and kissing her, his pulse raced ahead of his steps. Any minute, any second . . .

When he got to the field where he always met her, she wasn't there. His heart sank.

A GREAT HALL, THE FAERY REALM, EVER-THE-PRESENT

The full moon! Making her way from the common area, where many of the Moonstone Circle Faeries were entertaining themselves with dancing and singing, to the quiet of her aunt's suite of rooms, Aisling stopped in her tracks. A small gray-and-white owl, silently swooping past her, had hooted a soft greeting, drawing her attention to the sky.

Oh, no! She'd lost track of the days! The full moon had risen already! This was the night she'd promised to meet Sloan again, the last night they would have together before he would be returning to America. She must hurry, or else he would believe she wasn't going to keep her promise!

It was all too easy in the Faery Realm for time to flow like a stream, perpetually moving along to somewhere else, yet paradoxically always *there*. The Faeries themselves paid little attention to the practicalities of the Mortal world, relying as they did on magic, deception, and creative misplacement. There were no clocks, and no Faery cocks to crow the sunrise. Living Under-Hill, she'd had to measure the passage of time by the phases of the moon, the length of the days, and the seasonal changes in nature. But somehow between her last visit with Sloan, when she could appear to him only as Luna, and tonight, when she would

appear as herself, she'd lost count of the sunrises and failed
to notice the moon waxing toward full.

She began to run. By the time she reached her aunt's
suite, and the chamber she used for her own room, she was
out of breath and her heart was racing. There was little she
could do to fix her appearance, especially without a mirror.
She did her best to shake the leaves and butterflies out of
her hair and wipe any telltale smudges of Faery dust off
her face. Her dress was fresh and clean, as it always was,
but it needed her other two petticoats to make it look right.
They were hanging on a hook made of a thorn that refused
to release them, no matter how she tugged.

"Oh!" Aisling flung out her hands in defeat.

"What's troubling you, Niece?" Aunt Rainbow appeared in the doorway, a sympathetic frown on her lovely
face. Her aunt's expression suddenly brightened. "Ah! 'Tis
the full-moon night!"

"I'm late meeting Sloan, and now I can't get my petticoats," Aisling wailed. "He'll be thinking I'm not coming."

Rainbow swooped in and drew Aisling to her feet.
"Then you mustn't be keeping the man waiting." With a
wave of her graceful hand, Rainbow summoned Aisling's
petticoats. "Here you are, Niece. Would you like flowers
for your hair?"

For a brief moment, recalling her aunt's earlier betrayal,
she wondered if Rainbow were trying to hinder rather than
help her prepare to meet Sloan. But then she shrugged off
the suspicion. Her aunt had given her word not to interfere,
had vowed to allow Aisling to make her own decisions.
And she'd sworn on the Sacred Hawthorn to keep Raven
from creating any magical interruptions. Grudgingly, Raven
had sworn likewise. If she couldn't trust Aunt Rainbow,
then she had no one but herself and her belief in True Love
to rely on. 'Twas too lonely to hold such a view for long.

"I would like flowers, Aunt, but 'tis already so late, I'm
afraid to linger."

Her fingers shook as she fumbled with the ribbons at the
waists of her petticoats. Rainbow gently brushed her hands

away and tied them in secure bows. Their eyes met and
they shared a smile before her aunt turned away to arrange
her skirt and brush a lock of her hair off her forehead.

"I must go!"

Aisling darted toward the doorway, but halted when her
aunt called her name. Turning, she saw that Aunt Rainbow
was doing something Aisling had never seen, nor indeed
ever heard of, any other Faery doing: She was crying! Not
loud sobbing, of course, for that would be too strong a
display. But Rainbow had huge, glistening tears sliding
down her alabaster cheeks, each one turning to a glittering
diamond as it landed on her aunt's simple white gown.
Within seconds the gossamer fabric sparkled with hundreds
of diamonds. Fey gems were as precious as those of the
Mortal realm. The rarest of those gems, therefore the most
precious, were the jewels made from Faery tears. 'Twas a
Faery king's ransom in the precious stones, but as real as
daydreams. They would become bits of coal if a Mortal
tried to steal them.

Fey riches didn't interest Aisling at all. "Why do you
cry, Aunt? Are you not happy for me?"

Rainbow gave a most un-Faery-like sniff. Gliding closer,
she touched Aisling's cheek with cool, gentle fingertips.
Her usually brilliant smile seemed strangely dim. "I fear I
am cursed with uncommonly Mortal-like feeling, Niece.
We *Sidhe* seldom experience strong emotions, the way
Mortals do, and generally we prefer to avoid the influence
of Mortals with passionate hearts. But I feel deep affection
for you, Aisling, as if you were my own daughter. I truly
wish to see you find Mortal happiness."

Aisling wiped at a tear welling up and spilling over before she could blink it away. Unable to speak, she nodded
to her aunt.

" 'Twould cause me terrible pain to see you hurt, my
dear Niece. Last full-moon night you and Sloan were per-
ilously close to taking a step that, once taken, can never be
undone."

As she understood the meaning of her aunt's words, a
rush of heat flared up Aisling's neck and cheeks. Her mouth

opened but no sound emerged. Truly, they had been close to . . . to making love, a step she would never take lightly, for in her mind, making love and loving were yoked together, each sharing strength with the other. 'Twas the reason she had refused to marry Ambros O'Hara so many years ago. 'Twas how she'd fallen into Acorn Bittersweet's trap. 'Twas the belief that had sustained her for nearly a century of her enchantment.

When she was with Sloan, was it only the heat of the moment that melted her reserve? She did not think that was so. Was she, then, in her heart and soul, wanting to take that irrevocable step with Sloan? Why else did her heart and soul feel so restless, so discontent? But did that mean she loved Sloan? Surely, it must be so. Mustn't it? 'Twas very confusing!

After all the trouble she'd been through, all the trouble she'd brought down on poor Luna, she couldn't be changing her mind now! If she was willing to make love with Sloan—and she was thinking, truly, she was—then she must love him. But did he love her? Would he be the man whose True Love broke the gnome's curse, or was he only looking to have his way with her? How would she know? Perplexed, she stared into Rainbow's purple eyes. Her aunt smiled and patted her cheek.

"I only thought to cool your ardor, before inexperience swept your mind clean of good sense." Aunt Rainbow sighed and shook her head. "Rest assured, Raven will keep his promise to refrain from interfering in family matters between you and me. He must impress me somehow, or he shall not rest." The smile Rainbow gave Aisling then was close to normal brilliance. "Mortal or Fey, men are such vain fools!"

Aisling caught her aunt's hands in her own and smiled brightly at the blush coloring Rainbow's pearly cheeks. Her aunt, it seemed, wasn't objecting to the Faery man's courtship, but only to his extraordinary efforts.

"Then you understand why I must go to Sloan tonight? 'Tis my last opportunity to be learning if he loves me, before he departs for America tomorrow." She searched her aunt's eyes for empathy. "If Sloan loves me, 'twill give me strength to endure until the end of this century of enchantment, or to the end of the world."

Aunt Rainbow squeezed her hands gently. "Do not be too hasty, Remember-Fear-Not. Hear me well: Sloan is not the man you wish him to be." Aisling opened her mouth to protest, but her aunt shook her head. " 'Twas the O'Haras I cast my complementary spell on, yet you refuse to consider the last of the O'Hara men."

"Never!" The word burst from Aisling's lips, but the sentiment came straight from her heart. "Never! I shan't consider the O'Hara men for anything but food for the crows!"

Rainbow touched a fingertip to Aisling's lips, halting her indignant outburst. "The shorter the time remaining until Acorn Bittersweet returns to claim you, the better an O'Hara may seem." Once more, Aisling opened her mouth to protest, but her aunt spoke too quickly for her. "Go to your Sloan now, but don't be letting your heart shout down your head."

With a quick kiss on the forehead, Aunt Rainbow released Aisling. Her heart gave a great leap, like Luna soaring over a high wall. Gathering her skirts with cold fingers, Aisling turned and dashed to the passageway leading from the depths of the Faery *rath* to the Mortal world. As she ran, she heard Rainbow say, "Forethought and maternal instincts! I shall develop a Mortal conscience next! What kind of Faery shall I be, then?"

THE PADDOCKS, O'HARA HOUSE, CO. SLIGO, WEDNESDAY, JULY 31, 1985

Lying on his back, gazing blankly at the black sky and the huge white globe of the moon, Con listened through to the end of his new Dire Straits tape. The music didn't move him the way it usually did, and he knew why. Aisling wasn't coming tonight. He might as well just accept that he'd been stood up and slink back to the house before someone discovered he was gone. With his luck, it would be Leon, who'd probably convince his mother to have him committed.

Stiff from the cool, damp ground, he rolled over to stand at the exact moment that Aisling appeared out of nowhere.

Con felt his heart stop. When it started beating again, it was in the wrong place, too close to his throat, pounding on his ribs. He sat back on his heels and stared at her, a part of his brain pretty sure he was hallucinating. For a moment, Aisling stood like a statue, the moonlight turning her face and dress a silvery white that didn't look real. Maybe she wasn't real. There was one way to find out.

Without breaking his gaze on her face, he got to his feet. She was still there, so beautiful he could hardly believe his eyes. He didn't think he was sleepwalking, so she must be real. That meant she really was there! She hadn't stood him up! She'd kept their date! But, a cynical voice in the back of his head nagged, was she playing games? Stringing him along, making him desperate?

Aisling broke the impasse before he could. She came toward him in a rush, her golden hair streaming around her, that long, old-fashioned dress rustling with her movements. The look of uncertainty in her eyes, plain to see now that she was closer, told him everything he needed to know but didn't have a clue how to ask. Without a word, he spread his arms wide. A smile chased away the doubt in her eyes, and then she ran to him.

She was tiny, but she almost knocked him over when she fell against his chest. He closed his arms around her and pressed her close, feeling her heartbeat syncopated with his. Feeling her breasts pressing against him. Feeling a rush of heat roar through him, making him so hard so fast, he had to struggle to breathe.

"I was so afraid I would be too late!" she said into his shoulder.

"Me, too." His admission came out sounding choked.

And then he couldn't think of a single thing more to say. He stood holding her, fighting to control the trembling that was shaking him from the inside out. To hell with talking! He wanted to kiss her until neither of them could breathe, wanted to peel away all those layers of clothes she was wearing and bury himself inside her.

The question was, how to get from here, from standing locked together and not saying a word, to there, to lying on the blanket and not needing any words.

Aisling answered the question for him by suddenly wiggling out of his arms. After stepping back from him, she crossed her arms in front of her middle and looked up at him. Uh-oh. She was waiting for him to do something. Or say something. But what?

Oh, God, his mind was totally blank!

Sixteen

With the heat of a blush stinging her cheeks, Aisling gazed warily at Sloan. There was a look of uneasy surprise in his eyes, and he was staring at her without saying a word. Was he thinking her terribly forward for rushing into his arms? If she'd only thought before doing . . . But wasn't that the cause of most of her troubles? And now, the silence between them seemed to be turning into a living thing, pulsing and breathing, pushing them apart until Aisling wanted to scream.

Instead, keeping her voice soft, she asked, "Are you leaving for America tomorrow, truly?"

"Yeah." His brief answer echoed in the swelling silence separating them.

After another wait, Aisling decided *Might as well be hanged for a sheep as a lamb*. If Sloan thought her forward already, there was no helping it, and standing here, facing each other without a word of conversation, was going to be the waste of a perfect night. Their *only* night this Mortal year. Taking the risk of his rejection, she gestured toward the blanket he'd spread on the grass a good distance from the edge of the Faery *rath*. 'Twas on the tip of her tongue to thank him for his thoughtfulness toward The People's home. The memory of their terrible argument at the last full moon stopped her.

"Could we sit for a while? And could you be telling me more about your life in America?"

A strange look crossed his face. He made a low groaning sound, then cursed under his breath. "Sorry! I . . . Sorry. Please."

Aisling smiled, hoping to reassure him. His answering smile was endearingly crooked. Seeing that his cheeks had darkened, and not wishing to embarrass him further, she went to the blanket. Sloan followed her several steps behind, waiting silently while she sat and arranged her dress around her ankles. He continued standing over her until she patted the blanket beside her. He seemed to be taking care not to touch, or even to look at, her. Confused, Aisling picked up a leaf lying on the blanket and fingered it. After another pause, Sloan cleared his throat, startling her.

"I . . . I brought a bottle of wine. And glasses. Would . . . Would you like some?"

Aisling considered Sloan's question carefully. Mortals must not eat or drink anything in the Faery world, for doing so would ensure that they could never leave. Having a tiny portion of Fey blood was protecting her from that fate, although even she had to avoid certain of the most magical Faery refreshments. If Sloan's wine had the same properties as Fey comestibles, perhaps 'twould ensure her return to the Mortal realm. Would that also ensure Sloan's help in breaking the Leprechaun's spell?

"I've never tasted wine," she ventured, wondering if he would consider her inexperience unappealing. From books Faeries sometimes borrowed from absentminded or careless Mortals who left them lying about, she'd been reading of changing manners and customs. Until recently, however, she hadn't understood how out-of-date her knowledge of society and the world was. 'Twas shocking how some of the customs between men and women had been changing! But there was no holding back time, even in the Faery Realm, so she gathered her courage.

"I'd like to be sharing some wine with you, yes."

Sloan gave her a smile, then reached into the back pocket of the odd-fitting trousers she'd learned were called

Gene's—although why he said they belonged to someone else, when they were clearly *Sloan's* trousers, puzzled her. He withdrew the red-handled folding knife that seemed to have once belonged to the Swiss Army. She followed the movements of his hands as he was opening the knife, then twisting it into the cork.

Watching Sloan gave her pleasure. He had lovely masculine hands. They were strong, square hands, with solid wrists joining them to well-muscled arms and shoulders. To be sure, he was not so powerfully built as a laborer, but surprisingly muscular for a scholar. She didn't know that she ought to be studying his bare arms so boldly, but tonight he wasn't wearing a coat or long-sleeved shirt that would hide his flesh from her spying. Instead, he was wearing a short-sleeved garment similar to the summer undershirt her father often wore when he was working with their horses. But her father's shirts were of a plain and dull cloth, generously cut. The garment Sloan was wearing was made of soft, dark fabric that had the privilege of hugging his torso the way she was wishing to.

Sloan began working at the cork in a tall, clear glass bottle with pale liquid inside. The black and gold letters on the label made it look to be a costly wine. She'd never seen such a lovely bottle for wine, as her father had only drunk *poitín,* wickedly strong homemade whiskey kept in crockery kegs. The cork came out of the bottle with a soft *pop!* Noticing the two tumblers lying on the linen tea towel beside them, Aisling took them up and held them for Sloan to pour the wine into. The chill of the wine as it filled each tumbler surprised her. She would have liked to know if it was now the custom to keep wine in an icehouse, but she was afraid that asking would reveal her ignorance. After he'd set the cork back in the bottle, he took a glass from her, his fingers brushing her as light as a butterfly's kiss. Startled at the way her skin began tingling at his touch, Aisling stole a glance at his face.

The smile Sloan gave her could have melted a stone, and she was not nearly so hard nor so cold! With her cheeks flushing hot, she turned away and looked into her glass.

Her hand was trembling slightly, making the liquid ripple and shimmer in the moonlight, giving it the look of a magical potion. And perhaps it was. Didn't the Irish often say, *Scílidh fíon fírinne:* "Wine divulges the truth"? Surely, anything with the power to discover truth must be magical! Aunt Rainbow was forever insisting that Sloan wasn't the man Aisling wanted him to be, but she could never get her aunt to explain her dire warning. Perhaps the wine had the power to reveal this truth Rainbow believed he was hiding. Would that this wine could discover Sloan to be the man whose love would set her free of the living death of marriage to a Leprechaun!

Sloan touched the edge of his glass to hers. She looked up to find him watching her, his eyes sparkling with a smile. He raised his glass in a salute. With an answering smile, Aisling lifted her glass to mirror his gesture.

"Sláinte!"

They spoke together, then laughed softly together. Aisling watched Sloan lifting his glass to his lips. She watched, fascinated, as his lips shaped themselves to the rim, the glass tilting in his strong hand, the wine flowing to his mouth. When he lowered his glass, she lifted hers to take a sip. At first, the wine felt as cold and refreshing to her lips and tongue as a mountain stream. It tasted crisp and thin as fresh springwater, before bursting into flavors of fruit and honeyed sunshine as it warmed in her mouth. When she swallowed, the wine ran cool and smoothly down her throat, then surprised her by sliding through her insides trailing a soft heat.

"Oh!" A laugh followed her exclamation, which brought an answering grin from Sloan. "Oh, Sloan! 'Tis lovely! I was thinking it would taste sour, like vinegar does, or strong and sharp like whiskey, but this is sweet and gentle. It tastes of fruits and honey, does it not?" Without waiting for an answer, she took another sip, savoring the complex sensations in her mouth. This second sip surprised her yet again by warming her insides even more than the first. Perhaps that was the magic beginning to work.

Aisling's laughter, her excitement about the wine, sent a

new kind of warmth flowing through Con's veins. For a few minutes, after she'd stepped away from him, he'd been convinced she regretted meeting him. She seemed to be happy now, and he didn't want to do anything to make her change her mind again. Whenever she moved, her golden hair rippled with silvery moonlight that seemed to be inviting him—no, *daring* him—to reach out and touch her again. He kept one hand clenched around the glass, the other out of sight beside him. And another silence oozed up between them.

Damn! What good was a high IQ if his brain went numb whenever he was with her? He'd done a little dating, mostly in the past year when he'd finally stopped being one of the youngest guys on campus. His brain didn't shut down like this with other women, but other women didn't make him feel anything like the way Aisling made him feel. Maybe he should have considered a monastery instead of a Ph.D. in computers. Then celibacy wouldn't have been an issue. He wouldn't have had to worry about thinking of halfway intelligent conversation with his tongue tied in knots.

Aisling's wistful smile caught his attention. He couldn't help smiling back. Just the thought that she liked being with him turned his insides to warm Jell-O. Con couldn't keep his grin under control. The way Aisling had tasted her wine, the way she obviously liked it, was a silly, simple thing to feel so . . . so *happy* about. But he couldn't think of another way to describe his reaction to her surprise and her pleasure. Until that moment, it hadn't occurred to him how much her reaction might matter.

Aisling took another sip of wine, then smiled. Her lips were wet from the wine, her eyes were sparkling. He wished he could tell the color of her eyes. In the silvery moonlight, they seemed as dark as the night sky, but they must be blue. She was too pale and too blond to have brown eyes. He didn't know why the color of her eyes was important. It just was. Debating whether to be blunt and ask her, or just leave it a mystery, he took another drink of the wine.

"Is this the sort of thing you do for courting in America?"

Her question caught him about to swallow. The wine slid down the wrong way, choking him. Aisling made a soft sound and angled toward him. Coughing too hard to say anything, Con raised his free hand to tell her he was okay, but for a moment, he wondered. Tears filled his eyes as he coughed and struggled to breathe. She watched him with wide eyes and her free hand across her throat.

"I . . . I'm okay," he finally croaked. "Just swallowed wrong."

She let out a long sigh. "Truly, Sloan, I thought you were dying on me."

So did he, but he shook his head to deny it.

"Was it my question about courtship that nearly strangled you?"

The smile she gave him was a little shy, a little naughty. The grin he gave her back was more than a little rueful; she was too sharp to fool. At least she wasn't bent out of shape by his totally uncool—and uncouth—reaction. It made her easy to be with. Maybe this was going to turn out okay after all.

She spoke before he could. "I wasn't implying that you and I are courting, understand. 'Twas only curiosity about your customs, as you're the only person from America I've met."

She'd been right about his reaction: He didn't want her to think they were *courting*. But now that she'd let him off the hook, he felt a twinge of disappointment.

"Honest, Aisling, it was just the wine," he lied earnestly, his voice still a little hoarse. He cleared his throat, then took a careful drink of wine. Aisling drank also, watching him over the edge of her glass, laughter in her eyes.

"Anyway, Americans don't usually talk about *courtship* much anymore. It's a pretty old-fashioned concept."

Their glasses were empty. He reached for the wine bottle and pulled out the cork. Aisling held both glasses while he poured. It was the kind of simple thing his parents used to do for each other when he was younger and they were happy together. Now his mother fluttered around Leon, and his father treated his bimbo like some kind of princess. Maybe that kind of fading away was inevitable in a relationship. If it was, then he should treat the way he and Aisling fit together like a fragile, precious gift.

Taking his glass back from her, Con deliberately let his fingers overlap hers. Aisling released the glass slowly, prolonging the contact, then lowered her head a tiny bit and glanced up at him through her lashes. That little gesture, a moment that lasted maybe five seconds, pumped his ego and made his pulse do some weird kind of dance step in his veins. Suddenly, he felt like he could leap tall buildings and stop runaway trains. Or kiss her until they were both gasping for breath.

Unfortunately, Aisling still wanted to talk. "If not courtship, then . . . ?"

"Dating. Going out. Courtship sounds too serious."

She took a sip of wine while he spoke, then frowned. "But marriage *is* terribly serious, and shouldn't be entered into lightly."

Whew! At least her expectations weren't unrealistic. "That's exactly my point. Don't people in Ireland play the field before they decide to settle down?"

Aisling gave him that cute little frown again. "Play in the field? Is that what we're doing now?"

Oh, how he wished! Somehow, he kept his face straight and tried to explain dating, as if he were an expert.

"No, I mean going out with lots of different people, sometimes just for fun, sometimes seriously. Some people click right away, but it can take years to find someone who makes you want to settle down. Or it can take years to decide you're ready to get serious. Then you might have to look for the right person to commit to."

Aisling considered Sloan's answer. "I see," she finally said, although she was fairly certain she didn't see at all. Lots of different people? Years to find someone you want? Truly, times have been changing! Now people not only could choose whom to marry, they could choose when!

She'd thought herself wildly out of step with society nearly ninety years ago, wanting to marry for love. Now she feared she was out of step again, uneasy with the notion that people could flit from one to another like bees gathering nectar, before making up their minds. If ever they did.

The thought of Sloan returning to all of these women he was dating made her frown. The thought of him kissing another woman the way he kissed her, when she was so certain he was her True Love, hurt too much to contemplate. Worse, what if he chose to commit to one of those other woman, and didn't ever return? What if he chose not to commit himself to anyone until it was too late for her to escape the Leprechaun's enchantment? Strange, too, that he didn't mention love. There were many things she didn't understand, but she would have to be sidling up to the matter. If she told him why she wanted to know, she might be influencing the magic. He could choose freely, and he must love freely, too.

Carefully, she framed a question to test the depths of the waters. "And how is it people do this dating?"

Con frowned. How could Aisling not know what people do on dates? It was one thing not to understand some American slang, but Ireland wasn't exactly the back of the moon. Did this aunt of hers keep her locked up? Maybe the aunt was some kind of weirdo who practiced some airy-fairy New Age religion that kept her busy when the moon was full. Was that why Aisling could only get out on those nights? With any other girl—woman—he'd have suspected she was setting him up, seeing through his bluff and preparing to humiliate him just for fun. Like Maddy. But Aisling wasn't any other woman. He'd believe her until she gave him reason not to.

"The same thing as here, I suppose." He shrugged, striving for a casual tone. "Movies, concerts, hiking, skiing, tennis. Sometimes sightseeing. Maybe a party, or dinner out."

"Living with my aunt the way I do, I . . . I don't have much experience in those sorts of things." She looked away from him for a moment. Then she met his eyes, and something in her expression made his heart do a slow-motion back flip. "I imagine you must know many women, then. That you . . ." Her pale cheeks flushed and she lowered her gaze. "With all that dating you're doing," she said softly, "do you find time for studying?"

It took a few seconds for him to translate what she was asking. Then it took him a few more seconds to get over the shock. Aisling thought he was some kind of Casanova! He snorted at her mistake, but the sudden hurt in her eyes choked the laugh building to rush out. Damn! He'd done it again, making fun of her when she was being serious. This time, unlike their disagreement over Faeries, apologizing wouldn't require bending the truth.

"Not a problem. With all the dating I'm *not* doing, I have plenty of time for studying."

Aisling frowned and shook her head. "I'm finding that difficult to believe, Sloan. Are you so particular about the women you keep company with, then, that you prefer to keep yourself to yourself?"

To hide the sudden idiotic grin he couldn't get off his face, Con lay back on the shadowed half of the blanket. He balanced his wineglass on his chest and looked up at the stars, thinking about how to describe his life to Aisling. His grin faded. If she laughed at him now, it would be like being skinned alive.

"I've spent most of my life between ages," he confided. "I skipped a couple of school years, so I was two years younger than the rest of my graduating class. Most of those years, I was at an all-boys school. When I transferred to a co-ed school for my last year, I was sixteen, with the social skills of a twelve-year-old. The girls in my classes thought I was a dork, and the girls my age thought I was some kind of freak." He laughed dryly. "You met me when I was sixteen that summer. They were right. I was a total jerk."

"Ah, well, you were young and fresh, 'tis true, but you had a promising way about you." He didn't have to see her face to hear her smile. But it was a smile, not a laugh. "Thanks, but I know the truth when it bites me. There

I was, sixteen, and a jerk, at university. I crammed a four-year degree into three years, so it felt like I was getting younger than everyone else every year. I wasn't a hermit. I dated some, but I studied most of the time.''

He paused to swallow the pride lodged in his throat. The quick brush of her hand on his arm could have been an accident, or a gesture of comfort. He'd have rather it had been an accident. He wanted her to know something about him; he didn't want her to feel sorry for him. When she didn't touch him again, he figured she'd touched him by accident.

Then she spoke. '' 'Twas admirable that you were studying so much of your time. If I'd gone to university, I would be studying around the clock, too.''

"A lot of people study like that," he told her. "But they don't all live like monks. For me, it's always the age thing. The freshman women were eighteen when I was sixteen, and light-years ahead of me. I barely caught up, but this fall, I'll be nineteen in classes with people who are over twenty-one. And computer science isn't exactly a field crawling with babes." A derisive snort punctuated that understatement.

Aisling felt tears filling her eyes as Sloan was speaking. She didn't understand half of what he said, but the loneliness of being an outsider, of wanting something beyond his reach, resonated within her heart. She knew how he was feeling, knew how he was aching, sensed that he was saying less than he was thinking, less than he was holding in his heart. Her tears spilled over, making a hot trail down her cheeks. Not wanting him to think she was pitying him, she turned her head and wiped at the tears with the back of her hand. More welled up and spilled to replace them, so she kept her head turned away.

The sudden weight of his hand on her knee, through the layers of her skirt and petticoats, startled her tears dry. She jerked her head around to look down at him, preparing to give him a piece of her mind for being so forward. The sweet smile he gave her undid her indignation. The gentle squeeze of his hand on her knee undid her every other way.

Unexpected and disturbing tingles ran from her knee up the
inside of her thigh, then became waves of heat as the sensations moved farther up inside her. The heat built until it
stole her breath and left her gasping.

"Hey, don't feel too sorry for me," he murmured. "If
I'm out partying, I won't be able to take the computer industry by storm. With all the time I save for studying and
working, it won't take me long to make millions and have
gorgeous actresses throwing themselves at me."

Until Sloan laughed, Aisling thought he was being serious about having beautiful women chasing after him once
he'd made his fortune. But his laugh was short, sharp, self-
mocking, telling her plainly that he didn't believe it was
possible. She didn't understand why he was thinking
women wouldn't want to be with him. To be sure, he was
young, and perhaps too full of schooling for his age. Even
so, he was lovely and sweet and pleasant to be with, and
promised to be turning into a handsome and good man. Any
woman who wasn't in love with another would surely see
that. Indeed, hadn't she told herself she was already in love
with the man, because she felt willing to make love with
him?

True, she enjoyed kissing him and being held by him,
thrilled to his hunger for her. But this feeling she had now
for him was different from the heat he stirred in her body.
Now she was feeling his sorrow, his loneliness, his injured
pride, and longed to heal his wounded heart. She was feeling a bond with his heart, as well as a dizzying attraction,
almost a compulsion. 'Twas like she sometimes felt standing beside a rushing river, drawn toward its power, thinking
that if she dove into the water's center, she would become
part of the forces within. Ah! But this attraction, this pull
she was feeling toward Sloan was deeper, stronger. It made
her want to be so close to him that they would become part
of each other.

Was *this* love? The breath caught in her throat.

She was thinking maybe it was. She was hoping it was
worth the waiting nearly a hundred years, neither living nor

dying, but waiting and longing. And she was praying that Sloan could love her, too.

Without her knowing how, she found he'd set aside their wineglasses, and drawn her down to the blanket with him. Startled, she stiffened, but her first breath brought the scent of him to her, and she felt herself melting. His warm arms held her snugly, pressing her chest to his. Her legs, tangled in her skirts and petticoats, lay so close to his that she could feel the heat and shifting power of his muscles. Just as she was thinking that kissing would be impossible like this, Sloan rolled her onto her back and followed so he was covering her with his body.

Suddenly, his mouth was on hers, and for a second, the fierceness of his kiss frightened her. But then, his kiss was stirring an answering fierceness within her, turning her fear into hunger. Then, all she knew was that the taste of him, mingled with the taste of the wine, the feel of his body pressing hers, was as right as the stars shining in the sky.

Oh, yes! This was love!

Con felt a change, physical, but beyond physical, in Aisling's body, in her kiss, like she was melting under him. Her mouth was so soft, so warm, so responsive! The taste of her, the smell of her hair and skin, the soft little noises coming from her throat, the tightening of her arms around his neck fueled a fire growing inside him that already had him trembling. Somewhere under all those clothes, she shifted restlessly against him. Every press of her body against his was like another gallon of gasoline on the fire inside him, but he wanted, needed, more.

Freeing one arm without breaking their kiss, Con found her waist, then slid his hand slowly upward. When he covered her lower ribs with his palm, she drew in a sharp breath. Did he scare her? He didn't think he'd hurt her, but she was so tiny compared to him. Under his fingers, he could feel her ribs moving with her breathing, could feel her heart pounding. He could feel tremors shaking her. But when he tried to break the kiss, tried to lift his head to make sure she wasn't afraid of him, Aisling gave a muffled cry and tightened her arms around his neck.

Something wild inside him woke up and roared. Thinking was suddenly almost impossible. And just when he didn't believe he could get any harder, any hungrier, a surge of adrenaline flooded his veins with a wave of heat that pooled in his loins. Suddenly, he had to concentrate just to breathe. His pulse vibrated in every part of him, pounding a rhythm that goaded the wildness inside him to take over.

But he wasn't out of control. Not yet. He was still stronger than the hunger. He could stop, if he had to. If Aisling asked him to, he could stop right away. He knew he could. So it was safe to tempt himself a little more, because he could stop if he had to. He wasn't that wild beast. Yet.

Sloan's hand—warm, strong, his touch firm—was moving up her ribs toward her breast. Aisling's muscles began quivering. His kisses were so lovely, the taste of him like spices and honey. The wet, silky feel of his tongue on hers was shockingly sensual at first, an irresistible invitation to her to draw closer. She almost resented having to divide her attention between her mouth and any other part of her. Then his fingers stroked the underside of her breast, and she lost the focus of kissing him.

This was nothing like the way he'd touched her thinking she was Luna, and him not knowing she could feel every touch as herself. Then, she'd been too startled to understand what was happening to her. Only once before—nearly a hundred years before!—had a man put his hand on her breast. But Ambros O'Hara's hasty, rough groping had frightened and repulsed her. He'd pressed his mouth to hers, his teeth biting into her lips, and his hand had squeezed her flesh, hurting her, with almost a cold greed, as if he were assessing a broodmare. Ambros had stirred none of the melting heat, the surprising trembling, the leaping eagerness now wakened by Sloan's kisses and slow, questing touches. Ah, no, she wouldn't be thinking of Ambros now!

Sloan's lips eased away slightly, leaving her suspended between wanting more of his kisses and wanting to find out what magic he might work with his hands. A soft moan expressed something deep inside her that she couldn't put words to. His hand slid up her ribs, gently covering her breast, trembling a little, and then he paused, as if he were gauging her reactions. The desire to arch into his hand, to feel the press of his hands on her breast, came over her, and she gave in to it. As she rose up to his touch, Sloan moved his hand in the softest of kneading caresses, creating a riotous tingling in her flesh. The tingling coursed from her nipple, firming under his palm, right down into the deepest, most private part of her.

The more he stroked, the more she felt that tingling, such a strangely restless, seeking, yielding sensation, traveling inside her. And the more she felt the heat he stirred within her, as if he were a roaring fire and she too close. But how could she be too close, when her body was urging her to move closer still?

Without warning, Sloan broke their kiss, but before she could protest, he was burying his face in her neck and his lips and tongue were trailing tiny sparks along her skin. Aisling let her head tip back, exposing more of her neck to him, tasting the cool night air on her sensitized lips. The lace tucked into the neckline of her dress gave way easily to his fingers, and then she was feeling the wet heat of his mouth on the skin above her breast. It was lovely, but it wasn't enough! Giving in to the restless urging of her body, she freed one hand from its grip on Sloan's shirt, working it between them so she could unfasten the buttons of her bodice. She knew the instant that he understood her actions, for the sudden breath he drew sounded harsh, and a low groan rumbled in his chest.

When she'd undone the last button to her waist, Sloan pushed the fabric of her blouse aside and the heat of his mouth seared her nipple through the sheer barrier of her chemise. Oh! There was lightning flashing between her breast and the deepest feminine core of her. Now, with his lips and tongue teasing at her, it was her turn to gasp for breath. Sloan's answer was to turn his head and take her other nipple into his mouth, his suckling stirring a restless yearning, a heated aching, a melting and softening in her loins. Oh! This was wondrously sweet!

Con couldn't believe he wasn't dreaming. Instead of slapping him away, she unbuttoned her dress for him! Struggling to control the trembling inside him, he nibbled at her tender flesh through the flimsy top she wore under her dress. He must be doing something right, because she was making soft, whimpering sounds and squirming against him. Even so, she managed to tug his shirt out of his jeans. At the first touch of her fingers on his bare skin, every nerve in his torso synapsed wildly. Her hands skimmed over him, trailing tiny sparks wherever they traveled. She found the small of his back, and her touch there sent him arching against her. She made another soft little whimper and tangled her legs and all the layers of her dress with his legs. Immediately, without conscious thought from his brain, his legs pinned hers, and his hips pressed into her. His lower body had a life of its own, a mind of its own, desires of its own.

The force gathering inside him threatened to explode, to take over his mind and his body. The need to feel her under him, to bury himself inside her, was blinding. He didn't want to rush her, didn't want to scare her or hurt her. He knew he had to give her the choice, give her the final word, but his conscience battled with the urgency, the hunger raging inside him. It was like being caught in white-water rapids, struggling against a power outside himself.

For the moment, he was still in control, but he didn't know how much longer that moment would last.

Seventeen

~

Con felt her bare ankle graze the skin between his jeans and his sneakers. The shreds of his control nearly went up in flames. Before he thought about how to do it, his hand was dragging at her skirt—skirts! He didn't have a clue how many, just that finding her under all those layers was like unwrapping a gift. A gift he'd wanted for a very long time. With each layer he pushed out of his way, he felt that force, that hunger inside him growing stronger. He was almost groaning in frustration when his hand found the warm resilience of her inner thigh, under one last layer of something very thin and silky. She made a soft noise and flinched slightly. He froze then, but she didn't pull away. Now all he could focus on was making that journey up her thigh.

Aisling startled him by cupping his face in both her hands and drawing him back to her mouth. For a while, he forgot everything except kissing her, until kissing her sent his libido into high gear and he remembered the hand he still had clasping her thigh.

Kissing her mouth, drinking in her whimpers and sighs, Con slid his hand up the silky inside of her thigh, seeking, teasing, silently pleading. He felt her thighs tense, trapping his hand between them, and he forced himself to wait until she relaxed. Prayed she would. Concentrating once again on kissing her, Con finally felt Aisling's tension gradually

easing. Once again, he moved his hand up her leg until he
knew he must be close to the part of her he was aching
for. Then he waited, fighting the urge to reach a little farther, to claim her. This had to be her decision. Would she
let him touch her? Would she take him in? He knew he
had to ask.

Before he could find his voice, Aisling's thighs parted
slightly under his hand. Even then, he waited a few seconds, trying to prove to himself that he was still in control
of his urges. Trying to prove his willpower was stronger
than his lust. He had a strong sense of decency. Sure, he
was horny, and she seemed willing, but he could stop anytime. It wouldn't be easy. In fact, it would be damned hard,
in both senses of the word. But he wasn't an animal. He
thought, he hoped, he prayed she wouldn't say no. He
prayed that if she did, he had the strength to stop.

He better find out before it was too late.

Con lifted his head, breaking the kiss, trying to catch his
breath. Reluctantly, he withdrew the hand that had almost
succeeded in making its way through her layers of clothes.
He didn't want her to be able to say he didn't let her think
clearly. Assuming, of course, that she actually liked the way
he'd been touching her. God, this was so complicated!

"Do you . . . want me . . . to . . . stop?" he choked out,
then waited, dreading her answer more as her silence grew
longer.

At first, Aisling didn't understand Sloan's question. For
a moment, she simply lay staring up at him, not comprehending what he was asking her. Even with the strong
moonlight shining down on them, she couldn't see his face
except as shape and shadows above her. She blinked, feeling as if she were trying to waken from a deep dream,
through layers of hazy warmth and pleasure. Did she want
him to stop . . . what? This lovely, floating sensation? The
delicious quivering of anticipation, of discovering further
delights? The pledging of her love by the joining of their
bodies?

She touched her fingertips to Sloan's lips. "And why
would I be wanting you to stop?"

He sagged a little against her, as if he'd been holding his breath waiting for her answer. "Lots of reasons you should want me to stop," he told her in a husky whisper that was giving her shivers. "You don't know me very well. I'm leaving tomorrow. I don't know when I'll be back, so you can't believe any promises I might be tempted to make. You're here, and I've gotta be where the computer industry is. And I'm not ready to consider any kind of commitment. You're the one who'll have to deal with any consequences, like, you know, *baby* consequences, if . . . if . . ." As if he couldn't say the words, Sloan gave a shrug. "You know. I . . . I've got something with me . . . I can try to protect you, but nothing's foolproof."

"You already are protecting me," she told him softly, seeing the proof that she was right to give him her love. Knowing, too, that when he was ready to be declaring it, his love would set her free. As to the consequences of their loving, she was only now considering the matter. Having Sloan's children would be the greatest joy she could imagine! But while she was under the Leprechaun's enchantment? Was it even possible? 'Twould be horrible if the enchantment ensnared the child, as well!

Ah, but there was another question! Would the Leprechaun still be wanting her if she gave herself to a Mortal lover? Perhaps that would make him release her from this awful curse. Aunt Rainbow might have the answers to these questions for her, but Aisling wasn't planning to run and ask! No, indeed, she was staying right here, with Sloan, until the rising of the sun chased her away. Only when this precious time with Sloan ended would she seek her answers. Only then would she seek the means to draw him back to Ireland, to her, before it was too late to break the curse.

"Aisling, I want you to be sure." Sloan's hoarse whisper broke into her musings. She touched his cheek softly, absorbing his warmth and the subtle scrape of a tiny patch of whisker stubble his razor must have missed. " 'Cause if you say yes now," he went on, "and change your mind later, I don't know if I'll be able to stop. I can promise to try, but . . . I'm only human, Aisling, and I want you so bad. Do you understand?''

His ardent words had her blinking away a sudden welling of tears. ''You're a sweet and lovely man for taking such care, Sloan. Never you mind about having to stop. I won't be asking that of you.''

Sloan turned his head away for a few seconds, then bent over her again, leaving her wishing she could see his face more clearly. ''I'm *not* a sweet and lovely man, damn it!'' he growled. His sudden anger startled, dismayed her. What had she said wrong? ''I'm a horny, selfish bastard. I'm not taking care of *you*. I'm taking care of *me*. I'm going after what *I* want.''

Now Aisling understood his anger, which he was mistakenly aiming at himself. ''Well then, it seems we're both wanting the same thing.'' She spoke softly and brushed at the lock of hair falling on his forehead. ''Hadn't we best be getting on with it?''

His groan echoed through her own body, sounding almost like the cry of a wounded beast. Startled by his ferocity, Aisling tensed, but it was too late. Sloan was already moving toward her, his arms tightening to hold her down. Panic started to rise inside her, slicing into her certainty with sharp-edged doubt about her wisdom. She expected his kiss to be rough and crudely possessive. But Sloan's lips were covering hers softly, sweetly, and so tenderly that his kiss wrung tears from her closed eyes and a whimper from her throat. Her panic dissolved, and with it, her doubts.

She'd said yes! Con couldn't control the trembling that shook him down to his toes, couldn't hold back the groan of relief that tore out of him. But he could—barely—control the urge to crush Aisling to him and devour her. The effort made him shake like a scared puppy, which wasn't far from how he felt. Now that she'd said yes, and he could taste the sweet eagerness in her kiss, he was petrified that he wouldn't know what to do. Or that he'd fail to do it. Or he'd hurt her. Or scare her. Or not make it good for her. Or—wasn't this every guy's worst nightmare?—he'd do something to make her laugh at him. He knew plenty about sex in theory, but there was nothing theoretical about the woman lying in his arms. What if—

The slide of Aisling's tongue along his flipped a switch that turned off his brain. Thinking in words became impossible. Suddenly, he was all raw nerve endings, all heat and hunger. One hand was tangled in her hair, supporting her under him. The other found its way to her breast. Her nipple peaked as soon as he touched her. Carefully, he teased her through that thin shirt type thing she had under her dress, and Aisling arched into his hand. He swallowed her gasp, smothered his own groan at the way her small, round breast fit into his palm. He needed to get her out of her dress before he exploded, but he couldn't find a way into her clothes from the top.

Leaving her breast, he ran his hand down her side until he could find the bottom edge of her dress. With his hand shaking so badly he almost couldn't grasp the fabric, he again peeled the top layer back, then the next. And the next. And two more layers of cloth and lacy stuff. Finally, he rediscovered her legs and let his hand rest on her thigh for a moment, giving her time to get used to him feeling her up again. And giving him time to figure out his next move. Except Aisling was ahead of him. Her thighs parted enough to tell him he could keep going, and a rush of adrenaline twisted through his insides.

He took his time exploring the silky kind of long underwear she wore. It was like something out of an old-fashioned movie, or a museum, but maybe rural Ireland was a lot farther behind the times than he'd guessed. Con caught a breath between kisses, then inched his hand up her thigh. On the assumption that this garment was like panties, only longer, he intended to find the waistband and slide it down her legs. In theory, that should have worked. But when his hand reached the top of her thigh, theory dissolved as the fabric simply parted and his hand slipped inside too unexpectedly to stop. His fingers brushed soft curls, then, at the sound of her sigh, he cupped her. She was hot and moist, and his first thought was, *I did this for her!* Then Aisling

twisted closer and his next thought never made it into
words. A sensation like lightning zapped him in the groin,
and he felt another rush of blood. He had to lift his head
to breathe.

"Oh, Sloan! 'Tis magical, what you're doing!"

He was in too much pain to grin. Too much pain to talk.
He managed a grunt. Aisling lifted her hips and he slid his
fingers farther into the damp tangle of curls and hot folds
of her flesh. When he thought he'd found the place he was
searching for, he hesitantly stroked her, pressing gently, just
in case he wasn't there yet. The sudden stab of her fingernails in his back and arm let him know he'd guessed right.
That distracted him from the ache of an erection harder than
iron, so he kept stroking and pressing, wanting to give her
pleasure now, because he didn't know if he would be able
to later. Aisling writhed against his fingers, her breathing
turning rapid and shallow. Suddenly, she arched up, burying her face against his chest, and gave a muffled cry. Her
body pulsed hard under his fingers, as if he were touching
her heart. Not knowing what else to do, Con held her in
his arms until she could stop trembling and gasping.

Aisling clung to Sloan, trying to calm her shaking and
her panting. What he'd done . . . ! She had no words to
describe how he'd made her feel. All she could do was
hang onto him as if he were a raft and she were being
buffeted by a stormy sea. Indeed, she felt almost as if she
had the sea flowing through her body, wave after wave
surging, cresting, ebbing within her. But the sea inside her
was hot and full of life, not cold and deadly.

"You all right?" he murmured. His lips pressed warmly
against her temple.

She caught a deep breath. "Oh! I've gone beyond all
right, and straight past glorious, to . . . To I don't know
where!" Her own words came out in a whisper. She'd no
strength to speak. He gave a short, smothered chuckle that
made her smile. "You've reason to be pleased with yourself, you have," she teased, then grew serious again. "Oh,
Sloan! I never knew a body could feel like that! Truly,

'twas wonderful! But . . . Surely, there is something more to this, that we do together?''

His arms tightened around her and he pressed a kiss to her cheek. "Why don't we get out of our clothes," he murmured in a pleasantly raspy whisper, "so we can find out?"

"Take off our clothes?" she echoed. "If we go taking off our clothes, we'd be naked!"

"That's the general idea." There was a smile in his voice. He closed his teeth gently on her neck, giving her shivers. His tongue, following his teeth, sent more shivers after the first.

Aisling swallowed hard. "Is that a necessary thing? Being naked?"

What she'd experienced so far had been perfectly lovely without being . . . naked. She hadn't thought beyond that! But Sloan seemed to think they could make love even better without their clothes, and surely, he knew more than she did about such things.

If that sound Sloan made in the curve of her neck was a laugh, 'twas lucky for him that he smothered it quickly enough. "Necessary, no. But it would, um, enhance the experience . . . for both of us."

Aisling considered his answer. *Enhancing the experience* certainly sounded like a fair reason for taking off their clothes. She did want to be making him feel as wonderful as he'd done for her. And truly, she didn't want him to be thinking she was selfish. "Well, then, I'm trusting you to know what to do," she told him. "I'll need to be standing to shed all these layers."

To Con, Aisling's faith that he had a clue what to do was the scariest thing he'd heard since his parents had told him they were splitting up. For a couple of seconds, he almost thought he was about to lose his erection to a panic attack. But Aisling didn't give him much time to dwell on his mental list of things that could go wrong. She wiggled out of his arms and stood up on the blanket, and the sight of her renewed his lust with the force of a tidal wave.

Lying back on the blanket, he watched her under the cold light of the full moon. It was still hard to believe how bright the moon was here, in the middle of nowhere. The light turned Aisling to pewter, washing out details, but highlighting enough of her for him to appreciate. She peeled off the top of the old-fashioned clothes. Then she stepped out of the skirt and dropped it with the blouse. Now she was wearing another full skirt that reached down to her toes, and a white tank top that was so thin he could see the shadows of her nipples through it. Her hands went to the ribbon at her waist and she untied the bow. Letting the skirt drop, she stepped out of it and placed it on her dress. But she was still wearing a skirt! Three more times, she went through the untying and stepping out of the skirt routine. Down to the last skirt, Aisling hesitated, then took it off, and stood in front of him in that thin tank top, which turned out to reach her hips, and—there was no other way to describe them!—long underwear! Long, loose pants with lace at the edges, hanging down past her knees.

Standing barefoot in the moonlight, wearing almost transparent old-fashioned underwear, with her hair covering her back and arms like a golden, silken shawl, Aisling looked like some kind of nymph from a painting. It occurred to him that he'd never asked her why she dressed the way she did, when everyone else in the area seemed to wear jeans, but he was too stunned to speak. For a long moment, all Con could do was stare at her and remind himself to breathe. Then she slid her hands up under the long undershirt, fumbled with something, and those silky white long johns hit the grass at her feet, and he forgot about the breathing. The last layer she wore, that see-through long undershirt, barely covered the juncture of her thighs.

Finally, the breath rushed from his lungs, and his brain started to send signals to the rest of him. He pulled his T-shirt off over his head and tossed it without looking to see where it landed. Still gawking at Aisling, he yanked off his sneakers and dropped them somewhere nearby. Aisling was staring back.

Despite the sudden doubt and fear that sank in his gut—
What if she laughed at his naked body? Worse, what if she
screamed and ran away? What if he had trouble with the
condom? Worst of all, what if he went limp?—Con stood
and undid the button of his jeans. As he slid the zipper
down, Aisling's eyes went wide, but she didn't look like
she was ready to run. Just before he shoved his jeans down
to his ankles, he retrieved the condoms from his pocket.
The cool air hit his legs as he was kicking his jeans off
near his shirt and shoes, and the hair on his legs bristled.
Aisling's lips parted . . . No, her jaw dropped. Con braced
himself, but she didn't move, didn't speak.

Aisling couldn't help staring at Sloan. He looked like the
statues of Greek gods she'd seen in the library! She'd already seen his strong arms, but the rest of him was more
of the same. Lovely wide shoulders, sculpted muscles covering his chest and belly. Powerful legs. Narrow hips. And
the strangest black garment fitted tightly around his hips,
like a . . . a loincloth! Ah, well, surely undergarments had
been changing with the times, as much as anything else.
But black—?

Sloan hooked his thumbs into the waistband of his oddly
short drawers and slowly drew the garment down his hips.
As he revealed more of himself to her, a wave of heat rushed
up to her cheeks, making them sting. Oh! He was . . . ! He
was . . . !

For a moment, Aisling feared she'd be fainting at the
sight of Sloan's fully erect manhood. From childhood,
she'd seen stallions in this state, had even witnessed them
mounting mares. But Sloan was a man, not a stallion, and
she'd never before seen a man naked . . . in any state. To
her eyes now, there was little difference between Sloan and
a stallion. He was . . . very . . . very . . . Fighting dizziness,
she took a deep breath. Indeed, he was!

Damn! Aisling looked petrified. Con felt like a wolf siz-
ing up a tender doe. Keeping his eyes locked on hers, he
advanced a half step. And another half step. Almost within
reach. *Please don't run! Please don't be scared! Please!*

The words turned into a mantra in his brain, the only clear thought in a fog of instinct and hunger.

Another half step, and he was close enough to touch her if he reached out. Her head was tipped back, their eyes still locked on each other. In that transparent little *whatever* she wore, with her hair drifting around her, she looked like something from a fantasy story, a fairy tale. And she still looked like a doe facing a big, bad—and very hungry— wolf.

"Don't be scared." The words came out choked and hoarse, probably scaring her more. Somehow he managed a lopsided grin. "One of us shouldn't be."

The smile she gave him looked shaky, but at least he knew she'd understood. "Perhaps if we were both only half-afraid, that would be adding up right," she murmured back.

Suddenly, the only word he could say was her name, all his fears and hunger turning his voice into a harsh plea.

"Aisling?"

Without answering, she just took that flimsy under-dress thing by the edges and lifted it off over her head. Out of the corner of his eye, he saw it float to the ground like a cobweb, but the only thing he really saw was the incredibly perfect woman standing totally nude two feet away from him. *Perfect?* No, she was *beyond* perfect. Her skin was as white as pearls under the moonlight, her hair silvery gold, and the shape of her . . . ! He had to swallow hard to keep from howling like a wolf. Oh, God, she was so beautiful! And so small. So . . . fragile.

His heart sank. She couldn't weigh more than a hundred pounds, barely more than half his weight, but she was less than half his size. He wanted her so badly, he felt sick inside, from fear, from hunger. He would die if he couldn't have her. But . . . he was going to crush her, tear her apart, hurt her, and that was the last thing he wanted to do.

Aisling felt the cool night air swirling over her flushed bare skin, but the shivers rippling through her weren't from cold, nor even from her earlier fears. The way Sloan was staring at her, like he would be devouring her if he could, yet almost worshiping, too, was speaking silent volumes to her of his feelings. She smiled at the whimsy of her next thought, then voiced it in the hush of all Ireland surrounding them. "It's like Adam and Eve we are, alone in Eden. I'm thinking they might have been feeling the same way then, at the dawning of the world. A little afeared, a little greedy."

Sloan blinked once before giving her a sweetly crooked smile, but he was just standing, still as a statue, when she was expecting him to be reaching for her. He was waiting for her to be taking the next step, saying the final *yes*! Oh! Truly, Sloan was the only man she'd be wanting to save her from the Leprechaun's spell! Her heart felt bursting with love.

Lifting her arms to reach for his shoulders, Aisling stepped toward Sloan, and his strong arms closed around her, wrapping her in a blaze of wanting and needing and giving. The next moments became cloaked in a haze of sensations, a magical mist that heightened her perceptions while floating her above reality. He held her tightly for a while, and she felt the pressing of his manhood against the flesh of her middle. It was hot between them, hotter than either of them, and pulsing with the beating of his heart. And so much larger than she'd imagined! How was she ever going to be taking him inside her?

Just then, Sloan bent his head, capturing her lips in a kiss that began softly, slowly, and fueling the heat within her. His strong hands began moving over her skin, igniting tiny sparks wherever he was touching her. The closing of one of his hands on her bottom, lifting her higher into him, startled a gasp he caught in his kiss. Her breasts were now being crushed against his chest, soft yielding to hard, hard cradling soft. His skin felt hot. Curiously, she began exploring parts of him she could reach: his neck, with silky hairs tickling her fingers; his broad back, with muscles flexing under her palms; his shoulders and arms, with muscles taut with holding her.

Her courage to go on touching him ran out before her curiosity to be learning more of the feel of him was satisfied. She stopped her questing at his waist, not ready to reach lower to touch his manhood. Truly, she didn't know if he would want her doing so.

Sloan's other hand started combing through her hair, sliding up to cup the back of her neck, applying a delicious pressure to the joining of her head to her neck. Then the invasion of his tongue was stirring the flames higher, and she felt a heaviness inside drawing her down, whispering to her to lie with him now. She let her head fall back into his waiting hand and opened her lips to him. The melting inside her, at the core of her, like honey beginning to boil, told her she needn't worry about them fitting together. Loving Sloan was all the magic she'd be needing.

When he lowered her to the blanket, his mouth never leaving hers, Aisling felt herself floating. As they were stretching out on the blanket, he slid one hand from her hip to her breast, trailing sparks along her skin. Without thinking of what to do, she arched into his palm. He startled her by breaking that long, lovely kiss, but at the first touch of his hot, moist lips on her breast, her faint protest turned swiftly into whimpers of delight. As his lips and hands went roaming over her, pleasuring and promising, Aisling lost all sense of time, even a sense of herself as separate from the man loving her, the man she was loving. His touch melted into her, and her touch melted into him, so she could swear she was feeling his pleasure, and he was feeling hers.

And then he was kneeling between her thighs, murmuring of how beautiful she was, and how he didn't want to hurt her. He was trembling, and so was she. Aisling touched his face, shadowed above her, haloed by moonlight, telling him without words that she had no fears. And his fingers were creating such magic in the secret places deep inside her! She fixed her gaze on his face until the flames Sloan was stirring engulfed her and her eyes squeezed shut with the shuddering of her body.

A lovely, languid feeling washed over her, cooling the fire only enough to let her breathe. Before she could float away in the dreaminess enveloping her, she felt Sloan entering her. Slowly and gently, to be sure, and the effort to do so was making him tremble and groan, but he was pushing steadily, and a sliver of icy fear pierced her. He was so much bigger to feel than to see! A little farther he went, stretching her, invading her. Just when Aisling was certain she would tear in two, Sloan retreated, letting her breathe, then pressed into her again. The fear melted under the flaring of heat his movements were fueling. When he gathered her close, she clutched his straining shoulders and wrapped her legs around his back, trying to draw him closer, offering all of herself.

Sloan went still. Unsure of what was happening, of what would *be* happening, Aisling held her breath and waited.

His harshly whispered ''Oh, no!'' startled her. She tried to ask what was amiss, but found she had no voice. Sloan trembled in her arms, and she wondered if she'd done something wrong. Then she heard him whispering again, too indistinct to make out his words at first. When she did hear him, fear flashed hot and cold through her veins. ''Sorry! Sorry! Sorry!'' he was chanting in a choked voice, and Aisling didn't understand why.

Without warning, Sloan uttered a roaring groan. He reared up above her, his hips bucking between her thighs as he thrust hard and deep into her, tearing into her, filling her with himself. Searing pain followed. Tears sprang to her eyes, but Aisling was too overcome by the sensation of holding him inside her to be dwelling on the pain. She wanted to see his face, but when she opened her eyes, he was a dark shadow surrounded by stars in the black sky.

Giving another groan, Sloan tightened his arms around her, and she felt his muscles shaking with tension. Moaning her name against her neck, he flexed, withdrew, and thrust deeply again, and this time, wild shudders rippled through him over and over until he collapsed over her.

His hard, heavy weight sent the air whooshing out of her, and made it difficult to breathe in. Still, she liked the feeling of his body on hers, a moist, mingling warmth binding their flesh wherever they pressed together. But why had he been saying he was sorry? Seeking to rouse him, Aisling stroked his face with her fingertips. He remained motionless, his weight growing heavier by the second. With the little air she could take in, she whispered his name. He remained silent. Silent, unmoving, not even breathing!

By all the saints in heaven, she was truly cursed! After making love to her but once, Sloan had gone and died on her!

Eighteen

"Sloan! Oh, Sloan! Why did you go and die on me?"

Aisling's soft wail pierced the fog surrounding his brain. Con couldn't make his voice work, couldn't tell her he wasn't dead. Hell, he was so wasted, so wrung out, he might as well be. All he could do was draw in a wheezing breath, let it out in a moan, and hope she got the message.

"Oh, Sloan! Thanks to heaven, you're alive!" She jostled him. "Ah, but not very," she muttered when he didn't respond. "Get off me, you great oaf! Y're as heavy as a horse. I'll never breathe right again!"

There was lead in his limbs, cotton in his head. All his nerves begged for sleep, but he was crushing Aisling. Somehow, he made himself move. Still holding Aisling in his arms, still joined to her, he rolled to his side, carrying her with him. After several tries, he found his voice, which sounded pretty rusty.

"Sorry. I . . . I didn't realize . . . So fast . . . *Too* fast! Couldn't . . . slow . . . down. All right . . . are you?" Stupid question! How could she be all right after what he'd done to her? "I hurt you. God, I'm . . . sorry! I didn't mean to, but . . . Your first time . . . It should have been better for you. I should have made it better . . . made it special for you. I'm sorry."

He felt her fingers stroking the hair off his forehead. "No need to be apologizing, Sloan," she said softly. "That was lovely. And truly special. How could it not be, with you taking me in your arms like that?''

His heart gave a thump and swelled in his chest. He'd never imagined himself falling for anyone, never thought he'd have the opportunity. He'd never wanted to be in love. After his parents' marriage had turned sour, he'd told himself having love for a while wasn't worth the pain of losing it. But he ever loved anyone, he'd want her to be as sweet, as sexy, as bright, and as forgiving as the woman whose virginity he'd just taken. And Aisling was unique, so could he be falling for her? Already?

He needed to know she was okay. "I hurt you. I didn't want to. I tried not to be rough, but everything happened so fast. Too fast. I wanted you to enjoy it, too, but I couldn't slow down."

Aisling didn't reply to Sloan immediately, but kept stroking his hair. Then her hand went still as his meaning came clear. He truly was a sweet, lovely man, no matter that he didn't think he was. A new playfulness came over her, tempting her to tease him.

"Hmm. Being ignorant in such matters, I'm wondering. Now, I've no complaints, but that thinking you'd died gave me a terrible fright. Now you're saying what we've done isn't as fine an experience as you would have liked it to be? If we were to be trying again, do you think we'd be improving?"

Con swallowed hard. Did she just say what he thought she just said? Oh, yeah, she did! Con felt a telltale rush of blood to his groin, felt himself stir and harden inside the clenching heat of her body. No question, he was ready. But what about Aisling? The way he'd torn into her . . .

"It might be too soon," he warned her, when he really wanted to just start pumping into her again. He cupped her face in his hand. She was so small, so soft and warm. And he was the opposite: big, and hard. "I don't want to hurt you again."

Aisling rubbed her face against his hand. " 'Tis only the first time that should be hurting, isn't it?"

He'd have had to be made of stone not to hear the doubt

in her voice. Or the trust. She was the most wonderful girl—woman—in the world. And he was the lowest form of life to take her virginity on his last night in Ireland. Somehow, he'd have to find a way to come back soon. At Christmas, between semesters? No, probably not till next summer. Then he'd be a year more ready to be in love. If he wasn't already.

He leaned toward her and found her lips with his. There was no hesitation when he touched his tongue to the fullness of her lower lip; she opened to him with a tiny sound in her throat, like a welcome. She tasted sweet. Sweet and hot, and still innocent. Wanting to make love to her again argued with not wanting to hurt her again. The battle between the two urges made him shake all over.

"You must be sore inside. I don't want to make it worse. We don't have to, just 'cause I'm ready to." Brave words. Noble words. Noble lies. He really didn't want to hurt her, but he might just die from being this ready to make love again.

Aisling gently broke the kiss. "Sloan? 'Twould make saying farewell easier for me." Her whispered words sent shivers over his skin. "'Twould give me another lovely memory to be treasuring until we're meeting again."

Her words turned his brain to dust. He found one small breast and felt her nipple bead under his fingers. He followed his fingers with his lips, and when he took her nipple into his mouth, her little gasp sent another surge of blood to his growing erection. Her skin tasted so sweet, he couldn't decide where his favorite place to kiss her was. Not that it mattered. Eventually, he planned to kiss her all over, so choosing favorites was purely hypothetical so far. Any self-respecting mathematician or scientist would test his theories as rigorously as possible. And definitely try to duplicate results. For now, he'd taste her other breast and see if it was as sweet as the first one. He rolled her onto her back and bent to take her other nipple into his mouth. Oh, yeah, it was at least as sweet as the first. But just to be sure—

"Oh, Sloan! You're creating a terrible craving inside me!"

Aisling worked her hand between them and stroked his chest. He wasn't sure if it was her words or the feel of her fingers on his own nipples that sent his internal temperature up a few more degrees. Both, probably. She was writhing under him, and every wiggle, every advance and retreat, every tightening of her body made him harder. Every touch was making it damn near impossible to quell the urge to thrust into her hard and fast until they were both howling.

Just before taking her mouth again, he gasped, "Aisling, stay with me!"

Then, Con called on every shred of self-control to keep his thrusts slow and deliberate. He braced himself above her and tried to think of something unpleasant to distract himself from the silky friction of their flesh as he slid into her. He withdrew from her a little, his arms shaking with the effort to maintain control. Then he eased deeper as Aisling lifted herself to meet him, her body holding him tight inside, her arms holding him tight outside. How could anything distract him now? Even the thought of riding a horse took on erotic features. Worse, the thought of riding a horse with Aisling in his arms played like a movie in what was left of his conscious mind. Control evaporated. His body took over. His only focus was the surging, reaching, scorching drive to satisfy the raging hunger deep inside him.

Then he felt a change in the way Aisling moved. Her body arched like a bow strung tight, and for a moment, she held still even as his hips continued to pump. The tension in her tiny frame vibrated through him. Her slick, hot muscles closed on him, increasing the fierce craving inside him. He hoped to hell she was okay, because he was helpless to control the forces driving him. Suddenly, she gave a cry, and the tension gripping her seemed to break.

Then it was her body leading him into the fire. The urgency raging inside him exploded. A wave of heat washed over him. He felt himself being wrung dry, felt Aisling shaking and shivering beneath him. Con tightened his arms around her, but he didn't know if it was to protect her or to save himself.

Aisling clung to Sloan as the wild tremors tightening within her went on peaking and ebbing. She was still trembling from the sensations gripping her, but now there was a soft, unfolding feeling beginning to blossom inside her. As she slowly regained her senses, she realized that the tiny, almost sobbing cries she was hearing came, not from some night bird, but from her own throat. Then a strangled shout from Sloan drowned out all other sounds. He gave one final thrust she could feel all the way to her heart, and collapsed above her. She braced herself to take the weight of him, but he rolled to his side, taking her with him, protecting her.

Aisling felt her heart swelling with love for this sweet, tender young man. Whatever terrible secret Aunt Rainbow thought Sloan was harboring, her aunt must be mistaken. How could Sloan be turning her against him, disappointing her in her quest for True Love? Nothing about him could be dreadful enough to destroy this love she was feeling within her. Sloan was her True Love, and nothing would be persuading her otherwise. Certainly not her aunt's insistence that Sloan wasn't the man to be breaking the spell.

With Sloan in her arms and in her heart, she'd no need of any O'Hara. No indeed. If an O'Hara was to be lying at her feet, bleeding, she'd not be feeling a single twinge of remorse. Sloan was man enough for her love, man enough to break the curse, and to hell with any and all O'Haras! Even the thought of him leaving tomorrow couldn't dim her optimism, for she felt sure he'd be returning in time to save her. Now that they'd experienced this glorious lovemaking, she'd no doubts that Sloan would be returning to claim her. Her earlier precautions—sending two young Faeries to ensure that, this time, the horseshoe nail of Faery gold accompanied him to America—now seemed foolishly unnecessary. She'd no need of Faery magic. This love between them was the magic that would be bringing him back to her when the time was right.

Con fought against the drugging urge to sleep. They had

so little time left to spend together, he wanted to be conscious for all of it. Besides, his theoretical research indicated that women tended not to be flattered by their lovers
snoring within seconds of orgasm. He stroked her hair,
damp from their sweat, and listened to her breathing. She
was so quiet, so still in his arms. What was she thinking
about? Was she sorry she'd given her virginity to a guy
who was leaving almost immediately? She probably had
some expectations of him now. But what? Hell, maybe they
should have spent more time talking before they dove into
having sex.

Time? This time tomorrow, he'd be home, halfway
around the world from Ireland, from Aisling. Damn, damn,
damn! He didn't want to leave her. Should he ask her to
wait for him? If he didn't get back to her soon enough, she
might find some other guy. No, Aisling wouldn't. Even
three years ago, there'd been a special connection between
them. Now that they'd made love, whatever that bond was,
it was even stronger.

Oh, God! He was going to miss her! Just his luck to find
a girl—woman—he could love when he couldn't do anything about it. For his own sake as well as hers, he would
assure her—*promise* her—he'd come back as soon as he
could. How was he going to make it through a year of grad
school without her, unless he knew he was coming back?

He felt Aisling sigh deeply and kissed the top of her
head, nestled under his chin. Her sweet scent, mingled with
the smells of fresh Irish air and the grass under them, filled
his head. He wished he could bottle the scent to take home
with him. Then he'd be able to call up this moment anytime
he wanted to remember exactly how it felt to hold Aisling
under the Irish sky.

Something inside him seemed to expand, something
sweet and aching at the same time. Oh, God! Was he in
love? He might be. He could be. He probably was, but . . .
How did anyone know? He needed to know, but there was
no time. Oh, hell! How could he leave her like this, not
knowing how he felt? How *she* felt? She sighed again. Con
put his fingers under her chin, tipped her head up toward

his, bent his toward her, and kissed her softly. For a second, he considered taking the kiss deeper, letting the banked hunger for her flare again. But there was something so peacefully sweet about this kiss that he didn't. As if she could read his mind, Aisling also kept the kiss sweet and simple.

"Ah, Sloan!" Her voice came out as a sigh. "There's a sweet magic to making love with you. I wish tonight never had to end."

Con almost, *almost,* said the *L* word, but the feeling was so new, the words he'd never spoken stuck in his throat. Instead, after kissing Aisling, he blurted the next thing on his mind. "I feel kinda stupid telling you this now, but my name isn't Sloan."

In his arms, Aisling's body stiffened a little, and guilt made his cheeks burn.

"Not Sloan? Then what is your true name?" Damn, her tone was like dry ice.

"My given name is Conlan, but I almost never use it. Sloan is my last name, but it's what I'm used to answering to at school. Most of my friends call me Sloan, so I didn't think twice about telling you. Sorry." He nuzzled her neck, then tickled her ear with the tip of his tongue, grinning when she relaxed and squirmed against him. "But I think . . . we can be a little more . . . personal . . . now that we've made love."

"*Conlan* Sloan." Aisling said his name softly, like she was testing the feel of it. It sounded special in her voice. " 'Tis a fine old Irish name, Conlan is," she told him. Dumb as it was, he liked the approval in her tone. But then, why not? He wanted her to like everything about him. That way, they'd be even.

"So, what about you?" He picked up a strand of her long silky hair and let it flow like water through his fingers. "What's your real name? Your true name?"

" 'Tis Aisling Ahearn."

Aisling listened to him repeating her name, the way she'd repeated his. The sound of his voice speaking her full name gave it a magical, special feeling. Wasn't it strange that she felt even closer to him, now that they'd exchanged names the way lovers exchanged tangible tokens of their love. *Conlan Sloan and Aisling Ahearn.* Yes, there was a kind of magic in their names together like that. She dropped a slow, wet kiss onto Con Sloan's shoulder, amazed at how his hard, smooth body seemed heated from within, and impervious to the chill of the air. A sudden need to tell him about herself, to give him something to take with him tomorrow, sent her words tumbling out.

"In truth, my name is Aisling de Burgh Ahearn. My mother, Fiona, died when I was born. She was barely seventeen, and the last daughter of one line of the old de Burgh family. We owned these very lands and buildings before our neighbors, the dastardly O'Haras, stole everything and caused my Da's ruin."

His chuckle rumbled under her ear. Irritated, Aisling tried to sit up, but Conlan Sloan's arms held her too tightly. "The misfortunes of my family amuse you, do they?"

"No. Not that. It was that melodramatic bit about the 'dastardly O'Haras' that cracked me up. My mother is an O'Hara. In fact, my full name is Conlan Ambros O'Hara Sloan, but that's—"

Con was about to say his full name was a pretentious mouthful, but Aisling made a cry, part screech, part sob, that startled the hell out of him. Still sounding like an injured kitten growling, she struggled against him. Con's first impulse was to try to hold her, to ask her what was wrong, but she wrenched herself out of his arms and leaped away from him like he'd burned her.

Another muffled cry, nothing like her cries of pleasure, sliced into him. Something had frightened her, but what? A wild animal? A Peeping Tom? He glanced around them, but the moonlit fields were silent and uninhabited, except for them. Confused by Aisling's sudden and strange actions, Con felt foolish and helpless. Damn it! He was lying there, butt naked, when he should be defending his woman from whatever was threatening her. Some hero!

By the time he'd gotten his legs under him to sit up, Aisling was gathering her scattered clothes, keeping her face angled toward him and backing away. Then she paused, as if she wasn't sure what to do next, the dress and all her other stuff bundled in front of her like a shield. Watching her for any other clues, he reached for his jeans and pulled them on, then stood to fasten them. To his horror, Aisling cried out and raised one arm defensively. Something or someone must be coming up behind him, but he didn't care about his own hide. Whatever it was, he'd deal with it after he made sure of Aisling's safety.

He moved toward her to offer protection.

She took a step backward. "Keep away from me, you O'Hara devil!" Her words came out in a high, thin wail that gave him chills. "You've done me enough harm to last *another* hundred years! Tricked me, you did, into giving myself to you, with your lying and cheating and pretending."

Con's jaw dropped. Oh, God! He didn't know what she was talking about, but it was clear as glass that she'd changed her mind about what had just happened between them. Because he was an O'Hara? It didn't make sense, but she wasn't bluffing. The pain in his heart hit so hard, it nearly doubled him over. Breathless, he struggled to speak, without thinking about what he would say, could say, to fix whatever had gone so wrong.

"Aisling, I . . . I never lied to you. Honest. I thought you wanted to make love with me. I . . . I . . . I love you!"

The words burst out of him and hovered between them while he waited for her reaction. For a moment, she simply stood frozen, just out of reach, her lips parted, her eyes wide and dark in the moonlight. Then, without warning, she began to laugh, a strange, almost crying sound, that made him wonder if she'd gone crazy. Just as he was considering pouncing on her, to calm her down, she stopped abruptly, but her laughter continued to echo in his head.

She gave a shake of her head that made her hair ripple with pale moonlight. "Love! Hah! What does an O'Hara know of love? I'll none of your lies, none of your deceptions! 'Tis ruined I am, and by a lying, thieving O'Hara!" Her voice rose in a shriek, then broke into sobs. "Believing you were the one, I was. More fool me! Dying couldn't be more cruel than false hoping!''

Oh, God! Was she threatening to kill herself? Over him? Her reaction didn't make sense. Neither did half of what she said. He sure as hell didn't want to end up facing rape charges because of his family connections. Somehow, he'd have to calm her down, get her listening to reason, get her explaining coherently.

He took a breath, and plunged in. ''Aisling, I don't understand. I—''

Shaking with an inner coldness so fierce she feared it would be killing her, Aisling backed away from him. With what little was left of her wits, she noted that she was but a short distance from the secret passage to the Faery world. She took another step backward. Conlan Ambros O'Hara Sloan took two steps toward her, shrinking the gap between them too much. She had to escape!

''A curse on your black heart! I hate you!'' she cried.

In the chill light of the moon, his shocked, hurt expression sent an answering pain through her heart. As swiftly as she felt it, she shut her feelings to him and seized the moment to bolt for the secret doorway.

Before Con could register what was happening, Aisling was sprinting away into the darkness. He shook off his mental paralysis and started after her. God knew what could happen to her, frightened and naked, running away in the dark. Let her hate him, he had to take care of her.

Several times, he slipped on the damp grass, and then suddenly, he lost sight of her. He stopped running, straining his eyes to gaze through the darkness and shadows beyond. He held his breath, listing for a snapping twig, a slapping branch, the sound of her breath. Nothing. She'd disappeared.

For several minutes, Con waited, but there was no sign of Aisling. Finally, disgusted with himself for getting into such a bizarre situation, angry at Aisling for making a fool of him, worried about her getting home safely anyway, Con turned back to the blanket and the rest of his clothes. No point in bothering with his underwear or socks now. Bundling everything except the blanket into the backpack, he trudged toward the manor house.

When he reached the back steps, Con glanced over his shoulder at the full moon, now most of the way across the dark sky. The face in the moon looked . . . sad. Disappointed. He shrugged and opened the door to get whatever sleep he could before dawn. He felt like he'd been through the roughest white-water rapids without a raft.

When he dragged himself out of bed a few hours later, he felt totally wretched. Even the discovery that his mother and Leon had broken up sometime during the night didn't give him some mean-spirited satisfaction. His soul had sunk to the absolute rock-bottom. Nothing would make him feel better. And nothing he could imagine would ever make him feel worse.

Until Gramps issued his ultimatum the next morning.

Book Four

"*The lunatic, the lover, and the poet*
Are of imagination all compact..."
—*Shakespeare,* A Midsummer Night's Dream

Nineteen

~~~~

When McKeogh had stopped howling like a hyena over
that stupid book, and impulsively offered to go with him,
Con had decided just as impulsively not to refuse. All the
last-minute activity kept the memories at bay. But when he
stepped onto the Air Lingus jet, Con ran out of defenses.
The women flight attendants' voices, with their lilting Irish
rhythms, jolted him into remembering so acutely, it was
like a physical blow. They didn't really sound like Aisling,
but they made him remember, damn them. Damn her!

Damn him!

Overnight, stretched out in first class, there was nothing
to do after dinner but stay awake and watch McKeogh
sleep, or fall asleep. And dream of Aisling. Aisling, and
warm, misty summer nights. Aisling, his first love, his first
heartbreak. Awake, he could tell himself he never loved
her, didn't care if he never saw her again. But asleep, his
brain lost the battle with his heart. She filled his persistent
dreams with unbroken promises, unconditional love. He
knew it was all as insubstantial as Irish moonlight, but the
knowledge couldn't stop him aching for the illusion. In his
sleep, his fingers stayed closed around the gold horseshoe
nail in his sleep. The vivid memory of pulling the nail from

Luna's golden horseshoe collided with a vague recollection of delicate gold leather sandals on Aisling's feet. Was it just an illogical, impossible connection suggested by the legend of Lady Moonlight, or . . . ?

The swirling, beckoning visions in his dreams argued persuasively for magic and true love and happy endings. With the droning of the engines muffling any ambient noises and his eyes shaded from the sunlight above the clouds, he drifted between sleeping and waking. The illusions dared to stray past the boundaries of sleep, into the half-conscious, semi-trance state of waking in flight. For a while, he let himself believe that magic and love existed, let himself believe that most tantalizing of all illusions, enduring love, love that healed.

The static preceding the morning announcements woke him thoroughly. Even before he sat up and prepared for breakfast and landing, he tried to pretend he was still cocooned by his dreams. But just as noises were sharper now, just as the brilliant sunlight filtered under the edges of his eye shades, reality chased away the illusions. There was no magic, except what science had yet to discover and explain. The only kind of love that endured was the kind that lacerated the heart until it grew hard to protect itself, or bled itself dry. And there was no love that could heal such a damaged, lifeless heart.

They were about to land at Shannon Airport and McKeogh was glued to the window like a little kid. Con tried to contain his impatience. He wanted to be done with the unpleasantness of confronting his grandfather, of getting the old man evaluated, of whatever else had to be done. Then he and his partner could alternate pub crawling with castle touring, maybe catch some trad music, and do the obligatory trace of McKeogh's very Irish roots. That sounded like a plan to him.

The jet bounced once on landing, and several passengers gasped. McKeogh white-knuckled the armrest between them. Con gritted his teeth and, reflexively, closed his fingers around the gold nail. The thing was so hot, he dropped it in surprise. What was it he'd read in that book Gramps sent, about Faery gold having emotions? Jeez, what if . . . ? He looked down at the nail.

A shaft of sunlight was streaming through the window, touching his chest where the nail had been lying. Talk about a self-inflicted "gotcha!" Laughing silently at himself, he tucked the chain inside his shirt. It was just a horseshoe nail that happened to be pure gold. It was a souvenir of another trip, not some magical charm. *Faeries, magic and enchantments! Been there, done that.* What was it about Ireland that made even a robot like him get fanciful? Whatever it was, he didn't want any.

When they were finally off the plane and cleared through Irish Customs and Immigration, they retrieved their luggage and stepped outside the airport terminal building to find the car rental kiosk. Despite the surge and noise of the people coming and going, McKeogh stopped short on the walkway and gawked. Amused, Con looked up at the sky at the exact moment the sun broke through the clouds, scattering rainbows.

Momentarily blinded by the golden light in his eyes, Con took a deep breath of Irish air. He shut his eyes briefly to erase the dancing spots of color interfering with his sight, and a vision of Aisling, frosted by moonlight, sprang into his mind. He'd never seen her in daylight, but for some reason, the sight of a rainbow always conjured her image.

McKeogh's elbow in his side brought him back to reality. He pointed to the car rental sign, and they started across a small grassy area between the drive and the car park. The instant he stepped onto the springy green grass, he felt a searing pain inside his shirt. A bee? He dropped his suitcase and felt at his chest. The only thing he could feel was the nail on its chain, tucked inside. Well, *something* had burned him.

It had to be lack of sleep, too much coffee, all those memories, that stupid book, the harrowing confession in the letter. Disgusted at his suggestibility, he pulled the chain away from his neck, then felt the nail to prove it was his imagination. Hissing at the heat searing his fingers, he dropped the nail onto his shirt.

"Hey, Sloan? What is it?"

"Nothing."

McKeogh briefly caught hold of the ring, winced, and dropped it, then gave him an odd look. "Nothing, huh? How do you explain this? Your good luck charm is just about red hot, and it's pulsing like a heart."

"Oh, that." He shrugged. "Faery gold always does that." McKeogh's stunned reaction gave him the first genuine laugh he'd had in days. "Gotcha! Let's go shed the light of reason on my grandfather's irrational behavior."

A PALACE, THE FAERY REALM, EVER-THE-PRESENT

In the aftermath of yet another Faery *rade,* in which the Moonstone Circle inadvertently crossed paths with the Sun-Dancing Troop, Aunt Rainbow discovered a smudge on the hem of Aisling's dress. The instant their quarters had been magically furnished and all the pictures and pillows arranged to her aunt's taste, the chime of a silvery bell and a shy giggle announced the arrival of a laundress Faery.

At first glance, Aisling didn't recognize the little female Faery who followed Aunt Rainbow into their parlor. The blushing girl—now a mere adolescent of one hundred and twenty-three years!—was Juniper Bilberry. After instructing young Juniper to remove the smudge from Aisling's clothes, Aunt Rainbow glided away to join an impromptu *fleadh ceol,* a music festival. With Juniper's assistance, Aisling removed her skirt and passed it to the little Faery, who disappeared from view under the volume of fabric.

From within the folds of the skirt, Juniper's voice emerged. "Be it true, miss, that Acorn Bittersweet has chosen ye as his bride?"

Aisling shuddered at the unadorned reminder of her fate, should she fail to find anyone able to fall in love with her in time. And time was passing more rapidly every second that she continued to fail. " 'Tis true he has claimed that choice."

Juniper's gamine face popped out from the layers of cloth she was cleaning. She sighed deeply. "How fortunate you are, miss! Acorn Bittersweet is a wonderfully talented shoemaker who will provide well for ye and yer offspring.''

At the notion of bearing the ugly, inhuman creature's children, Aisling shuddered again. She opened her mouth to protest that she felt anything but fortunate at those prospects. The sudden rush of bright red in Juniper's plump cheeks caught her attention. Rather than speak, she smiled to allow the girl to feel encouraged to continue.

'' 'Tis no wonder he's so taken wi' ye, miss. Ye're very pretty, for a Mortal.'' Juniper gave Aisling a shy, sweet smile. ''I'm too young for him, Mother says. Once, I found a button from his waistcoat, and kept it to wear on a ribbon around my neck. At night, I dream about marrying Acorn Bittersweet, though I know 'twill do me no good. I do wish he had chosen me instead!'' The girl clapped a tiny hand over her mouth and the color drained from her cheeks. ''Oh, miss! I'm sorry! Mother would feed me to a cat if ye were to tell her what I blathered!''

Aisling's heart began beating faster as she stared at the Faery's contrite and worried little face. Managing a smile she hoped to be reassuring, she put her hand on Juniper's green velvet-covered little shoulder. Her magical name, Remember-Fear-Not, popped into her mind, imparting its strength to her century-long resolve to escape from the Leprechaun's clutches.

''Worry not, Juniper. I shan't betray your confidence to your mother.''

The brilliant smile and rush of color back to Juniper's round face touched Aisling. No matter that the girl yearned for a mate Aisling found repulsive. 'Twas the girl's own feelings that spoke so eloquently. Too well, she also knew the heart's aching sorrow at loving an unattainable man— only in her case, 'twas because the man she'd loved was a beastly fraud.

''Oh, miss! Ye're so kind!'' Juniper held out the now sparkling clean skirt. ''If ever there's aught in my power to repay ye . . .''

For a moment, their gazes locked in ageless, universal feminine understanding that erased all the differences between them. The first ray of hope since she'd run from Conlan *O'Hara* Sloan peeked through the clouds that had surrounded Aisling's heart and soul with the unrelenting darkness of despair.

The sudden swell of Faery harmonies from the *fleadh* broke the silent communication. With magical assistance from the little Fey laundress, Aisling's skirt drifted down over her head and settled itself over her petticoats. Then Juniper fastened the ties and buttons at Aisling's waist, and gave a final tug to the skirt to smooth it.

" 'Tis perfect, now, Juniper. You shall take some of the sweets from the crystal dish before you go to the *fleadh*." Aisling pointed to Aunt Rainbow's never-empty bowl of bonbons. She knew the little Faery understood her oblique means of expressing her gratitude. But would Juniper also understand the suggestion to seek Acorn Bittersweet out at the music festival? She'd heard no word of his return, but the dread event was imminent, and Leprechauns loved dancing.

Juniper dropped a hasty curtsey before slipping several of the rich, stolen candies into the pocket of her apron. Then, flashing a smile that showed she certainly had understood, the blushing girl darted toward the source of the music. Alone again, Aisling curled up on several cushions piled in a corner of the bower. She opened a recently "borrowed" copy of *The Complete Works of William Shakespeare*, which, judging from the notes in the margins of many pages, belonged to a university professor who no doubt thought himself rather absentminded to misplace this book.

A leaf marked her place in *Romeo and Juliet,* but she no longer felt inclined to dwell on the star-crossed lovers' fates. Turning instead to *A Midsummer Night's Dream*, Aisling began to read. When she reached her favorite line of the play, where Titania, Queen of the Faeries, says "Methinks I was enamored of an ass!" she paused, as she always did at that point, to conjure in her mind's eye an image of Conlan *O'Hara* Sloan. Truly, *donkey* was the most flattering of all the insults she could be heaping on his head!

O'HARA HOUSE, CO. SLIGO, FRIDAY, MAY 28, 1999

The heavy wooden door of the O'Hara manor house swung open only a few seconds after Con dropped the heavy brass door knocker. A rounder, slightly grayer Mrs. Penny welcomed him with a more enthusiastic hug than he'd expected. He had to drop his suitcase to keep his balance. The memory of all the times she'd secretly left treats for him thawed his lingering reserve and he returned her hug. Anticipating disaster as usual, McKeogh grabbed his briefcase before his computer hit the stone stairs.

Mrs. Penny stepped back, frowning as she stared past him. "Oh, dear. And this is . . . ?" Her voice trailed off oddly. Con introduced his partner and they shook hands briefly. Mrs. Penny's stiff smile puzzled him. She'd always taken pride in her role in maintaining O'Hara hospitality.

"Himself is in the library. Best go in now. Your usual room is ready, Conlan, and I've aired out another for your partner. Unless . . . you and your partner . . . ?" As her voice trailed off she looked from one to the other. One silvery eyebrow rose in a question, and then her ruddy cheeks turned redder.

Finally he understood her confusion about McKeogh. Laughing, Con shook his head. "Two rooms. We're *business* partners."

Mrs. Penny's face creased into her usual warm smile. "That's all right, then. You both just leave your cases here and I'll see to them. And you can tell himself I'll be bringing in morning coffee and cakes in a shake."

Con started toward the library door as soon as Mrs. Penny scurried away, but McKeogh grabbed his sleeve. "Sloan, I can stay at a hotel if I'm imposing."

He shook his head. "Stay cool, McKeogh. You're not imposing. There have to be a dozen usable bedrooms in this place. Besides, I'm the one frying their circuits, not you. Okay?"

Without waiting for an answer, Con pushed open the paneled wood library door and stepped inside. A glance over his shoulder showed his partner trailing behind him.

In spite of the warm weather, the tang of wood smoke wafted toward him as he scanned the room. His grandfather sat in his favorite leather wing chair near the hearth, angled toward the doorway but looking away from it, as if he were talking to someone seated across from him.

"Hey, Gramps."

The room seemed to echo with hasty silence, as if he'd interrupted a private conversation. The old man started and swung his head to frown at him. Their eyes met, and then Gramps surprised him with an actual smile. "Come in, Conlan, come in."

The rich voice still had the familiar boom of authority. The old man's hair had turned a startlingly bright silver, but there was little sign of his true age in his face. The broad shoulders were still squarely held, and the rest of him looked as fit as a man twenty years younger. If Gramps wasn't well, Con couldn't see any signs of it, excluding his recent irrational behavior.

With a hand on McKeogh's shoulder, Con opened his mouth to introduce them. Before he could say a word, Enid McDermott, the owlish junk-shop woman, popped out of a chair that stood with its back toward the door. The wide smile she gave him turned into a look of alarm when she saw McKeogh.

"Oh! Oh, dear, oh, dear! Conlan!"

Puzzled by Enid's strange outburst, Con walked across the dark hardwood floor, across the thick Persian carpet, to shake his grandfather's hand. There was nothing feeble, nothing ailing, about the grip the old man clamped around his hand. The gray eyes sparkled like ice.

"Gramps, Enid, my partner, Erin McKeogh."

Erin crossed the room toward them, her usually bright smile a little shaky as she extended her hand toward Gramps. The old man left her standing with her hand in the air while he glared at Con.

"*Partner,* you said? What's that mean? Your girlfriend? Your lover?"

Normally, Con's temper had a long fuse, but the shock and hurt on Erin's face as she withdrew her hand made him feel like exploding. Keeping his hand on Erin's shoulder, he glared back at his grandfather.

"What the hell difference should that make to you?" He didn't shout, but bit off each word, making up in intensity for what he lacked in volume. "Where are your self-righteous Irish manners, for crying out loud? I told you I was bringing a friend. That's more than you should need to welcome her."

Erin tried to back away. "It's okay, Con." Her usually clear voice sounded thin, like she might cry. "There must be a bed-and-breakfast around here. I'll wait outsi—"

"You will not!" She flinched at his bellow, and Con wanted to kick himself. He wasn't angry at Erin, damn it, and now he was making things worse. Lowering his tone, he continued, aiming his glare and his words at his grandfather. "This sanctimonious old man backhanded me when I was sixteen, because I complained about the way everyone in the village had to stop to talk to everyone else, and all they were saying was a whole lot of nothing. Said my rudeness was an embarrassment to him, and a disgrace to all of Ireland." Gramps turned red. "How is your snubbing Erin any different, except for being deliberate?"

Rising from his chair, Gramps cleared his throat and held out his hand to Erin. "My apologies, young lady. Welcome to O'Hara House. McKeogh, eh?"

There wasn't much light in Erin's smile, but she shook the old man's hand. "No need to apologize, sir. I told Con we should warn you, but . . ."

"But I never listen." Con flashed her a quick, apologetic grin. "Okay, you were right." He turned back to Gramps and Enid. "What's going on? You're acting like you've got some kind of guilty secret."

"Just answer me one question, Conlan," Gramps said, his voice more subdued than before. "Define 'partner' with respect to this lovely Irish girl." The old man was something else! Still on the same subject, now he was flirting and insulting at the same time!

"Partner means *partner,* damn it!"

Erin shook her head. "Sloan, chill. I think I understand

what the issue is." She gave Gramps one of her usual smiles, and the old character puffed up his chest like a pigeon. "Con and I have been in business together for over ten years, Mr. O'Hara. We're best friends, or like brother and sister. That's all."

Before Gramps could say anything, Mrs. Penny pushed open the door. She was carrying a silver tray loaded with a silver coffeepot, creamer and sugar bowl, cups, plates, and a loaf of tea cake. Con crossed to her and took the tray from her.

"Thank you, dear," she said with a smile. "Enid, if you'll pour, I'll be taking myself off to town before the shops close for lunch. There's plenty of sandwich makings in the kitchen, if you find yourself hungry before I'm back."

"Come, Erin McKeogh, make yourself comfortable." Gramps took Erin's hand and drew her to the chair he'd been sitting in when they arrived. Then he nodded over his shoulder toward the farthest corner of the library. "That scowling pup over there is Enid's son, Phelan McDermott."

Con saw Erin's reaction before he saw Enid's son. Her smile faltered, her face went white, then her cheeks got bright pink. With a wordless nod, she looked away. Expecting to see Quasimodo, Con peered into the shadows across the room. A tall, lanky man about his own age, wearing faded jeans and a dark sweater, stood leaning against the paneling. Con supposed the guy was handsome, in a dark, predatory sort of way. Wolfish. Probably a brooding Irish poet. Definitely not Erin's type. She preferred guys who could go out in daylight.

"Sit yourself down, Conlan," Gramps commanded.

"Thanks, but I've been sitting nearly around the clock. I need to stretch my legs." He picked a spot along the heavily carved wooden paneling surrounding the marble fireplace, and leaned his shoulder against it. "You look good, Gramps."

"Looks can be deceiving."

Enid moved to the coffee service and, without a word,

began pouring. Except for polite murmurs about cream, sugar, and cake, no one spoke while she served Erin and Gramps. Her son walked over to take a cup from his mother, paused long enough to make Erin look nervous, then walked back to his corner. Enid handed Con a delicate china cup of filtered coffee. The rich scent went right to the foggiest part of his brain. While he took a drink, Enid set a china plate with two slices of cake next to him on the mantel.

Con had just taken a taste of the buttery cake when Gramps took Enid's hand in his own. He gave her the kind of soft look Con hadn't believed the old man capable of. Did the two of them have something going?

"Go on, Ambros dearest," Enid prompted.

But Gramps drank his coffee and didn't even glance at him. A second before Con's patience snapped, the old man met his eyes.

"Your grandmother was a beautiful woman, Con, but she was a harpy, a cold-blooded shrew. Our marriage was miserable. The only joy I had of it was Corliss, and then you. When Moyra passed on, I swore I'd rather die alone than risk the hell of marriage again."

Astonished by the intimate confession, Con waited silently.

Gramps cleared his throat. "I've known Enid all her life. She's always owned a special corner of my heart, but things kept us apart: She's so much younger, I was married, then she was married. I thought of us only as friends, even after young Phelan's father passed on. It's taken her the better part of a decade to convince me we should be together. We're asking you to ensure our happiness."

It was a weird request, but at least he wouldn't be trying to commit Gramps to a loony bin. "So what are you saying, you want my blessing to marry Enid?"

"Blockhead!" Gramps snapped. A guffaw burst from Phelan McDermott. Erin made a noise like a muffled sneeze. Gramps shook his head. Enid fixed him with a look of patience mixed with a little irritation. Con shrugged and stuffed a piece of cake into his mouth. He was too jet-lagged to deal with this.

"Calm yourself, Ambros," Enid murmured. "Conlan, dear, what Ambros is trying to explain is this: 'Twas on account of Ambros the Second that the O'Haras have been cursed. 'Tis why none of the O'Hara marriages this century have been happy ones. You are the only one with the power to end this curse."

In panic, Con shot a glance at Erin. She looked as shocked as he felt. "C'mon, Gramps, Enid. You don't really believe that stuff. The book you sent was a joke, right? A way to trick me into visiting, right?"

Enid rose and stood beside him. Putting her hand on his, she looked straight at him, her expression dead serious. "'Tis no joke, Conlan, dear. The legend of Lady Moonlight and your grandfather's own grandfather is as true as the sky is blue and the grass is green. Poor Aisling Ahearn must be released from her enchantment before this July's full moon, or the O'Hara Curse shall never be broken. And unless you succeed, Conlan, you shall be the last unhappy descendant of Ambros O'Hara the Second."

He stared at her for a long moment, and Enid and Gramps stared back at him as if they meant every insane, ludicrous word. Then his patience snapped.

"Let me get this straight. You invited me here to go out under the full moon and fall in love on command, with some legendary babe who got turned into a horse by a Leprechaun, so the rest of the clan can shack up happily ever after?"

Enid smiled and patted his cheek. Gramps harrumphed and nodded. In his corner, Phelan snorted. Erin squeaked, but it could have been a reaction to Phelan. Con's blood pressure soared. He was going to need a group rate at the loony bin!

"What the hell have you all been drinking?"

Gramps sputtered invective, *blockhead* being the mildest. Erin gasped. Phelan snickered. Enid sighed. With his teeth and fists clenched, Con swore under his breath.

When Erin stood up, he expected finally to hear something sensible. "Sloan, let's look at this situation as if it were a system we're analyzing. Once you step outside normal parameters of expectations about reality, it seems to me there's definite, and quite simple, logic operating here. For starters, every action is calling for an equal and opposite reaction."

Con stared at her as if he'd never seen her before. Erin looked the same as always: slender, pale, with green eyes and a mop of long, curly red hair, her pointy little chin leading. An alien abduction—Irish pod people!—was the only reasonable explanation for her astounding comments. "Not you, too. Please don't say you've gone over to the lunatics."

"Lunacy is the operative word. There are but a few days to the next full moon." Phelan came out of his corner as he was speaking. The man had the rich, melodic voice of an Irish bard, and the closer he got, the more obvious it was that he was closing in on Erin. She stepped toward Con, and Con got between them, scowling. Phelan lifted an eyebrow at him, then gave Erin a smile that didn't quite look innocent. "You've barely time enough to prepare yourself to challenge Acorn Bittersweet."

Prepare himself to challenge . . . ? Con swore under his breath. "Get real, man. Even if I believed in Leprechauns, I'm not going *mano-a-mano* with one over who gets the horse lady who hates all O'Haras."

Without another word, he turned and strode out of the library. Ignoring the combined voices calling after him, Con took the stairs two at a time and slammed into his usual room. It looked exactly the same as it had fourteen years ago, but there wasn't much comfort in the familiar now. His suitcase stood near the antique wardrobe, his briefcase stood beside the desk. He sat on the edge of the old four-poster bed, then, too restless to sit, he stood up and paced across a time-faded Oriental carpet.

A knock on the bedroom door halted him. "Sloan? May I come in?" It was McKeogh's voice, unusually subdued.

Furious with himself for treating his best friend like a piece of furniture, he yanked open the door. "C'mon in."

As she stepped past him, he gave her a rueful grin. "Sorry about this whole crazy thing. I don't want you to waste your first trip to Ireland. As soon as I can throw Enid and Phelan out and find a shrink to examine Gramps, we'll do some touring."

Erin walked to the tall double windows and looked outside. Con stood next to her, not studying the formal garden just coming into spring bloom, but gazing beyond the fence around the garden, beyond the stone walls to the farthest paddock.

"Sloan?" Erin spoke quietly, still gazing out the window. "I don't believe in magic any more than you do. But can't you see an inherent logic to the story?" She smiled up at him, then turned her face away again. "Let's assume there are some historical facts we can verify. Take a leap of faith about some of the metaphysical details, and it's really a simple matter of symmetry."

Feeling strangely as if Erin had somehow betrayed him, Con moved away from the window. "It's simple, all right. Either you all had something very strange in your coffee, or you're all in some elaborate conspiracy to drive me crazy." Erin shot him an indignant glare. "I'm not sure which option I like better."

The sudden sparks in Erin's eyes reminded him acutely of the night he'd argued with Aisling over the existence of magic and Faeries. And the many times his mother had laced into him or his father over some affront to her sensibilities. He was surrounded by beautiful Irish lunatics. Some guys had all the luck.

But he didn't want to jeopardize his friendship with Erin. "Look, McKeogh, even if there had been an Aisling Ahearn a hundred years ago, and even if she'd made a bad bargain with a Leprechaun, it doesn't logically follow that a woman with the same name today is the same person. And even if *that* story were true, I'm sure as hell not gonna go falling in love with anyone at the drop of a shamrock, as a favor to O'Haras everywhere."

Erin shook her head. "You really are a . . . a blockhead! You've been in love with Aisling since—"

"Just drop it, okay? I saw the way you reacted when Enid's son was checking you out. Hell, I'm surprised the guy didn't start salivating. Want me to talk to him, tell him to back off?"

Erin shook her head. "Thanks, but I'll be okay. And you've got enough to deal with."

Con dropped into the big, overstuffed reading chair. "The offer to bust McDermott's chops stands. But you're right. Gramps is—"

A pillow from the bed flew across the room and landed on his head. "Not him, you cretin! Lady Moonlight and the Leprechaun."

He grabbed the pillow and scowled at her. "Wasn't it you who always said never date outside your own species?"

She flashed him a wicked grin, the familiar Erin again. "That was a hockey player. Horses are more highly evolved."

"McKeogh, *I hate horses*! The last thing I want to do is marry one."

At Erin's snort of laughter, he threw the pillow onto the bed and glared at her. "Anyway, if there's a nano-bit of truth in that story, it's pointless waiting for me to be a hero. That quaint little concept of *True Love* requires something called a heart. I have it on good authority that mine is made of stone."

Erin walked past him and opened the door to the hallway. Then she turned and met his eyes with the most sorrowful expression he'd ever seen in hers. It baffled him, but Erin seemed to be taking this enchantment thing more seriously than he'd thought.

"Most of the time, I believe you're wrong about having a heart of stone. But sometimes, Sloan, I'm afraid you really do." She shut the door quietly, but the click of the latch sounded like a shot in the silence around him.

Terrific. Erin had totally gone over to the lunatics' side.

He'd been staked out naked on a hillside, a sacrificial O'Hara. He felt like the kid who'd cried "Wolf!" Except he was crying about his heart. Before, he'd tried to fall in love, because no one wanted to believe his heart was an impenetrable rock. Now he didn't want to fall in love, but he couldn't convince anyone that he was the one who could get hurt.

Twenty

~~~~~

While he was unpacking, movement outside the windows caught his eye. He went closer to look out. In the garden below, Gramps was showing off his roses for Erin. Behind them, Phelan and Enid walked arm in arm, and Enid's lips were moving rapidly. Phelan was nodding occasionally to whatever his mother was chattering about, but Con could see the man's entire attention was focused on Erin. It was like watching one of those nature shows, with big cats pouncing on unaware gazelle-type creatures. Usually, he admired the cats' hunting prowess, their speed and agility, their stealth. This time, with Phelan stalking Erin, he was cheering for the gazelle.

The leather-bound book Gramps had sent him, the one that started him on this ridiculous quest, sat looking innocent on top of the gleaming old mahogany desk. Con picked it up and stared at the gilt lettering on the cover. *Inherent logic,* huh? Sure. And pigs wear pajamas. With a humorless laugh, he put the book back in his briefcase, peeled off his clothes, and took a shower. When he came out of the bathroom to get clean clothes, a thick towel around his hips and his toothbrush clamped between his teeth, the book was lying open in the middle of the bed.

Okay, so maybe he was too tired to remember where he'd put the damn thing. Grumbling around the stem of the toothbrush, Con shut the book with a loud slap, and latched

the briefcase after he'd tucked the book inside. As soon as
he was wearing clean jeans and shirt, he checked to see
that the others were still wandering around the gardens.
Then he went downstairs to root through the desk in the
library for the name and phone number of his grandfather's
doctor. With luck, he'd get the old guy referred to a shrink
right—

Con stared into the open desk drawer. That was impossible! He'd shut that damn book into his briefcase upstairs
not five minutes ago. No one else was in the house, and he
would have noticed himself carrying the thing around. How
the hell did it get in the desk?

"Must be more than one copy." Satisfied with that *logical* conclusion, he slid that drawer closed, then opened
another drawer. He found the disintegrating old address
book Gramps must have gotten sometime before the inven-
tion of the wheel, and went back up to his room to look
through it in private. Feeling more than a little foolish, he
couldn't resist glancing at the bed, but there was nothing
on it except the heavy white bedspread. His briefcase stood,
still latched shut, next to the desk. His notebook computer
lay alone in the center of the desktop. With a derisive snort
at his own lapse of logic, he pulled out the desk chair and
felt the universe tilt an extra degree.

The leather-bound, gilt-lettered book lay on the seat of
the chair.

A PALACE, THE FAERY WORLD, EVER-THE-PRESENT

Aunt Rainbow drifted into the corner of their shared parlor
where Aisling was critically examining the daisies she'd
just embroidered on a tiny linen baby dress. The dress was
a gift for one of the infant Faeries, although her finest
stitches, using gossamer silk and gold threads, looked
coarse beside the needlework of the Fey seamstresses.
Someday, she prayed, she would embroider her own babies' clothes, but *someday* seemed farther out of reach with
every passing day of her enchantment. She could not bring
herself to consider what sort of offspring a Mortal woman

and a Leprechaun might produce. To be sure, she'd never envisioned her own children being anything but human!

Hearing the faint chiming of bells, Aisling looked up, still frowning at her handiwork. Her aunt scattered a handful of fragrant rose petals over her, making her laugh when one landed on the tip of her nose. Gently, she blew it away, laughing again as it turned into a butterfly and flew up to perch prettily on the top of a lily-of-the-valley lamppost.

Aunt Rainbow gave her a saucy grin. "Magic would easily make your stitches ever so much finer."

Aisling set the dress and her embroidery frame down. Despite her laughter seconds before, she grew serious. "Perhaps, but magic is never free, is it? And seeking a magical solution is the cause of all my troubles, is it not?"

Her aunt's exquisite features became as solemn as a Faery's could. "Perhaps. And perhaps not. 'Tis true, there is always a price for accepting magic, but the cost is not always so dear as the one you've paid." A tiny frown line briefly marred Rainbow's perfect brow. "Methinks 'tis time you learned the truth behind the truth."

"You're speaking in riddles, Aunt." Riddles were a favorite Fey pastime, the more obscure, therefore more Mortal-confounding, the more highly praised. Aisling hated riddles almost as much as she hated Ambros O'Hara—and *all* of his descendants.

Sinking gracefully onto the velvet settee with Aisling, Aunt Rainbow patted her hand. "An abandoned web may catch an innocent butterfly long after the greedy old spider has gone."

"What's a spider doing in all this?" Aisling gave a little, involuntary shudder. "Aunt, why can't you be saying what you want me to know, instead of this riddling?" From a distance, sounds of Faery trumpets reached them. Aunt Rainbow glanced toward the entry of their quarters. 'Twould take little to distract her, and then Aisling would be left puzzling alone. "Aunt, please! 'Tis maddening, the riddling and obfuscating! What—?"

Raven's voice, calling for Rainbow, drifted melodiously to them, and Aisling knew she'd lost her aunt's attention.

What did Aunt Rainbow see in that swaggering Faery? To be sure, he was handsome enough to turn any female's head, Mortal or Fey. But his arrogance, his vanity, had turned his own head first, making him his own fondest admirer. Still, Aisling wished her aunt the happiness she feared she'd never find for herself, so she tried quieting her misgivings with the certainty that Rainbow always—at least till now—had been an excellent judge of character.

Raven appeared in the doorway. ''Rainbow, my love, the games are beginning.'' He bowed with irritating graciousness toward Aisling. ''Would you be accompanying us to the tournament?''

Certain he didn't mean the invitation, Aisling smiled and shook her head. ''Another time, perhaps.'' Then, as Rainbow darted toward the doorway to take Raven's arm, Aisling rose. ''Wait, Aunt! You've whetted my appetite with your riddles. Please—''

Rainbow's tinkling laughter rang delicately around them. '' 'Tis a mystery for you to solve, Niece. Your Sloan may help you, now that he's returned to his grandfather's house.''

The news of Conlan Sloan's return, so casually tossed at her, stunned Aisling. By the time she regained her sense and was chasing down the passages after her aunt, the swirling crowds of Faeries eager to watch the tournament turned her around until she grew dizzy. Sitting on a mushroom to catch her breath, she was startled to find Aunt Rainbow and Raven suddenly standing before her. Raven was scowling and trying to tug Rainbow toward the games, but Rainbow laughingly shook him off.

'' 'Tis true, Niece. My Wise friend's Wise granddaughter, Enid, sent me word only this day. Did you not see the white owl flying over the *rath*? 'Tis her magical shape. Your Sloan has become a prosperous but hard-hearted young man, and he holds the key to all your mysteries. 'Twould be wise to seek him at the next full-moon night, or even, perhaps, before, in the guise of Luna. The time of your enchantment is fast running out in the Mortal world. Ninety-nine years have passed. You've only one full moon after the Solstice, before Acorn Bittersweet claims you.''

Heart pounding, her breath rasping in her lungs, Aisling slid off the mushroom to face her aunt squarely. ''Never will I beg an O'Hara for help, or secrets to mysteries, or True Love!''

Sadness crossed Aunt Rainbow's lovely face. ''Ah, Niece, your Mortal pride will be causing your demise.''

''Come, sweet Rainbow.'' Raven tugged at her aunt's hand. '' 'Tis Mortal business. Let the Mortal make her Mortal decisions.''

For once, Aisling found herself agreeing with Raven. Her Mortal pride had gotten her into this dilemma. Her Mortal pride had complicated everything with her obstinate obsession over Sloan—truly, as her aunt had warned her, not the man she'd wanted him to be. And somehow, her Mortal pride would either be getting her out of her dilemma, or helping her accept her fate as the bride of Acorn Bittersweet. Having lost everything else in the Mortal world, her pride was indeed all she had remaining to call her own.

O'HARA HOUSE, COUNTY SLIGO, FRIDAY, MAY 28, 1999

After breaking the seal on his own bottle of Midleton's Very Rare Old Irish Whiskey and pouring some into the crystal glass on the tray, Con sat down to reread the book. This time, he took notes on the computer, determined to isolate anything that looked like a verifiable fact. Then, with increasing tension twisting inside him, he read the photocopied letter supposedly written by Aisling's father. It was such a private letter, like a diary entry, a confession intended for someone who could provide absolution. In a figurative way, Eamon Ahearn's pen had been dipped in his own blood. The man's guilt and shame were painful to witness, even from so far in the past. Almost a hundred years in the past, if the letter was legitimate.

Thinking about the age of the letter tightened the knot in his gut. If the letter was authentic, if the events were verifiable, did that mean the Aisling who'd crushed his heart fourteen years ago was the Lady Moonlight of the O'Hara Curse? That would make her over a hundred years old! In the story, the spell the Leprechaun cast preserved her youth all that time. He sure could attest to her being a young woman—and definitely *not* a horse!—when he'd—

Damn! His hand shook when he poured more whiskey, and when he raised the glass to drink. The whiskey seared its way through his insides, then sank through the ice in the pit of his stomach.

Con swallowed another sip, then turned back to considering the authenticity of the book and letter. It was all fairy tale nonsense. The stuff dreams, and nightmares, are made of. There was no such thing—it defied all the known laws, even all the suspected laws, of physics!—as magic. No such thing as a spell to turn a beautiful young girl into a white mare for one hundred years, a beautiful young girl who could only be rescued by True Love from certain death as the bride of a Leprechaun. No such things as Leprechauns and True Love, either.

If this was some elaborate scheme by a de Burgh descendant to get family land back, he'd be damned if he was going to let her finish grinding the remnants of his heart to dust. On the other hand, he wasn't a totally heartless bastard. If Aisling was in any *real* danger, he would do what he could to rescue her. Erin was right—magic aside, there was a kind of logic to all of this. Once he'd figured it out, he'd do whatever had to be done to convince Gramps and Enid he'd broken the O'Hara Curse. Then they could live happily ever after and leave him alone.

With his decisions made, Con set the book down on the desk and joined the others in the garden. Being outside in the warm sunshine, listening to the birds and smelling the fresh air, seeing the amazing range of greens and the profusion of colored flowers, he had to admit he did feel comfortable in Ireland. He felt the tension inside him starting to loosen—although that could just as easily have been the effects of two generous portions of Irish whiskey on top of jet lag, as the effects of the pastoral beauty. By the end of the evening, as they all headed toward their rooms, Con could even laugh when Erin handed him a book advising witches about how to contact Faeries.

The moon wasn't quite full, another two nights according to the calendar, but it was bright and high overhead when something woke Con. He went to the window and stared across the fields, but saw nothing but shadows and splashes of moonlight. Curiosity wouldn't let him get back to sleep. He dressed and snuck out the back door, like the gap of a decade and a half didn't exist.

As he trudged the familiar path, a distant dog barked a challenge. Another one barked an answer. Then, except for the rustling of night creatures—probably rodents trying to evade the white owl he'd seen circling overhead earlier—the fields were quiet. The fields were a little more overgrown beyond the first two enclosures. Gramps had sold off most of his horses, keeping only three older broodmares and his prized, but aging, stallion for breeding, plus two geriatric geldings for occasional riding. Con's mother was breeding the next generation of O'Hara horses at her farm in Napa Valley. The only horses *he* cared about were under the hood of his new black Ferrari.

By the time he'd reached the third wall, he was feeling colossally stupid. He closed the gate behind him, wincing at the way the clank of metal on metal rang in the open, moonlit fields. He didn't expect to find Aisling tonight, but he wondered if he'd see Luna. Granted, he'd never seen them together, but they couldn't be the same person . . . horse—whatever!

The snapping of a twig sounded like a shot in the quiet night. Adrenaline surged though his nerves, and Con froze halfway over the last stone wall. Warily, he surveyed the moonlit field where his figurative heart had broken fourteen years ago. Nothing and no one stirred. The silence continued to swell, like the resonance of a bell long finished ringing. Scanning the empty field, he almost expected to see the white mare clear the stone wall and gallop toward him. But hell, for that matter, he almost expected to find fragments of his heart, glittering in the moonlight, where they'd been scattered in the grass.

Swinging his legs over the top of the wall, he dropped into the last field, the site of his most painful lesson about love: The negatives far outweighed the positives. He'd tried to fall in love again. Lord knows, he'd tried, and he'd hurt several terrific women who deserved better. He'd rather live alone and lonely, than make another woman cry.

AN ENTRANCE TO THE FAERY REALM, EVER-THE-PRESENT

Aisling saw Sloan the instant he climbed over the stone wall of the paddock. As he dropped down to the ground, her heart dove into some cold pit deep inside her. So her aunt spoke the truth. Sloan had indeed returned to Ireland, and there he stood in the very field where he had seduced her with his lies of omission.

She stared at him as if the sharp edge of her glare could cut him down. The deceiving O'Hara! She hated him! 'Twould salve her pride to be seeing him fall to his knees, to be hearing him beg her for mercy! For what he'd done to her, she had no mercy for him. He'd renewed her dreams of True Love, and given her enough strength to endure and hope for deliverance from the Leprechaun's enchantment. Then, after he'd taken what he'd wanted, with one word— *O'Hara*—he'd crushed her dreams. Scalding tears welled suddenly in her eyes and spilled over.

Ignoring the tears coursing down her cheeks, Aisling stood as still as a tree, hidden by densely tangled vines and branches. Scarcely breathing, she watched as Sloan walked the inside perimeter of the field. There was still a vigor, a virility, about him, a masculine grace like that of a stallion in his prime. The breadth of his shoulders, the length and girth of his thighs, they spoke of his physical strength. Mortal time had been kind to him. Ah, but when she peered closer, the face of her seducer looked older, a little haggard, but still so . . . so deceptively handsome.

'Twas a fallacy that beauty outside reflected beauty inside.

Sloan stopped in the center of the field and turned his face up to the nearly full moon. Aisling gazed at him. With his arms crossed in front of his chest, she could plainly see his hands gripping his elbows. Such beautiful, strong hands . . . How gently they could touch her, how surely they could make her hunger for more than the touch of his hands. Memories of their lovemaking—what *she'd* thought was lovemaking—hovered, never far from the surface of her mind. Haunted, she was, by vivid images of his sweet kisses, the caresses of his hands, the heat of his body, the power of him thrusting into her, carrying her away with him.

Skilled at deception, he was! He had known she would never succumb to either roughness or sophistication. She'd willingly been seduced by his counterfeit awkwardness, his false innocence. Such tenderness, such pleasure he'd shown her! 'Twas no wonder she'd fancied herself in love with him. Damn him!

She closed her eyes against the sight of him, but the image of him stayed burned into her mind. Even after she'd learned the truth about him, she'd not been able to forget him. If she could not forget Sloan, she could never truly love anyone else. He'd ruined her heart—and her body!—for any other man, thus dooming her to a living death as Mortal wife of a Leprechaun.

When Aisling opened her eyes, Sloan had climbed the wall of the far paddock and begun walking toward the O'Hara manor house. Daringly, she moved away from her hiding place, watching him until she lost sight of his figure moving through the shadows beyond. Briefly, she weighed the temptation to reveal herself, to race after him before he disappeared into the house. Disguised as Luna to his eyes, she could have freely touched him, smelled him, felt his touch and heard his voice. He wouldn't have known 'twas she.

But her pride would know.

O'HARA HOUSE, CO. SLIGO, BEFORE DAWN, SUNDAY, MAY 30, 1999

In his dream, Aisling was whispering his name and shaking his shoulder. But then Con realized he wasn't really sleeping. He was hearing a voice calling him. Disoriented, he glanced at the lighted dial of the alarm clock: half-past three in the morning. As he tried to roll over, he realized the duvet was tangled under him. It didn't pull free after the first try. With a grunt of impatience, he tugged harder. The duvet gave suddenly and flipped over his head. Too tired to care, he closed his eyes.

" 'Tis an odd time, Conlan Ambros O'Hara Sloan, to be engaging in combat with your bedclothes."

The sound of a woman's voice sent him sitting bolt upright. His jaw dropped at the sight of a woman perched at the foot of his bed! A small, incredibly beautiful woman with silvery blond hair that flowed around her like a shawl and pale skin that gleamed in the dark dressed in some kind of white, gauzy dress. A woman he'd never seen before, but who apparently knew him.

"Wha—?" He snapped his jaw shut and rubbed his eyes, but she didn't disappear. Must be a very vivid dream

"Calm yourself, Conlan Sloan. I am the great-great-aunt of Aisling de Burgh Ahearn, called Remember-Fear-Not in the Fey world. My name is Rainbow-and-Silver-Lining, but you may call me Rainbow." She gave him a dazzling smile.

Con shook his head hard, but the beautiful woman stayed. "*You're* the aunt she lives with?"

"The very one." Then her smile faded, and she sighed. " 'Tis a paradox, Conlan Sloan. The O'Hara Curse dooms you to unhappy prosperity, until you break the spell on Aisling by loving her, as you're an O'Hara and cursed to be without love until you fall in love with Aisling." She tipped her head to the side and blinked at him. "My beloved niece will be forced to marry a Leprechaun at the full moon of your Mortal month July, if a descendant of

Ambros O'Hara does not declare his love, and prove his love, thrice before then.''

Another one! Didn't anyone in Ireland have anything better to do than torture him? Ignoring the reference to the Leprechaun, Con addressed the only important issue Rainbow had mentioned. ''Your *beloved niece* hates my guts because I'm an O'Hara.''

''Ah, but you love her''—he opened his mouth, but the woman lifted a silencing hand—''and if you lose her, you will never heal the aching in your heart.''

''Lady, the only heart I have is a lump of stone. Aisling broke the rest of it into little tiny pieces.''

'' 'Twas the shock of discovering herself in love with an O'Hara after all.'' At his snort of disbelief, the Rainbow woman shook her head. Her hair rippled, and the sound of tiny bells echoed around him. '' 'Tis myself I blame, for giving her riddles instead of the plain truth. But Aisling had so set her mind against any O'Hara, and wisdom is never best gained secondhand.'' She patted his leg through the down quilt. ''You must act swiftly, or all shall be lost. And my dear niece will suffer most of all.''

''This is such a crock!''

''Methinks your parents and your grandfather wish to be happy in their love.'' The look in her eyes told him she knew she'd scored a direct hit. ''Unless you break the spell on Aisling, they will never be so, together or apart.''

''My family is none of your business.'' A new thought occurred to him. ''How'd you get in here?''

Rainbow gave him another bright smile. ''Magic, of course!'' Then her smile faded. She held out her small hand, three stones balanced on her palm. Two of them looked like fat, dark crystals. The third was flatter, shaped like a cross. ''Take these.''

Without thinking, he did as she said. The woman placed the stones on his palm, then closed his fingers around them and tapped his knuckles three times, gently, with her fingertip.

''Keep these always with you, on your person, the way you keep the golden horseshoe nail. Should Acorn Bittersweet trick you into our world, they will aid your safe return from Under-Hill. The ruby will increase your strength, protect you from injuries, and help you resist negative magic. The amethyst will lend you courage, sharpen your senses, heal you, and guide you back to your own world. And the Faery cross will give you luck, and power over elemental forces.''

No point in dignifying that nonsense with an argument. He narrowed his eyes at her. ''How do you know about the gold nail?''

''Did you not read the book your grandfather sent? 'Twas all explained in there.'' Her tone made him feel like a little kid who hadn't done his homework. ''The horseshoes and nails are Faery gold, which always returns to its owner. You were to have taken the nail away with you after your first visit, a seemingly innocent souvenir, but you lost it between floorboards of this room. 'Twas Aisling herself who sent two helpers to tuck the nail into your traveling case last visit, where you would find it.''

Con opened his mouth to tell this Rainbow nutcase to buzz off. She lifted her finger in the air, and his voice stuck in his throat. Startled, he shut his jaw.

''Heed me, Mortal.'' Now the woman looked as serious as her tone. ''You must tell Aisling the truth Eamon revealed about the fire that destroyed the de Burgh great house, so she can make amends to The People. Before the spells can be broken, twice more must you tell her, and show her, that you love her.''

Con tried to tell this lunatic he didn't love Aisling, but his voice still didn't work. Furiously, he shook his head. She gave him another one of those serious looks. '' 'Tis no prank, Mortal. If you fail, Aisling will die. Only you can save her.''

Then, with a puff of light and sparkles—Faery dust?— she disappeared, right in front of his eyes. A moment later, Con woke up with a start. He laughed to find himself sitting up. That would teach him to read fairy tales before bedtime! Chuckling softly, he lay down and pulled the cover up.

It was after eight the next morning when he opened his

eyes again. The spring sun filtered through the lace curtains. The shaft of light illuminated millions of particles of dust floating on air currents. Well, there was his Faery dust! To his immense relief, there were no stones—magic or otherwise—in his bed.

After breakfast, Con invited Erin to drive with him to Sligo Town, and check out the public records for information about the de Burgh and Ahearn families. Telling Mrs. Penny they'd be back for lunch, he stuck his hand into the back pocket of his jeans for the key to the rental car. An odd feeling settled in his gut as he closed his fingers around several objects crammed in with his key. Standing beside the car in the bright morning sunlight, he withdrew his hand and opened his fingers. On his open palm lay a roughly cut ruby-colored stone a little larger than a shirt button, an amethyst the size of a grape, carved in the shape of a heart, and a thumb-size, dull brownish stone shaped like an equilateral cross.

Before Erin could see his handful of talismans, he jammed them back into his pocket. He tried to ignore them, but they seemed to get bigger and sharper as the day went on. By the time the sun was setting and the full moon was rising, late that evening, Con was convinced he had a back pocket full of boulders. When he took the stones out again, he was surprised to see that they looked exactly the same as they had that morning.

But something *was* different. With Erin's help, he'd verified enough of the facts about the de Burghs, Eamon Ahearn, and his daughter Aisling, who had disappeared the night of her planned betrothal to Ambros O'Hara II, back on July 22 of 1899. He'd even found an archival recording of an itinerant storyteller who'd recited the legend of Lady Moonlight into the tape recorder of a cultural anthropologist.

He still wasn't ready to *believe* . . . but he was ready to open his mind to alternate explanations under the full moon that night.

Twenty-one

~

"Ah! Here you are, Niece!"

At the sound of tiny bells and her aunt's musical voice, Aisling reluctantly looked up from her latest *borrowed* book. 'Twas an engrossing, modern romantic tale about a handsome ghost in love with his lady barrister—*attorney*, they said in America. Delightful as her aunt's company was, discovering how the ghost and his True Love might be reunited was claiming her attention.

Rainbow swooped down and dropped a quick kiss on Aisling's brow, then danced gracefully across the leafy floor, humming a spritely tune. Watching the lovely Faery, Aisling reflected that she was truly well named, for her Fey aunt had been like a rainbow, a silver lining, in the horribly dark, foreboding clouds of this century-long enchantment. Truly, if not for the spell cast on her and Luna, she might never have known her aunt.

"Know you, Niece, the moon is full tonight?" Reading between the lines, Aisling merely shrugged in answer, then lowered her eyes from the too-perceptive purple gaze fixed on her. "Hear me, Remember-Fear-Not: There remain but two full-moon nights before your marriage to Acorn Bittersweet. 'Twould be a shame to miss your last hours in the world, simply to avoid Conlan Sloan."

So little time? A cold wave of fear and dismay washed through her. How would she find another One True Love with so little time standing between herself and death? 'Twas impossible! And 'twas all the fault of Conlan *O'Hara* Sloan!

To hide her fear, Aisling set her features into a hard mask of defiance. "I shall die before I marry Acorn Bittersweet."

But Rainbow didn't even glance at Aisling, as she twirled about the room in her graceful dance. "Truly spoken, Niece! Die you shall, and most unpleasantly. Did you think to remain as your Mortal self after the Leprechaun claims you?"

Her aunt's silvery laughter rang cruelly in Aisling's ears. Shocked, she leaped to her feet and grasped Rainbow's hands, forcing the spinning Faery to halt and face her. Her voice came out shrill and brittle. "I do not mean to die to *become* the bride of that grotesque creature! I mean to die so that I may not!"

Rainbow gave her a dazzling smile. "Then you will not care that Conlan Sloan stays here with a lovely young Irishwoman from America. He met her at university, and is exceedingly fond of her. Each is a perfect match for the other, so I have heard; she knows all about the computers, and cares little for horses."

A rush of heat and a roaring in her ears forced Aisling to release her aunt's hands and sink to the soft floor. Darkness closed in around her and her stomach twisted into a writhing knot of pain. Oh, God! This could not be true! Sloan and another woman . . . ? Aisling buried her face in her hands. A *university educated* woman who knew about the computers Sloan spoke of with such . . . reverence? The way *she* might speak of horses? This could not be true! Oh, this *must not be true*!

"Perhaps you are wise not to venture into the Mortal world tonight. Sloan surely will be showing off the magic of an Irish full moon to his American woman." The Faery ran a gentle hand over Aisling's hair, but the words her aunt spoke came at her like poisoned darts. "I cannot offer you company tonight, as I shall be joining Raven at a *feis*."

Rainbow, more than two centuries old, gave a girlish giggle. "Can you imagine, black-eyed, black-hearted Raven plays pipes like an angel?"

And then, with a quick pat on Aisling's head, Rainbow hurried away. Aisling sat unmoving, her head still bowed into her hands, her eyes burning with unshed tears, her heart leaden. Gradually, she became aware of the relative silence settling around her as the Moonstone Circle Faeries left their Under-Hill palace to attend their full-moon festivities. When Aisling lifted her head, she discovered she was quite, quite alone.

O'HARA HOUSE, CO. SLIGO, SUNDAY EVENING, MAY 30, 1999

It was a strange experience to be crossing the moonlit fields toward the far paddock without having to sneak out after midnight. The assembled guests at O'Hara House had tried to throw him out at nine P.M. Now just before half-past ten, as Con vaulted over a stone wall, he wondered if his grandfather was watching him through binoculars. He wondered, as he strode across the next enclosed field, if Erin was sneaking around with her video camera. Or if Phelan was sneaking around Erin while her erstwhile protector was off skulking around for some phantom female, horse or human. Con was tempted to call her brother Nolan to join them, so he wouldn't have to divide his attention.

That Lady Moonlight story was such a load of . . . of what he almost stepped in. Muttering at everyone else's gullibility, and his own obliging stupidity, he made his way to the far paddock. As he scaled the last wall, he paused to look at the sky. Against the endless blackness, the full moon, with a rainbow-tinged haze shimmering around it, loomed huge and brilliant, almost blinding. Con had to blink several times to clear his vision.

Coming over the top of the wall, he blinked several more times to see past the afterimage of the bright moon. When he did manage to focus, he saw a figure, pale and radiant in the moonlight, standing in the middle of the paddock.

His feet hit the ground, and then his knees buckled, his heart pounded, his lungs shut down. *Aisling!*

For a long moment, he stood and stared, searching for every familiar detail, for any new ones. She hadn't changed at all. She wore that same old-fashioned long dress, the one his research had determined was similar to local styles of the 1890s. Her long, silky hair cascaded around her like a golden shawl, reflecting moonbeams, sparkling with light when the breeze ruffled the strands. Almost expecting her to disappear, he took a careful step, then several more, toward her. He halted about five feet away and let his eyes feast on the beauty in front of them.

The moon shone on an exquisite face, on skin as perfect as fine porcelain. If she bore any signs of age, the only proof was in the luminous sadness of her eyes. If she had any magic, the proof was in his reactions: shaking, tongue-tied. He fought a raging urge to run to her and hold her in his arms.

The tension made him say the first thing that came into his head, lame as it was. "How have you been?"

She stared back at him for a few endless seconds. He saw her swallow before she answered, "Well enough, thank you. And yourself?" The stilted tone of her words couldn't dull the sweetly musical lilt of her voice.

This was going nowhere. He shrugged. "I'm doing okay."

Aisling tipped her head to the side, studying him. "You've been successful with your computers?" He nodded. "I'm pleased for you, then. 'Twas good seeing you." Without warning, she bowed her head and turned away. He thought he saw her shoulders shaking.

"Aisling?" When she failed to react, he stepped toward her and repeated her name gently. Now that he was close enought to touch her, he could hear the soft catches in her breathing, and see that her whole body was quivering. Guilt, and a tidal wave of protective instincts, flooded through him.

"Please don't cry. I'm really not worth it."

"I know."

The choked sound of her soft voice canceled his amusement at the speed of her agreement. He took another small step, closing more of the remaining distance between them. If Aisling, her head still turned away from him, noticed, she gave no hint.

" 'Tis not the first foolish thing I've done. 'Tis certain not to be the last.'' She spoke into the night, but the pain in her soft voice reached him. Her self-reproach caused his breath to hitch.

"I never meant to hurt you. I still don't understand what went wrong.'' But he wanted to, needed to, understand, if only to set this all behind him and get on with his life. "Can we sit and talk awhile?'' He shook out the blanket he'd carried over his shoulder. "I promise not to smother any of The People this time.''

Aisling turned toward him, her pale face streaked with tears, her eyes glistening with them, her full, soft lips quivering. She seemed to be trying to smile, but not succeeding. Wordlessly, she held his gaze, and he caught a glimpse of how hard she'd tried not to love him, how painful the failure had been. Or maybe he was reading his own feelings in her eyes.

Whatever was happening, he knew he was in trouble. No matter that he'd tried to avoid this moment, Con felt something cold and hard and invulnerable deep inside him start to warm, to soften, to open to her. Dropping the blanket, he reached for her. He was making a colossal, potentially painful, mistake, but it was too late. And when he looked inside himself, he discovered that strangely enough, he didn't care.

When his hands closed around her upper arms, she felt so fragile, he was almost afraid to draw her to him. Moving carefully, respecting the resistance her pride needed to make, he brought her closer. A light breeze ruffled her hair and lifted the sweet scent of her skin to him. Closer still, and the layers of her skirt swirled around and between his legs. Close enough now to slide his arms around her back and gently engulf her, gently bring her against his chest.

Her hands, touching him lightly, slid up and around his

neck. A hesitation, a sigh, and she swayed closer. Her breasts brushed his ribs, her body trembling under his hands, then softly, warmly she nestled herself against him. The heat flaring in his loins wrenched the air from his lungs. At the harsh sound of his indrawn breath, Aisling started, then relaxed into him.

The sight of Aisling's silent tears had started a thawing process deep within him. Now the sensation that his cold stone of a heart was melting accelerated with sudden and painful speed. The inexplicable but undeniable *rightness,* which holding Aisling had always given him, now sent another wave of stinging heat through him. God, he'd never understood that healing could *hurt*!

Shivering and flushing hot at the same time, Con gently cupped Aisling's head and pressed her to his heart. He felt a warm, wet patch spreading on his shirt—her tears. She was shaking against him, sobbing soundlessly. Her arms tightened around his neck, and that frozen, dark, chambered part inside of him cracked with a searing, wrenching pain. His breath shuddered in his lungs, and hot tears filled his eyes and spilled down his cheeks to fall onto Aisling's golden hair.

If he didn't sit down, his knees were going to buckle.

Wracked by deep, silent sobs, Aisling could only cling to Sloan and let herself follow him down to the blanket rumpled on the ground near their feet. He cradled her against him as gently as he might a feverish infant, and despite her self-loathing, she could not bring herself to resist. Instead, she burrowed closer, breathing in the scent of him, absorbing the warmth of him, hearing his heart pounding a frantic rhythm inside his ribs. The press of his body felt so achingly, wonderfully familiar.

Lying in his arms, Aisling tried to summon the anger, the pain, that had lodged in her heart for nearly a century, but the hot splash on her neck of one tear from Sloan washed them away. All that remained was love . . . and fear.

Intending simply to look into his face, to memorize his features for her uncertain future, Aisling wiggled so that she could tip her head back. Tears glistened in his eyes, shining silver in the moonlight. She caught her lower lip between her teeth to keep it from quivering and steadfastly held his gaze until he closed his eyes, shutting her out. How cruelly fate had conspired against her, to taunt her by letting her find Sloan again just in time to lose him. Once, he had claimed to love her, but if he did not love her, then perhaps fate was more kind than cruel. And surely, he could not love her, for he had stayed away so long, returning to bring another woman to his ancestral home.

Thinking of that other woman, Aisling found the strength to struggle against the gentle prison of Sloan's embrace. She expected the tightening of his arms, holding her against him, but she didn't expect the anguish she saw in his eyes when he looked into hers again. Transfixed, she ceased her attempts to escape and lay quietly, listening to his breathing, watching his face, wishing she could read his thoughts.

Without warning, Sloan lowered his head and crushed her mouth under his, trapping her indrawn breath in her lungs. His kiss was more fierce possessing than caressing, but the fear she expected to feel never arose. Instead, like a spark meeting dry tinder, her own passion ignited. Heat roared up within her, wringing a muffled cry from her throat. Aisling tightened her arms around his neck and let her lips part at the first touch of his hot, wet tongue.

As suddenly as he'd begun the kiss, Sloan broke away. Torn between protesting his kissing her, and protesting his stopping, Aisling held herself rigid, waiting for him to be making the next move. Instead of pushing her away, as she expected, he cupped her head in one hand, gently pressing her face to his chest. Warily letting her resistance soften in his embrace, she realized his entire body was trembling.

"Sloan?"

She felt and heard him swallow, heard him draw a deep breath, felt him press a kiss to her head. "Sorry. I didn't mean to do that."

Resigned as she was to the knowledge that he did not love her, his words still surprised her with their ability to wound. " 'Tis no matter." The huskiness in her voice betrayed her denial, so she hurried to distract him. "We have a little time, if you'd care to be telling me what you've done since you were last in Ireland."

Con heard the wistfulness in her sweet voice and wanted to kick himself for hurting her again. He really had a way with words. "Yeah, I'd like that. Mind if we just lie here like this for a while?" She stiffened a tiny bit. "If you're comfortable."

After a pause, she nodded against his chest. "Talking like this would be fine." ·

Instead of talking about himself, however, Con decided to confront the unresolved issue between them. "Your Aunt Rainbow snuck into my room about three o'clock this morning." Aisling burrowed even closer, as if she were trying to hide, and she muttered something he couldn't hear. "What did you say?"

"I said, 'tis no wonder she knew you were not here alone!" A second later, he heard her yelp *"Oh, Aisling, you fool!"* and burrow even farther under his chin.

His grin made it hard to sound annoyed. "It's none of her business, but I was definitely alone in bed."

After a long silence, he figured Aisling wasn't going to respond. It was tempting to torture her a little, see how jealous she could be. But he'd hurt her too much already to deliberately feed his ego at her expense.

"Rainbow obviously made the wrong assumption about Erin."

Aisling mumbled something again. This time, Con poked her ribs. She jolted against him, sending a new rush of heated blood to his loins, then said tartly, "If Erin is a flame-haired, green-eyed Irish beauty who understands your computers and shares your disinterest in horses, 'tis she my aunt mentioned."

"Yeah, that's Erin McKeogh." The sudden tightening in Aisling's body made him want to reassure her. "We met at a party about twelve years ago. By the end of the evening, my date and hers had left together, and we were getting ready to draw up a partnership agreement." Carefully, he rubbed at Aisling's tense shoulders until she relaxed a little. "Erin has always been like a sister, never a girl-friend," he told her gently. "We nearly went broke to-gether, and we just closed a multimillion-dollar deal together, but we've never been lovers. She's my best friend, the only friend I've ever told about you. Okay?"

After a brief hesitation, Aisling nodded against his chest. "I hope Aunt Rainbow did not say anything embarrassing to you. She can be terribly forthright, but she means well."

Reaching down, he cupped her chin and angled away so he could look into her eyes. "She told me I better get my butt in gear to save you from Walnut Butterscotch."

Aisling's luminous eyes went wide, and she inhaled sharply. A giggle sputtered from her. Seconds later, she was shrieking with laughter. Curling herself into a fetal position, she pressed against him and howled. It was the first time he'd heard her laugh like that. The slowly thawing part of him warmed another couple of degrees. To his surprise, it no longer hurt so much.

"Oh, Sloan!" She giggled again, then drew several shaky breaths. "The Leprechaun's name is Acorn Bitter-sweet!"

"Whatever. I got the idea that time's running out for you." Gazing up at him again, her expression now com-pletely serious, she nodded. "Aisling, I've got to be honest with you, I still don't believe in magic and Faeries and spells and Leprechauns. But I've done some investigating, and there are some things that I'm not sure I can explain any other way."

She wiggled out of his arms and sat up, leaving him feeling cold without the pressure of her body against his. He pushed himself up to sit beside her. "What kinds of things, Sloan?"

"Gramps sent me a book about Lady Moonlight and the O'Hara Curse." The eager catch in her breath made him feel guilty for not believing her, and defensive for the same reason. "You know the story?" Wide-eyed, she nodded. "Erin and I checked on names and dates, and the people in the story existed, but—"

"Do you doubt I exist?" Eyes flashing, she thumped him in the chest with her small fist.

He grabbed her hand and drew it to his lips. Her skin was warm, soft, and smelled like flowers. "No, I don't doubt you exist. But I'm having a little trouble getting my mind around the idea that you're a hundred and sixteen years old."

She gave a quick laugh and shook her head. "Doesn't the book explain that I'm only to age one month for every Mortal year of the spell? 'Twill make me something over four and twenty years of age, if . . ." Her voice trailed off, and she turned her face away.

Con brushed his lips over her knuckles again. "Rainbow told me you need to know the truth about the fire that destroyed the de Burgh great house. I used to wonder about that, but no one would tell me. The records of the day— that would be 1882—say the fire started in the barn, then spread to the house while the horses were being rescued."

"That much, I do know." Aisling turned glistening eyes to him. "Acorn Bittersweet rescued the horses, hoping to impress Fiona, but Eamon Ahearn impressed her more by saving her life."

Even if Eamon Ahearn were a distant ancestor, not Aisling's father, this was the part of the story that would cause her the most anguish. Wishing he could do more to comfort her, Con slid his arm around her and pulled her close. "Aisling, along with a book about . . . about this stuff, Gramps sent a copy of a letter written by Eamon Ahearn in December, 1899. The Ambros O'Hara who was engaged to Eamon's daughter hid it in the wine cellar. I don't know how many years later, my mother hid the book down there, too. Gramps found them when he was rearranging old wines. The letter . . ." He paused for the right words.

Sloan's reluctance to tell her what Da had written sent a shiver of foreboding along Aisling's spine. When he pressed his lips to her hand again, she uncurled her fingers and spread them on his smooth, warm cheek, and waited silently for him to speak.

"Aisling, I want to soften this for you, but I don't know

how. Whether he's your father or your great-great-grandfather, Eamon's letter tells an ugly story.'' Sloan took a slow breath before going on. She could feel the pain in him, pain he felt for her, and the ache in her heart grew stronger.

''Eamon set the fire in the barn, intending to impress Fiona's father by saving the horses. De Burgh caught him, and they fought. A spark . . . ignited the man's clothes. The flames spread when he . . . when he ran to the house . . . for help.''

Aisling pressed her free hand to her mouth to hold back the moan threatening to escape. Only the solid feel of Con's chest kept her calm enough to continue listening.

''Eamon wrote that he tried to help, but de Burgh had some kind of seizure. Probably a heart attack. While Eamon was trying to revive him, the fire got out of control. De Burgh's wife and her mother were killed by the smoke. Eamon rescued Fiona, then lost her less than a year later. He confessed that he was jealous of anyone else doing anything for her that he couldn't do, so he refused to bring in a midwife for her labor. After his own daughter disappeared, he couldn't handle the guilt. According to public records, he died in December of 1899.''

'' 'Twas by his own hand, was it not?'' Sloan's silence was answer enough. Aisling sighed. '' 'Tis no wonder he drank.''

Sloan's arms tightened around her, lending her strength. His lips brushed her temple. ''There's more, but it can wait.''

''Tell me the rest, Sloan. I've little time left for waiting.''

''Here's where your Faeries come in. The de Burgh family used to leave cake and milk outside for them. Eamon got mad at Fiona for doing it when they had so little, and he liked to place the occasional bet. So he chopped down the hawthorn bush Fiona's grandmother used to say was sacred to the Faeries on de Burgh land. From then on, Eamon couldn't control his urge to gamble.''

'' 'Tis where the O'Haras come into the story.'' Speaking softly, Aisling related what her aunt had told her about how the O'Haras bought her father's gambling debts and tried to force her to marry Ambros the Second. "I spoiled their plans by running away," she concluded, "but foolishly accepted the Leprechaun's offer of magical assistance. He saw his opportunity for getting revenge against Da and seized it. In doing so, he acquired a sacred white mare of mixed Mortal and Fey bloodlines, and a future bride of Fiona's mixed Fey blood as well."

Con tightened his arms around her. Inhaling the delicate fragrance of her skin, he touched his lips to her forehead. This was the part of the story that stretched his credulity the farthest. The strange thing was, he wanted Aisling to somehow convince him that the legends of Lady Moonlight and of the Ambros O'Hara Curse were more than folktales.

"Okay, let's back up a bit. You ran away. Why do you blame my family for anything that happened as a result?"

At his question, she lowered the hand that had been lying against his face and the kiss of a breeze chilled his skin. "I ran away from being bought like a broodmare. I had a legal right to my legacy, and a legal right to accept or decline an offer of marriage." She spoke quietly, but anger and hurt vibrated in her voice.

"Couldn't you go to the police, or a lawyer or someone like that?"

"I knew no one, and Da never let me out of his sight. There I was at sixteen, too oddly raised, too ill-educated, and too poor to belong in my mother's society, and too well-born to belong anywhere else. Marrying into a prosperous and landed old family like the O'Haras was no doubt a prudent solution to my predicament, but I'd always dreamed of marrying for True Love. I'd never even met Ambros the younger, not since I was a tiny girl, until he arrived to claim me."

A shudder ran through her small frame, and he held her close until she calmed. Remembering what it was like to be a sixteen-year-old misfit, Con stroked her hair and frowned. The sixteen-year-old girls he could recall had been pretty sophisticated compared to Aisling, but he couldn't imagine any of them being ready to marry anyone. Or letting themselves be forced into it.

Aisling pressed her head against his hand like a cat. The trust implied in her gesture touched him in the vulnerable core of his heart. "He frightened me, Con. He was so rough when he grabbed at me." Her softly spoken words pierced his heart. "I feared he would hurt me. At first, all I was thinking of was getting away from him. Later, I thought that if I must marry Ambros to save Da, myself, and Luna, my running away might convince him to court me awhile. Perhaps, I thought, in time we would fall in love. Then I heard Ambros telling Da he did not believe in marrying for love."

The knowledge that, if her story was true, Aisling had clung to her belief in True Love for a century, shook Con's certainty that the concept was a delusion. Someone with so much steadfast faith would probably be able to love unfathomably deep, and infinitely long. It shook him to realize he envied that in her.

"Ambros the Second had a wife he loved very much, according to family diaries. After she and their son died in childbirth, he decided to marry for property and progeny."

"Ah, that poor man! If only I'd known something of his loss, I might have persuaded Da to let us be working out our own feelings in our own time."

Her compassion humbled him. "They didn't really give you a chance, did they?"

Aisling's deep sigh pressed her breasts closer to his ribs. A sudden surge of heat prompted him to tighten his arms, holding her there. One of her fingers traced the edge of his shirt collar and Con could swear she'd created sparks.

"I wonder if Ambros O'Hara, the First and the Second, thought a judge might rule against them and Da for cheating me of my inheritance. Perhaps they considered my marrying into the O'Hara family was recompense for their stealing."

Aisling's unflattering opinion of his ancestors gave Con a brief moment of ironic amusement. "Okay, most of these facts can be proven by diaries, public documents, that sort of thing. Where I'm really having trouble suspending my disbelief is the Leprechaun and the Faeries, and all the magic spells.'' He felt her stiffen against him and went on before she could interrupt. ''Anyway, for the sake of argument, let's say I believe these things are possible. Maybe I'm dense, but I don't get the logic behind a curse on the O'Haras.''

'' 'Twas Aunt Rainbow's brilliant scheme to preserve my legacy for me. But 'tis no matter. Unless I find True Love with a descendant of Ambros O'Hara within two full moons, I am doomed.''

To Aisling's chagrin, a laugh rumbled through Sloan's chest, shaking her from her very comfortable position in his arms. She pushed against him, but he restrained her, still chuckling. ''You must have a heart of stone and ice to laugh at me, Conlan Sloan! In barely two months' time, Acorn Bittersweet shall be claiming my immortal soul, and condemning me to a living death.''

''I'm sorry. Honest. You know, I almost believe you. But even if this whole legend is true, we still have the paradox your aunt explained to me. How can a lowly O'Hara of the Ambros line fall in love with anyone, let alone with a woman who hates his guts?''

There was a softening in Sloan's voice, almost as if he were asking her for a solution. For the first time in longer than she could say, hope soared within her heart.

'' 'Tis indeed a paradox.'' Her pulse skipped and raced as she dared to tip her head up under his chin. ''But if that woman did not truly hate this lowly O'Hara . . . ?''

''Hmm. Are we changing one of the variables? Because that would definitely change the results.'' His tone was light and teasing, but she felt the seriousness under his words.

A trembling began deep inside Aisling. She had to clutch the edge of Sloan's shirt to keep her hand from shaking. ''And if we change another of these *variables*? If this lowly O'Hara was to be finding a tiny corner of his heart where horses are welcome . . . ?''

Sloan's laugh rang out on the night air. He began rocking her as he continued laughing, making her cling to him to keep from tumbling over. There was a warmth to his laughter that, for once, did not make her feel foolish. The sound of it brought a smile to her lips, and caused her to lower her guard. With no warning, Aisling found herself again lying in Sloan's arms. She'd only time to be noticing his laughter had stopped before his lips were covering hers. And then, that was all she was noticing for a timeless moment.

Con broke the kiss and lifted his head to gaze down at the woman in his arms. Moonlight gilded her skin with a pearly glow. Her eyes shone like the sky. Her lips curved into a tentative smile that widened when he grinned down at her. He didn't know where this was all going, where it would—could—end, but right now, he felt more human, more alive, more *connected* than he had since Aisling had run away after they'd made love.

''You're incorrigible,'' he told her, dropping nipping kisses along her jawline. ''But . . . I can take a hint. Does Luna like sugar or carrots?''

A laugh of pure delight burst from Aisling's heart to her lips. ''Luna prefers kisses to either.''

Sloan's answering snort of laughter shook another laugh from her. ''The real Luna will have to wait for an appropriate guy horse for that. A very wise friend of mine once advised me never to date outside my own species.'' He kissed her softly, his laughter gone. ''Let me show you why.''

Twenty-two

Just before the sun peeked over the horizon, Aisling hurried along the glittering passageway toward the Moonstone Circle's great hall. Night after night, since the full moon of May, she had slipped away from the others, spending the hours between dark and dawn at Sloan's side. 'Twas terribly frustrating to be trapped in Luna's form, yet deliciously tantalizing to have the mare's heightened senses. The delights of listening to Sloan's voice, breathing in his scent, tasting his skin and feeling his caressing hands roaming over her, all were magnified.

Each time they parted, she felt the yearning within her growing stronger, and her impatience twisting more wildly toward thoughts of their next meeting. The old moon had waned and the new one had begun waxing, marking the passing of the days until the next full moon, when she would be meeting Sloan as herself once more. And on that night, soon after the summer solstice, on that night they would be lovers again, she was sure. She'd been willing— and Sloan had been ready!—at the last full moon, but he had not done more than hold her and kiss her until her head had been spinning and her senses reeling. Even now, her skin tingled from the stroking of his hands on Luna's coat.

"Are ye so pleased, then, to be seeing yer intended return?"

The sound of Acorn Bittersweet's reedy voice startled her to an abrupt halt. With her heart leaping wildly against her ribs, she scanned the passageway but saw no one. A rusty cackle of laughter behind her sent her spinning around, and there he stood. He looked no older for the past century, for Leprechauns lived at least ten hundred years, doing most of their aging in their earliest decades. He looked no better for the past century, too, Aisling thought as she stared at his grotesquely grinning face.

"*You* have never been *my* intended, Mr. Bittersweet." His amber eyes narrowed, but before he could reply, Aisling gave him a polite nod. "If you'll excuse me, I must be joining my aunt."

A sputter of Fey invective echoed behind her as she rushed along the passageway, including several variants of the phrase *meddlesome Bahn Sidhe* directed at Aunt Rainbow. "I shan't lose another bride, I shan't!" he shouted as she neared the end of the magical tunnel.

O'HARA HOUSE, CO. SLIGO, SUNDAY, JUNE 20, 1999

"If you two are going to be acting like two wet cats in a sack, you can take yourselves outside!"

At the outburst from Gramps, Con looked up from the chessboard. His grandfather, his mother, and his father marched into the library, each one of them scowling and glaring. Enid trailed after them, carrying a tray with cups for after-dinner coffee. Suddenly, his knight's next move didn't seem nearly as interesting or entertaining as the dynamics of another O'Hara family evening.

" 'Tis all your own fault!" Corliss dropped into a fat chair near the hearth and glowered at Gramps. " 'Tis your fault for deceiving Jonathan and myself, and Conlan, too, into coming all the way over here for your foolishness! Now you can reap what you've sown."

A tiny sound escaped from Erin, but Con didn't dare look at her or he'd be on the floor laughing, and it really wasn't very funny. Gramps had fed Corliss and Jonathan some bizarre stories to manipulate them, not letting either one know the other was about to arrive. His parents had taken one look at him, one look at Gramps, then stalked away in separate directions. Today, two days after their arrival, their silence was giving way to verbal sniping. Gramps kept needling them. Enid couldn't get the old boy to back off. No one could get Corliss and Jonathan to be civil.

It was just like old times, before the divorce, Con reflected, only now they had almost eighteen years of new ammunition to hurl at each other. After the rest of the assembled family and guests had spent the day dodging verbal shrapnel, his lingering nostalgia for the way things used to be had withered away. He understood what Gramps was trying to do, but he seriously questioned the wisdom of it.

After thanking Enid for a cup of rich filtered coffee, Con wandered toward the windows to evade the squabbling. In the irregularities of the old sheets of glass, he watched the reflection of the others. The distorted image of Phelan McDermott, who had turned up every evening for dinner, looked menacing as he moved toward Erin. McKeogh wasn't saying anything, but even a guy as socially dyslexic as he was could see McDermott was stalking her. As long as nothing bad happened to Erin, he'd have welcomed an excuse to clean McDermott's clock on behalf of her absent brother, Nolan.

"C'mon, you guys, act your ages." He spoke up after his mother had taken another shot at his father, and Gramps had threatened to horsewhip both of them. "You're making things really unpleasant for everyone else. Some of us are here on vacation." Erin faked a sneeze to cover her laugh. Con turned in time to see Phelan McDermott wiping a grin off his face. It took extra effort for Con to control his impulse to grin back.

"Corliss, dear, have your tea. I've made something special for you." Enid carried a cup and saucer across the room and smiled when Corliss obediently drank. "Jonathan? Coffee or tea?"

"Coffee, please, Enid." Jonathan took the cup she offered, then turned to face Gramps. "That old stallion of yours is in good shape, Ambros. He's over twenty-five now, isn't he?"

"Closer to thirty, isn't he, Da?" Corliss spoke gently, more than civil. She took a sip of her tea, but when no one spoke, she added, "Wonderfully sound, and he's thrown some lovely foals."

The surprise on Jonathan's face, when Con met his father's eyes, almost destroyed his control over the laughter trying to erupt. He shrugged. Horses always were the common bond for them.

"Speaking of offspring," Gramps said, "that son of yours is one to make a parent—or a grandparent—proud." Con's coffee slid down his throat wrong, choking him. "Didn't think I'd ever see the day when I'd say that about an O'Hara who wasn't in the horse breeding business." Con gaped. Gramps heaved a sigh. "But then, I didn't think I'd ever see the day when there was an O'Hara who wasn't." Then Gramps met Con's eyes and winked. "Be a terrible shame if he's the last of our line."

Corliss set her cup down with a loud clank. "Da, what on earth are you saying? There's nothing wrong with Conlan . . . Is there?" Jonathan set his own cup down and moved to sit on the arm of Corliss's chair. She reached up, he took her hand, and they both turned their eyes to Con.

"Nothing the right girl can't fix," Gramps announced.

Con stood up. If he didn't leave now, he was going to do or say something he'd be sorry for later. "Okay, that's enough. I'm outta here." Setting down his coffee, he started toward the door.

"Would you be saying hello to that little white mare from me, Conlan? I saw her once, when I was a child, but my mother talked me out of believing my own eyes."

Gramps's voice stopped him in his tracks. For a full count of ten, with the library vibrating in tense silence behind him, he stared at the door. Several replies came to his mind, but he rejected them all, and finally just wrenched the door open and walked out. He didn't stop walking until he'd let himself drop down over the last stone wall into the far paddock. Then, while the quarter moon sank toward the western horizon, he waited for Luna.

He was still waiting—alone—when the sun rose a little before five the next morning.

A PALACE, THE FAERY REALM, EVER-THE-PRESENT

Aisling was almost at the passageway to the Mortal world, to keep her rendezvous with Sloan, when she heard pitiful crying. 'Twas such an unexpected sound in the Faery World, where sorrow was unwelcome, that she knew something must be terribly wrong. Torn between her sense of compassion and her aching need to be with Sloan, even if she must appear to him as Luna, she halted. Following the sound of muffled sobs, Aisling peeked around a rosebush and saw tiny green shoes just beyond the shrub.

"Juniper Bilberry?" She pitched her voice as softly as she could, not wishing to alarm the little Fey laundress, nor bring unwanted attention to her un-Faery-like emotions. " 'Tis Aisling Ahearn, Juniper. Would you be needing a handkerchief?"

Several sniffles later, the leaves stirred and Juniper's little face peered around a large pink rose. Aisling opened her arms and her heart, and the unhappy Faery fell against her with another torrential round of sobs. Patting the girl's back and murmuring comforting nonsense, Aisling subdued her own impatience to wait for Juniper to calm herself. Finally, the Faery stepped back and loudly blew her nose into Aisling's handkerchief.

"Oh, Miss Aisling! Please don't tell my mother you found me crying! She'd feed me to a cat for sure!"

"No fear, Juniper. Oh, do keep the handkerchief," she added hurriedly when the girl held it out to her. "Would you be needing to talk to someone?" At Juniper's nod, she put her hand on the girl's shoulder. "Come with me, then. I know a corner where no one will be disturbing us."

When Aisling was satisfied that they were out of sight of all but the nosiest and most persistent of intruders, she gave Juniper an encouraging smile. 'Twas all the prodding the girl needed, to begin pouring out her sorrow.

'' 'Tis Acorn Bittersweet, miss! He has danced with me every night since he returned from his travels, yet he's been boasting to everyone who'll stand still, and anyone who won't, that he'll soon be marrying you. Oh! I'm so unhappy, miss! Why must my poor heart be setting itself on someone who loves another?'' Juniper blew her nose again, then sniffled a few times and blinked away the tears clinging to her lashes. '' 'Tis impossible to be hating you, Miss Aisling, much as I'm wishing I could. In spite of your own troubles, you've been so kind to me.''

The little Faery's confession brought a brief, small smile to Aisling's lips. ''Console yourself, Juniper Bilberry. Acorn Bittersweet may covet me, but he loves me not. Even if he were to find himself loving you, he'd likely choose choking on his pride over admitting his mistake. And the man I love . . .'' Juniper's eyes widened. Aisling sighed. ''Well, they're very much alike, Mortal or Fey, aren't they?'' Juniper nodded agreement, and Aisling gave her a quick smile. '' 'Tis up to you and me to be thinking of a solution, or else I fear we all shall end unhappily . . . or dead.''

O'HARA HOUSE, CO. SLIGO, SUMMER SOLSTICE EVENING, JUNE 21, 1999

The good news about the solstice, Con reflected as he let himself into the farthest paddock shortly before ten P.M., was that the nights couldn't get any longer after this one. If he had to spend another night like the last one, waiting for Aisling—or Luna—who never showed, he'd be a candidate for a rubber room. His right foot came down on an uneven spot, and a ribbon of pain slid up his back in protest. It was a damn good thing this situation with Aisling was due to be resolved—somehow—within the next month. He was getting too old for much more stonewall climbing and making love on the ground.

The moon was most of the way across the sky at this

hour. Con settled himself on the folded blanket and hit the *play* button on his portable CD player. Every night that Luna had visited him, he'd played different CDs and told her about the music and the musicians. He'd figured that, if the mare he saw as Luna really was Aisling under a magical spell, it was a way to bring her up to speed on late-twentieth-century culture. And, if the mare really was just a friendly white horse, who happened to wear golden shoes, that was no reason he couldn't talk and play music.

The opening bars of a Garth Brooks song floated out of the small speakers plugged into the disc player. If he got stood up again tonight, at least he had the right kind of music to feel melancholy by. But even before the first chorus, approaching hoof beats vibrated under him. The white mare cleared the far wall of the paddock with plenty of sky between her belly and the top row of stones. He had to admit she was a beautiful creature, but he still didn't think they'd make a compatible couple.

Luna landed, galloped a few strides, then slowed to a prancing trot that brought her to his side in seconds. He was already on his feet. When she reached out with her velvety muzzle to touch his chest, he looked into her eyes and ran his hands over her face. Was it Aisling? It was torture not knowing if she really was trapped in some alternative dimension by a force that reason and logic said couldn't exist, or if he was the butt of an elaborate joke.

The mare nickered softly, then took some of his shirt in her teeth and gave a playful tug. He chuckled and rubbed her nose. She gave another low nicker, then exhaled sharply. Con jumped back and wiped at the front of his shirt.

"Hey, quit it, whoever you are! You're not making me like horses any better by spraying me." The mare bobbed her head several times, then nickered again. "Okay, okay. You win." He moved beside her and began their nightly ritual of combing his fingers through the long, silky strands of her thick mane, massaging her favorite places, giving her another installment of the soap opera going on with his parents, Gramps, and Enid. And just talking about whatever

came into his mind. As long as no one caught him having
heart-to-heart chats with a horse, Con figured that it was
either a great way to share his thoughts with Aisling, or a
useful way to think about things out loud.

"Where were you last night, Luna? You had me pretty
worried." The mare lowered her head and pressed her muzzle against his belly. Con grinned. "Apology accepted. I
guess I can wait a week to find out what happened. The
important thing is you're okay now, right?"

The whine of a poorly tuned car engine drawing closer
caught his attention. He stopped rubbing her neck to listen.
Luna lifted her head and her delicate ears flicked forward
and back. She sniffed the air, then snorted hard and turned
back to nuzzling Con's belly. The road running along that
side of the O'Hara grounds was narrow and unlit, so it was
used mainly by locals and adventurous tourists. Sometimes,
lovers looking for a little privacy took a chance climbing
into an empty field, but this car kept whining and chugging
into the distance.

"Anyway, mare, I fell asleep out here, and woke up as
stiff as an old man. So if Phelan McDermott makes any
moves on Erin, it's your fault."

Luna bumped his shoulder with her nose. He moved
around behind her and began finger-combing the ground-
trailing strands of her tail. "McDermott makes Erin nervous, even if she doesn't want to admit it. My partner
would rather risk her neck than her pride." He paused to
work out a tangle, then, without thinking first, patted her
rump. A split second later, he was sitting on the ground
about five feet away, seeing stars from the force of his
landing. His gut, where her hock had caught him, ached
fiercely. Cursing, he stayed seated to collect his injured
pride and rub his muscles.

Luna swung around to gaze innocently down at him, then
snorted, as if she were surprised to see him there. He was
about to stand and scold her when the sounds of hushed
voices and hurrying footsteps on the gravel shoulder of the
road caught his attention. Puzzled, he waited.

A head, then two more, appeared over the top of the

stone wall to the east. In the partial moonlight, he could only see forms and shadows, not details, but as a fourth, then a fifth, head popped into sight, he thought there were four women and one man. The five heads froze in a row above the wall.

"There she is!" A wheezy old man's voice rang out in the night. "There's Lady Moonlight! I told ye, I did!"

Luna wheeled to face them, and the neighing sound she made was as close to a scream as Con had ever heard from a horse. As the mare fidgeted, the five heads dropped out of sight, but their excited voices, from outside the paddock, rang on the night breezes. Con realized that, at least for the moment, he was out of sight below the slight rise in the paddock, and behind the dancing, agitated mare. He decided to stay crouched low to keep the element of surprise in his favor and be ready to protect Luna from the five intruders.

A metallic clank briefly puzzled him, until he deduced that the trespassers had propped a ladder against the wall. Even though Luna was now neighing and rearing frantically, even though people were invading the paddock, Con stayed low. Over the sounds of panic coming from the mare, Con heard shrill female voices, some American, some British.

"Oh! She's beautiful! Where's your camera, Margie?" Several quick flashes of light sent Luna up on her hind legs again, pawing the air with her gold-shod hooves. Three more flashes, lots more shrill talking. Then, "Mr. Sweet, you were absolutely right! Lady Moonlight exists, and you knew exactly where to find her! I'll never forget this day as long as I live!"

Luna dropped to four feet, and Con saw that every taut muscle under her silvery white coat was bunched for flight. He wanted to comfort and reassure her, but he had to pick the right moment to spring on these people. Too soon, and they might get away before he could find out what the hell was going on. Too late, and they would probably frighten the mare away. A scared, running horse could get very badly injured in the dark.

"Can we touch her?" The speaker sounded breathless.

"Oh, aye, ye can touch her, ye can." The strangely rusty-sounding man's voice came out in measured tones. "But first, ye must slip this rope around her neck, to hold her fast."

Taking that as his cue, Con leaped to his feet and planted himself next to Luna's quivering shoulder. Laying one hand on her neck, he glared at the five trespassers, four women and one elderly man, who stood gaping at him.

"What the hell is going on here?" At his bellow, the four women stepped backward. The old man, holding a coiled rope in his hand, winced, but stood his ground. Con scowled harder. "This is O'Hara land. It's not open to the public day or night. I'll give you thirty seconds to get out before I call the police."

"But . . . But . . . We . . . We just wanted to see her . . . the mare called Lady Moonlight! At dinner in the pub, Mr. Sweet told us the legend of her enchantment, and he promised us . . ."

Con glared at the American-sounding speaker until her voice trailed into silence. "You're trespassing on private property, *my* property. I don't see any legends here. I see you five attempting to steal a valuable mare. You've got fifteen seconds left."

The four women suddenly turned and dashed for the wall. They pushed and shoved one another, but finally three of the four were on the other side. The fourth woman paused at the top of the ladder. She looked at Luna, then shifted her gaze to Con.

"We did so want to believe the legend." The wistful tone of her voice didn't come close to tugging at his heart. "But your little mare is just an ordinary horse, isn't she?" Con looked at her steadily but didn't answer. "We . . . We're sorry we disturbed you, sir. Thank you for being decent about it." When he continued to simply return her gaze, she looked at the little old man who was fingering the coiled rope in his gnarled hands. "Mr. Sweet, we're happy to give you a lift back to the pub."

Mr. Sweet shifted his weight from one foot to the other.

Under Con's hand, Luna was still trembling. Realizing that the old man and his rope had snuck closer, Con stepped between him and the mare. He crossed his arms over his chest and glared.

"Take your rope and go, or I'll use it to hold you for the Guarda. No one steals an O'Hara horse."

To Con's surprise, a wide grin split the wizened face. Then the little old guy touched two bent fingers to the brim of his felt hat, turned, and skipped—*skipped!*—to the ladder lying against the wall. With the warmth of Luna's breath on the back of his neck, Con watched as the grotesque Mr. Sweet scrambled up the rungs with unusual agility for such a bent, elderly man. A moment after he disappeared over the wall, the ladder was drawn up, and it went over behind him. The car sputtered to life. Long after it had whined and wheezed away into the distance, Con continued to stand on guard.

When he turned back around to Luna, the mare was gone. Her absence left him with a strangely hollow place inside him. He still wasn't ready to believe that Luna was really Aisling, but he was almost ready to concede that he . . . *cared,* for both the woman and the horse. Unwilling to leave, in case the trespassers returned, Con spread the blanket on the ground and prepared for an all-night vigil. As he searched through his backpack for the refreshments Mrs. Penny had packed for him, a melody he didn't recognize started winding through his head. Just as his hand closed on a bag of cookies, he recalled some of the words: "I'm not in love, I'm not in love . . ."

THE FAERY REALM, EVER-THE-PRESENT

Aisling raced through the Under-Hill passages to her aunt's suite, frantic over her encounter with Acorn Bittersweet. Indeed, she ran so quickly that several Faeries began shouting for the others to join the *rade.* By the time she reached Rainbow's rooms, most of the Moonstone Circle Troop were packing up and preparing to troop away. Aisling's panic increased. This was a terrible new complication! If

they all rushed to another site to set up their palatial head-
quarters, there was no telling where she'd be in a day. Even
as Luna, she could travel no faster than a real horse, and
she might be too far away to return to Con tomorrow night.

Just as she burst into Rainbow's parlor, a tapestry fell
off the wall and covered her. While she thrashed under its
gossamer but tenacious folds, laughter—Rainbow's and
Raven's—reached her ears. Furiously, she pushed the tapestry off herself and faced them, biting her lower lip.

"Ah, Niece! Just in time. Someone has called for a
rade."

" 'Tis a mistake, Aunt! A terrible mistake! I was running
to tell you . . ." Aisling paused at Raven's smirk, and
fought to compose herself. "I must be speaking privately
with you, Aunt."

Rainbow sent her a brilliant smile, then cast her sitting
room furniture magically into hiding. "Quickly, then,
Niece, before the noise begins in earnest."

Aisling gave Raven a pointed glance, but he was busy
casting carpets into rolls of moss and had turned his back
to her. " 'Twould be more private if 'twere just the two of
us, Aunt."

Trumpets began blaring, and the din of tiny voices rose
outside Rainbow's suite. Desperate now, Aisling tugged at
her aunt's hand, interrupting a spell to disguise a chair as
a mushroom and leaving the mushroom cap ill-formed.
Rainbow began laughing, but stopped when she looked into
Aisling's face. With a smile and a graceful gesture, she sent
a scowling Raven away, then took Aisling's hands in hers.
Speaking rapidly, Aisling described the encounter with the
four women escorted by a Mr. Sweet, who Aisling knew
could only be Acorn Bittersweet.

Hadn't she smelled him with Luna's sensitive nose?
Hadn't she heard that reedy voice with her own and Luna's
even more sensitive ears? Hadn't she seen, with Luna's
sharp vision, that he hadn't been able to transform his ears
perfectly, when he disguised himself as a Mortal storyteller? Faeries all might take on Mortal guises, but even the
most skillful at such transformations could not work them

to perfection. There was always some little detail wrong, revealing their true identity to the knowledgeable observer.

The noise grew around them as Aisling described Sloan's bold words and protective actions. "And did he then declare his love?" Rainbow shouted over the din.

Lifting her hands to protect her ears from the now deafening noise, Aisling shook her head. Aunt Rainbow's brief frown sent her heart sinking. There would be no more conversation, Aisling knew, until the *rade* ended and the members of the Moonstone Circle resumed their amusements in their new palace. Her aunt turned away and began casting the rest of the packing-up spells.

As the chaos and cacophony swirled around her and carried her along, Aisling kept her ears covered and prayed that she would be somewhere close to this place when the moon waxed full. If she were too far away, she would not meet Sloan again as herself before the July full moon, when Acorn Bittersweet would be claiming her.

Twenty-three

The full moon was just rising above the eastern horizon as the sun was sinking into the sea to the west. 'Twas a perfect moment of suspension, Aisling mused. There she was standing at the threshold between the Mortal and Faery worlds, and at the threshold between day and night. Suspended between them all, she was a woman appearing as a white mare, a white mare about to be turning into a woman. As soon as the blazing sun finished its setting, and the purples, pinks, and golds streaking the sky were fading, the cool white light of the moon would be lighting the way for Sloan. Until then, she'd be staying suspended, fighting the yearning inside her that would see her risking Sloan see her changing, from Luna to herself, before his eyes. If she must go to her living death as the bride of the Leprechaun, knowing she did not have Sloan's love, she would do so without his pity.

As the sky darkened, the air began to cool. In trees and shrubs all around, birds were chittering their good-nights to one another, sounding almost as loud as Trooping Faeries on a *rade*. With each minute passing toward night, Aisling let herself be inching away from the invisibility of the Under-Hill passage. The place where she and Sloan would be meeting was just out of sight from her niche, but as she still possessed Luna's acute hearing, she heard him approaching the paddock. Another inch toward him, and she was hearing the sounds of the music he brought for her. She liked the music he called "classic rock," and "new country," but tonight, surely, she was hearing something by Mozart.

Music, the moving pictures, the computers, the jet planes and spaceships . . . Luna truly had become a well-educated mare! Just thinking of the care Sloan had been taking, sharing with her the wonders of the real world, brought a smile to her heart. Imagine! She'd gone and done the unthinkable thing: she'd fallen in love—knowingly, in love!—with an O'Hara! Ah, and wasn't he worth loving? He was gentle, and kind, and wonderfully brilliant! Handsome, he was, too. If only . . .

With a hushed whispering of her wings, the white owl swooped past Aisling's hiding place. 'Twas safe now to be showing herself to her lover, but the memory of Acorn Bittersweet's abduction attempt made her wary. Taking a different path than she usually followed, she approached the farthest O'Hara paddock, which used to be the farthest de Burgh paddock. A warm breeze played with her hair, and the cool leaves of trees and bushes kissed her skin as she walked. The scents of flowers, grasses, horses, even foods cooking in the homes dotting the countryside—they all drifted to her, as did the sounds of the birds, and distant cows lowing and people laughing, music playing. 'Twas as if they were all bidding her senses farewell, on her last night living as a Mortal woman.

The sight of a strange object standing in the middle of the paddock brought her feet and her thoughts to a sudden halt. 'Twas like a hut, only much too small for living in, round like a deep, overturned bowl, and . . . bright purple. She scanned the enclosed field, but there was only this round thing, and no sign of—

Seeing Sloan, emerging from the depths of the purple mound and scowling toward the horizon, startled a tiny sound from her throat. 'Twas enough to alert him to her

presence, and the frown marring his handsome face turned
into a smile so sweet that it drew tears to her eyes. Giving
in to the impatience that had been tormenting her, she ran
to him and fell into his open arms. Then he was holding
her tight and fast against his strong body, kissing her hair
and murmuring her name, and the drumming of his heart
was shaking her with every beat. Hungry for the taste of
him, she tilted her head up, and laced her fingers into his
hair, drawing his head down. His mouth met hers, and she
opened to him, feeding on his kiss, slaking his hunger and
thirst with her own.

Con lifted his head long enough to confess, ''Oh, God!
I was so afraid you weren't going to make it!''

Then he covered her lips with his own and told her without words how he felt now that he held her in his arms
again. Under the sweetness of Aisling's kisses, he tasted
the same desperation poisoning the pure bliss of being with
her. He felt it in the way her hands clutched at him, heard
it in the tiny whimpers escaping from her throat as she
burrowed closer. His body was trembling with the need to
peel away all their layers of clothing and all their layers of
emotional defense, and make love until the end of the
night—no, until the end of time. But before he could give
in to that urge, there were things he needed to tell her in
words carefully chosen so there would be no misunder-
standings between them.

Reluctantly, Con lifted his head again. The deep breath
he drew in filled his senses with the sweet musk of Aisling's skin and the grassy sweetness of the night air. Bowing to rest his forehead against hers, he let his breath out
slowly. ''Aisling? I'm about to say one of the lines all
normal men dread more than having teeth pulled without
painkiller: We need to talk.''

She giggled softly. ''Is talking such a torture, then?''

Smiling at her teasing tone, he brushed a kiss to the top
of her head, then tucked her snugly against his body. She
wrapped her arms around his waist and pressed herself
close. ''Not if it's about baseball or cars. But having to talk
about relationships, about feelings . . . Most guys would

rather take arsenic, 'cause it can hurt less, and they know it'll end sooner or later.''

''And are *you* one of these cowardly men?''

''Honestly? Yeah. I'm probably world champion at avoiding any discussion that contains the words *relationship* and *emotions*, particularly in the same sentence. But . . . we've got some heavy-duty issues to resolve, things that go way beyond just us, don't we?'' She nodded against his chest. ''Let's get inside. I'll try to get all our talking done before I start tearing off your clothes, but I won't make any promises. We'll have more privacy in the tent, especially if those tourists come back.''

Con kept one arm around Aisling while he led her to the flap of the tent. She hesitated briefly, making him wonder if she were claustrophobic. Then she ducked inside so quickly that she left him outside. He followed her, grinning at her wide-eyed exploration of the interior of the tent, the double air mattress, the battery-powered lamp, the portable stereo. She squeaked, then covered her mouth with her hands, when she saw the wine, the chocolates, and the flowers. They were no less than she deserved.

She sat on the mattress, then laughed. '' 'Tis a marvel!''

He lowered himself beside her. ''I'm getting too old for roughing it. And . . .'' Even before the words came out, his neck and cheeks flushed with heat. ''. . . I wanted tonight to be special, and private.''

Aisling lifted her hand to his face and smiled into his eyes. ''Every second I'm spending with you is special, Sloan, but this privacy is a brilliant idea.''

He pressed a kiss into her palm. ''If I'm so brilliant, how come I was almost dumb enough to let you get away?'' She gave him a little frown. ''I was so sure you were scamming me, with all that Leprechaun and enchantment stuff, all the magic spells and counter-spells. But I convinced myself you were just a harmless lunatic, because you were so beautiful, so sweet, and you didn't seem to think I was the sorriest excuse for a male human being ever to walk the face of the earth.''

Taking her hand in his, he paused to give her a chance

to argue that last point. When she didn't, he shrugged mentally. "I was a horny dork at sixteen, and a hornier jerk at nineteen, but I . . ." The words stuck in his throat. "When we made love, I . . ." Nope, the words still weren't ready to come out. "I've spent the past fourteen years denying what I felt—what I feel."

Aisling's fingers tightened around his. "Ah, Sloan, after nearly ninety years of being neither alive nor dead, neither Mortal nor Fey . . . All that time, I yearned for a True Love to free me from the Leprechaun's spell, hated Ambros O'Hara, and I still had the foolish heart of a sixteen-year-old girl. But from our first meeting, I believed you would be my One True Love."

His heart did a standing broad jump at her softly uttered words. Envious of the ease with which she could express her feelings, stunned by the surge of his own feelings, all he could think to do was kiss her knuckles and wait for her to continue.

"Even with my aunt warning me with her riddles, and reminding me that only the True Love of an O'Hara could end the enchantment, even with you nearly calling me a liar, I believed you were the one. Aunt Rainbow must have discovered your O'Hara blood. She stopped flatly discouraging me from you, and began saying only that you weren't the man I was wanting you to be. 'Tis fortunate that my stubbornness blinded me, as I was wanting you to be a True Love who *wasn't* an O'Hara!"

"Fortunate?" He traced the outline of a heart on the silken skin of her wrist. "You acted like it was the end of the world when you found out." At the petulant sound of his own words, Con felt heat rise up his neck to his face. But instead of laughing at him and telling him to grow up, Aisling bowed her head.

"I'm sorry," she whispered. Then she lifted her head and looked into his eyes. "When we were making love, Sloan, I did not come to you as a mare in season. 'Twas indeed my love I was giving. But after, when you declared your love, I threw it back at you, smothered in my hate. 'Twas the shock of thinking all my suffering was for naught, and believing I'd been deceived by another O'Hara.''

Con opened his mouth to defend his innocence, but she pressed the fingers of her free hand to his lips. ''And I accused you falsely of lying, and of having a heart of stone. 'Twas my own hurt that made me cruel, but causing you pain has been a shadow on my heart since then. Can you be forgiving me, Sloan?''

Aisling held her breath, waiting—it seemed forever!—for Sloan to answer. Instead of speaking, he gave her a slow, sweet smile and pulled her into his arms, where she could hear his heart beating under her cheek.

''Forgiving you isn't an issue. Keeping us together is the issue.'' His voice rumbled under her ear. ''What do we do now?''

She reached up to lay her hand on his shoulder, following the hard shape of his muscle with her fingertips. ''To be breaking the enchantment on me and the curse on the O'Haras of Ambros's line?''

There was little encouragement in Sloan's grunt. Smiling at his mulish resistance to believing in magic, she slid her fingers up the warm, bare skin of his neck and tickled his earlobe.

''You might be a genius about the computers, but you've the brains of a boiled turnip about other things.''

Sloan's silent laughter vibrated beneath her. He caught her hand in his and kissed her fingertips. ''Okay, okay, you win! I've read the damn book. But a doctorate in computer science doesn't cover this kind of logic. Your Faery aunt said something about you making amends for the tree your father destroyed, and that I have to prove I . . . how I feel about you, and tell you, three times. Then, *poof!* Right?''

Aisling opened her mouth to point out that the working of magic required *specific* words and deeds, not general ones. Some inner voice urged her not to be pressing him about his feelings just yet. '' 'Tis near enough for now,'' she told him instead, and he hugged her a little closer, the gesture saying she'd made the right choice. ''You've fulfilled some of the conditions already, did you know?'' At his silence, she gathered her courage. "You've declared your love once . . . ," his body tensed under her, ". . . and proven it twice. Now, if you'd be asking your friend Enid for me to acquire a young hawthorn and plant it at the next new moon in the place where the old one grew, beside the de Burgh great house, I shall be watering it with my tears that night."

"Why Enid? Hell, this is *our* problem. Don't you think I can buy a hawthorn tree, or whatever it is, and plant it for you?"

There was hurt in Sloan's voice, and knowing she'd caused it mixed her sadness with a strange happiness. "Enid must be doing it for me, Sloan, as she's a Wise Woman, a witch, and a friend of my aunt. She knows the way to consecrate a Sacred Hawthorn."

Con digested Aisling's words. "A witch. Enid's a witch. And I thought she was just psychic." But he found himself chuckling instead of blustering that there was no such thing as witches. At the rate his credulity was stretching, any day now he'd be a card-carrying member of the Flat Earth Society.

He needed clarification of something far more important. "Let's go back to something you said earlier. I know I told you I . . ." Damn! The *L word* kept sticking in his throat like a burr. "Once, I did . . . say it. But I proved . . . how I feel about you *two times*? When? How?" He couldn't remember doing anything extraordinary for her, but if he'd done the right thing twice already, he wanted to know what it was, so he'd know what to do the third time. That would only leave having to blurt the *L word*—and mean it—two more times.

She wriggled against him, stirring the half-arousal he'd been able—until then—to sublimate. Leaning back, she looked up into his face with an expression in her eyes that he couldn't name, but it went straight to his brain like fine Irish whiskey. "You saved me from the Leprechaun. He was trying to capture me, using the touring ladies as his unknowing accomplices."

"Son of a bitch! That ugly runt was Acorn Bittersweet?"

Aisling nodded solemnly. "I should have cleaned his clock!"

"Oh, I doubt he has a clock, Sloan. Time is meaningless in the Faery World."

Con bit the inside of his cheek until the urge to laugh faded. "Okay, that was one proof. What's the other one?"

The expression in her eyes changed, and her lips curved into a smile reminiscent of a cat about to dine on canary in cream sauce. " 'Twas the way you treated me the first time . . ."

In the dim light of the tent, her pale cheeks seemed to glow a little pink. Con suddenly realized what she meant. He could have let her off the hook, but he owed her some squirming after she'd teased him over the L word, so he waited for her to finish her thought. Aisling's tongue slid along her lower lip, and Con felt his body tighten with a rush of heat.

"The first time we made love, you put my wishes, my fears, above your desires. 'Twas not an easy thing for a . . . a healthy young man to do."

And here he'd been imagining he was supposed to fight dragons or move mountains, or something impressive. He grinned. "You're right. It was . . . pretty damn . . . hard . . ." Her gasp widened his grin. "You had that effect on me."

She pressed against him, then arched an eyebrow. " 'Tis a similar effect to the effect I'm having on you now, I believe."

"For once, you and I believe exactly the same." She smiled and slid closer, her hip pressing against him, but Con hesitated. "Aisling, I want you to be sure . . . about this."

"And are *you* sure about this, Sloan?"

Her whisper sent arousal rippling through his entire system. "I'm not sure if the earth is round or the sky is blue," he answered in a suddenly choked voice, "but I'm as sure of wanting you as a man can be."

One second, she was staring up at him, her eyes large and luminous in the shadowy light. The next second, her

mouth was hot and wet on his, her cool hands bracketing
his face, her body squirming around until she straddled his
lap. After a moment of surprise, Con grasped her hips in
his hands and pulled her hard against him while their
tongues played a very tantalizing duet. In some foggy corner of his brain, he noted that there seemed to be less bulk
to her dress this time. Curious, he slid his hands under the
edge of her skirt and almost immediately encountered
warm, silky bare flesh. New underwear? Intrigued, he ran
his hands up her bare thighs, and found himself cupping
her bare bottom. Oh, God! *No* underwear!

Spontaneous combustion was a distinct possibility.

Con touched her carefully. Aisling pulled her mouth
from his and inhaled. He felt her trembling, but she didn't
flinch when he let his fingers explore her more intimately.
Uncertain of his stamina after wanting her for so long, Con
intended to make the overture last as long as necessary to
satisfy her. He found her already swollen and moist, and
as soon as he began stroking her, she cried out and arched
her back, her tiny frame quivering with her release. Then,
almost bonelessly, she flowed toward him, her hair falling
around them like a golden shawl. He held her against his
heart until he knew that if he couldn't bury himself in her
body soon, he was going to die.

Kissing her, caressing her, Con lifted her and stood with
her. Her dress was a three-dimensional puzzle. He solved
it with little finesse but no ripping, leaving her in her transparent little slip thing. His shirt was a straitjacket, but he
was Houdini. His jeans were an instrument of torture, but
he withstood the pain of Aisling slowly lowering his zipper,
the anguish of not being able to make them magically disappear. Relief at last! His jeans landed across the tent. His
briefs . . .

A laugh sputtered from Aisling. "Red?"

He grinned. "I wore them for you."

"Ah. Then I must thank you. But . . ." She tipped her
head to the side and touched the tip of her tongue to her

teeth. Even in the dim light, her eyes sparkled. ". . . I wore none, for you."

"For which I intend to thank you very, very thoroughly."

She tossed away her last sheer scrap of clothing. Con peeled out of his briefs, hard and heavy with arousal, aching for her, but he forced himself to wait for Aisling to give him a sign. She lifted her arms toward him. He scooped her against him and lowered them to the air mattress. He meant to go slowly, he meant to relearn every inch of her silky body, he meant to protect her, he meant to give her everything before he took anything. But somehow he was on his back and Aisling was astride his hips, eyes shut, guiding him to her. She was hot and tight. He was afraid to hurt her. She opened her eyes and smiled. Con was lost.

Aisling lay, limp as seaweed, on Sloan's chest, listening to the rasp of his breathing, the drumming of his heart. His hands on her back were warm, strong, gentle. What a sweet man he was! Had she truly accused him of having a heart of stone? How wrong, how cruelly wrong, she'd been!

"I love you, Conlan Ambros O'Hara Sloan," she murmured.

Without warning, he reversed their positions, startling a yelp out of her. Above her, he was staring down into her eyes, and there was a look of surprise on his face that puzzled her. Had she misspoken herself? Had she mistaken him?

"Aisling, I love you." His voice sounded a little hoarse, a little tentative. He shook his head. "No. *I love you!*"

At his triumphant shout, a sensation like a weight lifting from her heart, like a breeze filling a sail, like a fledgling taking flight, sent tears spilling from her eyes. She touched his face and he turned to press a kiss to the inside of her wrist, his lips warm at her pulse.

"I never thought I'd hear myself saying anything remotely like this, but before the next full moon, I'm going to be the leading expert on outwitting Leprechauns and breaking spells, or die trying."

Aisling arched up to kiss him, to cast her fate with his, but she couldn't silence the echoing fear that if he could not truly outwit the Leprechaun, at least one of them would certainly die.

Twenty-four

"Mrs. Penny sent you some fresh lemonade."

Erin's voice came from around the highest of the black-ened foundation stones. She followed it a few seconds later, a large glass in each hand. Grateful for an excuse to stop working and stretch his knotted back muscles, Con took a long drink; he was too parched to say thanks until after his first swallow.

"How'd you like touring with my mother?"

Erin chuckled. "It was, as they say, a trip. I thought I was in pretty good shape, but after two days with Corliss, I doubled my vitamins." She made a rueful face. "After a dozen years working with you, I thought I could follow almost any tangent without missing a beat. Not with Corliss. Her thoughts bounce around like atoms repelling each other."

Long since resigned to the phenomenon of his mother's brand of logic, Con laughed at Erin's indignant tone. "Bet she thinks you're hopelessly square, with your lists and color-coded notes."

"Touché." She shot him a smug grin. "However, it turns out we're both, in our own ways, awesomely world-class shoppers."

A chip of stone caught his eye. Stooping, he worked it out of the soil and tossed it into the plastic pail half-full of similar chips. "Get me anything?"

"A wedding present." She paused. "Matching horse blankets."

Con lunged for her, threatening a dunk in the fishpond. With a shriek of laughter, she leaped out of his reach, then gave him a suddenly sober assessing look. "How goes this?"

He handed her his now empty glass, then waved his hand in an arc that took in the area beyond where they stood. After a slow scan of the space surrounding the remains of the de Burgh great house, Erin gave a long, low whistle. "Wow! You did all that by yourself? No wonder you're rubbing your back."

"Yeah, well, Enid said I had to do it alone, but she didn't say why. Phelan mumbled something about a rite of passage, sorta like the tasks of Hercules." He shrugged.

Erin arched a brow at him. "The Faeries will love it."

"They better. I must have hauled a half a ton of rock to clear this place." But it wasn't the Faeries he hoped would enjoy the sight of the newly cleared area around the old foundation. He scowled at the land he'd been working on for the past week, so that Enid could plant a hawthorn bush to replace the one Eamon Ahearn had destroyed a century ago. If everything turned out right, he intended to rebuild the mansion for the last de Burgh heiress. "Enid wouldn't let me use a trowel, or a shovel. Said traces of the iron in the soil would repel the Faeries."

Grinning slyly, Erin sniffed in his direction, then wrinkled her nose. "You better leave time for a shower before the ceremonial tree planting, or you'll asphyxiate them instead."

Pausing to glower, Con grabbed the shirt he'd taken off hours before, when the sun had been blazing down on him. "I'm on my way now. Phelan and I are supposed to do some kind of ritual sauna to open up the channels to my right-brain spiritual side." He snorted derisively, but uneasily. Unlike some computer types, he'd never been superstitious or ritualistic. Hell, did he even have a right-brain spiritual side? He shrugged. After a week of grubbing in the dirt, his physical side could use some heat.

A last look around confirmed his sense that the site didn't feel so forlorn now that a lot of the debris was gone. Noting the low position of the sun in the western sky, he felt the first stirrings of anticipation, and anxiety. Tonight—and Aisling—couldn't arrive soon enough. He started down the path leading back to the O'Hara great house, with Erin following close behind.

"Hey, Sloan, exactly what's supposed to happen to-night?" There was a hint of worry in her voice. He wondered if his mentioning Phelan had anything to do with that. Probably. Now he was sorry he hadn't called Nolan to come over and look out for Erin.

"Enid's going to plant trees and do some kind of cere-mony to consecrate them to the moon, so the Faeries will be happy again."

Erin caught up with him. "What about you? Isn't all this supposed to be for you and Aisling?"

"My assignment was to get the space ready for the trees," he hedged, hoping she would forget about the L-word requirements detailed in the old book about Lady Moonlight. "I let that crazy woman talk me into fasting since last night, so I don't have any food clogging my spir-itual arteries. And after this sweat bath, I'm even going to let her give the gold horseshoe nail and . . ." Erin didn't know about the talismans still tucked into the back pocket of his jeans. No point in complicating things further . . . "give the nail a salt bath to cleanse the bad vibes from it."

She put her hand on his arm, and he stopped walking. Her green eyes looked more solemn than he'd ever seen them. "Con, I'm sorry I hassled you to be logical about this whole situation, 'cause some of the things going on have got me just a little freaked. You're being a much better sport about all these weird rituals than I'd be." She took a breath. "I hope it's worth it."

It was easy to offer a reassuring smile. "Aisling is worth any amount of weirdness. Except . . ." His smile turned to a scowl. "I will *not* wear the dress Enid gave me, even for Aisling."

A PALACE, THE FAERY REALM, EVER-THE-PRESENT

"Wait!"

Rainbow's whispered command held such urgency that Aisling's heart skipped a beat. Her aunt motioned for her to slip behind an enormous fern, then positioned herself in front of Aisling. With her heart pounding so hard she was afraid it would strangle her, Aisling waited. A moment passed in which all she heard was the usual sounds of a Faery great hall: bell-like music, laughter, and occasional trumpet voluntaries. Then a nasal, tuneless humming reached her ears and the tiny hairs at the back of her neck stood up. Oh! Let her aunt be mistaken!

"Mistress Rainbow!" There was no mistaking that voice!

"Greetings, Acorn Bittersweet." Her aunt's reply sounded formal, but gracious enough, Aisling hoped, that the Leprechaun would not suspect her of any deception. Solitary Faeries were not known to be forgiving. 'Twould weigh terribly on her conscience if any retribution came to Rainbow because of her.

" 'Tis nearly time for me to claim yer niece for my bride, it is! Would ye know where I might be finding her?"

"Surely, Remember-Fear-Not lingers somewhere in this hall. But as there is still some little time remaining to her, perhaps she is amusing the little ones in the nursery." How clever of her aunt to suggest that! Even a Leprechaun determined to sire his own offspring seldom truly liked children, Fey or Mortal. And the nursery lay in the same direction they must take to travel to the de Burgh great house that very night, the night of the new moon. Sloan awaited her, and 'twas their last and only chance, with the help of Rainbow and Enid, to break the enchantment.

"Ah. The nursery. Well." No doubt, he would not be going that way in search of her. "Then wait here for her, I shall."

"Unless, of course, she's in the great hall dancing," Aunt Rainbow said as if she'd only just had the thought. Even more clever! Dancing was irresistible to Leprechauns, and once they were dancing, there was no stopping them until the music no longer played. "Do you not hear the fiddling? Raven promises to play reels for us. Yes, my niece must be with the dancers."

"Ah! Dancing, now! If Raven plays reels, dancing until dawn we shall be, we shall!" The Leprechaun gave a gleeful cackle that faded into the distance with his retreating footsteps.

The breath trapped in Aisling's lungs rushed out the moment she no longer heard him. But just as Aisling was about to emerge from behind the fern, his voice came at her like the lash of a whip.

"If I find yer niece is thinking to escape me, I'll be coming after her, I will, and well before the July full moon. That young Mortal won't be cheating Acorn Bittersweet as her sire did. Acorn Bittersweet has become ruthless, he has, and I'll not deal mercifully with Mortals deceiving me." As Aisling's heart dropped, the Leprechaun uttered another laugh. "Come wi' me, Mistress Rainbow, to find yer niece among the dancers."

After a hesitation, Rainbow cleared her throat. "'Twould amuse me indeed, to help you find my niece among the dancers."

Frozen in panic, Aisling huddled behind the fern until their voices had receded. The new moon would be setting soon. If she did not return to the Mortal world in time to consecrate the Sacred Hawthorn Enid would be planting on her behalf, she'd be failing to fulfil a key requirement for ending her enchantment.

DE BURGH MANOR RUINS, CO. SLIGO, DUSK, TUESDAY, JULY 13, 1999

Con felt slightly dizzy, as if he were standing at the edge of the Cliffs of Mohr, being lured by the sea and the wind and the drop straight down to the rocks and surf below.

Maybe he was just tired and hungry. Maybe the pain of
Erin's fingernails digging into his arm was getting to him.
Maybe it was the fear, settled like a glacier in his gut, that
Aisling was a fraud. And maybe it was the fear that she
wasn't. Whatever the cause, there was a distinct possibility
that he'd end up passing out.

As dusk fell, he stole occasional glances at the others.
His parents were holding hands, their faces as solemn as if
they were at a funeral. Gramps, alone opposite Corliss and
Jonathan, looked a little embarrassed, but Con detected
pride and affection in the way he watched Enid. Funny
old guy. Erin had started the evening alone also, but she'd
grabbed Con's hand in a death grip the instant Enid and
Phelan had joined them. Con felt her trembling. He wondered if she was breathing. He could see why she was tied
in knots.

Enid and Phelan hadn't given any advance notice of what
they would be wearing. Their appearance had shocked
everyone into an awed silence, an awareness that they were
about to participate in a ceremony, not just plant three little
trees. Con had laughed that afternoon when Enid explained
she'd bought a small hawthorn bush, plus an ash and an
oak sapling, at a plant nursery; it was the same mundane
solution he'd suggested, and Aisling rejected. But when
mother and son appeared in their long, hooded white robes,
with dark green scarves over their shoulders, his breath
caught in his throat. That was when Erin started clawing
him.

Now the five of them stood in a circle drawn on the
ground Con had cleared by hand, while Enid and Phelan
performed a ritual they called "drawing down the moon."
Con tuned out their words and let their actions, the sounds
of their voices, mesmerize him. The sky was growing dim,
the sun and moon sinking nearly in tandem, the darkness
slowly thickening outside the circle. Inside the circle, the
flickering lights of dozens of black and white candles
seemed to get brighter as dusk faded to evening.

With flames dancing at the edges of his vision and all of
his senses simultaneously heightened and softened, Con

watched Enid and Phelan gently tucking the three young plants into the holes he'd dug with his bare hands. The lyrical, chanting voices in the purple and gray night, the light breeze, carrying the scents of candle wax, herbal incense, and summer's mix of flowers and grasses and earth, swirled around him. The pain of Erin's nails biting into his arm faded into a vague awareness, as if his arm had become numb. An image of the roots of the new plants, stretching out through the soil until they were entwined with one another, made him smile. He was in some kind of mellow zone. He didn't have a clue to what or where, but it felt great.

Only vaguely, Con registered new sounds around him, but he couldn't pull himself out of his strange state of mind to focus. It took Erin shaking the arm she'd been mauling, his father grabbing his other arm, and his mother patting his face to make him realize he was about to fall. Phelan materialized where Erin had been a second before, and he and Jonathan hauled Con upright. When Erin and Corliss started squealing, the three of them, Con sagging between them, staggered around to see what was happening.

At the sight of a white horse emerging from the dusk, Con's knees and mind suddenly went straight. Enid went to Luna and spoke softly, passing through what she'd called the "door" of the magic circle, and leading the mare to the new plants. Con shook off the hands that had been holding him up but now felt like they were holding him back. Watching Luna move wide-eyed past the flickering candles, he held his breath. She lowered her head to sniff delicately at the little hawthorn bush, closing her eyes in an expression of equine bliss. When the mare's dark, luminous eyes opened again, tears slid from them and fell toward the hawthorn. Con wanted desperately to go to the mare, to touch her, to reassure himself she was real, reassure her he was there for her, but he couldn't move.

Corliss gasped and pointed. "Oh, Jonathan! Everyone! Look!"

Con forced his gaze from Luna's face to the shrub she stood over, and his heart skipped a beat. Blinking didn't clear his vision. Shaking his head didn't change what he saw. Taking several deep breaths didn't do it either. Right under their noses, the newly planted hawthorn, as well as the ash and oak saplings, were growing and sprouting new leaves as if they were in a time-lapse film instead of real life. *And I'll water it with my tears,* he heard Aisling saying in his mind.

Aisling, with Luna's heightened senses, felt Sloan's presence even before Enid brought her into the circle. She quivered in anticipation of his touch, but it seemed forever until he closed the distance between them. She blinked away the last of her tears, and pressed her face against his chest, breathing in the familiar, beloved scent of him. His hands shook as he cupped her face between them, as he stroked her neck and whispered sweet nonsense to her. Only vaguely was she aware of Enid and Phelan ending their ritual. At that moment, Sloan was the entire world to her.

"What a lovely little mare!" Aisling lifted her head at the sound. The woman Aisling believed to be Corliss, Sloan's mother, took a step toward her.

"Ah! Lady Moonlight!" The oldest man, who bore a striking resemblance to Ambros O'Hara II, joined the woman. "She would have been my grandmother in her own time. Now . . .'' The man smiled, but in the candlelight Aisling saw tears sparkling in his gray eyes. ". . . Now, if all goes well, she may be my granddaughter-in-law, eh, Conlan?''

Aisling knew horses couldn't blush, but she felt heat washing up her neck and cheeks. Her embarrassed laugh came out as a horsy snort. Laughing softly, Sloan rubbed her forehead.

"Oh, Jonathan! Isn't it romantic?" Corliss turned to the tall man who must be Sloan's father and threw her arms around his neck, laughing and crying. "The curse is broken! We can be happy again!" And, as if they were the only two people there, Sloan's parents began kissing like, well, like she and Sloan did, when she was herself and not Luna. Another blush washed over her.

Averting her eyes and leaning into Sloan's gentle caresses, Aisling watched the others. Aunt Rainbow's Wise friend, Enid, held out her hand to Sloan's grandfather, and they, too, began embracing. Enid's son, Phelan, was gazing at Sloan's friend Erin with the hungry eyes of a wolf, but when he gathered himself to close in, Erin backed away toward Sloan and Luna. Sensing the other woman's unease about Phelan but unable to speak, Aisling settled for expressing comfort with a gentle touch of her chin to Erin's shoulder. Their eyes met, woman to woman, although to any observers, it would appear woman to horse. Erin smiled, and Aisling felt a special kinship forming in her heart for Sloan's friend. As Erin was like a sister to Sloan, then Erin likewise would be like a sister to her.

Still feeling a little unsteady in his knees, Con pressed his forehead to the hard, flat bone of Luna's cheek for a long moment. She was a nice enough mare, but he wanted Aisling, wanted her with an intensity that felt like an explosion inside him. He hated feeling ignorant and helpless, but this wasn't like a programming glitch he could troubleshoot his way out of. Enid was probably the only one who knew how this magical ritual was supposed to work. Con straightened and met her eyes.

"So, when does Aisling become herself again?"

She smiled at him. "I do believe that as soon as you meet the conditions of Rainbow's spell, the Leprechaun's enchantment shall indeed be broken, and the curse on the O'Haras of Ambros's line shall be ended." Gramps slid his arm around her and whispered in her ear. She giggled like a teenager and her cheeks turned pink. Turning again to Con, she gave him a long, studying look. He wondered if she was reading his mind. "Thrice must you declare your love, and thrice must you prove it. I believe your current tally is two and two."

With all eyes on him, he felt heat sting his neck and face. He used to be a pretty private person, Con reflected. Now, it felt like half the world knew more about him than he knew about himself. "Yeah," he muttered. "Now what?"

"You must—"

Luna's shrill scream stopped Con's heart in mid-beat. He turned toward her just as she tossed her head and bumped him backward. He staggered into Phelan and fell to one knee. As the pain of landing on a shard of partly buried broken stone sent shock waves up his leg, he saw movement in the shadows beyond the mare. Luna gave another shrill neigh and sidestepped enough for Con to see a small, twisted figure carrying a length of rope. As adrenaline flooded his senses, the pain in his knee dissolved.

Just as the Leprechaun tossed the rope over Luna's neck, Con sprang, preventing it from wrapping around her. He landed hard on the scrawny little man, then froze as the mare's gold-shod hooves danced a fraction too close for comfort. His prisoner was struggling under him and squawking curses, but Con kept up the pressure, flattening the Leprechaun. As soon as he heard Corliss's voice murmuring soothingly to Luna—and to Aisling, as well—he turned his entire attention to his sneaky little rival.

"Give it up, Bittersweet," he snarled, thinking he sounded a lot tougher than he felt.

"Never! They're mine, they are, the girl and the mare, and fairly won!"

Con knew he outweighed his opponent, and he had relative youth on his side. Ignoring the voices around and above him, he held onto the little man's collar with one hand and his belt with the other, keeping his own upper body pressing down on the back of the squirming runt. Eventually, the Leprechaun would get tired, wouldn't he?

Suddenly, Con felt himself being lifted off the ground. Still clutching at the Leprechaun's collar and belt, he looked down. In place of the scrawny little man, something large and black was rising to its feet under him. A horse! The sneaky little cheat had turned himself into an untamed stallion! With sickening clarity, Con instinctively understood the new rules. It was a test. The last time he'd stayed on a moving horse, he'd been eight or nine, but if he couldn't stay on this demonic horse, he was going to lose Aisling. While the others yelled, the huge black beast lurched toward the dark field.

"Oh, shit!"

Snorting, rearing, and bucking, trumpeting like a demon, the beast tried to dump him. With no saddle or bridle, all Con could do was clamp his legs tight and take a death grip on the thick mane. His teeth banged together every time the horse landed, but he stayed on. The beast's stiff-legged jumping nearly bounced him off, but he caught his balance just in time. Then the magical horse started spinning and kicking out with its hind legs, and Con almost slid off the side of the broad, slick back. Knowing what he could lose, he fought gravity and stayed on.

When the horse suddenly went motionless in the middle of the paddock, Con grinned. All right! He'd beaten the sneaky little—

The beast exploded into a gallop. Con's head snapped back so hard he saw stars, but he kept his grip on the mane and the sides. The ground rushed away under him. The wind whipped at his eyes and stole the air before he could breathe. He was riding a runaway locomotive, an avalanche, a volcano, a tidal wave. The speed was dizzying. The force of every landing was bone-jarring. Yet Con clung—his strength came from knowing that if he failed, Aisling would die.

With no light from the moon, the hill came at him from the shadows too rapidly for him to react. The horse gathered his muscles and leaped—

Straight at the hillside! The damn Leprechaun was going to kill them both! The sod rushed up at them like a slamming door. There was no time to plan, to panic, no time even to breathe a farewell to Aisling.

He braced himself for the impact. With hardly a jolt, the horse touched down in thick darkness. They had passed right through the ground, into the hill! The coarse strands of mane cut into his fingers, but Con couldn't have released his hold now, even if he'd wanted to. They galloped onward, harsh breathing and the pounding of hooves reverberating off unseen walls.

As they sped on, the horse's muscles bunching and exploding under the grip of his legs, the impenetrable darkness faded into a dense fog of swirling colors. Everywhere now, Con saw flickering lights in the mist, like candle flames, or fireflies dancing, but the horse ran too quickly for Con to fix his gaze anywhere. Over the bellows sound of the horse's breathing, over the rush of the wind and the surging of his own pulse in his ears, over the rhythmic pounding of galloping hooves, Con heard tiny bells. The high-pitched chiming surrounded them, followed them, rising into a maddening din the farther the horse galloped.

A strange calm took over his body as he realized that he'd begun to feel almost comfortable on the bare, muscular back of the racing horse. As if time had folded back on itself, he felt again the pure joy of riding his beloved pony, Sergent Pepper, along trails. The stiffness of panic eased and he let himself sink into the horse's movements, let himself flow with them. His grin nearly erupted into a triumphant laugh: He was going to win!

The horse stopped with a jolt. Without that connection to the stallion's movements, inertia would have launched him over the powerful neck and into humiliating loss. He recovered just as the horse abruptly reared high, trumpeting and pawing the air with lethal hooves. The interminable moment the horse stayed poised at that steep angle nearly dumped Con off backward. Heart pounding, he leaned forward and dug his heels into the horse's shoulders. The flailing front legs came down barely a second before Con would have lost his struggle with gravity.

'' 'Tis a dishonest act you commit, Acorn Bittersweet!'' A woman's voice came out of the mist. Aisling's Aunt Rainbow? Con couldn't see over the thick, arching neck and upheld head of the black horse now dancing and snorting under him.

''Mortal!'' That musical voice rang out, echoing around him, claiming his attention. ''The gold horseshoe nail shall lead you back to Aisling. The talismans in your pocket shall protect you. But only your own heart shall give you the strength to ride Under-Hill through our world and emerge safely.''

Figures, Con thought. There was always a catch to these

magical things. He opened his mouth to ask the speaker what he was supposed to do about his heart's notorious weakness when she stepped to the side. It was Rainbow, standing with one hand raised, as if she were magically controlling the horse. Her slender figure was surrounded by an aura of sparkling light; her purple eyes glowed in a pale face more translucent than fine china. As the horse jigged under him, Con gawked until he finally remembered to shut his mouth. Rainbow gave him a smile that refreshed him as if he'd taken a cold drink and a cool shower.

"Aisling's Fey name is your heart's strength, its talisman: *Remember-Fear-Not*. Repeat her name as you struggle with the Leprechaun's shifted form, and you shall defeat him. Forget your heart's talisman, and you shall fail."

Before he could thank her, she lowered her hand. Without warning, the stallion bolted forward, snapping Con like the end of a whip. A cold shot of fear laced through him as he fumbled to keep his hold and his balance on the powerfully galloping horse.

Remember-Fear-Not, Remember-Fear-Not. He chanted Aisling's Faery name silently, and the ice in his gut began to melt. But the horse was still running hard, and Con had no idea where he was or how they would get out of this Under-Hill place—or even *if* they would get out. Then the horse made a sharp right turn that nearly unseated him and a surge of adrenaline ripped through his nerves. Lurching and slipping, Con wondered if he could hang on any longer, if he could regain his balance. As soon as that doubt snuck into his mind, he felt his grip loosening. *No!*

"*Remember-Fear-Not, Remember-Fear-Not!*" The drone of his voice echoed in the mists they were passing through. As the sound came back to him, so did the strength to cling to the rampaging horse. He felt hope replacing doubt. This time, he bellowed the words: "*Remember-Fear-Not!*"

Suddenly, the horse stumbled. Its sides were heaving and slick with sweat. Con slipped, then shouted Aisling's Fey name, and regained his balance. Repeating the magical name loudly, he felt his strength increasing, maintaining his balance becoming effortless. That thick, blinding, smoth-

ering darkness settled around them again. Con called out
"*Remember-Fear-Not*" as their pace began to slow. The
horse gave one more enormously powerful leap—

And collapsed under Con, transforming back to the Leprechaun at the instant that they fell to the cool sod of the
old de Burgh paddock. Every muscle in Con's body felt
like overcooked pasta; his nerves were deadened by sensory
overload; his lungs refused to inflate for any more than
quick, shallow gasps of air. He could hardly lift his head
enough to look around; all he saw was six pairs of human
feet and four gold-edged hooves forming a semicircle
around him and his rival. The little creep struggled to escape. Whispering Aisling's Fey name gave Con the strength
to keep the Leprechaun flattened.

Ignoring the runt's whining and twisting, Con snarled,
"I win. You lose. Swear you'll honor your promises to
Aisling."

"I swear! Now, get off me, ye great ox!" his prisoner
gasped.

His enemy had conceded defeat. Con started to relax,
then tensed again. Had the sneaky little bastard really conceded, or had he given an answer that was vulnerable to
interpretation? Everything he'd heard and read about Leprechauns emphasized their legendary cunning and trickery,
and above all, the ability to outwit Mortals by twisting their
words. Leprechauns, like computers, were extremely literal-
minded, but they used it to their advantage against anyone
who tried to outsmart them.

What were the exact promises, all of them, that the little
cheat made to Aisling? Increasing his pressure until the
squirming under him ceased, Con added a qualifier to his
offer: "Admit you have no right to marry Aisling. Release
her and Luna from the spells you cast on them." He
paused. Even that might not be thorough enough. "If her
aunt is satisfied, I'll let you go."

The Leprechaun squirmed like a trapped bug. "I'd
sooner make myself die, I would," he wheezed, "than admit such a thing as that!" Abruptly, he stopped squirming.

"If I die without properly removing the enchantment, Fiona's daughter shall die with me!"

The words sent a chill into Con's heart, but at least the Leprechaun had stopped fighting him, giving him a moment to think. He'd been right not to trust the trickster, but that wasn't going to save Aisling forever. What should he do next? Rainbow would know, but she wasn't here. Was she still in the Faery World, that Under-Hill place where she'd given him the key to defeating the Leprechaun? Enid! Enid could probably reach her.

Con lifted his head to ask Enid for her help. He looked into Luna's luminous, dark eyes and tried to smile encouragingly. Suddenly, the white mare disappeared setting off a chain reaction of gasps. Expecting Aisling to take Luna's place, Con held his breath. So did the other six people gathered around.

He held his breath until he thought his lungs would explode.

Twenty-five

~

With every breath searing her lungs, Aisling ran along the misty passageways and through flower-festooned archways until she reached the crowded great hall. The Faeries were celebrating the consecration of the new Sacred Hawthorn, with its sisters Ash and Oak. Pausing at the edge of a whirling group of dancing Faeries to get her bearings, she pressed her hand to her heart to calm her panic. 'Twas only her imagination that her energy seemed to be ebbing, that her vision was growing dim and the sounds of the Faery dancing music were becoming faint. This couldn't be happening yet! Surely, the Leprechaun could not have made himself die so quickly?

Where, oh, where was Aunt Rainbow? Aisling called for her aunt, but her voice came out as weak as that of a newborn kitten. Frantic now, she started toward the corridor leading to her aunt's suite, but with her first step, her knees buckled and she was falling to the soft ground. Before she could land, however, she heard a cry of dismay and felt hands reaching for her. Dizzy now, she tried to focus on the faces wavering before her. 'Twas Aunt Rainbow and Juniper Bilberry holding her upright despite her trembling legs. Understanding that the Leprechaun was indeed willing himself to die rapidly, Aisling felt her eyes filling with hot tears. *Oh, Sloan! I love you!*

Summoning her last bit of stamina and leaning on the two Faeries, Aisling spoke in urgent, halting whispers. Her sight was growing more dim with every passing heartbeat. She could not draw enough breath to repeat the words Rainbow and Juniper failed to hear over the din of the Faery *feis*. When she finished speaking, the draining of her strength had left her limp. She could not even answer Rainbow asking her if she could help herself walk between her aunt and Juniper.

Then the dimming lights and sounds grew dark and silent, and Aisling could no longer fight the closing of her eyes. 'Twas over, she thought sadly. Her quest for True Love had ended before she and Sloan could be joined together in the Mortal world, but her love for Sloan would be living on as long as there were stars in the sky. 'Twas the magic of True Love that, somehow, Sloan would know.

DE BURGH MANOR, CO. SLIGO, TUESDAY EVENING, JULY 13, 1999

Con stared at the place where Aisling, as Luna, had stood a second ago, unwilling to believe she could vanish like a puff of smoke. He turned to meet Enid's eyes and saw that she was just as shocked. There were no answers in her eyes, no answers in Phelan's eyes, either. Erin stood between his parents, ghostly pale, visibly shaking. All three had tears sliding down their cheeks. Gramps had bowed his head, the first time Con had ever seen the old man defeated. And the cause of everyone's misery was peacefully willing himself to expire while Con held him prisoner.

Rage shattered Con's shock. No! The sneaky little weasel was not going to get away with this! If he had to pound the Leprechaun into a green pulp, he was going to save Aisling! With a growl erupting from his throat, Con sat up, clutching his enemy's narrow shoulders, and shook the limp, child-size body.

"Don't you dare die, you cheating son of a worm!" His voice cracked and tears filled his eyes. He drew back one fisted hand and glared at the ugly, wizened face of the Leprechaun. "Don't you die, because I'm going to kill—"

"Oh! Mr. Conlan Sloan, sir! Please stop!"

A tiny voice, high-pitched like a cartoon child's, screeched at him. Con choked on his words and looked around for the speaker. A very tiny figure broke through the legs surrounding him. The size of a kindergarten child, she was nevertheless a mature woman who stood wringing her hands in front of her white apron. Con gaped at her, too stunned to move or speak. After a moment, she knelt in the soil and clutched the lapels of the Leprechaun's green jacket.

"Acorn Bittersweet, 'tis Juniper Bilberry. Ye must listen to me!" Juniper Bilberry's shrill voice pierced the night like a siren. The limp Leprechaun twitched. "If ye will yerself to die, then so shall I, and all for you!"

Con felt signs of stirring in the small creature he still held tightly by the shoulder. No wonder. That was a voice that could wake the dead! Little Juniper cast a desperate glance at Con, and in the flickering candlelight, he thought he saw her blush.

"Acorn Bittersweet, ye've been deceiving me! Ye've been leading me to think ye would be choosing me to marry, instead of the Mortal Aisling. Now that ye've made me fall in love with ye, ye must be taking the blame if I die for sorrow at losing ye!"

The Leprechaun shuddered under Con's restraining grip, and blinked open his amber eyes. Con was about to shake him again. He wanted the little runt to release Aisling immediately. He'd be damned if he was going to let the creep get away with hurting Aisling and running off with this little Juniper creature. But Enid caught his eye. With a quick shake of her head, she pressed her forefinger to her lips. Reluctantly, Con gritted his teeth, then resumed watching the Leprechaun, who was waking up like a hung-over drunk.

Erin's gasp, followed by his mother's, caught everyone's

attention, including the Leprechaun and Juniper. Both women pointed in the same direction, to a point beyond him. Their faces were mirror images of shock. Right about now, heartsick over Aisling's disappearance, Con didn't care enough about anything else to be surprised or shocked, but he turned to look anyway. His heart leaped into his throat and trapped his breath.

Luna—Aisling!—was back! The urge to jump up and go to her, to touch her and make sure she was real—as "real" as an enchanted horse could be!—almost overcame the need to hang onto the sneaky little bastard in green. Flanking the mare were Rainbow and a guy who looked a little like one of the Three Musketeers. Con assumed he was a male Faery.

"I don't believe this is happening! This isn't real!"

Erin's wail caught the attention of both Faeries. Rainbow beamed a brilliant smile. " 'Tis real enough, whether you believe or no. Welcome to the home of your ancestors, Niece."

"Niece?" Erin went stark white and gaped at Rainbow. "You . . . You're a . . . a Faery?"

Rainbow and Luna both nodded. Even after the way Erin had razzed him about Aisling, Con felt guilty for wanting to laugh at his partner's expense. He bit back a grin.

"You can't be . . . You can't be *my aunt*!"

"Your great-great-aunt, truly. 'Twill be such a delight to have two beautiful nieces! We shall speak together soon, dear one. I should like to hear of my dear half-brother's adventures." Then she turned to Con and curtseyed. "I thank you, Conlan Sloan, for bringing me a descendant of my lost nephew, Ian Mac Eochaidh, the old form of the name McKeogh."

Poor Erin backed away, bumped into Phelan, shrieked, and shied away again. She finally latched onto Gramps, who patted her shoulder and spoke quietly until he'd calmed her the way he would a nervous filly. So much, Con thought, for Erin's *inherent logic*. When this was all over, he'd enjoy teasing her about her family connections. But it wasn't over until Aisling was safe.

Rainbow moved to stand beside the shrill little Faery Con now understood was the key to saving Aisling. "Juniper Bilberry speaks true, Acorn Bittersweet." The faint sound of tiny bells lingered after Rainbow stopped speaking. "You've led her to believe you were courting her. 'Twould be dishonorable of you to allow her to die for love of you, and all who dwell Under-Hill know that Acorn Bittersweet is indeed an honorable Leprechaun."

Acorn's face lost its color. Juniper, who was blushing cherry red all the way up to her hair, bobbed her head. " 'Tis true, Acorn Bittersweet. 'Twas my belief that ye were courting me. If that not be true, then I . . . I shall die of grief!"

The Leprechaun glanced at Con, and for just a fraction of a second, Con felt a flash of . . . Well, he wouldn't call it male bonding, but he knew where the runt was coming from: Private feelings should stay private. Acorn looked at Juniper and cleared his throat. Twice. "I'll not let ye die, noble Juniper Bilberry, I'll not! Acorn Bittersweet would rather admit to making a mis . . . a mist . . . making a mista . . . ," the Leprechaun's face turned so red, Con thought he might explode, ". . . than act dishonorably."

Rainbow nodded. "There is a more grave matter solved, Acorn Bittersweet. Your death before the proper canceling of the enchantment would be the death of the true mare Luna." Con swallowed hard. That was close. Rainbow aimed a disapproving glare at Acorn. "Juniper Bilberry has saved you from the disgrace of being the first of your race ever to harm a horse."

" 'Tis a great tragedy averted, it is!" Acorn twisted in Con's grasp, then scowled when he couldn't break free. "I swore to free Fiona's daughter of her enchantment on condition that she be finding her One True Love inside ninety-nine and one years. Mistress Rainbow, as the girl's goddess mother, are ye satisfied that this clumsy, ham-fisted son of an O'Hara Mortal be he?"

Luna bobbed her head and snorted, but Con couldn't even manage a smile. Rainbow stepped closer and gave Con a long, searching look. He tried to return it calmly and still keep his grip on the fidgeting Leprechaun. "Conlan Ambros O'Hara Sloan, you have now thrice proved your love for my beloved niece Aisling. But . . . ," she frowned and glanced at Luna, then back at Con, ". . . only twice have you declared your love." Rainbow gave him a radiant smile that sent a wave of heat up his neck.

"Once more must you declare your love, to break the spell on her, and to end the curse on Ambros O'Hara's line."

In all the action of pinning down the Leprechaun, Con had lost sight of the others except for Erin's brief distraction. Now, with his face on fire with embarrassment, he stole a glance at the witnesses—six Mortal, four Fey, and one equine—staring at him. Surprise, shock, amusement, and curiosity beamed back at him from the eleven faces. His mouth went dry as he turned his gaze from Rainbow to Luna, his enchanted Aisling.

His voice failed him twice. On the third attempt, he barely managed a croak. "Aisling, I . . ." He stopped to clear his throat. "I . . ." His voice cracked. "I . . . Damn it! I can't tell a horse I lo . . ." He swallowed. "Damn it! *I can't say that to a horse!*"

For some reason, he was the only one who didn't think that was uproariously funny.

Aisling's laugh came out as a delicate snort from Luna, but under the hilarity, she was feeling Sloan's awkwardness. Truly, she was needing to hear him say he loved her, but as herself, not as her mare. Unless the Leprechaun released her first, they might all be waiting until the birds mistook them for trees and built nests in their hair. But between young Juniper Bilberry grasping Acorn Bittersweet's hands, and Sloan gripping the little man's shoulders, Aisling doubted he was thinking as clearly as he might.

She picked her way past Raven, who earlier had astonished her by gallantly carrying her from the Faery World when she'd been too weak to stand, and past Sloan's grandfather and Enid, holding hands as tenderly as young lovers. Stepping past Enid's son in his cloak, and Sloan's parents

standing protectively by Erin, who might be a long-lost
cousin of her own, she stopped beside Sloan.

Although Rainbow, Raven, Acorn Bittersweet, and Juniper Bilberry were seeing her as herself, to the others she
appeared as Luna and so could not speak to anyone. Instead, Aisling could only point mutely to the Leprechaun's
pocket, where she'd seen him tuck the golden horse con-
taining Luna's true spirit. When he merely stared at her for
a long moment, her heart sank. Had she been mistaken all
this time, thinking that Luna was indeed safe?

Sloan said something so softly that she couldn't hear the
words, even with Luna's keen senses. Gently, she nudged
his arm. He looked straight into her eyes and said, more
clearly, yet still intimately quiet: *"Remember-Fear-Not."*
To tell him that her heart understood, Aisling brushed her
lips over his cheek. To her delight, he pressed his lips to
her nose. As the other Mortals would be seeing Sloan kissing a horse, 'twas all the more sweet.

Acorn Bittersweet suddenly reached into his pocket and
withdrew the tiny golden horse. He held it out to Sloan,
who was eyeing him suspiciously. "Take this over past the
Mortals." When Sloan still hesitated, the Leprechaun gave
him what Aisling was thinking could be a smile. "I'll not
be trying to trick ye," he said a little stiffly. "As a Lep
rechaun of honor, I keep my word. Take this trinket there
and I'll be setting all to rights again."

Con was torn between desperately wanting this all to be
over, and suspecting the Leprechaun of setting a word trap
for him to blunder into. Rainbow's nod tipped the scales in
favor of the little man in green. Closing his fingers over
the small object in his palm, Con felt movement and nearly
dropped it in surprise. The Leprechaun snickered, and Con
tightened his grip on the guy's bony shoulder. A gentle
nudge from Luna, like a soft kiss from Aisling through the
mare, prompted him finally to release his prisoner.

With the oddly animated object in his hand, Con stood,
expecting the Leprechaun to disappear as soon as he did. The
little man rose also, but instead of bolting away, he walked
with Con. Feeling every eye on him, Con crouched and set

the object down on the soil he'd spent days clearing of debris. In shock, he stared down at a tiny golden horse . . . a golden horse that was moving! The little man brusquely ordered him to stand back. While the Leprechaun spoke in a singsong voice, Con glanced at the white mare nearby, the one he'd come to know as both Aisling and Luna. He realized his heart was pounding rapidly, nearly choking him. Or maybe that was fear choking him.

Suddenly, Luna—the Luna who'd been standing between Erin and Phelan while everyone watched the Leprechaun—disappeared. A heartbeat later, Aisling stood in her place. Con stared at her, almost afraid to believe she was standing there in her old-fashioned dress, her eyes huge and luminous in her pale, beautiful face, her hair drifting around her like a long, golden cape. As he slowly let himself believe, he broke into a wide grin and took a step toward her. Aisling's dazed expression turning into a radiant smile . . . as she gazed past him.

Con glanced over his shoulder, and there stood a dainty white mare, snorting and shaking herself. After a quick thumbs-up to the Leprechaun, Con turned back to Aisling, and this time, her smile came straight to him. He wanted to savor the moment, wanted to howl at the moon in celebration, and above all, wanted to whisk Aisling away to some quiet, very private place. Immediately.

A hasty look at the others, however, suggested that introductions would have to wait for everyone to get over their astonishment. Gramps was scratching his head and glancing from Enid to Rainbow to Aisling. Enid was smiling and wiping at her cheeks with the sleeve of her ceremonial robe. Corliss was gasping and gawking, first at the Faeries, then at the real Luna and back to Aisling; holding her hand, Jonathan was alternately shaking his head and rubbing his eyes. Funny, Con thought, that these people were the same ones who'd tried to convince *him* to believe in Faeries and magical spells.

His poor partner seemed the worst affected. With Luna disappearing and Aisling appearing right beside her, Erin staggered backward and fainted. Before anyone else could react, Phelan dove to her side and cradled her head. Tearing off his ceremonial robes, he bundled them into a hasty pillow for her.

"Rainbow?" Phelan looked petrified. Con felt a certain bond with him. "I think this was all too much for Erin. Can you help?"

"Indeed, I shall, as soon as Conlan Sloan fulfills the last condition for ending Aisling's enchantment and the Ambros O'Hara Curse."

Con took Aisling's hands in his and looked into her eyes. He couldn't tell which one of them was shaking harder, but the smile she gave him was sweet and brave, and gave him the courage to go public with his feelings. Later, in private, he planned to go into detail, but for now, he'd think of this moment as just diving in when the water was cold. The initial shock would offset the prolonged agony of sidling in gradually. Besides, he'd be declaring more than his love publicly at their wedding.

He took a breath and felt everyone leaning toward them, holding their breath as well. No pressure. Sure. "Aisling, I—"

"Wait!" Gramps's shout cut through the silence around them. "With all the strange goings on tonight, I almost forgot . . ." Moving to Con's side, he frowned and fumbled in his tweed jacket pockets. Then he smiled, and for the first time since his childhood, Con felt the old man's love, approval, acceptance. Withdrawing his fisted hand, he held it out to Con.

"This was the betrothal ring my grandfather was to have given Aisling de Burgh Ahearn. It has been handed down through the men in the family, but never given to any O'Hara bride." Gramps shrugged. "Some foolishness about a curse," he said, then waited for the startled laughter to fade. "Take it, Conlan, and give it to this lovely girl."

After Con closed his fingers around the small object Gramps placed in his palm, the old man turned to Aisling. "Fourteen years ago, in hasty anger, I disinherited my only grandson, and mainly succeeded in punishing myself. On the day he returned, willing to help an old curmudgeon and a legendary damsel in distress in spite of his disbelief, I instructed my solicitor to reverse the disinheritance. In addition, as the O'Haras owe a moral, if not legal, debt to the child of Fiona de Burgh Ahearn, I have deeded the former de Burgh lands to Aisling Ahearn, along with funds to restore the home and stables of which her father and my grandfather cheated her.''

As Aisling stood on her toes to kiss Gramps's cheek, Con blinked away the sudden moisture in his eyes. ''Thank you, Grandfather O'Hara, but your blessings on Sloan mean far more to me than the return of the de Burgh lands.''

Gramps blinked and wiped a hand over his face. ''Go on! Get this over with. I've a declaration of my own to be making, and I'm not getting any younger waiting for you two!''

Swallowing hard, Con picked up the gold ring balancing on his palm. It was set with a large emerald, carved into a heart, surrounded by diamonds. He gave up trying to stop his hand from trembling. He took Aisling's left hand in his and carefully slid the ring onto her ring finger. Then he drew her hand to his lips and, looking into her glistening eyes, he kissed her knuckles.

''Aisling, I love you,'' he murmured. While everyone around them was sighing and cooing, he muttered, ''The rest of what I have to say can wait until these voyeurs go away.''

Her smile quivered around the edges. ''I love you, Conlan Ambros O'Hara Sloan.''

Slipping his arms around Aisling's slender waist, he pulled her close and bent to cover her mouth with his. Her arms circled his neck, pressing their hearts together, and she opened to his kiss. Con felt the last vestiges of cold stone melt away from his heart, and for the first time in his life, he understood the true meaning of magic.

''Oh, Jonathan! I'm going to cry!''

''C'mon, Corliss. Don't cry. You always wanted a daughter-in-law who loved horses.''

''True, but I never expected a daughter-in-law who *was* one!''

"I have an idea. We've still got a few days before we
have to get home. How about a romantic tour of Ireland
with your ex-husband?"

"Oh, Jonathan! I can't think of anything I'd like more . . .
Unless it was touring Ireland with my no-longer-
ex-husband."

"Well, Enid, you were right about that O'Hara Curse.
I'm thinking it's not too late for us to be happy, if you're
willing to be patient with an old man."

"Haven't I always been patient with you, Ambros dear?
I'd say now's the time for being *im*patient, for seizing the
gift these two fine young people fought so hard to bring
us."

"Ah, Enid McDermott, you're a wise Wise Woman, you
truly are. Would you be willing to take a wedding trip to
California? I've never been, but I understand they've some
wonderful horses, as well as people who appreciate the occasional magic spell."

"Anywhere with you, Ambros. Anywhere."

"Oh, Acorn Bittersweet! I'm sorry if I caused ye to lose
the bride and the mare ye've been saving this century! Will
ye ever be able to forgive me?"

"Forgive ye? I shall be thanking ye these next eight or
more centuries of my life, I shall, Juniper Bilberry! Ye have
saved me the shame of being the first Leprechaun ever to
harm a horse, a sacred white one at that. And ye've saved
me, ye did, from marriage to a virago of a Mortal! Indeed,
ye spared my offspring being both tall and unhandsome!"

"Oh! And I shall be thanking ye for not dying in shame,
Acorn Bittersweet, so that ye could save my life!"

"Ahem. Well, now, Acorn Bittersweet, bachelor Leprechaun, has died, he has. As I'm planning to wed such a
sweet and pretty little laundress, I shall need a name more
fitting a Leprechaun husband and father. Juniper Bilberry,
as the new-named Oak Steadfast, I'm asking ye to be my
bride, mother of my children."

"Oak Steadfast? 'Tis a perfect name for a husband and
father! But as I am only one hundred and twenty-three earth

years of age, ye must be asking my mother, Candleberry Burtree, for my hand.''

"We'd best hurry, then, we'd best! A full century I have waited already, I have!''

"Raven, why are you laughing?''

"My lovely Rainbow, do you know why Leprechauns are always so bad tempered?''

"Fact or riddle, handsome Raven?''

"Riddle and fact, beautiful Rainbow. Leprechauns are always cranky because they are all bachelors. See how the anticipation of a sweet little mate in his bed has turned the curmudgeonly Acorn into a protective Oak.''

"Ah! If you are thinking to persuade me into your bed, you shall have to be finding better arguments. Cranky and bad tempered you have never been.''

"Then I shall have to practice being sorrowful more diligently, until compassion moves you to become my lover.''

"Compassion, Raven? 'Tis a Mortal quality, is it not? If Mortal qualities appeal to you, perhaps you should be seeking a Mortal lover.''

"Shall we retire to your rooms, lovely Rainbow, to debate the question further?''

"Rainbow? Before you go, is there anything you can be doing for Erin? Witnessing tonight's magic has overwhelmed her senses.''

"Ah, Phelan! There are indeed many spells to remedy being overcome by magical events. But none so eloquent as the incantation penned by my dear uncle William. You may recite with me, Phelan, for I believe you shall find the words familiar:

> *If we shadows have offended,*
> *Think but this, and all is mended,*
> *That you have but slumb'red here*
> *While these visions did appear . . .*''

TIME PASSAGES

__CRYSTAL MEMORIES *Ginny Aiken*		0-515-12159-2
__A DANCE THROUGH TIME *Lynn Kurland*		
		0-515-11927-X
__ECHOES OF TOMORROW *Jenny Lykins*		0-515-12079-0
__LOST YESTERDAY *Jenny Lykins*		0-515-12013-8
__MY LADY IN TIME *Angie Ray*		0-515-12227-0
__NICK OF TIME *Casey Claybourne*		0-515-12189-4
__REMEMBER LOVE *Susan Plunkett*		0-515-11980-6
__SILVER TOMORROWS *Susan Plunkett*		0-515-12047-2
__THIS TIME TOGETHER *Susan Leslie Liepitz*		
		0-515-11981-4
__WAITING FOR YESTERDAY *Jenny Lykins*		
		0-515-12129-0
__HEAVEN'S TIME *Susan Plunkett*		0-515-12287-4
__THE LAST HIGHLANDER *Claire Cross*		0-515-12337-4
__A TIME FOR US *Christine Holden*		0-515-12375-7

Prices slightly higher in Canada   All books $5.99

Payable in U.S. funds only. No cash/COD accepted. Postage & handling: U.S./CAN. $2.75 for one book, $1.00 for each additional, not to exceed $6.75; **Int'l** $5.00 for one book, $1.00 each additional. We accept Visa, Amex, MC ($10.00 min.), checks ($15.00 fee for returned checks) and money orders. Call 800-788-6262 or 201-933-9292, fax 201-896-8569; refer to ad # 680

Penguin Putnam Inc.   Bill my: ☐Visa ☐MasterCard ☐Amex_____(expires)
P.O. Box 12289, Dept. B   Card#_____
Newark, NJ 07101-5289
Please allow 4-6 weeks for delivery.   Signature_____

Foreign and Canadian delivery 6-8 weeks.

Bill to:

Name_____
Address_____City_____
State/ZIP_____
Daytime Phone #_____

Ship to:

Name_____ Book Total $_____
Address_____ Applicable Sales Tax $_____
City_____ Postage & Handling $_____
State/ZIP_____ Total Amount Due $_____

This offer subject to change without notice.

ROMANCE FROM THE HEART OF AMERICA
━━ Homespun Romance ━━

__TOWN SOCIAL	by Trana Mae Simmons	0-515-11971-7/$5.99
__HOME TO STAY	by Linda Shertzer	0-515-11986-5/$5.99
__MEG'S GARDEN	by Teresa Warfield	0-515-12004-9/$5.99
__COUNTY FAIR	by Ginny Aiken	0-515-12021-9/$5.99
__HEARTBOUND	by Rachelle Nelson	0-515-12034-0/$5.99
__COURTING KATE	by Mary Lou Rich	0-515-12048-0/$5.99
__SPRING DREAMS	by Lydia Browne	0-515-12068-5/$5.99
__TENNESSE WALTZ	by Trana Mae Simmons	0-515-12135-5/$5.99
__FARM GIRL	by Linda Shertzer	0-515-12106-1/$5.99
__SWEET CHARITY	by Rachel Wilson	0-515-12134-7/$5.99
__BLACKBERRY WINTER	by Sherrie Eddington	0-515-12146-0/$5.99
__WINTER DREAMS	by Trana Mae Simmons	0-515-12164-9/$5.99
__SNOWFLAKE WISHES	by Lydia Browne	0-515-12181-9/$5.99
__CAROLINE'S PROMISE	by Deborah Wood	0-515-12193-2/$5.99

Prices slightly higher in Canada

Payable in U.S. funds only. No cash/COD accepted. Postage & handling: U.S./CAN. $2.75 for one book, $1.00 for each additional, not to exceed $6.75; Int'l $5.00 for one book, $1.00 each additional. We accept Visa, Amex, MC ($10.00 min.), checks ($15.00 fee for returned checks) and money orders. Call 800-788-6262 or 201-933-9292, fax 201-896-8569; refer to ad # 411

Penguin Putnam Inc.	Bill my: ☐ Visa ☐ MasterCard ☐ Amex_____(expires)
P.O. Box 12289, Dept. B	Card#_____
Newark, NJ 07101-5289	
Please allow 4-6 weeks for delivery.	Signature_____
Foreign and Canadian delivery 6-8 weeks.	

Bill to:
Name_____

Address_____City_____

State/ZIP_____

Daytime Phone #_____

Ship to:

Name_____	Book Total	$_____
Address_____	Applicable Sales Tax	$_____
City_____	Postage & Handling	$_____
State/ZIP_____	Total Amount Due	$_____

This offer subject to change without notice.

Presenting all-new romances—featuring ghostly
heroes and heroines and the passions they inspire.

♥ *Haunting Hearts* ♥

__*A SPIRITED SEDUCTION*
  by Casey Claybourne   0-515-12066-9/$5.99

__*STARDUST OF YESTERDAY*
  by Lynn Kurland   0-515-11839-7/$5.99

__*A GHOST OF A CHANCE*
  by Casey Claybourne   0-515-11857-5/$5.99

__*ETERNAL VOWS*
  by Alice Alfonsi   0-515-12002-2/$5.99

__*ETERNAL LOVE*
  by Alice Alfonsi   0-515-12207-6/$5.99

__*ARRANGED IN HEAVEN*
  by Sara Jarrod   0-515-12275-0/$5.99

Prices slightly higher in Canada

Payable in U.S. funds only. No cash/COD accepted. Postage & handling: U.S./CAN. $2.75 for one
book, $1.00 for each additional, not to exceed $6.75; Int'l $5.00 for one book, $1.00 each additional.
We accept Visa, Amex, MC ($10.00 min.), checks ($15.00 fee for returned checks) and money
orders. Call 800-788-6262 or 201-933-9292, fax 201-896-8569; refer to ad # 636

Penguin Putnam Inc.	Bill my: ☐Visa ☐MasterCard ☐Amex_____(expires)
P.O. Box 12289, Dept. B	Card#_____
Newark, NJ 07101-5289	
Please allow 4-6 weeks for delivery.	Signature_____
Foreign and Canadian delivery 6-8 weeks.	

Bill to:

Name_____

Address_____City_____

State/ZIP_____

Daytime Phone #_____

Ship to:

Name_____ Book Total $_____

Address_____ Applicable Sales Tax $_____

City_____ Postage & Handling $_____

State/ZIP_____ Total Amount Due $_____

This offer subject to change without notice.